THE MAN IN MILAN

THE MAN IN MILAN

VITO RACANELLI

The following is a work of fiction. Names, characters, places, events and incidents are either the product of the author's imagination or used in an entirely fictitious manner. Any resemblance to actual persons, living or dead, is entirely coincidental.

ISBN 978-1-951709-11-2
eISBN: 978-1-951709-27-3
Library of Congress Control Number: 2020944552

First hardcover edition November 2020
by Polis Books, LLC
44 Brookview Lane
Aberdeen, NJ
PolisBooks.com

POLIS BOOKS

For Lisa, Giovanni and Giuseppina

Chapter i

Friday

In the gutter lay a man, face up, between two parked SUVs on Sutton. He wore a pale gray suit with impossibly thin pinstripes. It was Zegna, because I'd seen one on my partner, Detective Hamilton P. Turner. The suit was still in good shape, a testament to its workmanship, but the man was not.

I squatted and looked at him in the evening of an April day. I put on my latex and turned him gently. Our fashionable boy wore no tie and his pink shirt had a large red-brown blotch right where his heart used to beat. His suit was ruined in the back, an exit hole right through the trapezius. That's what the coroner's report would probably say.

He was about six feet, one inch. Skinny, with fine brown hair, blue-gray eyes, *glauco*, they say in Italian, which is what the body turned out to be. My grandfather was called Glauco for his eyes. This guy was good-looking. Once. No sign of a struggle. Two wounds: a dime-sized hole punched through the back of the head and one more straight into the chest—probably the second shot as he lay prone—to make sure he stayed all the way dead. Below, burrowed halfway into the asphalt, was a slug.

The blues who'd found him already radioed for the NYPD photogs and CSU.

I walked back to my car to call my partner, who'd hadn't told me

1

why he couldn't come along to
the party. "I'm good," I said to Turner. "You're missing a beautiful spring evening in New York City, marred only by one dead body."

His voice crackled over the radio: "Just the one? Gonna rain later. Meet you back at the precinct, Paolino," Turner said.

I tossed the receiver back into our Crown Vic's front seat and walked back to the body. Turner liked to call me little Paul because I was taller than him. The photogs showed up and cordoned off the area around the body.

"Any other bodies, Detective Rossi?" the photographer asked me.

"I told you, one. Why does everyone think there's more than one?" I said.

"Yeah, but you know, sometimes you think there's one and then other bodies just start showing up when you look around. They're like rabbits."

I smiled at our photographer, Joe Rinn. He had a nice sideline doing weddings. "You never tell those brides what you do, do you? That you flash dead bodies all day. That your work graces medical school books about fatal wounds?"

"Nah," he said, smiling back at me, then turning to the job at hand. "I tell 'em I'm an *artist*."

I stood back and let the artist work. I tugged my right ear, tilted my head to get another look at this guy, and wondered what this poor fucker had done to deserve a dog's death.

Rinn circled the body like a vulture. "The geeks'll be here in a minute. And hey, a *Post* guy is comin', too. He asked me to keep the bodies fresh."

"A body. One body. We'll try to oblige, but if the fourth estate doesn't show in time, tough," I said.

After they took the first set of photos, the CSU geeks began. Hair, blood, and nail samples. They scraped his jacket, pants, and shirt with tape to pick up foreign elements, like someone else's hair or blood.

I looked around to figure some possible MOs. There was a small service alcove down a few steps and a few feet away. Our hunter knew his rabbit's habits. Maybe tailed him for a few days. He waited in the alcove and calmly skipped up to the victim as he walked between a Range Rover and an Escalade. That gave the shooter some tall cover, and then he did him. Bang. Bang. Or rather *Ping, Ping*, with a silencer. The killer had probably taken care after the first shot to lay the body down, so that they were partially obscured, on Sutton near 54st. And that's when he—or they—popped him a second time. His head, inches from the curb, was near enough that his blood had drained into the sewer nearby. Just when you think you've seen it all.

The body came conveniently with docs, a small black address book and an Italian identity card wrapped in a soft, dark brown leather case— Gaetano Muro, forty-six years old and a Milan address, so immediately I thought Mafia. Even the stupidest perp knows not to leave docs in a fixit job. The killer must have been spooked immediately and had to run. This was a botched execution. Two kill shots to rob someone? Not likely.

The address book had names and phone numbers but little else. No addresses. The ID was diplomatic, Capo Servizio something or other, Consolato Generale d'Italia, it said, with an embossed little star inside an olive branch and a mechanical gear wheel. My Italian wasn't bad thanks to my grandfather. Muro was a diplo and *Signore* Muro from Milan came all the way to New York City and found unexpectedly that this late April evening would be the least lucky night he was ever to have, and he was dropped in the gutter on Sutton Place. I suppose there are worse streets to die on.

I'd bet it wasn't the way he thought it would go. Nobody ever does.

Muro had no time to argue with his Angel of Death. I bent down again, to touch his still warm face. TOD? About 10 p.m., I guessed, pending confirmation by the geeks at CSU. Then a little surprise. The distinct smell of fresh urine on him.

I did a quick walk-through with the Crime Scene Unit guys, and then I shut the poor bastard's eyes, still open and staring heavenward. Even after eighteen years on the job, I hated to see them with their eyes open. I'd seen plenty but it still gave me the creeps. I expected the body to speak up suddenly, to ask "Why me, Detective Rossi?" The eyes had registered the moment his spirit had been shoved headlong into the *al di la*. It sounds so much better in Italian, as if there were no heaven or hell but just a nice airy place in the mountains. The *al di la*…just over there. That's what my *nonno*, Glauco, used to say to me when he was dying. That he wasn't really going to die but go to the *al di la*. He was actually dying most of the years that I knew him, in his eighties. He was dying of this, dying of that. Finally, one day, he did die. In the middle of a handball game. Heart attack. *Infarto*. Even that doesn't sound so bad in Italian.

Just the one bullet was found initially, in the street under Muro. The other slug? Likely somewhere in his skull since there was no exit wound in his face. The CME boys were going to have to dive in and get that one, since the mashed-up slug in the street probably wouldn't be much use as evidence.

The doorman up the street, a grandfatherly guy with a German accent, kept repeating, "I saw nuss-zing." Another doorman across the street should have had a perfect view of the whole thing but claimed he was attending to a tenant in the foyer.

The body had been discovered by an older woman, maybe sixty-five, a Suttonite with sparkling green eyes and expensively taut skin, walking her dog. We sat in plush leather chairs in the foyer of the building closest to where Muro was gunned down. She'd noticed a tall blond guy in a nice suit walking down the street quickly, passing her by the Escalade. She looked back over her shoulder at him because he "looked like he didn't belong," and didn't notice her Wheaton terrier pissing on Muro's head. She apologized. "I hadn't expected a body to be there," she said.

4

Of course. Nobody would on Sutton. Her thick gold bracelets shook and clinked against each other as she trembled.

But why had the body and docs been left? Didn't feel like a robbery to me. There had been a patrol car nearby when it happened, behind a doubled parked car on the corner of Sutton and 56th. One of the blues from that car stepped out to write a summons. When I asked him earlier—he and his partner were first on the scene—he remembered seeing a big blond guy looking in their direction just for a moment. But he couldn't give more than that.

"Excuse me, Detective Rossi, there are fucking blond guys everywhere," he'd said.

Maybe the patrol car scared our killer off before he could clean up the mess? Then I had a blue run the Escalade and Range Rover plates. Both owners lived nearby.

"Want me to grab the owners?" the blue asked me.

"Get a statement," I said.

"You think the owners are involved?"

"Nah. That would be too messy. They've already left the body. They're not gonna leave the car, too."

The blue was a rookie. "But I'll get a statement just in case?"

I just nodded and sat on the hood of my Crown Vic.

An ambulance arrived and took Muro for his last ride in the Big Apple, a short trip to First Avenue and the Office of the County Medical Examiner. A small crowd of locals had gathered behind the police cordon, and from a distance they sounded like excited finches. Mostly Old Money WASPs around here, that's the 19th precinct, with a sprinkle of nouveau riche to create some *frisson*. There are 217,063 people in the One-Nine, which covers less than two square miles, and lots of these folks make more in a month in what the accountants call passive income than I *earn* in a year. I wouldn't mind some passive income.

As the EMS guys eased the stretcher into the back of the ambulance, the taller one let out a cackling kind of laugh, as if he'd heard the biggest howler of his life. No sense of respect for the dead these days. Who dies in peace in New York City?

His short, fat partner asked me with an imploring look, as if I, the cop, were the arbiter, the court of last resort, "Hey, the Yankees beat the Sox tonight, right? Our radio's busted, and we been real busy."

"Yeah, three to two," I said, looking down the street, as if the perp were still hanging around.

They slammed the back door shut and high-fived each other. The flashers went on, but no *ee-wah, ee-wah* siren, no urgency. Muro wasn't coming back. Poor fucker. I don't know why I felt for the guy but I did. Most times, bodies are bodies. Half of 'em deserved what they got, anyway. This guy Muro was a real Italian, not like me. Like my grandfather.

The EMS rolled away. Just another spirit in the night.

"Ciao," I said aloud.

All of my grandparents had come from a little town in Basilicata. They'd come all the way to this country but nobody offed them. Both my parents worked and my *nonni* raised me. Gave me the language.

I was being sentimental. Muro could have been a drug dealing dirtbag, a murdering pimp, for all I knew, but he had me. I tugged my ear again, a habit so old I don't remember when it started.

I called my sponsor. I usually felt better after I talked to Harry. Harry Alimont. It used to be Alimonte, but on Ellis Island, his great-grandfather had somehow lost the E.

"Hello," Harry said.

"It's me," I said.

"Where are you?" he asked.

"On a job. Sutton Place."

"Nice," he razzed. Harry lived in Bensonhurst, where I grew up. I needed a neighborhood guy to help me. "So?"

"Haven't touched a drop in two years, nine months, four weeks, and two days, Harry."

"Good. Now make it two years, nine months, four weeks, and three days. Talk to you tomorrow." His dog barked in the background.

"Copy that, Harry." I hung up and got in the car to go back to the One-Nine. It was just as hard today as it was two years, nine months, four weeks, and a day ago.

It started to rain lightly, just as Detective Hamilton P. Turner predicted.

*   *   *

As I sat at my desk writing out the particulars on the latest recipient of New York City hospitality, I realized that my very favorite part of detective duty, informing the next of kin in person, had to wait as Muro's ID was not the kind we were used to. DMV found no driver's license in his name. I looked at the ID more closely. Inside the fold was a black-and-white picture, with his name, physical characteristics, home address in Milan, nationality, age, and occupation. Colonnello, AMI, Aeronautica Militare Italiana. The Air Force.

No criminal priors, at least in New York. We had a line out to the Feds, but nothing had come back yet. On Friday nights the Bureau always took its time. No social security number, no home phone, nothing else. I had no idea if this guy had a place in town or was just passing through.

There were seventeen Muros listed in the Manhattan phone book alone, none of them Gaetano. I tried Google. I'd read recently that the company had just gone public on the stock market, the IPO thing, and the shares shot up. Probably every resident in our lovely precinct had bought some. I didn't.

Some stuff came up in Italian but I was too tired to read it right then. My Italian is good but I make mistakes when I'm run down. Anyway, who knows how many Gaetano Muros there are in the old country. The Italian Consulate and the State Department were no help at this hour. In Muro's personal address book, which I found in his vest pocket, there were just a bunch of foners. So I would have to make calls to his friends, assuming he had some, and fish something out of them without telling them he was dead.

One-Nine's detective squad leader came by, Lieutenant Patrick Dunne. *Grand poo-bah*, as the detectives called him behind his back, among other things.

"Whaddaya got?" Dunne said. He was a short-sleever and had a sheaf of folders under his arm, which was fair-skinned and blotched that way redheads are prone. Even in the dead of winter, the only shirt I ever saw him wearing was a white short-sleeved number, not much different from the kind worn by a Catholic school boy, which he—like me—once was. It was a walking advertisement that he never spent a second outside our house on business. My partner and I called him the "two stepper." Two steps to the precinct front door from his car and in, two steps back and out.

"Dead white male. As usual, our particular precinct's criminals give much too much attention to these privileged types."

"I repeat, Rossi. Whaddaya got?" he said, standing over me as I sat.

"Age, forty-six. Bullet to the back of the head and one to the chest. They probably used a tiny, but final determination of weapon and caliber still pending from FID. No witnesses so far. No wallet. Apparent robbery but believe that's a cover."

"A small bore gun? Cover for what?" Dunne grunted. He had this wonderful habit of wearing truly ugly ties. The one he wore that evening was a pretty unappealing mix of Jackson Pollock-like drips streaked across a background of small N.Y. Giants football helmets. Awful.

"Don't know yet," I said.

"Bullet to the head?" he said, looking up from the files he was leafing through. "What the fuck is that?" When he got excited, you could hear a bit of Irish brogue left in him. One March 17th he'd enjoyed himself a little too much and at the morning's St. Paddy's Day toast, he revealed with a tear that he'd left Old Eire when he was just six. It was the only thing I liked about him.

"Yeah," I said. "Looks like an execution. We don't know who this Gaetano Muro is."

"He's a Wop?"

My neck muscles tensed. He thought he was being funny again. "He's the real thing," I said. "Italian diplo. Works at the Consulate. From what I can make out in the ID, he might even be in their military."

"Christ, a foreigner," he said, making brief eye contact with me, something he avoided as much as possible. He knew he wasn't much liked. The blues hated him, too, and years ago the Patrolman's Benevolent Association managed to unseat Dunne from a desk command. And he landed, legs down like a cat, among us detectives. I figured he had an Irish uncle way upstairs at 1 Police Plaza.

He eyed the brown ID I held in my hand. "Is this case doable?" he asked and started scribbling on a pad now.

"Italian national. Diplomat. Do-ability? No witnesses. No home address. Doubtful at this point," I answered.

"Drop it," Dunne said out of the side of his mouth, and he walked away. That meant fill out the papers, tell the next of kin, wave your hands to look like you did something, and move on to the next case, preferably one that could be solved and publicized, bringing him glory and vindicating the taxpayers' support for more cops.

"I still have to tell his wife, assuming he has one."

He stopped and turned. "You said you have nothing. How do you know that?"

"Ring on his left hand."

"Fine. Diplos don't pay taxes. Hell, they don't even pay their fuckin parking tickets. Don't bother with a 5. Fuck 'em," he said, meaning not to do a DD5, a complaint follow up and record of detective's investigation. He was already out of the squad room.

I had just barely registered the "'em" out of his mouth, but I could tell this was already out of his brain.

I glanced left, at my partner, Detective Hamilton P. Turner, sitting at the next desk. He'd been on the phone, with his back to us, and missed the Dunne act. When the case came up earlier, he'd begged off, saying he had something important to attend to. I went along, as always.

His rib cage was moving slightly under his shirt, as if he were holding back a soft laugh. He was giving his mellow-throated routine to a woman. I couldn't hear what he was saying but I knew because he was using his late-night disc jockey voice, low and full, yet weightless and honey-covered at the same time. It was as if his tongue had managed to smooth the edges of the nastier Anglo-Saxon consonants. He never seemed to lack for the company of women.

He looked at me, then turned away. He knew I knew.

Muro's address book in hand, I made a few calls. It was near 11 pm. Reached a lot of answering services until Dorothy Hochman, who said she was Muro's wife. She confirmed his Milan address. She paused and added ex-wife, because they had separated. I told her we needed to see her tonight about Muro, ask some questions, but couldn't say why. She said she'd been at a party all evening. Plenty of witnesses, she said, though I hadn't asked her. She didn't seem too upset. Maybe annoyed. She didn't want us to come over right then. It was late, she said. I told her we had to.

"Is he dead?" she asked.

Smart one. "We'll have to come over," is all I said. She gave in.

I had to stop for a minute after that call. I took a second look at the ID, hoping to find something new in it. Anything. Encased in plastic, the reddish-brown cover looked like it had weathered several decades. It was embossed with the letters GM in gold in the upper right corner of the cover, small and just barely noticeable. The G and M were so intricately intertwined amid tiny trellises of flowers that without knowing the owner's name, it would be nearly impossible to figure out the initials.

Felt sorry for Muro all over again. Not a good emotion in my line. My folks were from much further south, at the bottom of the boot. Still, we were practically *paisans*. I hoped he wasn't just another thieving scumbag who met with the ultimate payback.

I'd seen an ID like this one before, from an Italian model killed by her boyfriend a few years ago, a lowlife masquerading as a performance artist. Barry Mayew. Turned out his "art" was eating people and boiling the leftovers into his paints. Then he'd strip, smear himself with the stuff, and roll around on a canvas on his studio floor. He'd film the whole thing and show that, not the canvas, to a bunch of googly-eyed eggheads, who fawned over the shock of the new. I had guessed he tossed the canvases to get rid of evidence. I found one in the trash and that's how we nailed him. The paint had traces of her blood. Got medaled for it. Mayew didn't last six months upstate. His prison daddy shivved him one less than amorous eve, unhappy with the quality of Mayew's blowjob.

Turner got off the phone and swiveled his chair in my direction.

"It's in the pocket," he said, cracking a half smile. It was a toothy grin to be sure, full of big white, straight teeth. But when the corners of his mouth turned up to a point—like devil tails—they were so mischievous that you had to give in. He reserved the full treatment smile for special occasions. People broke out into song when he flashed The Full Crescent.

"What?" I said. I pulled the ID out of its leather protector. It was soft, a thick, cloth paper. I felt the barely raised letters of a very official looking stamp in red on the back of the document. *Commune di Genova*, it said.

"I *said*, It's in the pocket."

"Do I know her?" I rubbed my face with one hand and tossed the ID onto my partner's desk with the other.

"Alicia, the writer," he said with glee. "You met her at that party last week. The Madrid chick, so it's pronounced Al-i-th-ia."

11

"The one with the funny left eye. Looked like she had that thing. Whaddaya call it, wandering eye, right?"

"There is something fishy about her eye, but I'd say it is moderately divergent strabismus. Anyway, the rest of her is fine, very fine," Turner said. He picked up Muro's ID.

"Too brainy for you," I said, feeding blank paper into the printer. Out would come an NYPD UF61, the initial report, which went over to the coroner, who would ready the death certificate.

Turner seemed to appreciate the leather of the ID, too, turning it over and over in his hands. "She wants me to make her dinner," he said. "Diiiiin-huuuuuh," he repeated, heavily accenting the second half of the word. "You know what that means."

"Yeah. You diiiiin-her, you win her," I said, parroting Turner's way of saying it, and typing away. His theory was that if a woman asked you to cook for her, she wanted you to make love to her.

"Who's Muro?" he asked.

"Was," I said, not looking up. "You'd know that if you'd come with me tonight."

"Dunne was busting me. They're still bugging out about that skinhead cracker I arrested a little too passionately two months ago," Turner said.

"That took two hours?"

"I had to get some *Aida* tickets," he said quietly, then quickly and loudly added, almost with a whoop, "Hey, this guy's E-taliano. Fresh?"

"Two hours old. Diplomat from Milan."

"Sorry, Paolino." He grinned.

"Fuck you," I said. "He's not my cousin."

"Give me the Cliff notes."

He put the ID back on my desk, open. He had long, slim fingers, sinewy, like those of a gymnast. The left hand had a brown, drumstick-shaped blotch on it. He insisted the birthmark was the shape of Mother Africa. He was a Redbone, light-skinned with a reddish tint to his hair and freckles. Some white in him somewhere.

"You are staring at my hands, Paolino," he said in a tone just a bit higher than normal.

I recounted the particulars, noting Dunne's resistance. There was something protective about those hands. It was strange that I noticed that just then.

"Sounds delightful. I hope you're not calling this a robbery-murder," Turner said.

"Ask Dunne."

"Fuck him. Sounds like Muro got himself whacked. You said he's Italian, right?"

I turned to Turner, my head down slightly, eyes glancing over the tops of my reading specs, like a disappointed John Jay college prof. Fucking reading glasses. Forty-five and I was all going to shit real quick.

"Okay," Turner said, putting up his hands in surrender. "We will not assume Mafia. Any kin?"

"Wife. Gold band on his left ring finger. I just talked to a lady who claimed said title. They were separated, not yet divorced. I think," I said, finishing up the preliminary file. "Got a call into State and the Italian Consulate. You know how good their twenty-four-hour desks are."

Turner rubbed the whiskers of his thin goatee, another source of contention with Dunne. The first time our great leader saw Turner, he said, "Great. Just what we *need*. A black beatnik detective."

"Dunne wants it dropped." I ripped the preliminary from the printer and threw our copy on his desk.

"What else you got?"

"His phone book," I said. I grabbed an envelope, stuffed the second UF61 copy in it, and stood up. "Come on, I have to drop this with Dunne. We're off to see the wife...or whatever she is. She said they're legally separated and it's too late to come over. By the sound of her voice, you'd think maybe that her ice cream cone had melted."

Turner smirked.

"Even if we had something to give a judge—and we don't—by the time the warrant came down it would really be too late," I said.

Turner grabbed the address book. "I'll take A through M, you take N through Z," he said, following me. He fanned through the book as we walked.

We dropped off the prelim on the night clerk's desk. Little Jimmy—our resident paper pusher, or The Archivist, as he liked to call himself—typically wasn't around most of the time. He had a day job running Circle Line tour boats out of the West Side, so most of the time, at night, if you wanted Little Jimmy, you had to check the couch in the infirmary. Outside the captain's office, it was the only cushioned spot in the precinct house not worn to shreds.

Turner almost stumbled into the water cooler. "Oh, snap," he yelled, so loud that a couple of our law enforcement colleagues looked up from their desks. Turner snorted, the kind that comes out of a smiling crocodile as he invites you to dine with him. "I don't believe it," he said, and pushed the booklet at me splayed open to the Bs. "My friend Elena is in this goddamn book. She used to work at the Consulate. Look. Her number is right here," he said, one long finger under her name.

"You remember the number?" I said.

"Plenty of reasons to memorize it."

"Well, if she worked at the Consulate…he probably knew her. Maybe a girlfriend of his?" I said, hoping to raise a little jealousy out of my partner. Nothing. "Maybe Muro and his wife had an arrangement. Talk about taking things in stride. I know it was late, but this new widow told me she had a headache and insisted she couldn't see us until tomorrow. I told her we had to come over tonight."

I could tell my partner looked forward to meeting Dorothy Hochman, or Mrs. Muro, or whoever she was.

"You know, if I thought for a minute she did it," I said, "we'd have been at their apartment already. Not too many women executioners around."

"Maybe she did him for his dalliances," Turner said.

He seemed intrigued rather than upset by that thought.

"Sounded like she didn't do him at all. We're going uptown. The missus lives on 85th near Park Ave." We headed to the front door, speeding up as we passed the chief of detectives' office.

"Paolino, uptown is above 110th," Turner said, laughing, as if he were sorry for me. "How many times do I have to tell you before it gets through that thick white head?" He grabbed his raincoat from the rack.

I slipped on my shoulder holster. I could never type with the damn thing on. Never gave me a problem otherwise. I could sleep with it, but typing was something else altogether. I slipped the little phone book into my right pocket and automatically grabbed for my cigarettes, but they weren't there. I'd recently quit, sort of. Was tougher than booze. I took off my reading glasses and stuffed them back into the case.

Chapter 2

Friday

On the way to Hochman's home, I drove and with the windows down Turner blasted his *Tosca* CD, the first big solo by Scarpia, the Roman chief of police. I liked C&W music, the whinier the better, beer-soaked tales of infidelity, ex-wives, alimony unpaid, and drunks. It vaguely outlined my life, even if I was from Brooklyn instead of Nashville. Tosca was bigger than life, and bogus. Revolutionaries, barons, and Roman churches weren't for me. And as for the great Tosca, none of the women I had ever known would have thrown themselves off a parapet for me.

The church bells clapped louder and louder out of the car speakers, first majestically, then like a black mass, Scarpia crying "Tosca" over and over. People on the street were staring at an obviously unmarked police car with opera blaring out of its open windows.

When the music faded, Turner asked me again if I thought she'd done it.

"She *said* she was at a dinner party earlier, charity thing," I said. "She *said* she wasn't feeling well and went home early and has witnesses. Lots. Anyway, she'd have to be a pretty good actress—nobody can fake ambivalence like that. If she were behind it, she would have been bawling, right?"

As we reached Third and 85th, and I made a left, Turner said,

16

"Diplomat. Bullet in the head. Damn. Next thing you know, the Consulate will tell us that they've never heard of him." Turner stared out the passenger side window as we double parked. "Just a simple execution."

The doorman eyed us, particularly Turner, who generally didn't like it when doormen stared at him, particularly those on the Upper East Side. Today for some reason my partner didn't give any lectures, or worse. This guy looked a lot like the poor fucker we ran into on the first day we did a shift together two years ago, when Turner gave me his take on doormen. "Even white doormen have got this plantation house slave look on them. Like they were *with* the rich folk, you know, and not just hired serfs who could be turned out faster than you coughed."

That day, I saw him put his revolver—safety on—to the temple of a doorman who had made the serious mistake of assuming Turner worked for me. He advised him very nicely that he should never make that kind of assumption about a black man again. The doorman pissed his pants. Turner was appeased.

That's when I first noticed that in addition to the department-issue Glock 19 automatics we all wore, my partner liked to carry a spare, a barrel-fed Smith & Wesson Model 10, the heavy metal John Wayne would wear. How he lugged that fucking weight around all day, I could never figure. But I knew why. Any old timer could tell you the score: automatics can jam, but wheel guns are forever. They always gave you six bangs. If you need more than that, you're in trouble big anyway.

This Hochman doorman was smart enough to keep his mouth mostly shut. He knew we were coming. The missus had warned him. "Ms. Hochman is 12A," he said, waving us in after we flashed our shiny business cards. Turner asked him what hours he'd been on duty, if he'd seen Mrs. Muro leave or enter tonight, and if he was sure he could identify her.

"Yes, I am recognizing her. Ms. Hochman, you mean?" said the general of No. 47, East 85th St., one of those huge, ugly white brick

17

apartment buildings dotting the Upper East Side. He spoke with a heavy Russian accent.

"Did she leave the building tonight?" Turner asked.

"Yes," the doorman repeated. "She is leavink six thirty and comink back at nine."

"You certain she returned at nine? Were you at the front door at all times?" I asked.

"Yes, I am sometimes taking break. I go side room here when I do that. I no sleep, so still I am seeink ere-wee-budyi." He pointed two fingers at his eyes.

"Back door?" I said.

"We got cameras. I didn't see nobodyi. But you can check vit da tape."

When 12A swung open, the woman behind the door was wearing black, though I got the distinct feeling it wasn't for poor old Gaetano. It was a cocktail dress. And it looked like Mrs. Muro still had her party paint on and was about to go out. The large living room had wraparound views, dotted with furniture of mostly white leather or shiny black metal.

She pointed at the couch and without looking at us said, "Look, I know I should have a lawyer here, but as I said, I've nothing to hide. Guy's dead, right?" Dorothy Hochman or Muro was about five foot nine, with shoulder length, straight light brown hair. I guessed forty, a very good forty.

Turner and I exchanged glances. I nodded. I told her our names, began to tell her we were sorry for her loss, but she was already walking down the two steps into the living room.

She turned. "I know it looks bad, but I'm not crying because I'm not sad. I mean, I loved Guy at first. Then he got difficult to live with. You know how it is."

Yes, I knew how it was. "He's a diplomat?" I said.

"You fell for that too?" she said, smiling. "He's no fucking diplomat."

Then she apologized for the fuck and lit a cigarette as she moved to the couch. She was twirling her hair, like a teenager.

"Hey, I like Italian men as much as the next girl," she sighed. "He wanted to move to this country and take care of me. Not that I needed that. I've got money, but a woman likes to hear it. He was nice the first few years, but then he started to get paranoid, said Italian special agents were following him. Christ, I didn't think Italy even had special agents," she said, taking a drag. "Three years ago, the late night calls started—one in the morning, two o'clock. I would have gotten mad at him, but I could tell that the caller was a man, and the same one, too.

"Then he would disappear for days at a time. I never knew where he was. At first, I was sick with worry, but eventually it was too much for me to take. Guy said he had to hide. From what, he wouldn't say. But I don't know what he was up to. Maybe he was *finocchio*, for all I knew about Gaetano."

She looked at us as if she expected understanding.

We said nothing.

She sighed again and plopped herself down on the couch. "At a certain point I didn't care anymore." She looked to the windows.

Turner sat at the other end of the couch and I remained standing, looking the place over as discreetly as I could.

The tears were going to come eventually, I knew.

She went on. "I'm embarrassed to tell you that I don't even know what my husband actually did for a living. Oh, he gave me some bullshit about managing his family's money. When I first met him, he said his family had hundreds of millions of lira. Later, I found out that wasn't much money," she laughed. "This is *my* apartment, by the way. Not *his*. And I was at a benefit for sick children in Bosnia tonight with three hundred people. And right now, I'm not feeling well, so can we make this snappy?"

I almost winced at that one. I saw Turner mouth, "That's cold," to himself.

"Did he still live here?" I asked.

"Do I have to answer your questions, Mr. Officer-whatever-your-name is?"

"It's Paul Rossi, ma'am. And as I said when we came in, it's Detective," I said. "And my partner here is Turner, Hamilton P., also a detective." I nodded in his direction. Mrs. Muro looked at Turner for more than a second. "And no, technically, you don't have to answer my questions."

Turner rolled his eyes.

"But it would probably be better if you did."

"Better for *whom*, detective?" she shot back.

"For Gaetano, at least, and possibly you," I said.

"Look," she said. Her face tightened up. "This...marriage was over. We just never got around to an official divorce. I let him occasionally stay here because he had nothing—no money, nobody else to go to. But six months ago, I'd had enough, so I asked him not to come back. He dropped by here a few days ago, just for a minute. We spoke for literally two minutes, he used the bathroom, and he left. I felt bad. He looked terrible. And that was very unlike Guy. He liked to look good. That was one of the things I loved about him. He'd look so good in gabardine, like a model."

She stopped, rubbed her temple lightly. "Anyway, he wasn't taking care of himself, started jabbering about ghosts he was seeing at night. *La verita*, he kept mumbling."

"The truth?" I said.

She nodded.

"About what?" I asked.

"Hell if I know." She shrugged. "He looked like he was going over the edge. I haven't talked to him since Tuesday. And I haven't thought of him until you called about...about his murder." For somebody who didn't love him anymore, she looked like she was about to open both faucets now. But out it came in little streams. She wiped her eyes, and the mascara ran.

Okay.

"Mrs. Muro…" I said.

"Oh shit," she said, turning away and trying to wipe the paint from the top of her cheeks. "And cut out the Mrs. Muro stuff. I never used that. My name is Dorothy Hochman."

Something about that name, but I couldn't place it right away.

"Were you home all day, Ms. Hochman?" Turner cut in.

She straightened up. The tears stopped quick.

"Except for the charity thing I told you about. Yes. I came home around nine. I had…I have a headache. You can check with Yuri downstairs."

"We did," Turner said. He made it sound light, not accusatory.

She looked surprised, as if we were smarter than she had thought. "Oh, and in case you didn't know, there are cameras watching the service exits, too," she said.

"Naturally," Turner said, taking notes in his pad.

I turned my head to the left and saw that she was watching me, wondering what I was up to. "Are there any of Mr. Muro's personal effects in the apartment?" I asked.

"No," she said curtly. "I told you he doesn't live here."

I gave a tight smile. "Do you mind if I use the facilities?"

"Through the corridor, second door on the right."

I left her with my partner and popped into a couple of the rooms in the back. I had to move fast. The master bedroom was very neat. I checked the closet for men's clothes. None. I closed the bathroom door loudly from the outside, so that she could hear it. Then I slipped into the study, where I went through a couple of desk drawers. The second one down had an envelope with red and blue airmail trim addressed to Colonnello G. Muro from someone named Alfredo Dottori, with the rank of Maresciallo. I put it in my breast pocket. It was onion paper, the kind people use to keep the weight down and save postage, yet it was heavy with something inside. I tiptoed out of the office, quietly opened the bathroom door, went in, closed the door again, and flushed the toilet before opening the door again.

Then, in the hallway, the vertigo came. I occasionally got a bout of it and the doctors couldn't figure anything better than telling me it was inner ear related. Weather? Blood rushing to my head? Residue of my former Seagram's love affair? Who knows, but every once in a while it hits me and I lose my balance. The room spins, like one of those Whirly-Bird rides at Coney Island. My ex-wife wanted me to get a disability retirement but that was bullshit. She just wanted me out of the line of fire. It didn't happen often.

I could hear Turner and Hochman talking in the living room, but I couldn't move, for fear of toppling over. Usually, I lie down and minutes later it's over. But that wasn't possible, so I leaned hard and straight against the wall, flat palm grabbing it as best I could. In five minutes, it passed.

When I wobbled back into the living room, Turner and Dorothy were looking like they were enjoying their own little joke. My partner had moved along the couch, closer to her. Dorothy was leaning forward, drinking in his smile, their knees close enough to whisper to each other.

"So what's the P for?" I heard her coo, her voice more girlish.

Turner smiled and rose when I entered. "I'll tell you some other time, Ms. Hochman," then turning to me, "Paolo, you ready?"

I nodded, closing my eyes for a moment.

He recognized the wobble.

"Did you find what you were looking for detective?" Dorothy said to me, sounding more suspicious than I'd expected.

"Excuse me?" I looked over at Turner, who smiled and gave a minimal nod. He knew my MO.

"Did you find the bathroom?" she asked. "You took so long, I thought perhaps you got lost. It's a big place and a bit confusing back there."

"No. I'm fine, thanks. I found it." I couldn't tell if she knew. She was a cool one.

Turner saw I was still woozy and stepped in. "Unfortunately, Dorothy, we're going to need you to ID the body for us," he said. "I'm sorry, but the sooner the better. It won't take long. Then I'll give you a lift over to your father's place." He looked back at me for some sign of objection.

I had none.

Hochman smiled. "I'm not going to change." She picked up her purse, one of those tiny affairs that women carry around God knows why, and thirty-five minutes later—after the morgue run—we left her at her father's townhouse on East 65th. She'd even dropped a few more tears when the orderly pulled old Gaetano out of the icebox.

He didn't look so bad for someone shot in the head. I assumed FID would tell us it was a .22, which doesn't do much collateral damage, if properly placed. The skin on his face was drying out fast.

"You will tell me what the P stands for, right, Detective Turner?" Hochman said to Turner, as if I weren't there.

"In due time," he said, opening the car door. He wouldn't look at me right after that for about ten minutes.

Through the large parlor floor windows of her father's home, we could see the lights blazing, people milling, and the clinking of glasses and chatter came down to the street. Evidently, Mr. Hochman's parties went late. Double-parked black limousines lined the block, the drivers trading jokes with a couple of blues on duty. Probably extra security for some *pezzi grossi,* as the Italians say, VIPs. Then I remembered. Hochman. Sy Hochman was a big Wall Street banker. That was her father? We sat in the car a minute.

"Think she did it?" I said in mock worry, gripping the steering wheel lightly. I went for my cigarette box in my jacket pocket instinctively. Then I remembered that I had quit. I wouldn't have minded a drink right there.

"No." Turner scribbled a note into one of those Mead black-and-white pasteboard composition books that grammar school kids used to carry around. I don't know why but I remembered right then that for years my daughter Libby would accept no Mead notebook without a picture of Barbie on the cover.

I turned the ignition and pulled out. "I'd like to go to that party. Just for a look-see," I said. We turned onto Fifth Ave. He was still writing in the notebook. "The 'moos' again?" I said, elongating the vowels to sound like a cow.

"Never refuse the muse, Paolino. Otherwise she won't come back."

"What if she shows up just when we're under fire, and somebody's about to pop me, then what, Kerouac?"

Turner looked up from his lap, his eyebrows arched with irritation and face lined with a barely noticeable trace of pity, for he knew the muse didn't come to Paolo. "Never happen. My muse abhors violence," he said. "She will not come amidst violence. And Kerouac was more of a novelist than a poet, by the way."

"Amidst? Geez. You want to be dropped back at the House or you want to go home?"

"Drop me off at Nuyorican Café. I'm reading tonight," my partner said.

I didn't want to go downtown but I couldn't refuse to give him a lift.

"You want to come? Plenty of fine, arty girls there. They love poets."

I wasn't a poetry man, but if you measured a poet's triumphs by the number of women he seduced—which was maybe what the ancient Greeks intended—Turner was successful. He had some pieces published in *Lettre*, *Bleak*, and *Black Boom*, but he didn't mind the ancients' tally of success.

"Arty girls don't like cops," I said.

"We're not cops. We're detectives. The executives," he said with the

DJ voice.

"I don't feel it."

"You don't feel it? You're divorced, got no love life, and an ex-drunk, just like half the fucking cops I know. What's your alternative?"

"So my life hasn't been ideal. Fuck that and you, too."

He grunted and looked out the passenger side window.

I don't like pity. Didn't need any help with pussy.

I dropped him off, went home, poured myself a ginger ale, and started on the crossword puzzle.

CHAPTER 3

SATURDAY

"If he really is a diplo, you know State's gonna make us give back the phone book," I said to Turner. We drove over to the Italian Consulate on Park Ave and 66th, which opened at noon Saturday. The clouds from last evening were gone.

I thumbed slowly through the phone book again, as if the killer's name might pop out at me. "We don't have much time," I said. "I photocopied the address book this morning. Somebody in this book knows something."

"You'll call everyone in that book?" he said.

I nodded.

"Some of those numbers are in Italy."

"That's what I'm here for, *paisano*," I said.

At 66th we slowed. On the sidewalk, half a block from the Consulate entrance, dozens of people already were lined up.

"Damn," I laughed. "Just like Cracker Jacks, a little surprise inside."

Turner pulled the car over, narrowly missing a bike messenger, who gave us the finger.

I peeled back the inside cover of the address book and a small piece of lined yellow paper spilled out. A phone number was written on it.

We radioed the number in to the One-Nine. It turned out to be a line at the *Manhattan Morning Post*.

"Call it now?" Turner said.

"Let's see what the Consul General has to say first. Maybe he'll be a little bit more helpful than the wife," I said, opening my door.

That morning, Dunne had told us at first to drop it. From his cover-your-ass, keep-unsolvable-problems-away-from-me viewpoint, that made sense. The press wasn't interested. The Jews for Jesus had taken over the Belvedere Castle in Central Park again, and they vowed to hold it until the messiah returned. Another financial scandal involving a deputy mayor.

So even though Gaetano seemed to be a diplo, military, and it was Sutton Place, with all the other shit happening, the story rated three grafs on page eight of the *Post*.

What I didn't understand was why the Italians didn't care much, either. The Embassy in DC didn't find his name on any diplomatic roster. I finally got a hold of someone in the Consul General's office and the CG reluctantly agreed to meet with us. Once that was lined up, Dunne gave in, though only after telling us how we should be solving real crimes, not goddamn dago foreigner executions.

The CG, Ruggero di Gagliano, kept us waiting thirty minutes before Turner talked his secretary, *Signorina* Bianco, into busting into his office to remind di Gagliano we were waiting.

"Gentlemen, what can we do for you?" the CG said in almost perfect American vernacular without looking up from his desk. He was a small man, bald on top, with oversized tortoise shell eyeglasses, so he looked a little bit like a precocious child sitting behind his large oak desk, a beauty with crenellated corners and biblical scenes etched into the sides. It reminded me of altar paneling I'd seen in a church in Bergamo once. I almost wanted to kneel beside it and confess.

"I think from the beginning, Officer..."

"It's Detective Paul Rossi," I said. "This is Hamilton P. Turner. Also Detective."

Di Gagliano smiled obviously at my name.

"Yes, Detective Rossi. As I was saying, right away we must recognize the diplomatic immunity of the Consulate and all its Italian national employees."

I nodded.

"Actually, I don't even have to meet with you, even if the body and suspect turned out to be one of the Consulate's diplomats. But I want to show good faith to an important ally of Italy." Di Gagliano gave a smile, one that made it clear he was hoping this would be over quickly. He called someone from a side office, a beady-eyed guy in a natty three-piece suit, with high, narrow lapels and trousers fashionably a tad too short, who sat on the couch and took notes.

"This is Mr. Samuele. He's my right hand. He'll be taking notes, if you don't mind."

We nodded.

We talked for a minute about the upcoming World Cup in Japan and Korea. A big black and gold nameplate sat at the edge of his desk, advertising the lowercase "d" in di Gagliano. That typically meant a count or marquise, or some aristocracy.

"It's lucky for you I work most Saturdays," he said. "What can the Italian government do for you? And please, I don't mean to rush you"—which of course was exactly what he meant—"but I must be to a luncheon shortly, an EU-USA meeting."

Di Gagliano stroked the thinning, silvery hair on the sides of his head as we spoke and looked out the window often.

After explaining what had happened to our boy Gaetano and that his docs suggested he worked for the Consulate, I handed him Muro's ID.

The CG looked it over, up and down. "I don't recognize the name, but that means little. Between employees and their dependents, I am responsible for hundreds of people here, not to mention the needs of thousands of Italian nationals living in our region of competence. But this isn't a diplomatic ID, it's just an Italian identity card. All Italians have one. If he is…was accredited to us, I'll let you know. That's all I can promise, Detective Rossi." Then he turned a bit personal. "Paul Rossi. Rossi, hmm, where are your people from?" he asked.

"Basilicata."

"Are you perhaps related to the famous Paolo Rossi who won the World Cup for us in 1982? I forget where he was from."

I said no.

"Oh well. It's a common name, of course," di Gagliano added. "Do you speak Italian?"

"No, just a couple of words from my *nonno*."

Di Gagliano gave a perfunctory laugh, a tiny snort, pig like, and stood up, ready to show us out. It looked as if he felt sorry for me, the little Italian American who knows only a few words of the great operatic language. Isn't that too bad.

Seeing me lie, Turner couldn't resist. Di Gagliano had ignored him the whole time, barely glancing over. "My people are from Abyssinia, otherwise known as Ethiopia," he said. "Every Italian knows where that is, surely."

The CG was unflappable. He gave Turner a pallid smile. "Ah, Ethiopia, *un bel paise*…beeyu-tiful people," he said, staring down at Muro's ID as he turned it over in his hands absently. "I was born there in 1938, so I am African in a way. I was a boy when we had to leave, but I remember. The Negus, the thick-walled, ancient Orthodox churches, the monks… You know they have the Ark of the Covenant in one of those churches."

"I thought that ended up in Rome," I interjected.

"True. Most things finish in Rome," di Gagliano said, almost as if he were talking just to himself.

The meeting was over. I asked for the ID back, but he refused, saying that it was property of the Italian government, and then said, nervously, almost apologetically, that he needed it to get information about Muro. When I asked for a photocopy, he refused that too, claiming Consulate's only machine was broken.

"We will send you a copy," he said, not looking at us and putting the ID in his vest pocket.

I thought of the little brown phone book we still held and looked over at my partner. Both of us remained silent. We fooled no one. I figured they knew about Muro's little address book.

The forgotten legal adjunct, sitting behind us on the couch, piped in. "You will have to give us any other material you might have, Mr. Detective," he said to Turner. The way he said it, sharp and pushy from a little white man, with just enough sovereign contempt, made me fear Turner would lose his cool. He could handle bullets, mendacity, and murder, but not contempt or disrespect.

Turner showed a forced tight smile, behind which the molten lava seethed.

We moved to the door and the adjunct followed us. I pulled a business card out of my pocket and handed it to him. "Let us know if you find out anything on Mr. Muro. And thanks for your...cooperation," I said, closing the door behind us. The lock clicked solidly.

On the way out, Ms. Bianco offered us espressos again. Turner was about to accept when di Gagliano buzzed her on the intercom. He shouted at her in Italian: "Faccia uscire immediatamente quei rompicoglioni di poliziotti e chiami al telefono l'ambasciatore Marone. Subito!" ("Get those ball breaking cops out of here fast, and call Ambassador Marone right away.")

Sabato Sera

It was raining heavily, a soaking that more often hits Milan in the winter, as three men met on the fourth floor of a seventeenth-century Baroque palazzo just behind the opera house in the center of town. The building's entrance was guarded by thick, burnished oak doors, ten feet high. There was no house number on the building. There never has been.

Behind the doors, in the interior courtyard, two armored, silver

Mercedes C class limousines sat parked. The palazzo windows, on the exterior façade and the courtyard, were framed in delicate Italianate arches, almost Middle Eastern, soft curves at the top, simple pedestals below.

A tall, bony man walked to the library's balcony, which faced the cortile, or courtyard, and peeked out at the low clouds. He returned inside quickly, gently closing the glass doors behind him. Though in his mid-seventies, with thick, graying hair, Giovanni Montone seemed younger than his days, with a bearing of one who is rarely refused. He always held his head high, chin forward, just as he was taught in St. Eustace and at Charleton in England, between the World Wars, so many years ago. He was a Senator for Life, a unique Italian Parliamentary office awarded to those who have made a great contribution to the country.

While such an honor isn't supposed to be about money, it was, of course. He headed a family with far-flung business concerns that gave him effective control of many of Italy's major industries. Through Byzantine ownership structures, he typically only needed twenty to thirty percent of a firm's shares to control it. His companies accounted for one sixth of Italy's employment and ten percent of the annual gross domestic product. He was royalty in a country that had exiled its king more than half a century before. There were several Senatori a Vita in the Italian Senate, but the press—and everyone for that matter—referred to him and only to him as The Senator, Il Senatore. He took a sip from his negroni, a drink that dated his playboy days to the 1950s.

On the couch sat an even older man, eighty-five, short but thick, with a humped back and still, dark looks. This man, a Baron from Sicily, always walked with a stoop and hardly spoke to anyone besides The Senator. Gnome-like and wrinkled of face, he looked like a creature that might guard the bridge over a cursed river.

The two men had been friends and colleagues for nearly half a century. The Baron, chairman of MilanoBanca since World War II, steered money and investors to Il Senatore's projects and businesses, and

31

to important politicians in their stables.

A third man, robust, blond, about forty years old, stood before them, his posture military. He looked straight ahead, not at the two men. His English was good but German-accented. He was tired after having arrived from New York just one hour before.

"We agreed that you would take care of the body, did we not?" said Il Senatore. His English was without flaw, tinged slightly by neutral BBC British.

"Yes, but we could not wait for a more opportune situation. We were certain the target was about to break…at any moment. He had been speaking to a reporter. We believe he was going to meet a man named Gretzman at the newspaper."

The Senator walked back to the couch, so that now he was directly behind the Baron. He rested his hands on the top of the couch, framing the Gnome with his arms. "We were informed that the New York City police are investigating. This disturbs us."

The Baron sat there motionless, eyeing the man standing before them.

"It's routine. He had immunity so there won't be any trouble. Your people in New York say there will not be a problem."

"Why didn't you get rid of the body? We don't like bodies and we don't like broken promises in this country," The Senator said.

"A police car came up unexpectedly ahead of our van when I completed my mission. For some reason, the police pulled over and stopped just down the street from me. I had no choice. I couldn't stand there waiting for our van to come. They'd have noticed. There was no time to return for the body. I was afraid someone might come along, and a woman did. It was a small error. I'm sorry."

"Did she see you?" asked the thin man.

"Absolutely not," said the standing man without hesitation. He knew she'd seen him. His arms were straight at his sides, and he began to lightly rub together the forefingers and thumbs to dry the thin film of sweat *building up.*

Il Senatore invited the blond man to sit, but the Baron waved off the courtesy. The smaller man kept his gaze on the German the whole time, searching him as he might a tea leaf.

"It would be well for you to go back to America immediately and make certain the investigation ends," the Baron said. His dark blue eyes never left the target. They were the kind of azure mixed with the white of a fire, but they didn't give off any warmth. It wasn't clear if his reputation made his eyes scarier or if these strangely beautiful eyes made his reputation. Italians loved to say that if the Baron wanted something to happen, so did God.

Taking the Baron's threat as his cue, the standing man nodded his head and left.

When they were alone, Il Senatore put down his drink, and turned to the Baron. "He's lying. Perhaps we have made an error with this man, letting him take care of an important piece of business. But in this particular case we needed someone not at all traceable to us and disposable..."

The Gnome stared at the spot where the guest had stood. Then, "I did not want this done in America."

"Agreed. But as you know, there was little time. The colonnello wasn't going to return willingly, and he was becoming more and more...erratic over the past few weeks."

"Nor did I want your East German friends involved," the Baron continued with unadorned sarcasm.

"The colonnello was originally..." The Senator paused, not wanting to sound like he was blaming the head of the pride, but nonetheless wanting to shift some of the barely veiled accusation from his shoulders, "...your idea."

"Yes, yes," said the Baron. "That's my error. He's the grandson of an old friend. When I first met him years ago, it occurred to me that a fighter pilot might someday be useful to us." The Baron looked over to his friend.

"That proved well and true two decades ago. Now we have to clean up the mess made by these Germans you hired. It is too late for quiet methods. It could have been all so simple." He sighed. "Now we will need to send an unmistakable message to our new police friends in America."

"Though we are a bit old for battle, I am reminded of a favorite bit of wisdom," The Senator said. "'Experience has shown that princes achieve the greatest success in war when they themselves direct the movements of their own armies, while mercenary troops do nothing but damage.' I should have observed this rule closely."

His business partner began to chuckle at the Machiavelli quote. The great political philosopher's strictures were practically tattooed on his brain. Nodding his head, he brought his hands together in his lap, as if he were a pastor about to address the flock at a Black Mass. He remained seated there with his feet dangling a few inches above the floor. From his lips came a whisper that the thin man could not hear, "Niccolo' aveva ragione." (Niccolo was right.)

Chapter 4

Sunday

When I arrived at my desk, a working Sunday thanks to Muro, Turner was already hunched over his, eyeing Muro's little brown address book. I'd made a photocopy of all the pages and given him the original last night. But he was working from photocopies, too. "Where's Muro's book?"

"Dunne took it. State Department suit called him and gave him a foreign policy lecture. So I had to give it up, sans the yellow note, though."

I threw my jacket on the chair, sat, and swiveled over to him. "Any luck?"

"No," he said, not looking up. "Reached four out of six local numbers. They swore up and down that they didn't know him that well. Oh, and they were real sorry he was dead, too. I'll call them again later. Let their conscience work on them a bit."

"You're assuming friends of people like Muro and Hochman have such luxuries."

He ignored me. "I'm saving the Italiano phoners for you."

"Forget that. I called most of them from home this morning because of the time difference. *Niente.* By the way, my daughter's learning to play frisbee. It scares me," I said.

Turner stopped and looked at me. "You sucking the liquor tit again?" He rode me hard about my drinking. My former drinking.

I shook my head.

"Come again?" he said.

"Later I'm going over to the ex. Libby wants me to teach her Frisbee so she can play with some fourteen-year-old boys she and her friends have their eyes on…I think. They could be fuckin pedophile truck drivers she found on that Internet thing for all I know. I only see her one or two days a week."

He threw down his pen, and leaned back in his chair, hands behind his neck. "White girls are funny even when they're young."

I frowned what must have looked like a liberal's grimace.

"They are always toddling after boys. When I was twelve, I was afraid I'd have to learn to skip rope and braid hair in order to get this one girly I liked. I hope she learns to play Frisbee real well," he added a bit sheepishly, his eyebrows knitted together a little.

"Screw you," I laughed.

"You really want to spend time on this one?" He pulled out three other murder files and waved them in front of me.

A nineteen-year-old prostitute from Minneapolis who'd gotten stabbed at Neutrino's, a dive run by the Irish Mafia on 94th. There was a seven-year-old who had been beaten to death by his stepdad while his junkie mom shot up. I didn't even remember the other one. They all ran together in my head, like that slimy red crap they put in lava lights. Top to bottom, bottom to top, over and over again and no real changes, even though it looks a little different every time.

"Yeah, well, I'm intrigued," I said. "That Consul General was hiding something. You gonna tell me he doesn't know if a colonel from the Capo Servizio whatever is working for him? Bullshit. Muro was in the Service. That man has to know."

"What's he hiding? A drug scheme or a lover's spat. I hate to say it, but in this one case, once in a century, maybe Dunne's right," Turner said.

I gave him a sideways and disbelieving eye roll. "Murder's murder." I said, twirling a pencil in my hand.

Then I remembered the yellow note. "Hey, what about that phoner that fell out of the address book," I said. I dialed and Turner got on an extension. The phone rang three times before a guy with a high-pitched voice answered, "Metro. Gretzman."

"Is this the *Post*?" I said.

"Yeah. Who are you?"

"I'm a detective at the One-Nine, homicide. Rossi."

"I'm not the police beat reporter, you want Dan—"

"No, it's not like that," Turner cut in. "I'm Hamilton P. Turner. Don't you remember?"

There was just the slightest pause, as if Gretzman were sizing him up, wondering if this would be a page one story or buried in the back of the book. "I remember you," he said, "the black cop with the goatee beef? The brass wanted you to shave it. I wrote about it like a year ago."

Dunne really didn't like Turner much. He tried to hide it. He asked for a disciplinary hearing over the goatee, but Turner won. That got my partner a three-inch mention on page five of the *Post*. Civil liberties and all that. Of course, it also got his brother officers in the African American chapter of the Policeman's Benevolent Association mad, as they didn't think a goatee was a disciplinary matter worth going to the mat for.

"Yeah," Turner answered.

"Great, you won, right? What's the matter now? Afro problem?" When Turner didn't laugh, he said quickly, "Is it sexy?"

Turner looked over to me, and I came back on.

"Too sexy for the phone," I said.

I could almost feel Gretzman's mouth coming closer to the receiver.

"Look, I'm not interested in another departmental tiff. How do I know this is good?" he said.

"You don't," I shot back. "Maybe I'll call Dan what's-his-name."

"No. I'll handle it," Gretzman said even before I put the period on my sentence. "You know Moonie's on 1st and 13th? It's quiet, secluded. Nobody goes there."

Turner made a sourpuss face. He hated Irish bars in general. He looked at me and I shrugged my shoulders.

"Sure, I know it."

"Today, one p.m.," he said.

I put down the phone. "Think he knows anything?"

"I don't know," Turner said, "but if his taste in saloons is any indication, he probably doesn't know jack shit."

We spent part of the afternoon on the phone dialing the remaining phone numbers. The only one who would meet with us was Turner's old girlfriend Elena. She was so excited to hear from him; he didn't have the heart to tell her why. He'd tell her in person, right after he screwed her.

*   *   *

"Mooooo," Turner said as we stood waiting outside Moon's, which looked as run down as the three septuagenarian barflies we could see through the front glass. The place was hardly more than an East Village tenement storefront, with a neon sign blinking on and off, the last three letters dark. It blinked "Moo." The neon shamrock didn't work, either. It was the kind of place where the addition of barnyard animals might improve the smell and general level of clientele.

Two of the three at the bar were sleeping. One held a cigarette with a long ash balanced perfectly between thumb and forefinger, while his other hand was wrapped rigor mortis-like around a dirty yellow beer mug. The other was quietly oozing white, bubbly saliva onto the bar, and he was out for sure, though his eyelids had flapped up.

"It's one fifteen and he ain't here," Turner said, getting angry. "Ten to one, this Gretzman is one of those skinny, smartass Jewish fellas with round, wire-rim glasses. Probably went to Harvard or Yale, working on a dime novel and thinks he deserves a Pulitzer."

"You're giving him too much credit. I thought you knew the boy."

"Yeah, well. Talked to him a coupla times on the phone a while ago. That's all. I hate—"

"When people are late," I interjected.

Turner smiled when I finished his sentence.

"I'll double-check the back of the bar. The booths in the back are pretty dark." I didn't want to endure that smell again.

There are scores of these bars in each borough. The smells inhabiting these watering holes originate from generations of beer spill painstakingly worked into every crevice of the bar, cushions and chairs. There, the millions of bacterial spores, *glutinous stalis*, under the heavy pressure of cigarette and cigar smoke mixed with the oil from human fingers, eventually mutated to become a strange new life form. And when one of the patrons sits motionless on a barstool in one of these places just long enough, the mold can eventually take over his body, as these three bar hounds demonstrated.

Just as I came back out to give the thumbs-down, Gretzman showed.

He was just as Turner had pictured, short, slight of shoulder, with wire-rim glasses, sport jacket, old jeans, no tie, and dirty black shoes. If he was Jewish, he was Ashkenazi, pale as bone, pinkish lips, and reddish-brown curly hair. No suntans for this guy. His hands were thrust deeply into his pockets, so he appeared a bit hunched, like he had a bad back.

"Officer Turner?"

"Detective Turner."

"Right, sorry, Detective," Gretzman answered, not particularly sincerely, sticking out his hand. "Who's your friend?"

"That's my partner, Detective Rossi."

We went inside and directly to the last booth, and Turner made a point of making sure there was no one around us in adjoining booths. I thought maybe he laid it on a bit heavy. We didn't have anything to give this guy.

Turner asked about wine, but the waitress gave him a "you poor fucker, don't you see what kind of shithole operation this is" look. Gretzman got a beer and corned beef on rye. I asked for a Coke. Turner decided then he didn't even want water. We passed on the food.

I took the lead. "First, everything we tell you is on deep background, understand. We have an incomplete picture, and if you write about it now, you'll fuck it up for us...and for yourself. Everything's on background until we say it isn't. Understood?"

Gretzman half nodded. "So why'd you call me?"

"That's what we want to know," Turner chimed in.

"What are you talking about?" Gretzman said, his voice going high pitched again.

"We found your number hidden in somebody's little brown book," I said in a low voice. "Hidden inside the front cover flap."

"Yeah, so?"

"That somebody is dead. Executed, actually. We don't have much on him but we think you know who he is."

Gretzman figured it out right away. "You guys want the story from me. You have nothing."

"Not true," Turner shot back. "He was Italian, probably in the military. Gaetano Muro."

"You guys wrote yesterday that he was mugged and murdered Friday on Sutton," I cut in.

"Yeah, but the cops didn't give out the name," he said. "Pending notification of next of kin." Gretzman perked up now.

"He wasn't robbed but he was killed," I said. "Robbery was how it appeared in the police blotter because we have an ID but no wallet, and not much else. It was a stop 'n' drop. The man was whacked. Clean shot to the head, another to the chest. Muro was attached to the Italian Consulate."

Gretzman hunched forward, laying aside his sandwich. He took

40

off his glasses to wipe them. He had light gray eyes.

"Yeah, I remember him now. Gaetano Muro is…was Guy. I met him at a book party at the Italian Cultural House on 10th in the Village about two weeks ago. Great place to troll for chicks, by the way. Seemed like a nice guy. Handsome. Very European. He looked military, ramrod straight, very polite. His English was terrible though. I had a hard time understanding him. When he found out that I worked for the *Post*, he wouldn't leave me alone. I thought he was a little nuts."

Turner and I eyed each other.

I started to get that itchy feeling on the back of my neck that came whenever a case began to resemble a Russian nesting doll. You could spend a lot of time on it and in the end all you have is a bunch of cheap wooden dolls to show for it. "What does an Italian colonel want with a *Post* reporter?" I asked.

At that, Gretzman pulled back. He smiled weakly, took a bite of corned beef and chewed for a few seconds. It was clear he realized he knew about as much we did.

"Look, guys. I don't know if we got something or nothing here, but we gotta have an agreement. I'm all for helping the law, but you have to help the fourth estate. Me in particular."

"How?" I said.

"No other reporters. You can't talk to my competition."

"Come on," I said, protesting half-heartedly.

"After I break the first one, you're free to talk to whoever you want," Gretzman said. "Pretty standard. You guys know that."

"*Whomever.* I thought you were a writer," Turner corrected him. He looked at me and I nodded. "All right, deal. We won't talk about Muro, but you have to protect us. And you might have to hold off when we say so, if it compromises the investigation."

The reporter nodded.

"What'd Guy say?" I said.

"I couldn't make sense of his story. I'm telling you the guy's English was bad… Let's see."

Turner took out a pad and pencil, and Gretzman laughed. "I'm the one supposed to be writing this down. Like I said, he told me his name was Guy. But he wouldn't give me his last name. Said that would come later. He didn't have a name tag like everyone else at the party. Anyway, Guy said he had a story for me. Then he got quiet. When I asked him what story, I was pretty skeptical. *Post* readers don't give a rat's ass about stories about European countries, but, hey, I'd been to Rome once, so I asked him. That's when he looked around and pulled me into the pantry, off the lecture hall, away from the party. Now I'm thinking either he's nuts, or he'll make a pass at me, or both. When he closed the door behind us, I was ready for anything. He told me he was a fighter pilot for Italy. Said he has a very, very big story. 'People died, many people,' he says. 'I can no longer remain quiet. Their souls are bothering me now,' he says, and he asked me for my number and I wrote it down for him. 'We have to meet soon. Some place safe,' he said.

"Then the pantry door burst open and two guys come in. They didn't have name tags either but I remember one had a fat ruby red ring on his finger. 'Colonnello,' one of them says, 'we are missing you at the party.' Then he says something in Italian and they drag him out of the pantry. They didn't look at me for more than a second but they saw my name tag. Everybody had name tags except for those two and Guy. Then instead of going back to the party, they hustled him out of the building and into a cab."

Gretzman finished his sandwich. "Strange."

Turner pulled out the yellow sheet with Gretzman's number on it.

Gretzman pointed at it. "Yeah. How'd you get that?"

"We told you. That's what we found hidden in Muro's phone book," I said.

Gretzman said, "Can I see the phone book?"

"Too late," Turner said. He scratched the side of his face lightly. "State Department made us give it back to the Italian Consulate."

"Too bad," Gretzman said. "Somebody in there has to know something," he added.

My partner and I looked at each other. He smirked.

"One other thing," Gretzman said, ""Guy called me last Wednesday and left a message. Said he was going to come by my office. He was yammering a mile a minute. You know how many crazies call the *Post* each day with their hallucinations? Anyway, you could hear the panic," Gretzman said, looking down at his empty plate and moving crumbs with his fork. "At the end, Guy kept repeating, 'Ewe-stick-her, yewe-stick-her.' I don't know. Something like that, maybe five times, and then the message ended abruptly. I didn't think much of it at the time. *Post* wouldn'a gone for it anyway," Gretzman said. "Do you speak Italian?" he said to me. "What's 'ewe-sticker-her' or 'oo-sticker' in Italian?"

"Beats me," I said. "Doesn't even sound Italian. Gretzman, tell me you saved the message."

He shook his head with pursed lips. "Sorry." He stood up. "Got to get back to the office. I'm in the middle of a story about a dead prostitute with a heart of gold."

"Don't know how you guys do what you and keep a straight face," I said.

"I say the same thing about cops," he replied over his shoulder.

After he left, I wondered aloud if we shouldn't have shown him some of the names in the little address book.

"He can't be trusted not to write about this. Just tell him what we need to, when we have to," Turner said.

*   *   *

Later Sunday night I went home. Spoke with Harry for a minute. He was going fishing off the Long Island shore for a day or two. Wanted to know if I wanted to come along.

"Everything good?"

"Two years, nine months, four weeks, and four days."

"Make it two, nine, four, and five," he said, and hung up.

I walked over to the kitchen table and opened the *Times* to the crossword page.

"Any of several American shorebirds with webbed feet?" I wasn't one of those rapid *Times* crossword fans. Most of the time, I wouldn't finish, but I'd get about eighty percent done before I'd give up. As I was printing the letters for "tern," my phone rang. I reached up from the couch and grabbed the receiver.

"Hey," Turner breathed.

"What's up? I'm doing the puzzle."

"Graduate to one hundred pieces yet?"

"Funny."

"Come straight to Hochman's crib," he said.

"What?"

"Dorothy's. She's had visitors. She's okay. Her place is trashed."

"In ten."

There was little apartment left to come to. The four walls were still there, but the place had been scientifically upended. Furniture piled in the middle of the rooms. Drawers removed from the dressers and cabinets, their backs pulled out. Couch and chair fabric ripped open. These folks had made fist-sized holes in the walls at various points. Looking for what?

Maybe Hochman knew. After spending the day at her father's place, she'd come home, she claimed, to find a place that qualified for Federal disaster relief. Yet chunks of jewelry were left, strewn around the place. Sitting on a Persian carpet, a couple of diamonds the size of my pinkie knuckle blinked at me. The five-hundred-dollar-bill she had left in a Limoges vase on the kitchen table for would-be robbers was still there, amid smashed pieces of the French ceramic.

Here was the best part: the back of the refrigerator had been removed, even a couple of window sashes had been opened. Jesus. How'd they do this without neighbors immediately complaining to the co-op board?

Her father wasn't just a Wall Street financier, but the king *macher*, with his own powerful investment bank and brokerage, one of those Forbes 400 guys. I knew more than one cop whose kids' college tuition evaporated with the dot.com Internet crash thanks to Hochman's weaselly brokers.

Dorothy sat on a stool, calling her insurance company. She was still wearing black. There were a couple of blues around and Detective Louis Grasso from the robbery squad, our resident breaking and entering expert. He was the Bolt Whisperer. If it locked, he could open it. Grasso could have made a mint as a locksmith in New York, I figured, but instead he felt, like some of us, anyway, that somebody had to catch the bad guys.

The doorman told him that we had come by on Saturday. Grasso remembered the Muro murder and called Turner when he realized whose apartment this was.

"What are you gentlemen doing here?" she asked, looking up from the phone. "I thought you were *homicidal* detectives," she said, just a little bit too unmoved, I thought, for someone freshly widowed and then robbed. But then I wasn't insanely rich. I began to think that perhaps Gaetano wasn't so crazy, marrying this girl. Maybe his enemies had more to do with Sy Hochman. For a moment, with the way she said it, I'd have guessed she was slathering Turner a bit.

He didn't mind. "We are," my partner responded, and then corrected her, "that is, in the homicide squad."

She slammed down the phone. "Damn insurance companies. Just thieves. Take your money and when you need them at ten o'clock at night, their fucking eight hundred number tells you to call tomorrow." She took out a cigarette and Turner offered her his lighter.

"That and losing your husband added up to a bad weekend," I said quietly, but loud enough to be heard. She ignored me.

"You okay?" Turner asked her.

I went over to talk to Grasso for a minute, but still within earshot.

"Yes. I was out all day and came home to this."

Turner took out his pad and asked what she'd done today.

She probably didn't connect this to Gaetano. I also wasn't sure. Whoever did this had to have tailed her for a while. "Have you checked for missing valuables yet, Ms. Hochman?" I asked, coming back to the twosome.

"No," she answered flatly, as if to say, "Why should I, genius? Can't you see I've been robbed?"

"Well, Detective Grasso has found a good bit of money scattered about, and a lot of jewelry seems to have been left behind." I paused. "Ms. Hochman, he's been on the force for over twenty years and he said he's never seen New York City burglars take the time to silently drill about two dozen very clean holes in a victim's apartment walls."

Turner crinkled a little smile. I was giving as good as I was getting.

I couldn't tell if she really didn't get it, or was trying to hide something. Maybe Muro had stashed something in the apartment. "Ms. Hochman, perhaps whoever did this wasn't looking to rob you, at least not of money," I said.

She sat there patiently smoking her cigarette. She turned herself more in my direction.

"Now you are going to tell me this has something to do with Guy?"

"Don't know for sure," I said. "But can you give us some kind of explanation, like you're a Russian operative or something totally believable like that."

She smiled weakly. "No. But this looks like a robbery to me. Yeah, they left a few things. Maybe they were in a hurry. I haven't had time to check, and it's going to take time to find out what's here and what's not. I've got...I don't see my jewelry box around, for example. Yeah, there are some rocks on the floor, but I have...had a *lot* of jewelry," she said, "and maybe they left what they didn't like," she mused. "In fact, just looking at what's on the floor, I would have left that, too," she laughed, then looked at Turner.

"Do you have a place to stay?" he asked, and rather boldly, I worried. I thought he was going to follow that up with an offer of space at his place. "We can give you a lift," he added in a soft, thigh-weakening lilt. She warmed up to that. "Yes, if you could drop me back at my father's place. He's expecting me. That'd be welcome, Detective Turner," she said, not even looking at me.

Not wanting to watch Turner in action yet one more time, I gave the apartment another look. A minute later, my partner joined me. "You're going to give her just a lift, right?" I asked.

"Yeah, yeah, don't worry. Maybe I'll call her in a month, she'll still be charmed, and there'll be no conflicts," he said.

"You're assuming this is all over in a month." He didn't reply. "What do you think they were looking for?" I stuck four fingers into one of the holes and felt around. Nothing. I wiped the gray drywall dust from my hand, and the powder sprinkled to the carpet.

Grasso walked over to us. He looked like a grandpa who'd be more comfortable in a cardigan and soft slippers than a detective in a cheap suit. Twinkly blue eyes but breath like a shark. "The holes were so round and...professional. Drilled and not punched. Hand tooled," he said. I denoted a bit of grudging respect in his tone, as if the perp was a breaking and entering performance artist. "This was no sledgehammer job. That would have been too noisy. These people had the tools, alright," Grasso said. "The guys who did this, they're pros. Money. Museum quality, high-tech stuff. CIA? NSA? Maybe somebody's intelligence service, anyway. Even the front door locks still worked," he said to me, genuinely stumped. He bent down and picked up a braided gold bracelet from the floor, looked at it and whistled at what was clearly an expensive piece. He shook his head at the foolishness of leaving something like that behind. "We'll be finished in a minute," he said and he walked back to his team.

"I don't know," Turner said to me. "We can't be one hundred percent sure it's connected to Guy. Who knows what this society chick's been up to? She's pretty rich. She…her dad…they've got enemies, too."

Hochman, out of earshot, looked over and smiled. She was on the phone again.

Turner was thinking this was connected to Muro as well, but we needed to try out several explanations. The last thing we wanted to do was go to Dunne with some half-cocked international murder and high-tech robbery story that didn't pan out. With the way Dunne felt about Turner, he would have us reassigned to traffic duty on Staten Island.

"We'll have a little talk with Dorothy on the way tonight, huh," Turner said to me. "I'll drive slowly. Maybe she knows something, even if she doesn't know she does."

Hochman got off the phone and seemed to be in a better mood. She'd reached her insurance company. "Detective Turner, I'd like to leave now," she said, adding, "if you are ready," with just short enough of a pause that it didn't seem an order or afterthought. "I just have to get some things."

Her black pants were sharp. Tight enough to flatter an excellent figure but not enough to be trashy. She wore a white blouse, with fine black and purple stripes. Missoni, according to Turner. It was only now that I'd noticed her big black eyes. My partner was no fool. He was jelly for the doe-eyed girls, I'd noticed. For that matter, so was I. Maybe Guy, too. The blues and Grasso's team had packed up their chemistry sets and left, and it was now suddenly quiet in the apartment. Hochman returned from her bedroom, leather jacket in hand. A moment later the door locked loudly behind us, working as if nothing had happened.

When we reached the lobby, we needed to question Yuri again, so I brought Hochman out to our car, parked just in front of the building, and put her in the backseat. "We'll be finished with the doorman in a minute," I said to her, and she settled in. We were going to let her think about things.

As I turned to walk back to the lobby, where Turner was talking to Yuri, I saw a black Mercedes-Benz limo doubled-parked about a hundred feet up the street, toward Park Ave. Instinct made me look at the plates but I couldn't make them. They appeared to be diplo tags, red and blue. In a precinct with thirty-two missions, twelve consulates, and seventy ambassadorial or consulate residences, that didn't surprise me.

Back in the lobby, Turner was holding a wide flat binder, the building log, in his hands. "So you came on shift at one in the afternoon?" he asked.

The log showed names and times of entry and exits for service people. "Wery bizzy day, today. FedEx deliweeery guys is comink, UPS is comink, express mail packajez, kupla messengers, Werizon phone people. Vee get a lots of professional peoples in dis bilding," he said just a little too proudly, "and stuff comes and it goez. You know. Doc-ooh-ment, some box-hes, manuscrip, fruit basket, plant, ev-weee-ting! Maybe Andy, dee morning guy, he knows someting, but it's not like these robbermans come wit tools hanging from dare belts. Not when I was here."

"We'll take the book for a day or two, okay, Yuri?" Turner said.

"Yes, yes, but I need it back. You must not keep it," he said, getting nervous in only the way an Upper East Side doorman could, part subservient nervousness and part arrogance.

"We just need to double-check it with the companies who sent people today, that's all. They've got logs, too, and they should back up yours. The one that doesn't is the bogus one. You'll have it back." I patted him on his back.

"Give me Andy's phone number and address," I said to Yuri, who turned to go into a tiny office next to the mail slots.

As Yuri opened and closed a few drawers in the office, the intercom rang and he answered it. Turner stood behind the large, beige leather guest couch in the lobby, his face buried in the log. I looked over to check on Hochman, who wasn't looking our way, but just sitting quietly. That's when I noticed a black limo pull up next to our Crown

Vic.

It did a slow pass, far too slowly, I thought, and I kept watching. What happened next was over in seconds but felt much longer. The smoked windows, front and back, of the black car's right side came down slowly and evenly. I couldn't see inside the limo. It was too far away, but then when the barrels came out of the front and rear windows, the streetlight made them glint silvery blue, as if lit by moonshine.

I barely got out the first syllable of Dorothy's name before the windows of our car and the building's plate glass blew out, shattering and splintering everywhere. I dove backward into the side office, pulling Yuri down with me behind the desk. The phone receiver hung down over the desk and just out of reach. The receiver swayed back and forth along the side of the desk, like the balance mechanism in a grandfather clock.

I pulled out my Glock, which even with a full mag of fifteen wasn't going to do much good in the face of the mega power outside, and slid over to the door. If I hadn't seen the car, I'd have sworn somebody was crunching pavement with a jackhammer. It was that kind of pounding.

Outside, in the lobby, Turner squatted behind the couch. He was okay and alternately looking at me and trying to get a peek out front, though that was going to get him killed if he did it too many times. If they wanted Turner and me, they could have easily nailed us. I couldn't hear him but saw him mouth, "Holy fucking shit." A chandelier had crashed down where I was standing just seconds before and then, just as quickly as it started, the attack stopped. From the swaying intercom receiver, I could hear an older lady saying, in a voice that sounded entitled and displeased, "Yuri, Yuri, where are you? What's going on down there? Who's breaking glass?"

Turner nodded in my direction, one hand securely stuck to his automatic and the other to the S&W revolver.

I nodded back, though clearly this was a move we could regret. We raced out front, guns up, but the limo tires were already smoking.

Turner checked Hochman and I ran into the street to try to ID the plate. It was that black diplo Mercedes. But that's all I saw. Our car and the radio were history, so I had to call it in via Yuri's phone. I turned to see Turner trying to slam our car's backdoor shut, cursing. It banged and hung limply open. It was riddled and wouldn't close properly. I looked inside the back. Dorothy Hochman's Missoni blouse was ruined.

The Crown Vic was Swiss, peppered with slugs the size of Sacagawea dollars. At least it was quick. We sat on the sidewalk. There was nothing to be done for Hochman. In less than a minute I heard sirens wailing, and an EMS truck scrambled around the far corner and accelerated down the street.

"The car was bouncing so much from the shot that it seemed like it jumped into the air from the recoil," Turner said, wiping the sweat from his face with a hankie.

"See anybody?"

"No," he said, looking away.

"Fuck," I said. "Well, we have a dead taxpayer now. Maybe we won't have to hide the case from Dunne anymore." Neither of us laughed. I got up and started looking for witnesses among the bystanders. They stood back from the car quietly, like skittish ghosts. There were so many people hanging out their windows and jabbering, you'd think we were back in a South Bronx barrio instead of the Upper East Side.

"They got Tosca, too," Turner said with disgust, throwing the shot-up CD and jewel case into the street.

Chapter 5

Monday

I was more right than I'd imagined. Not only did Dunne cooperate, he had his arm twisted into giving us carte blanche. That was partly thanks to who Hochman was and partly to Gretzman. Hochman's murder, clearly a rubout, was so big that the *Post* put it on their website Sunday night and on the front page in the paper the next day: "Hochman Heiress Hit." "Muro was her husband and his murder wasn't a mugging," Gretzman wrote, "as originally thought, but some kind of skullduggery—according to unnamed sources close to the investigation." That was us. That got the rest of New York's whiniest calling us night and day for scoops. And it made it all the way across the Atlantic to Italy's TV news.

The death squad had used new Glock 21s with big bore .45s, lots of 'em, according to FID Ballistics. The two murders and Gretzman's story got the attention of the mayor's people. Dorothy Hochman was the only child of Sy Hochman, CEO and owner of Hochman, Ellis, Brown & Co., which happened to be the lead underwriting bank for most city municipal bonds. Hochman and the mayor were tight. If they weren't golfing together in Westchester, they were at Jay's Cigar Room on 42nd or sitting at the mayor's box at Shea Stadium. Hizzoner was a big-time New York Mets fan, and took every opportunity—it seemed to this

Yankee fan judging by the TV news—to be filmed goofily wearing a Mets cap. Seemed un-mayor-like to me. Gretzman told me that even though he wasn't on the crime beat, his editors threw him on the story because he "knew" Guy.

Mayor Francis X. Salerno had made his name more than twenty years before as the local Federal DA who'd cleaned out the mob. He'd won decades of hard time for five Mafia capos. The wiseguys themselves had christened him with the nickname of Peek-a-boo for his wiretapping and surveillance methods. That was supposed to be a dis, but it turned out to be like a medal pinned on him. For all the bullshit written about *omerta*, Peek-a-boo knew most of the street soldiers had a beef with one or another of the lieutenants, and that they, in turn, had a beef with one or another of their capos. Each underling was ready to do time for his own capo, but not for ones he hated or who had dissed him. Respect was the currency of the Mob. If you didn't have it, you might as well have been a nine-to-five schmo, one of the lambs. It was just a matter of time before Peek-a-boo, who worked with the Jesuit fervor and tenacity he absorbed in Regis High School, found the weak links in each of the Mafia families.

By the '80s we were already down to the third and fourth generations of wiseguys, and it turned out that one or two *would* turn against lieutenants and capos they hated, especially if the footman was facing a life rap. Capos didn't approve of turning state's evidence, but when it hurt a rival capo, well, with the Russians, Dominicans, and Jamaican gangs breathing hard on their rackets, then even in *La Cosa Nostra* there was wiggle room for informants. Peek-a-boo knew this and played them all. When the capos finally caught on, it was too late. Each time they brought somebody in for an indictment, Salerno'd play the incriminating phone recording or the video tape for them and laugh, "Peek-a-boo, I see you."

I'd met the mayor briefly at my academy graduation, when he was still DA. "Rossi, eh," he said to me, smiling at our common heritage.

"Remember one thing. Every Wiseguy makes our folks look bad, *brutta figura*. Every bastard who'd rather break heads instead of using his head. Capeesh? And we are going to get them. Every fuckin' one."

That morning, Peek-a-boo was in great form on TV. I watched him on *Your Morning Show at 8 a.m.* Slim and tall, receding but still-black hair, decent looking but not handsome. He was perfect for the tube, gravitas in form avuncular. He wasn't going to be a lowly mayor for long. Albany was next, maybe Washington.

"I want to assure everyone that this isn't the start of a Mafia war," Peek-a-boo said straight into the camera. "These murders will get the full attention of the police force. We will do the utmost to apprehend the perpetrators of these heinous crimes, and, in fact, we have several leads." He smiled directly at his viewers.

To me, it was as if he knew the perps were watching and he wanted to intimidate them. That made me lean off my couch and put down my coffee and bagel. I looked at the TV hoping he'd say it again. "Leads." Like maybe then I'd know what the fuck he was talking about. Then my phone rang.

I picked up the receiver with my eyes still glued to the TV, half expecting Peek-a-boo himself on the line to ask me for a progress report on the crime.

"What fuckin leads?" Turner asked.

"I don't know. Maybe Dunne's not telling us everything," I said, not able to take my gaze away from the TV set and Mayor Salerno.

*　　*　　*

Our own uberlieutenant called us into his office that morning. At 9 a.m., Dunne was already tired, more ashen faced than usual, like he'd been chewed out hard.

"The Consulate was starting to make a stink. Three days after Guy's murder, they finally acknowledged that he was on "temporary assignment" here. They refused to get any more specific. The commissioner called. Peek-a-boo wants arrests…soon. I've got Hayes and Sanchez back on Sutton asking everyone in the area if they saw anything that could be connected to Muro. You know there was a patrol car on that street approximately around the time Muro got dropped. The two blues now remember that they saw a tall blond guy, mid-to-late thirties, standing between two SUVs, poking his head out and looking at them for just a second before he walked away. There was a white van that took off, with speed. No tags ID'ed. Nothing more. Sanchez double-checked with the neighbors at Hochman's apartment. We've got a lot of zeros right now, and I'm feelin' the commissioner's spikes right here." Dunne tapped both shoulders, head bowed. "So, what have you got?"

"What have we got?" I sputtered, looking at my partner. "Lieutenant, what the fuck is that…with all due respect? Friday this was 'Drop it,' and now you're asking me what've we got…" I looked at my partner for support. "We got squat."

Dunne pushed back his squeaking chair from the desk and threw his feet up. He gave a sideways acknowledgment by sighing. "Okay. Let's start again. And I'll be nice. Gentlemen, what are the leads that our lovely mayor is promising the citizens?"

That's when Turner jumped in, thoughtfully caressing his goatee as he explained. "You know Muro wasn't robbed. He was executed. I don't care what the Eyeties said, but he's military. A colonel, probably in the Air Force, for a while, anyway. We got that from someone Muro talked to before he was drilled."

I pulled out my notes. "Muro was apparently estranged from his wife, Dorothy Hochman, probably for months, maybe longer. He wasn't living at the apartment, according to her. Where he was during that time, we don't know. Muro was trying to sell some kind of story to a *Post* reporter, the guy who wrote up the Hochman murder today. He doesn't know much, or else he's saving it for his book deal. Hochman herself said she didn't know what her husband was doing here. And when she was robbed yesterday, they were definitely looking for something. Just ask Grasso."

"For what?" Dunne asked.

"Damned if we know," I said. "Robbed is not the correct description. Looked like they'd done soundings for something metallic behind her walls. A couple of them were just plain pulled down. Whatever it is, I have a feeling there's a connection between the two murders. They nailed Muro for something he was about to say. And Hochman. Either she knew or there was something in their apartment, whether she knew it or not. I got the feeling she didn't know. Hochman was a warning to us."

Dunne seemed surprised by this. "Peek-a-boo pretty much decimated the Mob."

"Maybe this is bigger than them," I said.

The best Dunne could muster was a dejected "Fuck." He looked down. That was our signal to go.

"Hey, what about the leads Peek-a-boo talked about?" I said as we stood to leave.

"You're supposed to have them. He's running for governor," Dunne replied without even looking up from his desk, "so you better come up with some."

We shuffled out and into the squad room.

"What do you mean, 'Maybe this is bigger than them.' What are you going on about?" Turner asked.

"Maybe I don't know what I'm talking about. But the Mafia doesn't kill women. To use that firepower is to send a message."

"These people are evil, Paolo, evilissimo," my partner said. "I got a feeling Muro's murder might be the littlest detail in a very ugly quilt."

At my desk, I kept a small bust of Mussolini. It was a joke, but nobody seemed to get it. I'd bought it in Rome years ago. I loved that 1930s way he thrust his chin out. Mussolini thought he was being manly, but he looked like a buffoon, one with a glass jaw. I'd been meaning to throw the bust away but kept forgetting. Taped to it was a message from Gretzman to call him. Urgent.

"Rossi," I said when the scribe came on the line.

"I'm a fucking star," Gretzman laughed. "And I have you guys to thank."

"Fuck you. Whatta you got for me? This is a two-way street, and so far, I've been doing all the driving. Plus, you reneged, writing that story," I whined.

"Hey, I couldn't help it Hochman's daughter got nailed. That was a story itself. The connection I made was legit. She's Muro's fucking wife. Geez." Then Gretzman paused a moment. He was obviously weighing what he had.

"Okay," he said. "Since my story came out, half the newspapers in Italy have called me for comments. People from *R-A-I* are going to interview me for Italian TV today."

"Great. You're getting your fifteen minutes in Italy. Send me a tape," I said.

"I'm doing you a favor now. Do you know why this is a story for them?"

"I'm waiting."

"Mr. Detective, the Italian Consulate asked the police about Muro only this morning, nearly three days after he was killed. Funny how the Italians didn't even know he was alive before Dorothy's murder, but now they're complaining."

"Typical bureaucracy."

Gretzman went on: "The Italian press is all in a snit not only because the Consulate ignored it at first, but also because *Signore* Muro was a fighter pilot, and of no little renown. He was in a famous dog fight with some crazed Libyan fighters over Sicilian airspace about twenty-two years ago. Almost caused World War Three. I don't know much of the details yet, because I haven't had the articles translated, but I will. The Italian press is speculating that their government wants to sweep it under the carpet."

Turner was on the extension, and he laughed.

"Hey, Detective Beatnik," Gretzman went on, "I know you're there. Another thing. You guys ought to be careful. Whoever they are, they killed the girl as a sign. That's what the Italians say, anyway."

"We know, Gretzman," I said.

"And can I get a copy of Guy's phone book, the thing you didn't give the Consulate?"

"No," I said. "That doesn't exist, asshole. Remember that. If you mention it, you're cut off. We'll keep you posted, as in our deal." I hung up the phone and looked over at my partner.

He sat thumbing through the photocopy of Muro's phone book again. "Paolo, I'm getting that feeling you get on the Coney Island Cyclone when you go up the first incline, you know. You notice when it's too late how nineteenth century the damn thing is, made of hundred-year-old wood that's splintering in places, and you're already in the ratty, tattered seats and it's slow and rickety at first. In your stomach you feel the excitement but also like just maybe you might not get to the end of the ride in one piece." He threw the pages on his desk almost with disgust.

*   *   *

As I pulled into my ex's driveway Monday night, a black Mercedes pulled out of a parking spot near the corner intersection and drove away. Angela's home in Windsor Terrace, my ex's home—my ex-home—is on a long cul de sac. The cops and fireman who used to live here were selling out to lawyers, PR types, and financial consultants. I was getting used to Audis, Beamers, and Benzes parked in this hood, but that car pulled away just a little bit too quickly for someone going to the Key Food.

I looked at my watch. The whole ride over I was absorbed in the Muro case. Maybe I was bent out of shape for nothing. What if Hochman was the wrong woman? Unlikely but possible. Criminals fuck up. All the time. Maybe she ticked off the wrong person. Her greedy titan bastard of a father probably makes Russian billionaires look saintly. There were plenty of stories about his nasty MO. Water boarding was preferable to negotiating with Hochman, I read once. Fifty thousand vestal virgins praying for his soul every day for a century couldn't keep Sy Hochman out of Hell. That bloody signal could have been for him. Maybe nothing to do with Guy.

"You're early," Angela said at the door.

"Sorry. There wasn't any traffic," I answered, frowning.

"I don't mean it that way," she said.

Libby came charging into the foyer. She ran straight for me and dug her head into my chest, giving me a bear hug and a kiss. Libby was getting tall but she was still a snug fit below my chin.

"Hey, give me a donut, too. I'm starved," Libby said. I'd stopped for a box on the way over. We moved to the living room. "How's Uncle Hamilton? Will he be coming over?"

"Geez," I said, wondering if my jealousy was all that obvious. "He's fine. I don't know when. Sometime. Maybe *he'll* give you the Frisbee lessons."

Libby nibbled a donut edged with chocolate, when she raised her head in my direction. But those blue eyes were still on the donut and she spoke as if she were distracted by another thought.

"Dad? Remember when you told me I should always keep my eyes open in the neighborhood…for people who didn't belong or people acting a little strange?"

"Yes," I said.

"I keep seeing this big car parked on the block that was never there before. Today, yesterday, Saturday. I saw it this morning before I went to school. It was there again when I came home. Now it's gone."

I looked over at Angela, who shrugged her shoulders.

"Are you sure, Peanut?" I said, my voice accidentally slipping into detective tone, which immediately got them anxious. I walked to the front and peered through the shades at the street.

"Yes," Libby said.

"Libby, what color is this car?"

"Black," she said.

"Shit," I said before I could help it.

Angela jumped up from the couch. "Paul, what's wrong? What is this? Your job again?" she said, a hint of anger coming up in her voice.

"I don't know, Angela." I said. I pulled the thick satin curtains closed.

"Everyone take it easy. Peanut, can you tell me anything else? How many people in the car? Men only? What were they wearing?"

Libby replied, "Always two men, Daddy. They had jackets and ties, big heads and buzz cuts. And today, when I passed them on the other side of the street, one of them waved at me." Libby was now fast looking like she was about to burst into tears.

"I've got to call Ham. Just in case."

"Just in case *what*?" Angela's neck muscles were tight and she brought a hand to her temple. Her voice was now officially angry. Libby quietly wiped the tears from her eyes.

I put the phone down a second to restore some calm. "I don't know, but I am trying to find out, okay? It could be nothing. It could be something." That seemed to satisfy her.

If it was all because of Muro, what was this guy hiding? An Italian fighter pilot? That was bullshit. It had to be money. It's always money. Hochman had to have known what was going on. She lied to us. Fucking Turner. He should have pushed her hard instead of playing horn dog cop.

"Take the phone to the kitchen," Angela ordered, returning to the couch.

"Hello," I whispered into the phone. I pushed the swivel door and let myself into the kitchen, which reeked of Mr. Clean. I could barely make out what Turner was saying. In the background I heard Wagner's *Ride of the Valkyries* blasting out at neighborhood-bashing levels.

"Hey, lower the volume."

"But it's Wagner, man," Turner warbled. "He rules."

"Come on. He was a vicious anti-Semite and probably none too fond of Africans, either."

"Okay. Wait, wait. Here comes the part I love." He walked away from the phone and turned it up. I could hear him shouting, "Ho-jo-to-ho...Heia-ha!" Then all went quiet and Turner came back on the line. I could tell from his exhaling that he was excited.

"It's blasphemous to cut into Ric-*Hard*'s stuff," he said, giving the composer's name just the right Saxon accent. "You can still love the music even if you hate the man. If it sounds like I'm a little hopped up, it's because I just came back from a reading at Vishna's. Very successful. Some little freaky white boy wants to publish my poems. He's got his own publishing company. I think he just wants to fuck me, though. Some of these freaks, they just loves da big black men. Worse than arty white girls. God, this business is tough," he cackled.

"Very nice," I said. "Need you to do something."

"Okay, Detective. T'sup?"

"Out the window. Look for a black Mercedes or limo outside," I said. "And don't make it obvious." I heard him shuffle over. "Car there? Two big guys in it?"

"Yeah..." Turner replied slowly. "Down the street a bit. Damn if they don't have diplo plates. I can't make it because I'm not pulling up the blinds enough."

"Give me forty minutes. I'll call you when I arrive. Look for a flashlight when I'm behind them."

Before I hung up, I heard a clank that sounded much like the polymer frame handle of a 9-mm Glock 19 semi-automatic hitting a night table.

*   *   *

When I parked on 133rd Street, a few blocks up from Turner's place, I decided against backup. These guys were skittish and would bug out at the slightest noise. Frankly, I wasn't even sure our little ruse worked. I half expected to find my partner laughing at me on his front stoop. He lived on 131st, between 5th and Malcolm X. I needed to get the black sedan between me and him, otherwise the Italians would recognize me. Creeping around the corner at 131st, I eased up the street, behind a tree, behind a parked car, until I spotted the shiny Mercedes C-500 midway down the block. There was no one around right then. I got as close as I could, always keeping the car between me and Turner's building. I couldn't make the plates yet. Three cars from them, I could see my partner's window. I pulled out my flashlight and turned it on and off once.

Ten seconds later, Turner came strolling out his front door and down the steps of the brownstone he lived in. I pulled out my pistol, when I noticed he had a little dog with him. I didn't know he had a Jack Russell terrier, and I wondered if this was part of his act or if he didn't understand me somehow. He kept on coming on the opposite sidewalk from the sedan. Turner talked to the dog, pulled at his leash and cussed him when he stopped. Then he moved to cross the street right where the black sedan was.

That was too close. They turned on the ignition and that was Turner's cue. I always knew my partner had a fast hand but he pulled out his pistol between the time the car started and its headlights went on.

"Out of the car, motherfuckers! Out now! Police. Get the fuck out!" he shouted. I ran up on the passenger side, gun drawn, staying as clear as I could and still get good sight. Shit, I thought I was going to piss my pants.

The two in the car put up their hands but they weren't very cooperative. They were taking their time getting out. Too many seconds. Bad sign.

We started screaming. "Get out of the car. Out of the car. Now! If you're not out, you're dead!"

I hated it when people were slow. They were trying to figure a way out. "No thinking. Get out of the car, motherfuckers. Do it now!" I ordered.

The terrier was yapping at them. Then it ran to the curb on the far side.

Slowly, the driver moved out of the car with his hands up. "Ya. Ya. Mine hands are up. Vat is dis? Ve sitting here minding our bizness." He was huge, probably six foot six and two hundred fifty pounds, with a neck thick as an Indy racing tire. But it was the accent that I noticed. He sounded German, like Arnold Schwarzenegger. Where were the Italians?

The passenger side guy was sliding over. He was cover. As he passed to the wheel, I saw a shadow pop up from the back seat but it was already too late. Shots came out of the car and the driver, standing between my partner and the car, went down in the crossfire. Turner hit the ground behind the car, and I wasn't sure if he was hit or dropping in defense. I jumped back and ducked behind a tree and fired into the car blindly, screaming, "Ham, you hit?" Then the shots came at me, very big plugs again, tearing the bark off the Juniper that protected me. Another dog walker shouted, then ran for cover.

Suddenly, the tree seemed a lot narrower. I figured both were shooting now because I could hear bullets flying in two directions. They had too much firepower and in seconds they were down the street and around the corner. I ran out to ID the tag. I was too late.

Turner put his ear to the driver's chest. He held his wrist.

I pulled out my cell phone, "Ambulance or hearse?"

"Gunnar…or Dieter…or whatever the fuck his name is needs the latter," Turner said, vexed, and dusted himself off. He sat on the now vacant curb and wiped his face with his hand, leaving his fingers covering his mouth. They were tapping lightly at his lips and goatee.

I looked over the body and carefully turned his pockets. "Guess what?" I said.

Turner grunted. "You're contaminating the scene."

"No ID. No pistol. I think the guy in the backseat shot him on purpose."

"Got that right. Shit. Motherfucker."

The terrier had returned, still growling, his teeth securely sunk into the driver's bloodied pant leg. A red-black rivulet, glistening in the city's halogen streetlight, ran to the curb.

I could already hear the sirens and, in my mind, Dunne's screaming voice. I plopped myself down next to Turner on the curb and softly put away my pistol. "Hey, I didn't know you had a dog," I said, and patted the little fellow. "How is it possible I don't know you have a dog?" I asked, more to myself than him.

"Well, if memory serves, partner, this is the first time you've been to my crib in the time we know each other."

"What's her name?" I said, trying to change the subject.

"It's a he," Turner answered, distracted, picking up a thingamajig from the ground in front of him and throwing it down the street. "It's Basil…rhymes with cavil."

Chapter 6

Tuesday

"Lately, every time I see you guys, it's in connection to an *unsolved* murder," Dunne said. Sarcasm was blood in his veins. We were spending too much time in his office, certainly more than any of us wanted. "Fucking Peek-a-boo is roasting my balls on this. Got another call from the Commissioner this morning. Did you see the paper today?"

"Yeah," Turner said.

"You know the rules in this house. No blown covers. No pictures in the paper. Some criminals do read, you know, and the rest can recognize pictures. You fucking idiots."

Dunne was referring to a front pager, a *Post* Kodak of us sitting dejectedly on the curb last night, looking like Keystone Kops. The dead driver lay in front of us, Basil chomping on his leg, that thin sheen of corpuscles flowing away from his wounds. The caption said: "Cops Kill One Suspect but One Got Away."

"Wrong on both counts," Turner had said when he saw it earlier, before we'd gone into Dunne's. "But that's pretty typical. I wish I had killed him. Still, from a purely aesthetic point of view, I think it's a fine picture for news photography. He did capture the way we felt."

Gretzman wrote the brief story on it. Didn't renege this time, didn't connect it to the Muro case.

"Where do we stand?" Dunne barked.

"In quicksand," I replied distractedly. I'd been staring at the photo. Dunne grunted.

"We have three people," I said, "two of whom are related. Two foreigners. We have nothing on the driver. I think he's German or Austrian, from the accent he had." Turner nodded. "No ID on him. The Bureau report hasn't come back yet, but I'd bet that will be negative, unless he's military. We'll check with DIA, CIA, NSA, Interpol, anybody, but that could take who knows how long. Meanwhile, these guys…"

"What guys?" Dunne shouted. "That's what I want to know. What fuckin guys?"

I resumed quietly, hoping to calm him down. "Meanwhile…these guys have been following my family and they were snooping on Turner last night. That's how we caught up with them. They want *us* now. They think we know something and we have to start acting like it. We're the bait," I said.

"You got two days. A collar, not developments, not leads. I want a real live or dead perp. Got that?" Dunne said, closing his file on the case. "Out."

Once again, back at my desk was a message from Gretzman pinned to Benito. Again, it said, "Urgent. Return call request."

Right about then, shouting came up from the front lobby of the house, downstairs on the ground floor and just below us. Some pimp's mother or sister was there practically day and night crying loudly that their baby boy was innocent. Then it would graduate to cussing out the cops.

I called the scribe.

"Maybe you should tell him something, too. We have to act like we know something, right?" Turner said.

"*Post*, Gretzman."

"It's—"

"Rossi. Yeah, hi. I want to know what you wouldn't tell me last night, after you shot that Nazi."

"What Nazi? Forget it, can't tell you anything right now," I said, just letting out the bait a little, in case he had something.

"I have something for you, but you have to pay for it," he said.

"Maybe," I answered.

"By the way, nice dog, Detective Turner." Gretzman folded. "Fine, I'll go first. I received a call from an Italian woman today. She sounded very sexy...."

"Come on," I said.

"All right," Gretzman continued. "She said Muro's her brother and she's here to collect his body. Her name is Lori or Laura. Her English was good. Anyway, get this. She's some kind of cop. They have something called the carabiners—"

"It's carabinieri. Military police," I threw in. "Come on, Gretzman. What the fuck did she call you for?"

"Okay, okay. She's a cop. At the Consulate office, apparently they like to keep tabs on your newly high profiles in our little paper. She saw my Hochman article and today's exciting front page picture—man, our guy nailed you in that shot—anyway, Lowra or Lori or whatever-her-name-is is coming here to collect the body but she wants to see you guys. She also said she didn't get much help from that Gagliano guy."

"Great," I said. "That's all we need now. A meddler with an emotional attachment to the case."

Turner covered the receiver and made a "cut it" motion with his hand to his neck. "Maybe she can help," he whispered.

"Finish it, Gretzman," I said into the phone.

"Anyway. She says she knows some things about Guy that might help. She wouldn't tell *me*, though. So she asked for your address and I gave it to her." Gretzman stopped. He added sarcastically, "I hope you don't mind."

"Thanks," I said.

"Wait. Where's mine? I gave, now you give."

"What do you want to know?"

"What's the connection between last night and Muro."

"Deep background?

"Yes."

"None of this 'according to unnamed police sources'?"

"Fuck. Come on. I'm trying to make a living."

"Agreed or not?"

"Jesus," Gretzman cried. Then, "Okay."

"Neither one of us killed the driver."

"What?"

"There was a third man. In the backseat. He offed the driver and I'm not sure it was accidental. Maybe damage control, 'cause his guy was out of the car already. It was either drag him back into the car or leave him behind quiet."

"Third Man. Next, you're going to tell me you chased him down into the New York City sewers, Mr. Welles. What the—"

I hung up, because I wanted to leave him hanging and because Turner was tugging at my elbow. A blue from the front desk was trying to get our attention.

"Detective Rossi, there's a hottie downstairs making a ruckus and asking for you guys. She says she's an Italian cop and when she tried to go up the stairs without permission, we had to grab her. She kneed Croup in the balls, even." Croup was a nickname for one our big blues. A giant and a man whose coughing never seemed to end.

Just then the squad room door flew open. In came a tall, black-haired Joan of Arc. Reedy and regal, she asked in English just a bit tainted with an accent, "Agente Rossi?"

I nodded.

"I'm Laura Muro. Tenente. Italian Carabinieri. Gaetano's sister." Then we heard two blues clomping up the stairs and they grabbed her from behind.

And before another set of testicles was laid low, I raised my hands.

"It's okay, guys. Everybody, calm down," I said. "She really is a cop. She's working on the Muro case from the other end." Why I said that, I don't know, but I did.

The blues let her go. Croup arrived, out of breath, yet still coughing, red-faced, and still a bit stooped, but apparently mostly recovered. Physically. Unfortunately, he would be forced to hear about this for many years. His nickname would change. Mrs. Croup, I'm thinking.

It was my partner's idea to go to Sol's, on 57th and First. We weren't known there, and the food was supposedly good but cheap. Dunne had come out to investigate the yelling and we were just able to shuffle Laura out before Dunne noticed anything. We'd have to answer to him later.

We sat at one of Sol's heavy wooden tables, my partner and me on one side, Laura on the other. She had thrown her big black cape across the chair next to her. It was so long that the fur edge hung just above the floor. Her dress was black, too, befitting the occasion, but a tad too short, I thought, to be considered one hundred percent funereal. Still, it wasn't a sexy dress, though she herself was attractive when she took her sunglasses off. What surprised me was that she didn't wear much makeup, a rarity from what I remembered of Italian women on my visits.

Turner offered her one of his Rothmans, but she demurred.

"I'm sorry, you are very kind, but I don't like American cigarettes, Mister...."

In the confusion at the station, no one had introduced him, so Turner quickly retorted, "Hamilton P. Turner, Detective, NYPD. And these are Canadian, by the way."

"Ah, yes. You are the partner."

He frowned lightly and lit a cigarette, though he wasn't supposed to in my presence, knowing that I was trying again to quit.

I waved the smoke back at him pointedly.

"I saw you made a good picture in the paper, Detective Turner," Laura said. "You looked so...ah, *come si dice...doloroso*...what's the word...sad, yes?" she said. "But it was very beautiful."

"Thanks. We're not supposed to be *in the papers*," he said sarcastically.

"Miss Muro," I began.

"Well, since we're using titles. I'm Tenente Muro. Lieutenant in English."

I dropped my head a second. We were nearly assassinated, my family's in danger, and the investigation was leading nowhere, and this chick wants to be known as lieutenant.

The waiter brought two coffees and a Diet Coke for her.

"Alright, Lieutenant Muro," I said, perhaps too harshly. I noticed Turner wince, but the girl remained straight. "We are investigating your brother's death. And to be perfectly frank, we have very little to go on. He's dead, the wife's dead, and now a German guy who we don't know is dead. In fact, we don't even know if the guy's German. That's it."

"Don't forget Dorothy's house," Turner added. He could not remove his eyes from the girl.

"Right, my partner is reminding me that Dorothy Hochman's apartment, that is Muro's wife, former wife, was ransacked..."

"Methodically. Like somebody sifted the walls through a tennis racket," Turner explained. He was exaggerating for effect, and for her he turned it up a notch. He rubbed his slim, bronze fingers together as if the plasterboard grit were slipping through them.

"Yeah. It was no robbery. They were looking for something, and whatever that was, we figure your brother, the colonnello, had it. We're not sure they found what they were looking for."

"They didn't," she said quietly.

I looked at Turner. His eyes opened wider and then rolled slightly upward.

"Do you know what they want?"

"No. They think that maybe you have it or maybe you know where it is. Otherwise they wouldn't be following you still because you'd be dead."

"'Scuse me, Lieutenant," I said, again a little testily, "but we don't even know what *it* is. If I sound riled, forgive me. We've been shot at for who knows why, for a guy that the Italian government didn't acknowledge until yesterday, and a supposed colonel whose wife didn't give a damn about him…"

"The 'it' I don't know," Muro said. She started eyeing Turner's Rothmans but then seemed to think better of it. The lieutenant looked right at me. She had killer green eyes. Close up eyes. "*They? They* is maybe harder still. They supposedly no longer exist, except that maybe they do. They are a group of…let us say…like-minded, highly placed people in Italy. They share some old bad habits of the far right, the monarchists, a kind of…what do you Americans call it? Military-industrial complex." She trailed off. "Do you know Gladio?"

"I've read of it."

Turner made the time-out sign.

"Gladio," I said, turning to my partner, "was…is?" I looked to Laura for confirmation. "A general's cabal with roots in the royalist coup against Mussolini during World War Two. They never took over the country and the group's existence wasn't acknowledged by the government until only a few years ago. Gladio had plans to take over the country if the Italian Communist Party formed a government, a strong possibility at one point in the seventies. They had plans that were discovered in 1967 but not publicly acknowledged until much later. The generals had collected secret dossiers on thousands of people who'd be rounded up—or worse—in a coup if the *Communisti* came to power. They had very important big businessmen as allies, for obvious reasons. Banana republic stuff. Am I right, Tenente Muro?"

She looked at me closely. She must have been surprised, I guessed, that a dopey NYC cop would know such esoteric Italian history.

But I'd been over there a few times, and I liked to read history books. Military mostly. I looked directly into her startling eyes too long, and she looked away. I felt a tingle somewhere down below, and I had to bring my knees together tight. I had to admit they were splendid, all the more *verde scuro* because of that lovely black mane swirling around her face.

"Of course, American money was involved," she said with a wide smile. "The discovery of Gladio plans shocked the country. There are plenty of powerful people, military people, business people, church people, government people—even on the left—suspected of being the descendants of Gladio, actual or spiritual. But there's no proof. When someone from the far left is killed in a mysterious accident, the Italian papers smell Gladio," Muro said. "Its tentacles reach deep. Gaetano didn't tell me much besides that. I don't know how involved..." she paused, "...or even if he was compromised at all. There were probably many of them inside the upper reaches of the Air Force. Gaetano hinted as much."

I tried to tread lightly but there was no getting around the next question. "Was your brother a descendant?"

"No." Muro said. "I hope not, but I don't know for sure. My brother..." Muro hesitated and stopped.

Turner was impatient. "A nice history lesson. Some cloak and dagger, but what's this have to do with a fella getting killed on Sutton Place?"

"I don't think Gaetano is...I mean was part of Gladio," she continued. "I think mainly he was disturbed. About a month ago, my family became very concerned. He started phoning me, crying and saying there were ghosts visiting him at night." She hesitated, probably wondering if we thought the whole thing a joke. "Yes, I know it sounds silly. I don't believe in ghosts, but I do believe in souls. He said there were dozens and dozens of them. He began to know their faces. Sometimes, they were floating, hanging on to their suitcases for dear life, as if they were stranded somewhere in mid-air. '*Giustizia! Vergogna!*' 'Justice! Shame!' they would scream at him until he went running out of the house in a furious sweat, he said."

Muro fingered the Rothmans box, looking through it, it seemed. "Now, you perhaps understand why his wife reacted the way she did. Sometimes, he would not come back for days or weeks. She had to put up with that for a long time, I guess. The strange thing is that he'd never seen any real war action except for an occasional buzzing of Libyan MiGs straying into Italian airspace. The Soviets made the Libyans do it to test NATO's radar defenses."

"Maybe it's action you don't know about," I said as neutrally as possible. And I thought maybe it was action she didn't want to tell us about, like the dog fight Gretzman told us about. Or maybe the reporter got his info wrong.

Muro said nothing. I thought maybe she was going to cry.

"An American priest friend of ours here in Manhattan," she went on, "recommended a psychiatrist for my brother, but Gaetano refused to even begin therapy. He said it wasn't in his head. It was real. Everything would be righted soon. *Giustizia* would come and he'd be freed from their torments. Two weeks ago, he told me not to worry, that he had a way to fix things and he was finally going to use it," she said. "I guess he's free now."

"So, if he had *it*," Turner said, "then why did they cap him? Now, whoever they are don't know where *it* is." He was saying the words but looked as if he didn't know what he was asking.

"Maybe Gaetano really was losing his mind," I answered. "Remember Gretzman and the party at Casa Italiana," I said, looking to Turner. "My guess is they thought he was going to blab something. They couldn't afford his conscience and offed him. And now, whatever *it* is, they really want to find it. Could di Gagliano somehow be involved?"

"He's a bureaucrat," she said. "His instinct is to protect himself, his government, and not help you solve a crime. Gentlemen, I loved my brother. I don't know what he got himself into, but he wasn't a bad man."

"You're sure?" I asked as gently as possible.

"No, not entirely," she said quietly, taking a sip of her Diet Coke. The ice clinked as she drained the last drops. Muro suddenly put her sunglasses back on, grabbed her cloak, and stood up. "I'm returning to Italy soon. I have a few things to attend to. And the Hochman family is insisting on a brief wake. It appears they really were fond of him. Please call me if you have any information. I'm at the Waldorf," she added, and then moved away.

I couldn't resist. After all this to-ing and fro-ing about whether her brother was dirty, she, a cop—and I knew they didn't get paid well in Italy either—was staying at the Waldorf. "Not bad," I said, just loud enough for her to hear going away, "on a cop's salary."

Turner gave me a nasty look. He'd already fallen for her.

"The military is paying for the room, Detective Rossi. All perfectly regular," she answered without even looking back, throwing her cape over her shoulder.

As she swiveled through Sol's glass doors, Turner slouched down in his chair. "You're being awfully tough on her, Paolo. For Christ's sake, she just lost her brother in a brutal murder. On top of that, she's a mighty fine Eyetie, or should I say an Eye-Full."

At that moment I wanted very much to light up a nice Rothmans out of Turner's pack, which was sitting, blue on white crushproof box, on the table. Just as I reached for it, he snatched the box.

"Yeah, I know. She's not telling us everything, either. And she supposedly wants us to catch the bad guys, too," I said.

We went back to the One-Nine, not a word spoken in the car between us. It wasn't that warm out, but the sun shone brightly, and with the windows rolled up, the inside of the car turned hot.

My partner and I figured she could be just as dirty or even dirtier than Muro or the guys that dunked him.

"We're flying this plane blind," I said to break up the silence. "There's nothing."

"I know that."

"The Muro chick. I don't have a read on her."

"What do we tell Dunne?"

"That, I don't know," I answered.

When I got back to my desk, Mussolini was covered in more telephone message post-its, all from Gretzman.

"You know, Paolo," Turner said, pulling off the stickies one by one and placing them on my desk, "you have never publicly explained why you have the bust of a fascist dictator on your desk. Yes, he was a pale impersonation of Der Fuehrer, a *pagliaccio* from a cheap operetta, but a person of color—" he pronounced the word "kuluh" "—for example, could take it the wrong way. Now, I know you, I realize it's *ironic*," he said with heavy emphasis on the I. "It's a symbol of your rebellious nature, but an innocent citizen coming in here off the street might get to thinking terrible things about the police here in Gotham. God, if Brother Sharpton saw this, he'd probably sue," he said, laughing.

I smiled but was too preoccupied to respond. What the fuck had our Italian colonel been up to?

On my desk was a file with Italian language news clippings from the 1980s.

Saturday, I'd asked the Bureau to run a search for all Italian news reports that mentioned Gaetano Muro, and since I hadn't asked for translation it was back already. I leisurely opened the manila folder. The topmost article had a picture of some clothes, baggage, an airplane wing, all floating in the water. It was dated June 28, 1980. "Strage di Ustica!" ("Ustica Massacre!")

"Shit." I jumped up. "That's it, Ham. Fucking Ustica. That's what Gaetano was screaming at Gretzman in the pantry. 'Ewe-sticker' is

Ustica." I sat down and pushed myself back an arm's length from the desk and stared at the articles. Then I spread them out.

Turner ran over and looked at the file. "What does it say? Let's go, Paolo."

I read and translated at the same time, as quickly as I could. There were articles from the day, from investigations over the years. The fucking thing was running still. Ustica, an island in the Tyrrhenian Sea, off the shin of Italy near Sicily. A passenger plane crash happened there June 27, 1980, twenty-two years ago. Even now no one knows why the plane fell out of the sky. The pilots didn't report trouble.

I kept going with Turner hunched over me. "It dropped like a stone. Besides the Italian Air Force, there were secret NATO and French maneuvers going on nearby. Libyan MiGs. There was talk that Gaddafi was secretly in a plane in the same Italian airspace as the passenger plane. And look here," I said, grabbing a pen to outline a name in one of the articles, "Colonel Gaetano Muro was one of two pilots in visual contact with Itavia commercial Flight 870. A bunch of people died in the crash.... "

"Lemme guess, partner. Eighty-one?" Turner said, remembering the number tattooed on Muro's right forearm from the morgue report.

"Right," I said, looking up at him. His teeth showed big.

"Anyway, there was evidence of foul play but nothing conclusive," I said, rifling through the remaining articles. "At least not so far. These were the Red Brigade times, man. Shit, the Italian Parliament still has hearings on it every couple of years. From the looks of it, they still don't know what happened, Ham."

"I'm willing to bet Muro knew," Turner said.

I had to admit, I was excited. We had something, now. I didn't know exactly what we had, but we had a reason that *they* would kill for. Eighty-one reasons. I swallowed hard.

I looked up at my partner. He didn't look happy. Turner rubbed Mussolini's bald head. "Funny how our little Italian police lady friend didn't mention Ustica. Well, if we end up morgue meat, at least we'll know why. On the plus side, maybe we'll get a trip to Italy out of this," he laughed. It wasn't a ha-ha laugh. He was scared, too. He stared straight at Il Duce's face. "This reminds me. I guess we should tell Dunne."

I sat back and kicked up my legs onto the desk. "If we tell Dunne this, he's going to get reinforcements. That's assuming he accepts the connection. All we got is a crazy dead guy."

"A dead crazy guy," my partner interjected.

I ignored him. "Worse, the State Department will get involved. The politicians will get involved. Shit, who knows, the fucking CIA or NATO could be in this up to their eyeballs. If we tell Dunne, we're as good as off the case. Peek-a-boo will get involved. And Gladio or whoever they are will kill us anyway for nothing."

Turner showed nothing. Lips straight as a pencil.

"But if we don't tell him, at least not right away, we have a few days, maybe a week."

"Paolo, it's going to be all over the papers."

"The Italian papers."

"Yeah."

"Nobody gives a flying shit about Ustica at the *Post*. I bet you that even if Gretzman finds out—"

"When," my partner interjected.

I continued. "He won't even be allowed to write one paragraph about this. Ham, everybody but you and me gotta be in the dark about this. Everybody."

"And Tenente Muro?" Turner said sadly.

"Maybe she's part of the problem," I said, a little disappointed, too.

*　　*　　*

Later that afternoon, Tenente Muro returned to the house and I took her to see her brother's body at the Office of the Chief Medical Examiner on First Avenue. She wanted to finalize arrangements for transportation on Alitalia Friday. A lackey from the Consulate was waiting for us there, but that seemed only to make her mad.

I liked the way her nostrils flared at this.

"This wasn't necessary," she snapped at him. "My English is fine. I'd prefer to do this on my own," she said.

"I'm sorry, but the Consulate feels a responsibility for getting him home. Please, we only mean well," he replied.

Laura submitted but spoke barely a word to him, and she refused to go to see di Gagliano—at least that's what she told me.

"He's in pretty good shape given what happened to him," the morgue attendant said, trying to say something, anything, when we arrived.

As Gaetano Muro lay there in a large, clean metal drawer, a thin white sheet covering him, she touched the hand that was poking out. The rigor mortis had worn off. She pulled it up to kiss. Her lipstick, warm from her lips, smudged against his chilled fingers. She looked at his face. She brushed his hair lightly. It looked trim, as if he'd taken himself to the barber recently.

The attendant asked why he had the number eighty-one tattooed on a black and red cross on the inside of his right forearm.

"I don't know," she replied to no one in particular. She kept her gaze on her brother's body.

Well, there's lie number one.

Tenente Muro brought her right hand up to remove her sunglasses and covered her face, using the other hand to steady herself against the morgue table.

Through her fingers I could see her black mascara ran.

Other people had simply fallen straight down at these times, so I moved next to her, ready to catch her if necessary. Then I held her lightly by the shoulders. I felt her legs weaken and she fell against me.

"He was my brother," she whispered.

"I'm sorry," I said, looking at the body and then down at my plain black shoes.

CHAPTER 7

TUESDAY NIGHT

I took Laura back to the Waldorf. It was a nice night, so we waited outside for Turner to show. She wanted to smoke.

My partner pulled up his Passat to the Waldorf on the Park Avenue side and, after stepping out and giving the valet the keys, he smelled his left wrist. I knew he did this to make sure his cologne wasn't overpowering yet strong enough to send a few molecules wafting across a small table to a female.

He slipped a ten in the valet's palm. We exchanged hellos and went through the double doors, up the stairs, and then into the bar. I picked a booth at the far end, which offered a bit of privacy. An Aberlour Scotch on the rocks was placed in front of Turner wordlessly by the waiter, who acknowledged him with a barely perceptible wink, and then asked us what we wanted.

A moment passed quietly. We all seemed on edge.

"I've been thinking about this case," I said to no one in particular.

"Yes. Me, too," she said.

"Do you think Gladio is involved?" I said.

"I'm Italian," she laughed. "We are a nation of conspiracy theorists. It's an old country. We've been through two thousand years of republics, empires, monarchies, and dictatorships. There is no such thing as coincidence. When something happens, the Italian knows it happens for a reason. My family isn't without some money here and there, but hardly rich. But Gaetano lived beyond his means and didn't hide it. Something that I think now was not that smart, and perhaps his way of telling us something was wrong. Anyway, he had money somehow. Maybe Dorothy's. I ignored that. I loved my brother. Maybe I'm a failure as a carabinieri, but I'm his sister first and I didn't want him to go to jail or to have our family name dragged through the mud."

She looked at me. "We didn't get on so well this morning, eh, Agente Rossi. You and me?" She paused. "You are of Italian background, no?" It was flirty. Definitely flirty.

"He is," Turner said. "Even has a bust of Il Duce on his desk."

I think I blushed. My face was hot.

When Laura raised her eyebrows, Turner added quickly, now looking at me as a penitent for revealing a secret. "It's meant to be ironic, Tenente. Though most of the precinct's blues, I grant you, don't get the joke. They think my partner likes Mussolini. Eh, Paolo?" he said.

"Does he?" Laura said, pointedly ignoring me and speaking directly to Turner.

He smiled again and looked at me. "We don't talk politics much, but in my two years of partnership with him, I can say that he's not a fascist...anal retentive, a shitty former husband, and maybe a philistine, but no fascist."

"All right..." I said, trying to end this conversation. I shifted to something serious. "I have to tell you, Tenente, that I worry perhaps you aren't telling us everything."

"And you?" she said to Turner.

"I could be convinced of such a thing," my partner replied, sipping his scotch and not looking at Laura.

"What would you like to know?" she said, looking first to him and

80

then me.

"Was Guy part of Gladio?" I said.

"I don't know. Maybe not. Maybe he was taking some of the crumbs that fell off the big table where the pigs sat. I just don't know."

"But you mentioned Gladio right away."

"This is how they kill people. Bullet to the head and one to the chest. What do you call it? MO? Except for one thing. There's rarely a body. People just disappear into the *al di la*. That's why in this case I do not think it is Gladio."

I wondered whether to broach Ustica. If she were involved, it would tip our hand. At a probable thirty-five years old, she would have been too young to be actively involved, but maybe she was covering up. If she wasn't involved, she could help the investigation. Was she a good cop?

"So what about Ustica?" I said.

Laura raised her eyebrows and brought her lower lip under her front teeth. She laughed, "Why do you ask me about an island in the Tyrrhenian?"

I frowned.

"The plane crash?"

Turner nodded. "We know that he was very upset the last few weeks. You said yourself he was having those recurring nightmares."

I cut in. "That's all he kept saying to a reporter friend of ours... Ustica, Ustica, Ustica," I said, each time louder than the previous one. "Those may have been his last words. I'm guessing your brother wasn't crazy. I'm guessing there's a connection between those nightmares and Ustica."

Laura ran her hand through her thick hair and angled back in her seat. "I remember when it happened. I was in grammar school then. Gaetano was stationed at Ciampino, the military airbase near Rome," she said. "My brother was so handsome. He was a fighter pilot, and all of us, sisters, girl cousins, looked up to him. He was much older, a man

81

and we just children. It was bad times then. *Gli anni di piombo…*"

The years of lead. I remembered reading about it in the papers. La Brigata Rossa and right-wing death squads hunting and killing people, politicians and corporate titans –and each other. A month after Ustica, they blew up the Bologna train station in July 1980. A year later they shot *Il Papa*. The Cold War was hot. Coup rumors, the Communists were looking to enter the government. It was a dangerous, unsteady situation, even for Italy, which specializes in unstable governments.

"Difficult times then," Laura said. "To us girls, as silly as this sounds now, he was our protector against all that craziness. I wanted to be a pilot just like him, but I had to settle for carabinieri. They weren't allowing women pilots then."

Laura paused. "Anyway, my brother said…testified…he was on the ground when that plane went down. He said he was—how you call it—scrambled later, after the plane disappeared from the radar. It was a beautiful moonlit night, the kind of evening he loved to fly, he used to say. He saw bodies and luggage floating in the water. That's why he had those nightmares. Nobody knows what happened to that plane. There was an explosion on that passenger jet. That's been established by the official investigators, but most Italians don't believe them anyway. It might have been a missile, or a bomb on board, or just a catastrophic technical failure. No one knows what really happened.

"No one will find out now, twenty-two years later, after investigations by the Cabinet, the Parliament, the Aeronautica, SISMI, the military secret service. The plane was raised from the ocean floor in pieces, and they were still doing it in 1991, eleven years later! No one wants to know. Even if someone found the real story, no one would believe it now. Too much time has passed. Why would anyone care enough to kill Gaetano all this time later, even if he knew anything or was somehow involved? They could just say he's a crazy man."

"I'm not concerned with Ustica," I said. "We're pissed off that a man and his wife were dropped on our turf and we can't find out who did it. That's all, Laura."

"Okay," she replied, doing her best to muffle a sob, but the dikes would not hold and the tears rolled out.

I touched her lightly on the shoulder. I liked it. "Look, we didn't mean to suggest your brother was mixed up in that business. Ham and I, well, we're just a couple of New York cops. Only our mothers are above suspicion. I don't think you're holding out on us. It's just that we've been stonewalled by the Italian government, by his wife, and then you come along with Gladio and conspiracies. We don't know what to think."

Laura nodded and took a handkerchief from Turner's jacket pocket to wipe her face. I was jealous.

"We just want to catch the bad guys who killed Muro and Dorothy. That's all. We don't want to bring down the Italian government."

She laughed and got up from her seat. "Time for me to go."

"Wait just a minute, Laura. It's early yet," Turner said. "You're upset. Maybe you need a little cool down. Do you like poetry?"

"What do you mean?" she answered.

I couldn't believe my partner was doing this in front of me.

"Well, I don't let this get around much, particularly among my colleagues, most of whom don't appreciate the arts, let's say." Turner looked at me and nodded slightly. "But I am a published poet. And I like to go to readings. Get my competitive juices going, meet some interesting people. There's a place down on Avenue A. The cappuccino is probably not as good as you're used to…"

"We don't drink cappuccino at night," she teased him. "That's bad for the digestion." She looked at me, as if I should help her out of it.

My smile was wan. Much as I wanted to, I wasn't about to sabotage what little chance my partner had.

Laura cracked a smile. A standing row of mostly straight, white enamel stared at us. Her incisors seemed just pointy enough that it gave her a kind of almost goofy, schoolgirl grin. "Well, Agente Turner.

That's a first, I have to say. Men ask me many things, but never to attend a poetry reading." She grabbed his right cheek lightly between the thumb and index finger of her right hand. She squeezed just barely and then kissed him lightly on the left cheek. "But it is not a good idea, eh, and you know why, I think," she said, looking him straight in the eye. She grabbed her purse, patted his hand, and left.

The waiter came over to see if we needed refills. Turner covered his glass with his hand and I took another Coke.

"A good cop always has backup," he said mostly to himself as he got up. Turner fished out his cell phone from his breast pocket and his phone book and found Elena's number.

*   *   *

I drove out to Angela's Tuesday night for my weekly visit with Libby.

Before I could even get in the door and a say a word, Angela told me that the Mercedes had once again appeared in the afternoon, and as soon as she went out the front door and toward them, they took off.

"It's happening again, isn't it?" she said, her voice rising in tired anger. "It's those men from yesterday, right? They *are* watching us." I was afraid she was going to throw something at me, but she just turned and walked into the kitchen.

We were divorced and it was still happening. My daughter was in danger and it was all my fault. I could have easily moved to a desk job for my frequent dizzy spells. I had the magic pass from the MDs, an official diagnosis: nonchronic or transient vertigo. My piece could have been covered in dust and safely locked into my shoulder holster. I had the time in. But no. I had to play little Superman. I felt like a skunk.

I pushed the swinging door into the kitchen and Angela turned away to bend over the sink. Libby went out the other door without a sound. She knew when Mommy and Daddy had to "talk." The muscles at the sides of Angela's chest were heaving and she had her hands over her face. She stood up straight, then leaned over, arm raised against a cupboard.

"There are times when I really hate you."

"I'm really sorry, honey." Why I said "honey," I don't know. It just came out.

"Don't call me that."

"Sorry."

"Shut up," she said.

The light bulb finally went off and I realized it was best to say nothing and hunker down, to absorb the blows, like an animal in a cruel experiment.

She turned to me, her eyes big red welts. What little makeup she had on was a mess of black lines. Her long dark hair hung about face, wet with tears, too. I thought she'd scream but she didn't. Instead, she spoke in a low and determined tone: "I divorced you for two reasons."

I nodded my head.

"I couldn't live any longer with the risk of your job. I didn't want to be one of those women on the news with the big sunglasses and black scarf at the funeral, arms around crying children in front of her, with the fucking bagpipers from the Society of the Friends of Armagh playing a dirge behind your casket. And, more important, I didn't want Libby's life to be in danger. I realized the first was possible when I married you but not the second. I'll suffer for my mistakes, but she shouldn't have to."

"Angela."

"Shut up. Let me finish." She took a dishtowel and wiped her face with it, then realized it was a dirty dishtowel, smiled a second, and dropped it. She came over to the table and sat next to me. Even with everything smeared, the light was good to her skin, which was still creamy alabaster. That was one of the first things that drew me to her. I've always been a sucker for unblemished skin. She took my hand now and lightly rubbed it, almost absentmindedly. She didn't look at me. "Paul. This is it." Her hands were cold.

I nodded again, not knowing what she meant.

"I can't take these threats and moves anymore. Understand? I have divorced you. You are no longer my husband. Hurting me will not hurt you."

"They don't know that," I blurted out. "And it's not true, anyway."

She put her finger to my lips. "I won't put up with this anymore. The fear, the lowered shades. I've had it. Libby's got to go to school. She has friends, roots. We'll move away and we won't come back. Really. I'll take Libby far away for good, where none of your perps can find us. I'll go to California...my sister has a nice setup out there," she said, getting up slowly and wearily, her wooden chair making a loud scraping against the tiles.

The swivel door swung back and forth in ever-smaller arcs, creaking less and less until the noise disappeared, and I heard Angela murmuring to Libby in the living room. I stayed in the kitchen. Libby was crying. "I don't want to leave Daddy." On the table was a pack of Camel Lights and I grabbed one.

Fuck it. I stuffed the whole pack in my pocket and lit the one I had. The smoke alarm went off but I paid it no mind. No one else in the house did, either. I blew the smoke away and a few minutes later it stopped shrieking.

I left and thought about dropping in on Harry. I was already in Brooklyn. Would have been easy. But it was late, so I played a game with myself in the car while I drove home. I'd be me and Harry, too. He'd say what's up. I'd tell him my family life is two inches from imploding around me and I might be killed at any minute by persons unknown. That's all? Yeah. Come over. Nah, it's late. Come over. We'll talk. Okay, Harry. We'd sit in his living room reeking of heavy cigar smoke. Ship paintings hanging on the wall. A couch so old even the plastic cover was worn in places. His wife Bee would make us sandwiches and disappear. She knew the score. I wasn't Harry's only charge.

Harry'd tell me that no matter how bad things got, the booze makes it worse, not better. You know that. You absolutely—fucking absolutely—know that. You've been down in the gutter looking up at dogs pissing on you. You know that. When the drink wears off, your life will be the same shitty thing it was when you first poured. Fix your life with the booze and you're good for a day or two. Fix your life without the booze and you're good forever. "Look at me," he'd say, giving a mock arm sweep to his domain and a big smile on his face.

I figure it must have been real bad when Harry was a drunk.

CHAPTER 8

WEDNESDAY

At the One-Nine, on East 65th and First Avenue, the detectives' squad room wasn't much to look at. No windows save for the almost never cleaned, frosted plate glass topping the partition walls. A dozen standard issue municipal gray desks, a couple of them with computers, some without. Despite the introduction of floppy disks and too many Law Enforcement Information Technology classes, most of my brothers and sisters stayed as far from an electronic screen as possible. Detectives wore out shoes, not computers.

Beige manila folders papered the desktops. Metal filing cabinets lined the far wall. The den could have passed for any room in any New York City government department. Hell, if not for the pistol holders adorning all five men and one woman, it might easily have been a room full of social workers. Sometimes, I thought it was.

As ugly as that place was, I wouldn't put myself anywhere else. I was a certified fuckup in other parts of my life. Bad husband, put my family at risk, no real friends beside my partner, but I was decent at what I did. Put some bad guys away. This Muro case was bothering me.

There was a connection to Ustica, but I didn't really give a shit about that. We wanted the guys who did the tricks here. If that stirred up the Italians, so what?

Maybe I was getting old, or maybe I was beginning to think about my family like I should have all along. I didn't want them to touch Libby, and this thing was looking far more dangerous than I had anticipated. I hated to admit it, but maybe Dunne was right for once in his life. Maybe Dunne used to be a good cop who decided after risking his family one too many times that life is too short. We pay for our jobs with spectacularly failed marriages, screwed up kids, and loneliness. The more I thought about it, the more I realized solving this particular crime wasn't going to make NYC one bit safer.

It had to do with a time and place that doesn't even exist anymore. The Red Brigades were finished. We got ourselves caught up with the sex of it, the diplomats, a good-looking female cop, eighty-one dead bodies floating in the Tyrrhenian Sea, an international incident. I didn't like this Dunne feeling, but there it was, standing in front of me, making me feel like a huge shit for endangering Libby. I thought about bailing out.

Turner walked in. He seemed happy, but then he frequently seemed happy.

"Let's go for a walk," I said before he could sit down.

He immediately raised his eyebrows.

"Nothing. I'm dry," I said.

We grabbed coffees from Dino's around the corner.

"Whoever they are, Ham, they are leaning heavy on me. There's been a car sitting outside Angela's house every day. The fuckers even waved at Libby when she rode down the street on her school bus Monday. Angela's gone ballistic. She's threatening to move with my kid. No divorce court order can stop her when she tells them their lives are in danger 'cause of my line of work. They did Muro and Hochman in a blink. These guys are worse than the Mob, with tons more firepower.

I'll do a lot of things for this job. I don't care if they drop me, you know that. But I won't…I can't bear a threat to Libby for the common good. I want the bad guys, but not at that price."

Turner stopped. "I said last night you are a shitty former husband. I didn't say you are a bad father. Angela's not going to move. You know Libby needs a safe house. Right away. It's temporary."

"Yeah, I know." I didn't want to face the obvious. "This case could take forever. Governments, military, State Department, spies…who knows what this Laura chick is up to. I'm not sure she's been straight up with us. You think she's his sister?"

"Those were real salty tears last night, so she's a good actress if she's not his sister."

"I don't see what Guy could have possessed that they want. Italian fighters didn't have mounted cameras as standard equipment then. I checked. Was he taking Polaroids from the cockpit while flying a jet?"

Maybe it was the frustration of the case but a strange desire hit me. I'd never known what the P. in Hamilton P. Turner stood for. I didn't know why but I suddenly had to know. "Hey," I said. "What's the P for?"

"Petrarch," Turner answered without even looking, as if everyone asked him that question. "Took you long enough. My father taught Latin and Italian in high school. He loved Italian poetry. Hence Petrarch."

"Petrarch?" I asked, a bit too incredulous. How did I not know this about my partner? Then I made a stupid mistake. "How'd he know Italian?" I realized my error immediately and stammered out, "I mean…"

"How'd a black man come to learn the sublime language of art and opera?" Turner finished my question with one eye closed and the other wide open, eyebrow raised like I used to see on the toughest nun I'd ever had in grammar school. The disbelieving eyebrow. It presaged a smack across the face, but all he did was make me feel foolish. He looked away, like he wasn't going to finish.

"He was a lieutenant in the Army. Served in World War Two and fought in Sicily and Italy. Maybe even fought your people," Turner laughed. "Anyway, for some strange reason, he seemed to like the place and learned the language when he was stationed there a few years. He loved Italian poetry. Hence Petrarch."

"Oh," I said. I wanted to end the conversation.

"Want to know about the Hamilton?"

"Wasn't bothering me as much as the P," I said.

*   *   *

At the Consulate, di Gagliano knew we were coming, but he made us wait again. We sat thirty minutes with the receptionist, the same one who had offered us coffee the last time we were here. She was apologetic.

"I think there will be some time for a café this time, *agenti*. His Excellency is held up in a number of meetings this morning, I'm afraid."

"Two coffees, then, thanks. What's your name, *signorina*?" Turner said.

"Sylvia," she said. "Sylvia Ortelli. I am his Excellency's assistant." She walked into an alcove to grab coffees from the cappuccino machine.

"I hate that they have us over a barrel. I hate thinking we don't even have the slightest idea who *they* are. I hate thinking that if I didn't have Libby, I could really go heavy after these guys. I'd go to Italy if I had to."

"Oh, yeah," Turner said, "*if you had to*, he says. Come on, we should be milking this thing to get our asses to Italy, Paolo."

"That ain't happenin'."

Sylvia returned with the coffees, and left the tiny cups, which had a gold band circling the rim and were stamped with a small Italian flag, on the end table between Turner and me. She smiled and I remembered what Gretzman had said about all Italian girls being beautiful.

Sylvia was no exception to the fantasy. Reddish-blonde and she packed a lot of punch into her sweater. I walked back to the couch, but it wasn't long before Turner was sitting on the side of her desk. She was laughing. He was laughing and gesturing with those graceful hands of his. She had moved closer to him in short order. It wouldn't be long now.

I occupied myself with the Italian magazines lying around, like *Panorama* and *L'Espresso*. I eyed the cover of *Panorama* to find at the bottom left hand corner a small black-and-white picture of Muro staring at me. An old military photograph probably. The caption said: "Ustica Pilot Murdered in Manhattan."

I quickly thumbed to page five to find the story, a few lines in a box. It gave the few particulars on his murder and that it was unsolved. "Thanks for that," I whispered to myself. The article said that Muro had testified in numerous trials and maintained that he scrambled later and saw nothing. The other pilot had said the same thing initially and then committed suicide just six months after the downing. It could not be proven they had scrambled before the explosion, the article said, but unnamed military sources had said back in 1980 that they were in the air *long before* the Ustica flight disappeared. The article claimed that Muro had flown his F-104 in the vicinity of the downed Ustica airliner, the Itavia 870, and that he was one of only two Italian pilots with potential visual contact.

Then the kicker: the article referred to a *Panorama* story of the time, published in August 1980, that cited military people who had seen some lost radar evidence. The radar showed the two Italian planes *and* several others had flown very close to the commercial liner before it went down.

Laura didn't happen to mention that. That night the vicinity was thick with planes: Libyan MiGs, French Mirages from the nearby carrier Clemenceau, as well as some American F-14 Phantoms from the *Saratoga* that were involved in NATO exercises that week. A downed MiG was found on a Sicilian hillside one month later, the pilot's death dated back to around the same night the airliner went down. The Italian government quickly said he'd had a heart attack and shipped his body and the plane back to Libya, showing little curiosity in this invasion of its airspace. The magazine added an editorial comment: "The NYPD has no clues and isn't likely to solve the crime."

"Fuck," I said a little too loudly. I smacked the magazine on my thigh, then quickly ripped out the page. Seemed like everyone but us knew what was going on.

Turner and Sylvia stopped chatting and looked toward me. Her cheeks were red from smiling so hard.

Just then, di Gagliano walked in from his office, trailed by the same lawyer guy from before.

"*Pronto*," di Gagliano said curtly, and marched back into his office, though not without a quick and nasty look to Sylvia.

Turner eased off the desk as soon as di Gagliano entered but it was too late. The CG had seen him and made it obvious that he was none too pleased. Poor little Sylvia was going to pay a price for allowing herself to be entranced by my mellow partner.

I looked at Turner. I could tell he wasn't happy about Mr. Consul General's current attitude.

"Maybe, I'll wait here," he said to me. "Might be best if you handled it alone."

I nodded and left him with Sylvia, the lamb with the lion. Given di Gagliano's entrance, I was sure Turner would have lost his temper, and we didn't have much to say.

Inside the office, there were already espresso cups set up for four.

"Please, sit Mister...Detective Rossi, correct?"

"Yes."

"I thought you didn't speak Italian?"

"Excuse me?"

"I noticed the *Panorama* issue sitting on your lap."

"Let's just say I can stumble along."

"I'm sorry about the delay. My fault, of course. Bureaucratic meetings. Nothing gets done. The work we do here is…well, it's a long-term effort, sometimes measured in inches of documents." He looked up to notice that I wasn't much interested. "Where is your partner?"

"He's gonna wait outside. I won't be long, Mr. di Gagliano." I avoided calling him Consul General to annoy him. "There's nothing to add. I'm afraid we're a bit stymied here in the case of Colonel Muro. We have one intact bullet from the scene, and no witnesses. Mr. Muro seems not to have had many friends. His estranged wife was murdered."

"I know," he jumped in, looking down. "It's so sad that hooligans can go around killing people with impunity in this great city of America."

I wanted to throttle this fat pencil pusher. No international incidents. We'd had enough. "Anyway," I continued, "we have little to go on. I don't want you to think the case is closed. Technically, that can't happen until my boss has determined the facts of the case justify its removal from the active files."

"I see. Of course. Such a shame after your mayor came by yesterday to tell us personally that the case had his ear."

That threw me for a moment, and I hoped it didn't show. "I'm going to level with you. I'm sure you are disturbed by the murder and would like to see justice done. We have little to go on and any help you can give—"

"That's unfortunate," he interrupted. "I'm sure Mr. Muro's family would like to see the killer apprehended. I understand you met his sister. Tenente Muro. She's here to escort his body back to Italy Friday."

"I don't remember telling you we met."

"Well, she's part of the military police, so we are certainly kept abreast of things."

It was clear he was going to do his utmost to stonewall us. I got up and moved toward the door. I didn't want to even shake this slick bastard's hand. "By the way, may I ask you one last question?"

He made no move.

I stopped a few feet from his door. I said, "I couldn't help noticing in *Panorama*, and maybe I read it wrong, as I said my Italian's not so good, but the article suggested Colonel Muro was in the air in the vicinity of that plane that went down in Ustica so many years ago. He may have been the last eyewitness."

"This is a very old item, very old. But *I* remember that he said he didn't see anything, and that he scrambled—isn't that what you say in English—after the accident. Journalistic excess isn't new. To this day, no one knows what happened on that plane. So terrible, really," the CG said, and it almost seemed heartfelt.

"Strange that Muro should come to such an awful end three thousand miles away from Ustica, and here too there were no eyewitnesses to murder," I said.

Di Gagliano put his big oval glasses on and picked up a thin file. Standing up behind his desk, he walked over to me, put his hand lightly on my shoulder, and herded me to the door. "Yes. Well. It's best we move on, Mr. Rossi. You understand. All of us should move on, as you Americans say, given the circumstances." The door clicked behind me.

At Sylvia's desk, the giggle fest went on. When they noticed me, Sylvia was writing on a business card and handed it to him.

"Bye-bye, ciao-ciao, Detective Turner," she said, kissing him on both cheeks.

"Ciao, *bella*. I'll call you soon."

"You did well," I said as we walked lockstep out of there. I glanced at the business card he held in his hand.

He slipped it into his pocket. "What about you?"

"We're going to that place called nowhere fast, I believe," I replied as we headed out the Consulate's front door.

On the street, I called Angela on my cell phone. "They still there?"

"Yes," she replied.

"I'm coming out there. I think you and Libby need to move to—" She hung up before I could finish my sentence, "...a safe house for a little while."

Back at the One-Nine, Dunne busted our humps about Muro. Not because he cared. Peek-a-boo was keeping the pressure on. The mayor, being of the heritage and friends with the Wall Street uber-macher father, felt particularly embarrassed about the murders. That's why he'd made the unusual call on di Gagliano. And Hochman, the biggest contributor to Salerno's campaign last time around, would be needed to ante up again in the next one. Mayor Francis X. Salerno had personally gone to the Italian Consul General to promise his—and our—utmost attention to the case, Dunne told us. Talk was intensifying that Salerno would run for Senator in New York, an undertaking that would take a ton of brick, as Hamilton P. Turner would say.

"Whaddya got?" Dunne came into the squad room barking.

My Benito again had yellow stickie messages from Gretzman on it. I was picking them off one by one when I swiveled to meet Dunne's gaze. Turner avoided looking over and made himself busy.

"Who the fuck is that ugly bastard, anyway?" Dunne asked loudly, sitting on my desk like he owned it and me, pointing at Il Duce.

I ignored that. "Well, I could tell you I think I know who murdered Muro and his wife."

"I'm listening."

"Gladio."

A big smile came across Dunne's face. The first one I'd ever seen in my two years of working for him. It was frightening. And I wondered if he ever scared his kids with that smug, idiotic face that came along with the smile. He took a seat at the next desk, all happy, as if Peek-a-boo's shoes had been lifted from his neck, and then I realized with horror that Dunne had swallowed my little joke.

"Why isn't he here for questioning? Any priors?"

I looked over at Turner, who was now moving away from me, trying to dissociate himself from my flippant remark, which was about to detonate right there in a spectacularly bad way.

"It's not a person. Not like Jimmy Gladio. Gladio is a thing."

Dunne needed no more to realize I was jerking him around. His face tightened. The neck muscles appeared. "Look, Rossi. You don't seem to realize the gravity of this situation. It will be very easy for me to take you guys off the case."

That was something neither Turner nor I wanted. Being pulled from an active file was an altogether embarrassing option. It meant endless ridicule in the squad room. Then our nicknames would become Gladio. We'd be the Gladio Brothers. It also meant dropping to the bottom of the pecking order and getting the worst assignments in the future. Worst of all, neither of us relished failing.

"I'm not joking, Chief," I said finally. "Gladio is some kind of shadowy military/government/industrial complex in Italy. It's their version of the Black Ops helicopters. Government conspiracy, the Grassy Knoll, etcetera…" I said, trying to punctuate the whole thing with hands. It just looked like my hands were lamely fluttering in the air.

Dunne just stared at me. He picked up a pencil and twirled it. He must have thought it was total bullshit.

"We don't have much else. But what we've learned from his sister… you heard probably, the chick who marched through here yesterday. He was involved in some strange business twenty-two years ago, a downed airliner, and—"

"Twenty-two years later? You gotta be kiddin' me."

"I'll grant it's strange. But you know the Muro killing was pro. Then the search and destroy at Hochman's apartment. This isn't the work of some Bowery Boyos, not the Mafia. There's absolutely nothing on the German guy we dropped in Harlem. Not a stitch. And there have been diplo plates involved every time."

"You are telling me things that I know already. See, the thing is, Rossi, one of the most important job requirements of detective first grade is that you tell me things I don't know. Next, you'll be telling me you need to go to Italy to solve this case…or Germany."

That's when Turner sidled over and the ears of every other detective in the room opened wide. "I'd prefer Italy," he said, straight-faced.

"Yeah fucking right you would," Dunne added, looking at my partner. "Here's your options, as I see it. Either you take some help on this or you're off the case. Decide now."

"Sonny and Gabe," I replied before he could finish, risking that Dunne would not remember those two were set for a two-week vacation starting Monday.

"Sold," Dunne said, getting up to leave. "You two don't know how far up my rectum this guinea mayor's boot is. I can taste his fucking shoe leather. You'd think he lost his twin sister, mother, and father, the motherfucker. He's a twenty-four seven prostate exam. You fucking wops stick together, Rossi. I know that. He told me on the phone yesterday—called me up *directly*—to tell me that he knew you personally from your graduation from the academy eighteen years ago. Somehow, he remembers your sorry ass," Dunne said, huffing his way out of the office. He stopped at the door and yelled out loud so everyone could hear: "I don't give a shit if it's Gladio or Gladys Knight," he said, the latter pointedly at Turner, "all I want is the trigger. Got that? I don't give a shit who they work for."

When he left, I pushed back and angled my chair back as far as it would go and threw my feet up on my desk. A paper airplane loaded with all Gretzman's messages landed on my crotch. It had taken off from somewhere in the direction of Turner's desk.

My phone rang. It was Gretzman.

"What do you want?"

"Having trouble with the case?" Gretzman said with mock worry.

"Before I hang up, one more time, what do you want?"

"You haven't returned my phone calls."

"First, I don't like you. Second, I only return important calls," I said, and slammed the phone down. Turner made a face at me, like I was being too tough on Gretzman. I looked at my messages. The mother of another murder victim, a gay black male model axed to death in a swanky apartment on First and 62nd, had called. She had some info but wanted us to come over to talk to her. She lived in Coney Island. Maybe the ride would do us good.

My phone rang again.

"I got something," Gretzman said.

"Man, you don't give up," I said. I had to respect doggedness. "Go."

"No. We meet in person. This is good and I'll expect something in return."

"What have you got?" I asked.

"I told you it's good. Let's meet. Not at Moon's, either."

"Forget that. We have to make a run to Coney Island."

"What'd Muro do there?"

"It's a different fuckin' case. Your limited experience with police work might be holding you back, son. We often work on several murders at a time. We have to go and now. You can come in the car if you can stand the excitement of riding with two cops. Might even let you hit the siren."

"Nice. But you will be letting me do more than that when I tell you what I've learned."

"We're leaving in ten minutes. Be outside One-Nine."

Gretzman was on time. I always thought reporters wore suits or at least presentable sport jackets and ties. But he never failed to show up in faded jeans, a ratty jacket, and shitty sneakers. A tie seemed to be the last thing he'd ever wear.

As he came up to the precinct house, I said, "Don't they make you wear something better than that? I mean, you're representing Foxhound Publishing and all." We motioned him into the backseat.

"I don't like ties," he said. "Second, I'm dealing with real people, often lowlifes…not the swells you hang out with in One-Nine. Anyway, some of my sources get nervous when they see a tie. They think maybe

I'm a cop or something," Gretzman said with a big, smug smile.

"Funny," Turner said. He was driving and I was in the front passenger seat.

We pulled quickly onto FDR Drive. "Let's have it, scoop."

"I hear you guys are this close," Gretzman made a tiny space between his forefinger and thumb, "to being off this case."

Turner shifted in his seat and threw a cigarette butt out the window as we passed the Houston St. exit. I watched the butt land, wishing I had one. I'd finished the cigarettes I'd taken from Angela's kitchen table. We said nothing.

"You two ought to treat a guy more nicely. Hurtful remarks, not returning my phone calls… Are we ready now?" Gretzman said.

"Deal," I said.

"Well, a little hottie Italian correspondent that I ran into on this case had a couple of very interesting pieces of information. First, Muro was somehow involved in Ustica more than he let on. He was flying that night—"

"We know that," I interjected, "I read that myself in the fucking Italian paper, so you better have something else."

Gretzman looked hangdog dejected for a moment, as if that were his best shot. "Well, the other thing is that the head radar man, a guy by the name of Alfredo Dottori, committed suicide in 1982. He was the second one involved to off himself. The other pilot did it in December 1980, six months after the plane went down."

Gretzman pulled out his little reporter's notebook to refer to. "Dottori checked out on June 27, 1982, the second anniversary of the downing of the plane. He shot himself in St. Peter's on a day the Pope was giving a sermon on forgiveness. Unbelievable, huh? Anyway, what's more important is that this Dottori was the guy at the air traffic controls in Marsala, Sicily, or something like that, an Italian airbase, the night that plane went down. Here's the best part. Check this out. It's fucking Nixonian, this conspiracy. God, I'd love to be a reporter in

Italy…not just for the girls but for the stories…"

"Come on, Gretzman."

"Okay. It's 1980, right. Jet fighters couldn't record visuals then. No video cameras aboard. None of this Gulf War computer wizardry. Our friend Dottori testified at the first investigation that he indeed *had* recorded the doomed flight's progress on the routine radar tracking tape. It's the only one that existed. But then, get this, he said in later investigations that he *accidentally erased* the exact four minutes before and four minutes after the flight was downed. When Dottori's radar tapes were finally impounded from the Air Force by civilian investigators three months after the crash, guess what? Those eight minutes were missing. Is that fucking unbelievable or what! And they haven't shown up since, that is, assuming they haven't been destroyed."

We headed down the Gowanus Expressway just before the road forks for the Belt Parkway and Bay Ridge. For once, Gretzman could have something. Something was bothering me. That name, Dottori. I knew it and I didn't. "Didn't Dorothy mention a Dottori?"

Just then, Gretzman's cell phone squealed. "Sorry, I have to take it," he said, flipping on his phone.

Turner's eyes narrowed at Gretzman's ringtone: *The March of the Toreadors.* "That's a fuckin shame. Really. Bizet never figured his work would come screaming out of cell phones. Dead too soon. No royalties, either."

I was bothered. Dottori. Dottori. I knew the name. Where? "What about his address book, partner? Dottori," I said.

He screwed up his lips and gave it a thought. "No, I don't remember a Dottori. I'd remember that name. Italians are always calling each other that. Dottore this and dottore that. That's what Sylvia called us when we first went to the Consulate, before she knew we're cops."

"Yeah. I remember the name, too. That's why it's bothering me. Shit! Dottori. Shit! The letter." I almost jumped out of my seat.

"What?" he said, tapping the brakes softly. "What?"

I reached into my left side breast pocket. "I forgot. That fucking letter I filched at Hochman's before they pillaged the apartment. I slipped it into my vest pocket," I tapped the outside of my jacket, "and forgot all about it because I had a bout of vertigo at Hochman's house— remember?—when I was in the back, right after I put the envelope into my pocket. I had told her that I had to go to the john. I did some checking in a couple of rooms. Jesus Christ. The vertigo makes me forget things. There was so much shit going down. I haven't worn this jacket in a couple of days," I said, grabbing hold of the letter's edge.

"I don't have any gloves. I don't want to contaminate any prints."

"Take my hankie," Turner said, gesturing with his chin toward the clean, white handkerchief in his front left pocket.

"For once, these fancy whites you carry around have come in handy."

"Second time this week, actually," he said.

Using the cloth, I gently pulled out the still unopened envelope. The blue and red ink on the envelope had run a bit but the letter was readable. It was addressed to *Egr. Col. Gaetano Muro, Via Sanovino, 28, Milano. 20133.* The return address was: *Alfredo Dottori, Piazza Navona, 11, Roma 00180.* The postmark was barely readable but looked to be *27 Giugno 1982.*

I showed it to Turner, who was about to shout when I signaled him to shut up.

"Too late," said Gretzman, who, off the phone, had now stuck his head over the back of the front seat and could have practically eaten the envelope. "Holy fucking shit. That's from Dottori. Where did you get that? That's postmarked 27 Giugno…June 27, 1982, right? That's the day he shot himself."

I turned and grabbed him by his sweater, pulling him forward. "Gretzman, I swear, if you write about this, I will not kill you but instead paralyze you so that you feel nothing for the rest of your life, are stuck in a wheelchair, and never able to wipe yourself again. Never able to

pound a keyboard or a girl, assuming you get any. You understand?"
He was angry and unbowed. It surprised me. "Hey, without me,
you're nowhere. If it wasn't for me telling you about Dottori, you'd
have left that envelope in there until the next time you had to use that
breast pocket, which is probably for the pink slip you'll get for your
spectacular work on this case." He loosened himself from my grip and
straightened himself out.

We pulled off the exit for Ocean Blvd. and headed south. "He
knows now. We'd have to kill him to shut him up," Turner said in jest,
though I think Gretzman got a few degrees more nervous at that.

"Don't you want to know what's in the letter?" Gretzman cooed.
"Open it!"

"Hey, Paolo, that's a purloined letter and you know it. We'll never
be able to use it in court," Turner added.

"Maybe we won't need to use it in court," I said, holding it up to the
sunlight. Through the envelope, I could see a couple of words and then
what looked and felt like a pen or funny shaped piece of metal.

"You want to know what's in the letter, Jimmy Olsen?" I said.

Gretzman made a face. "Superman you ain't."

"Let's make a deal."

"I'm listening," Gretzman said.

"I'll open the letter right now but you can't write about it."

"That's not a fucking deal. That's diddly squat. No deal."

Turner interjected, playing the good cop, faithfully, "Now, Paolo,
come on, that's no deal. The guy has provided some useful info. And
he's right, we wouldn't have known this letter is useful—assuming it
is—if it wasn't for his legwork."

"Come on. I'm gonna write about it," Gretzman said.

"Fine. I open the letter right now and you can't write about it until
I say. Got that? We won't tell anyone else. You'll have the exclusive."

"Fuck that. No deal. What good's an exclusive I can't write about?
How about forty-eight hours. After that I can write about it and you

can tell any reporter you like."

"No deal. One month," I offered.

"One week," he replied.

I looked at Turner. He nodded. "Done, but you can never ever say *how* we got it. Even when they are pulling out your fingernails and stabbing your eyes," I said.

Gretzman nodded.

I pulled out a pocketknife and gently ran it along the top edge of the envelope. Inside was one folded memo-sized sheet, which I pulled out using the hankie. The letter wrapped a small but longish key. It wasn't shaped like a typical American key. It reminded me of the kind of room keys you'd get in a pensione in Italy, like a skeleton key. I dropped it on my lap.

"Can you read the letter?" Turner asked. Disappointment must have been all over my face, because he added, indicating behind him, "Aw, com'on, Paolo. He's in it up to his neck now. What does it matter if they kill him too?"

Before I read the letter, I wanted one thing to be clear. "Our deal covers everything. You can't write about even the existence of this letter, nor of the written contents nor the key. No veiled references until the week is up. Understood?"

Gretzman nodded again, this time with a look of exasperation.

I pulled out my reading glasses and translated the letter, just a few lines long:

27 Giugno 1982

Egr. Col. Muro:

Quella notte e' successo un casino, per poco non e' scoppiato la terza guerra mondiale. Ti mando la chiave di cui abbiamo parlato per quanto riguarda la quarta storia del quarto giorno. Fai come ti pari, ma io no posso andare avanti cosi'. Stai attento.

Tanti saluti,

A.G. Dottori, Mar.

"It's from Maresciallo Alfredo Dottori: '*Dear Col. Muro. That night was bloody chaos. We averted a third world war by the skin of our teeth. I'm sending you the key of which we have spoken regarding the fourth story of the fourth day*.' Fourth story of the fourth day? What the fuck is that?" Turner and Gretzman shrugged their shoulders and I went on: "*Do with it as you see fit, but I can no longer go on this way. Be careful.*" I repeated the last line. "There's nothing else."

I said the obvious thing on all our minds. "I wonder what this key opens and was it worth killing yourself for?"

Nobody said anything, but we were all thinking about the radar tapes. We dropped Gretzman off, and he jumped into a cab back to Manhattan.

"Hey, remember our deal…or you're a dead man," I yelled, perhaps a little too loudly. People stared.

We arrived at Neptune Avenue and hopped out in front of a decrepit apartment building complex. I'd been so wrapped up in the Muro case that I spaced out on our current destination. I stood there at the car, looking stupid, while Turner waited for me, hands on his hips, already at the front door. He had his new navy Zegna suit jacket on again. I had to admit it looked good on him, even if I kept telling him not to wear such threads to work. Not only did the rest of the detectives think he was putting on airs, but it was definitely not a work outfit. It wouldn't wear well while running down a good-for-nothing-shitface in a dirty alley or pushed up against a filthy door half open to a perp's pigsty.

"You are the one with the info, Paolo."

I blanked.

"The mother of the axe murder victim…lives here on Neptune… You having another vertigo episode?"

"Yeah, I mean, no," I said, pulling out my notepad. "It's building

3." While we walked up the entryway to a boxy, six-story apartment building, I said, "You know, Tenente Muro leaves soon, Friday, I think, with her brother's corpse. We have to see her before she does."

"Uh-huh." He nodded as he pushed the buzzer to 5A, Mrs. Junius Walker, grieving mother of a sweet, headless boy of seventeen. "Goddamn it, there's no elevator in this joint," I mumbled as she buzzed us in.

"This boy was a freak, eh? Let's put a hurry on this," Turner said, pushing open the graffiti splashed front door, which had green metal mesh covering the window.

Somebody had bent back part of the wiry protection, doubtless for the sheer fun of it, or what passes for that in this godforsaken tenement.

"I got a date with Sylvia tonight," Turner said.

Chapter 9

Wednesday Night

On the way to Windsor Terrace I had plenty of time to think over this case. I'd had cases I didn't solve. I've had to watch mothers crying for years over no justice for their baby girls killed by pimps or just because they were in the wrong place at the wrong time. I was frustrated often, but I never just chucked it. I had a good reason this time. Libby.

I didn't pull right up to the house, just in case our new friends were around. I parked a block over and walked to our—her cul de sac. Nobody was there. No Mercedes. I guess that was a good sign. I rang the doorbell. Angela took her time answering. I knew she was mad—this was just one of the many ways she would express her anger. She opened the door and left it open halfway. Not even looking at me, she just turned and went back toward the kitchen.

"Aw, come on. Don't be like that. It'll be a long night if you are going to be sore." I probably should not have said that.

She turned on me like a red-haired panther. Her eyes were big. "Fuck you. You don't think of anybody but yourself."

107

"What's wrong? Where's Libby?"

"Ask off the case," she said, walking away. "You're dealing with murderous psychos now, not hoods." That was the wife network. It revealed who was drinking, who was working what case, who was fucking around, who was doing a little blow, among other things.

"Libby's in a safe place. You should've let this alone from the start," she said, "from the moment they ransacked Hochman's apartment. You knew what you were dealing with then. We're divorced and you are still doing this to me." She came at me with a raised fist.

I grabbed her arm before she could take a swing and she went limp. I let her go and she walked back to the couch and threw herself on it. She pulled out a pack of Camel Lights.

It was quiet for a while. It was ten, maybe twenty minutes until she said, very matter-of-factly, "You know, Paul, we could have been good, you and me. A Paul that had a regular job. I did love you once. Yeah, I like to have nice things, and I'm bitchy sometimes, but I'd give up a lot for a regular Paul. Someone who I was sure would come home every night with his body and soul intact. Someone who I knew would be there, for me, for Libby."

"That wasn't me."

"It was you before you joined the force."

"Let's not do this to ourselves, okay? The die is cast, the roll was snake eyes. Maybe you don't believe this, but I'm sorry about it. This will all be over soon. It will be the last time."

"Right. Until the next one."

"Maybe I'll take a desk job. I don't know." Now I saw what was happening. This was the first time somebody took a shot at me since the divorce was finalized, the first blowback at her since we split. She had probably figured it was going to be smoother dealing with an ex-husband cop.

"Maybe we should get some rest, huh."

"Paul, it could have been different, right?"

"I don't know, Angie."

She smoked another cigarette and then went quietly upstairs. Not even a "No funny stuff" from her this time.

I pulled open the couch and lay down. Fuck the sheets, I was too tired. I didn't even take off my clothes. I lay there thinking about it. Maybe it was time to get off the street. Eighteen years of running up flophouse stairs after shits and down shaky fire escapes after fuckheads. A broken leg, a couple of punctures, a Police Combat Cross. My pension is there, if I can get to it in a few years. Started late on the force. Already twenty-seven. My physical reactions aren't what they used to be. Forty-five isn't old, but it's not twenty-one, either.

What if my vertigo hit at the wrong time and I didn't see the asshole with a gun in the dark corner? Or, worse, Turner ends up with a hole in his head. Not sure I could live with that.

I got up from the couch and walked over to the stairs. "No fucking way. What an ass I am for even trying this." I just stood there and leaned over the banister, on the first step. It was real quiet in the house. I could hear the grandfather clock in the dining room sounding the eleventh hour. Maybe she still loved me. Maybe I loved her. Maybe I was stupid. "Or just maybe I was horny," as Turner would say.

I knocked on Angela's bedroom door. First quietly and then a little bit harder. "Angie," I whispered into the doorsill. I heard the bed sheets rustle.

Angela pulled the door one-quarter open. Her long hair hung down around her face, so that I could only see her lovely brown eyes. I stood there, not really knowing what to say. There was something like an embryonic smile in the right corner of her mouth. Was it that? I couldn't tell. It was dark. I lightly pushed the door open.

As I opened my mouth to say something, anything, I heard a window break downstairs, an explosion and then a concussive force of air, and we were lifted clear across the room, landing in the bed. Smoke quickly filled the house. Broken pieces of glass were falling from window frames.

"Are you hurt?" I asked, still not understanding what had happened. Angela had indeed ended up underneath me. She was so shocked she seemed calm.

"Did you leave the stove on?"

"No, I didn't leave it on," I answered, a bit testily, "and stoves don't explode by themselves." I stood up. Dust was everywhere, sprinkled in the smell of singed wood and burned plastic. "You sure you are alright?"

Angela got up and looked herself over. "I feel okay." Her face was white.

I went to the door and looked downstairs. Some planks had gone right through the TV, and the couch I'd been sleeping on was now in cinders. A small fire burned in it. Through the broken front window, my neighbor, ex-neighbor, Vinny peered in. He was out of breath. Vinny was Old 'Hood.

"Hey, Pauly," he said, surprised to see me…and Angela. "You alright? You guys back together now?" He didn't wait for a reply. "You are not gonna believe this, Pauly," Vinny said, his hands gently cupped around his mouth as he shouted into the hole in the window. "I'm taking OJ for a walk down the street when these two…two…two fuckin' giants, you know, like that Bunyan guy, right. They walk up to your house. One of them does a pitcher's windup—but like a girl, like he never threw a ball in his life, and then something—I thought it was a rock—went crashing through your nice bay window there. They start running back to their car and in a couple of seconds…ba-boom!"

"Black Mercedes. Diplomatic plates?" I said.

"Yeah. Howdja know?" he replied.

"Wild guess."

Angela joined me on what was left of the upstairs landing. Sirens wailed in the background.

His dog, a huge rottweiler, was barking, his nasty snout peeking above the broken windowsill. Vinny named it O.J. because it had "killed a bitch or two," he informed us when we moved in ten years before.

My cell phone rang and all three of us jumped.

"It's me," Turner said. "I'm in the East Village and we got another little problem."

I didn't respond right away. I surveyed the damage to Angela's house, holding the cell phone at my side. I then noticed that I could just see into the basement, through a small hole in the living room floor, just to the side of the sofa.

"Hey, Paolo. You there. Did you hear me?"

"Yeah."

"I'm in Sylvia Ortelli's apartment. She's dead. Head blown off."

"Fuck. You okay?" I heard voices in the background. Cop noises. Police radio crackle. Orders being given.

"Yeah. I came over to pick her up for our poetry date," Turner said. "Didn't get to that. Goons busted in. No time. Glocks in our mouths."

I looked over at Angela, who was crying.

"'Where's zee fucking tapes?' they kept saying. And when I told them I didn't know what the fuck they were talking about, they threatened to kill Sylvia. And when I said it again, they did it. They said if you and I don't come up with the tapes, we're next. They tied me up and blew out of here. We might have our first break. Witnesses on the street said a black BMW took off like the Indy starter's flag dropped. One got a tag."

Angela wanted to know what Turner was saying. I waved for time.

"Before our new friends killed her—this place could be bugged by the Eyeties for all I know—Sylvia said she overheard di Gagliano speaking with that lawyer guy, who's a spook, by the way, SISMI. Di Gagliano says Rome wants the Muro thing closed right away. They are leaning hard on him to sew it up. Another thing: Sylvia said she never ever saw Muro at the Consulato. Ever. When she first heard of the murder, she looked him up in the diplomatic register and he wasn't there. Then after we showed up at the Consulate, he magically appeared in the register."

Angela was tugging at me wanting to know what Turner was saying. "You don't even know the half of it," I said into the phone.

"Why am I hearing a siren on your end? You okay?" Turner said.

"Yeah. They just firebombed my house, Angela's house tonight… while we were in it."

"Shit. Angela okay?"

"Yes, scared but unhurt."

"One more thing," Turner said, his voice turning quiet. "Can Angela or Libby hear me?"

"No," I said, pulling the cell phone tight to my ear.

"They said Libby's next."

"Thanks. I'm coming in." I put the phone in my pocket. Angela just looked at me. She knew. "I…uh…I don't think these guys will let us get off the case."

Angela looked around. Surveyed the damage. She wiped her face with her nightie. She didn't look at me.

"I'm going to pick up Libby right now. We're gone." She went back to her bedroom and tried to slam the door shut, but it would no longer close properly. The fireman broke down the front door and the EMS guys followed them in. Vinny's dog started barking.

Chapter 10

Thursday

"Well, at least it's a chance to see the city's political power plant again," Turner said as the three of us—Dunne had to come along—traipsed up the steps at City Hall to see the mayor. The sun shone on our right as we ascended. There were protesters of one sort or another beyond the security gate and inside the park nearby. I heard a blue on guard duty refer to them sarcastically as the nicest looking men he'd ever seen, a transvestite or transsexual group. I wasn't sure which. They were protesting that city run hospitals didn't offer free sex change operations. Somebody with a sense of humor had a boom box hidden in the gatehouse and was blasting out *Dude Looks Like a Lady* by Aerosmith.

I'd been to CH a couple of times, that medal for me and one for Turner when he caught a serial wife murderer named Stengle, but never for a papal audience with Peek-a-boo. I didn't look forward to it. He probably was not a happy mayor. Foreigners were getting popped daily on the street, while the Italian government and State were pummeling him to end the carnage. Friday morning's *Manhattan Morning Post* front page: "NY: Dodge City for Foreigners." My personal favorite was a front-page photo of a rifle sight view superimposed on a group of tourists waiting for the Statue of Liberty ferry: "Sight Seeing."

The Police Commissioner, James Frobish, met us inside and walked us to the mayor's office.

He casually mentioned that Peek-a-boo was apoplectic. Salerno was getting played by the *Post*. He was going to run for New York senator in the fall. Everyone knew but the official announcement hadn't come yet. He didn't want to have to field questions about this mess at his big press conference announcement, I figured. Dunne wasn't particularly happy. He must have been worried about his job. He wanted another chance at command someday and this was not helping his resume, Irish uncle or not. This was the kind of thing that could bury your career in the force.

Everybody in this town knew who Muro was now. We would be forever known inside the department as, "Oh, the guys who didn't solve the Muro case" and, "Yeah, isn't he the Muro guy?" Dunne was already sweating heavy. He was wearing that stupid Giants tie again, probably because he knew Salerno was a big Giants fan. He didn't say one word to Turner or me. I figured Frobish and Dunne would just cut us loose and ask for reinforcements. We would be the fall guys, and we deserved it, but a good squad leader takes some of the heat for his boys.

"Welcome, gentlemen," Peek-a-boo said at his door. He had actually gotten up to let us in. His desk, big enough to double as a dining room table, was at the far end of the room, but we all sat down on the two large beige couches. Two of the four walls were fronted by large, glass-enclosed bookcases. Six or seven "Olde New York" paintings and prints hung on the other walls, and on the east side. A large photo of the president, from the same party as Peek-a-boo, beamed at us from the far wall, along with one of La Guardia, a secular saint for the mayor, being of the same party and heritage. Right behind his desk was a painting of St. Sebastian, with arrows piercing his neck, chest, and legs.

If you sat facing the mayor at his desk, St. Sebastian's agonized eyes would be upon you. It supposedly belonged to the mayor and the papers all said it was done by a student of Caravaggio's, a copy of one done by the master himself but lost. The papers loved Peek-a-boo, for the most part, and nobody wondered where a man who has spent most of life in public service could get the money for such a painting, even one by a student of Caravaggio's. Of course, there were rumors it really was a Caravaggio.

Peek-a-boo sat in a large comfy chair with just one aide in attendance. That was David Holden, known as The Second Brain. Some said he was Peek-a-boo's alter ego, others his puppet master. The Second Brain himself couldn't get elected freshman homeroom president at Stuyvesant High School, where he graduated first in his class. As incredibly smart as he was, he had zero social skills and no ability to joust with reporters in public, all things Salerno had in his DNA.

Against all odds, he got Peek-a-boo, a Republican, elected twice in a Democratic city, and he was likely to get him to the U.S. Senate in a few months' time. Just a stop on the Bullet Train to the White House. The Second Brain eyed us quietly. He had a pencil and legal pad on his lap. He sat behind the mayor. Peek-a-boo didn't even refer to him. A white-gloved, tuxedoed waiter came in with coffee and Italian pastries.

The mayor started off. "Let's get right to it, boys. Jim, Lieutenant Dunne, I understand we don't have much in the way of leads."

Frobish wanted no part of this and just nodded at Dunne.

Our lieutenant cleared his throat and leaned forward in his seat, pulling out a sheaf of files, which Turner and I knew to be a huge pile of nothing. He cleared his throat again and the sweat really started pouring off him. He didn't even look up at the mayor. "Mr. Mayor, on Friday, April 25, about ten p.m., a Gaetano Muro, a colonel apparently attached to the Italian Consulate and having diplomatic immunity, was found shot through the head and heart near 50 Sutton Place. At that time, Detectives Turner and Rossi were assigned to the case."

"The bullets that killed Ms. Hochman, an American citizen and Mr. Muro's wife, and Ms. Sylvia Ortelli, another Consulate employee, match and are from the same gun as the weapon used to kill Colonel Muro."

The mayor lounged back in his chair as Dunne continued. He looked bored. He gave Holden a glance, the meaning of which was something probably only his aide could decipher. Holden leaned forward and whispered something in Peek-a-boo's ear. The mayor clasped his hands together. He let my boss ramble on a bit more but probably realized that Dunne wasn't going to give him what he wanted.

"That's fine. I'm somewhat familiar with the particulars of this case." He lowered his voice for a moment and said, "As you may know, Dorothy was the daughter of a great friend of mine." He paused. "Not that that matters, of course. What I'm searching for here are leads, gentlemen. I'd like to have some leads." His voice rose: "L-E-A-D-S. I'd like to be able to tell the people of this great city that the greatest police force in the world is on it, is on the trail—if not hot on the trail—of the perpetrators of these terrible crimes."

"I received a call this morning from the head of the New York City Hotel Association. Summer and fall tourist bookings are down five percent in the last week. That's not good, boys. Not good at all. I have the Italian General Consul and the Italian Ambassador to the U.S.—both friends of mine—unhappy with me. That's a first for this mayoralty. The State Department is on me like original sin. With all the problems in the world, it seems State doesn't have much to do besides call this office to see if we have a collar. A couple more of these folks go down and I might get a call from the president. That's a call I don't want."

We nodded in unison.

The mayor started to get a little agitated now. He stopped calling us gentlemen. I had a feeling the Temper was going to make itself known soon enough. I'd heard he threw things, telephones, books, files, desk blotters, half-filled cups of coffee, whatever he could get his hands on, even chairs. Holden had a scar on his forearm, the *Post* had written once, from a large ornamental Turkish letter opener the mayor hadn't expected to be sharp. The missile would have hit Holden in the eye, but he got his arm up in time to block it.

"What I need from you are bona fide leads. And a collar. Understood?" he said, looking from Turner to Dunne. I was uncomfortably in the middle.

Again, we all nodded, "Yes," a chorus of cheap bobblehead dolls.

This was where Dunne chimed in, "Mr. Mayor, I'll let my men do the talking."

Here, of course, was where Detectives Turner and Rossi would get hung high and out to dry. Staten Island here we come.

I turned to Turner, and he looked happy, unperturbed even. He had taken an unnatural liking to the idea of meeting the mayor, even though we were going to be chewed up and spat out like a stick of Wrigley's. He wanted to see City Hall, to see the mayor in person, he wanted to see the "Powah," he joked.

Turner began with a smile, a full devil's tail on each corner of his mouth. It was not just electric but fifty-thousand-watt neon. Or maybe it was fusion powered, I didn't know, and here the mayor got it all. He leaned out and put his fingers lightly on the elegant coffee table— nineteenth century teak?—in front of us. "Mr. Mayor. The unfortunate truth is that we have nothing solid in the way of leads."

"What about the license plate the witness made, Detective Turner?" the mayor said, his voice rising slightly again.

I waited for the Temper, the power of Saturn V rockets loosened upon us. Our careers would disintegrate in the afterburners. Instead, the mayor leaned in, as if to say, tell me more, son. Even the Second Brain, behind Peek-a-boo, leaned forward.

"The BMW involved in Ms. Ortelli's murder turned out to be stolen the same night from an Upper East Side public relations executive.

Other times it's been a Mercedes with diplo tags. Now, this is going to sound crazy, Mr. Mayor, but we, Detective Rossi and I, think that this is much bigger than three murders. There is a potential connection to very powerful people back in Italy. We don't know if the government is involved—"

The mayor winced. "Whose government?"

"Theirs…we think," I answered. "Maybe ours, too. And the Italian military…and ours, too. We think the good colonel was murdered to keep him quiet. He knew something about a plane going down over Ustica, which is a—"

"A small island in the Tyrrhenian Sea."

"You know it, sir," I said.

"Yes, of course. Ustica is where the plane crashed and nobody knows how or why."

Turner and I exchanged surprised faces.

"I was on vacation in Sicily at the time," the mayor said, "I think it was 1981…or maybe 1980. Visiting my grandfather," the mayor crossed himself, "who was alive at the time and lived in Messina. I read Italian decently. I know the basic story. So give me the Cliff notes. What's Ustica got to do with three murders and a little bombing in our city?"

"Well, as far as we can tell, and this is only an educated guess, you understand," I said, "the folks who killed Muro and the others have gotten the idea that we know or have something incriminating."

"And do you?" the mayor asked quickly. The Second Brain now stood up and walked around to stand next to the mayor.

Turner grabbed his chin lightly with his left hand, pulling on the goatee. "Now what?" his face said.

"Mr. Mayor," I said, looking him straight in the eye, "I don't want to compromise you in what has turned out to be a case already dangerous to my partner, my family, and myself. However, if you tell me we must divulge—"

118

Peek-a-boo stood up and gave the halt sign. He waved the Second Brain—who was about to whisper something in his ear—back to his chair. "You know, Detective Rossi, I like you. I like you both. Brave and discreet. Very good qualities in a police officer. What now, Turner and Rossi?" Peek-a-boo said. He smiled at what he'd just said. "Sounds like the ambulance chasing law firm that I worked for fresh out of law school," he laughed.

Turner said, "Mr. Mayor, right now we are a liability to you here. And there is a chance we will get killed here…and almost no chance we can solve the crime here, as most of the clues are probably in Italy."

"How do you know that?" the mayor asked.

"Again, Mr. Mayor, if you want to know…."

"Forget that question and go on."

"Let's just say we have what might turn out to be a key element," Turner said. "If we happen to get killed in Italy, that won't hurt you too much and the *pezzi grossi* in Italy will be happy and the murders will stop. And if we solve the crime…"

I knew where this was going.

"If we solve the crime, Mayor Francis X. Salerno gets the credit for the foresight of sending us to Italy to help the authorities there."

Dunne put his head in his hands. Frobish seemed completely blindsided. I was ready to clap at this performance. The mayor was all smiles. The Second Brain was not. He grabbed the mayor lightly by his jacket sleeve and they walked over to his desk to confer. It got animated. I made out a, "We can't just drop this on them," from Holden. "I disagree," I heard the mayor say. He returned to us without looking back at Holden, who remained near his desk.

"David, would you mind seeing if the other guests are here."

Holden was red faced. His arms straight down at his sides and hands in fists. He turned and walked to another door down the other end of the room.

"I've given the Italy idea some thought and I agree," Peek-a-boo said. "Boys, we'll have to keep this quiet, you understand. We'll call it the Petrosino Job," he said pointedly to me. "I'm not exactly sure of the protocol, but Holden will attend to that. We've got to convince the Italians of this, too."

Turner and I looked at each other. He was pretty satisfied with himself. This was a bet I would never have taken, and yet it paid off. Dunne signed off on it. He sounded more like a lackey than ever. "What a great idea, Mr. Mayor," he yapped aloud. I couldn't tell if Dunne was more excited about the idea because the mayor was or because it got us out of his hair and probably dead. "I'll be glad to work with the Italian authorities, as I'm sure my guys here will."

Turner was right. It was a tidy political solution for Peek-a-boo, a win-win for him. Maybe dead-dead for us. In Italy we might not make it off the tarmac to see the Coliseum. As long as Libby was safely hidden away, I wanted these guys bad.

Holden returned. "The CG is here," he said to the mayor.

"Let them in," Peek-a-boo replied.

In came di Gagliano, along with his little band, including the lawyer guy. Di Gagliano looked his rotund self in a dark blue pinstriped suit. They sat on the other couch, facing us. His eyes were pretty dark, the circles surrounding them nearly black. He wore a thick gold ring on his finger, with an almond-sized red jewel in it. It looked like a ruby. I don't know how I missed that the first time.

"Ruggero. I'm glad you came," the mayor said.

Di Gagliano, meanwhile, didn't seem particularly happy, just uptight, as if peeled lemons had been shoved up his ass. He was flanked on the couch by his posse, one of whom carried a huge brown leather valise. I didn't think they would go for this. It seemed unlikely to me that the mayor would spring this on him as a surprise. That didn't seem very politically astute.

"Your Excellency," the mayor began formally now, "as you know, these murders of Italian nationals have made all New Yorkers, and me in particular, very sad. I want to apologize on behalf of the City."

Di Gagliano nodded ever so slightly.

"We...these police officers here," Peek-a-boo pointed to us, a mistake since di Gagliano hated our guts for breakfast, lunch, and dinner, "the detectives here have been working very diligently on the case. I think you know that."

Di Gagliano didn't move. Said nothing. Just sat stone faced, looking at Peek-a-boo.

"They've visited with your office, more than once, I'm told," he said, looking over at us. "And while they do have some leads, it appears that the...the trail goes cold here in the U.S.," he said.

The phrase "in the U.S." perked di Gagliano right up. He seemed to sense what was coming. "With all due respect, Mr. Mayor, I find that hard to believe. Our nationals, attached to the Consulate, were killed here in New York City. I don't see how this—how you call it—this trail could go anywhere else. The perpetrators are still here, I would guess."

"Your Excellency, I disagree. The driver of the attack on Detective Turner in Harlem had no ID. But his prints have finally surfaced. We think he's Jens Dormon. Originally East German and former Stasi, in their commando department, I think." Peek-a-boo looked over to the Second Brain, who nodded slightly. "He was last known working for a private security firm in Milan called Atropos.

"It's unlikely that such a man would be working alone here in the Big Apple. We have no other records of him. His company refuses to talk with us, and, of course, we can't force them. The detectives think this is an Italian job, if you pardon my bad pun. They have evidence, which I'm afraid I cannot reveal to you yet." He looked again over to us for some support. I tried to look as firm as possible. Turner smiled. "It strongly suggests the trail leads to Italy. We're not sure where exactly or to who..."

Turner muttered, "Whom," under his breath, just loud enough for me to hear.

"We believe there could be some powerful people in Italy involved."

At this, di Gagliano's eyebrows arched, the give-me-time-to-figure-this-angle brow raise.

Peek-a-boo ended with hands extended and fingers open, a weird sort of supplication. He stood right in front of di Gagliano, with only the coffee table separating them.

I heard an arrogant sigh. Then the Consul General replied, "Mr. Mayor, this is highly irregular. I think perhaps you read the Italian newspapers too much, eh?" He laughed, as if to share a secret he knew about the mayor. "Always with the conspiracies. Like the true Italian you are. But maybe the solution is some bad powerful people *here*, no?"

"No," the mayor replied politely, walking away. "I'd like to send over Detectives Turner and Rossi to help the Italian authorities track down the killers."

"I'm not sure this can be done. There is protocol."

"We'll contact State and your ambassador in Washington and ask them to arrange this with the proper people in the Ministero del Interno and Giustizia. How hard can it be when there is good will on both sides?" he said pointedly.

Di Gagliano's lawyer leaned over and whispered into the CG's ear. The CG continued, his voice stiffened, "You have no jurisdiction. Worse, you have no leads that you can give me. There is nothing that I can legitimately forward to my government that suggests the trail leads to Italy. And to whom should we send these two?" he said, looking over at us. "Interior? Justice? The police? Carabinieri? SISMI? There are no Italian suspects. I object to what is a highly irregular procedure. You cannot just drop this on me like this. What will they do? What powers will they have? And will they read reports filed two decades ago? In Italian?"

The mayor said, "Yes. Detective Rossi is fluent." Well, that cat was now out of the bag.

Di Gagliano stood up, making his chess move. "Well, if this is what you wish. I'll try. It will probably take a few weeks to get an answer. Protocol, permissions, etcetera."

"We don't have that luxury, Ruggero," Peek-a-boo said bluntly and sternly. "I need it in twenty-four hours."

"Not possible." Di Gagliano was angry.

"With all due respect, Ruggero, make it possible. As your Excellency knows, Ambassador Marone is a very good friend of mine, so you won't have a problem there. I'm surprised I didn't see you at his birthday party two weeks ago. Anyway, I'm sure you know that he is well known in the halls of Palazzo Chigi. I understand that he is a regular visitor at the prime minister's vacation home on Sardinia.

"From our side you might note that my views have some weight with the City's Buildings Department. I know you've been fighting for years to get a permit to construct a nice addition to the Consulate on 67th street. Seems like the whole neighborhood is against it, eh, since you must build on what was once a small private park? And *your* park, too. That must hurt. Time is money, isn't that true, Consul General? Be a shame if you couldn't get that permit. Perhaps with the right approach the zoning board could look into a waiver for the Consulate."

"And here I thought I was in America," di Gagliano said, not totally indignant, but almost resigned. He was far too savvy a government mandarin for that. There was just a trace of a nasty and knowing smile on his lips. "I'll do my best, Mr. Mayor," he said, and walked to the door, his ducks following him.

"I'm certain that will be fine. Remember, Ruggero, I'm here to help you," Peek-a-boo replied, almost reveling in his power. He returned to his desk, not looking back at us.

My partner had watched the whole thing unfold with a student's eye. I wouldn't have been surprised to have found him taking notes. He liked the power. He wasn't going to be a detective forever.

Unbidden, he walked slowly over to the mayor, who now had his back to us and his hands locked behind his back, looking at Fiorello. Turner surprised him and he said something to Peek-a-boo, which I didn't hear, but Peek-a-boo had a big smile on his face as Turner returned.

"Definitely, Mr. Mayor. Definitively," was all I could hear my partner say to the mayor.

We made our way to the door, and the Second Brain looked at us as if we were mangy cats.

"What's the Petrosino Job?" my partner asked aloud as we walked the halls. Dunne had no idea, but I did.

"Giuseppe Petrosino was the NYPD's first Italian American detective, about a century ago. Investigated the Black Hand mafia," I said, "and founded the first bomb squad in the country."

"Nice," Turner replied.

"Yeah, but you're not going to like the ending to the story," I said. He looked at me for the punch line. "After he was sent to Italy to gather intelligence on the Black Hand, he was assassinated in Sicily."

"Oh," Turner said.

"If it makes you feel any better, over two hundred thousand people attended his funeral in New York City."

Walking down the front steps, the vertigo hit me. I staggered and Turner caught me. Everything was spinning. I felt nauseous. It always got me when I was standing or lying down, never when I was sitting. I could never figure out what would bring it on. There seemed to be no common threads to the period just before I was hit. It came when it came. My own muse.

"What's wrong?" Dunne, who knew nothing about it, asked.

"I'm just a little dizzy," I said, hanging on to Turner.

"Too much excitement for you, huh," Dunne said stupidly.

"Yeah, that must be it," I said.

On the way back to the One-Nine, Dunne, in the front passenger seat, was quiet, but it seemed a happy quiet. He figured his Turner problems were over. One way or another, we would be gone.

On the seat next to me in the car was the *Post*, full of tourist murder scare stories. Hotels were handing out advice pamphlets. Move in groups. Don't stay out past 11 p.m. It should have said, *Don't hang out with Detectives Hamilton P. Turner and Paul Rossi*. Security was tightened at the Statue of Liberty, MOMA, and the Met.

Gretzman covered the Ortelli murder. He linked my partner to the other three dead bodies, Hochman, Muro and the ex-Stasi kraut, but he stuck to our deal. Except for one thing. The last line said: "The key to solving the crime might lie in Italy, according to a police source who declined to be identified."

The quiet was broken by Turner. "Libby in a safe place?" he asked.

"Yeah…I think. They got on the first plane to LA this morning. Then off to the California hinterland. I didn't want to know where, just in case." I exhaled loudly. "What did you say to Peek-a-boo alone? Ass kissing?"

"I prefer to call it job prospecting," Turner said. "Assuming we live through this, I'm not going to be a cop forever."

*   *   *

Late Thursday, I walked over to the Grantham Funeral home on 79th street, near Lenox Hill Hospital. Muro's body had been moved there to be prepared for burial and the long trip back to Italy Friday. Laura didn't know we'd be traveling with her.

I found Laura in the chapel. Gaetano was laid out nicely, hands crossed over his chest with a small black and gold set of rosary beads in his cold grip. "The arrest with no bail," Turner called it, cribbing Shakespeare. A few people were in the chapel, three old ladies, two others, and us. Laura was at the front. She even had a veil on her head. I stepped up to the casket and knelt down in front of Gaetano. He looked good for a dead guy. He was in his pilot's dress uniform, big brass buttons, with what I guessed was the Italian Air Force insignia on them, AMI, and a strip of gold braid laced around his left arm. His pants were crisply creased.

I walked to Laura to give her my condolences. I put out my hand and found myself pulled toward her. I pecked her on the left cheek and moved back, whispering, "I'm sorry," only to find myself pulled forward again by her. It was the European kiss required. So I kissed her right cheek, this time a better kiss, my lips completely touching her face.

It was a lovely right cheek, soft yet firm. I could smell a faint lilac perfume about her, just enough to make me want to stay where I was. As I stepped back slowly from her, a small shock of her black hair fell upon my nose and swept along my muzzle; it was the softest, lightest flagellation. My whole body noticed it. She didn't let go. She wrapped her fingers around my hand.

"Sit here," she said. "Next to me. The skin around those green eyes was moist and the mascara had run. I don't know why that surprised me. She was a cop but she was a woman, and this was her brother. Military family. She looked up to him.

"Thank you, Paolo. It was very kind of you to come before we leave."

She simply thought I'd come to pay my respects.

We sat there for a while quietly.

Eventually, I got to it. "Laura, I think you should know that the higher ups have decided my partner and I should go to Italy to help."

"What are you talking about?" she said. Her black eyebrows arched. "Why are you doing this?" She let go of my hand.

"They think we could help the Italian police in this case. I do, too. We have evidence that can help." I wanted badly to tell her about the key, which was in my pocket. "I can't say more."

She shifted in her seat and seemed to mull it over. She took my hand again, very lightly, looking straight ahead, at the casket four feet from us. "You will help get yourselves killed is all. I wouldn't like that." Then, absently, she said, "What something? You were not able to catch

126

them in your own backyard. What chance have you got in theirs?"

"That's cold," I said, ignoring her question.

"I'm sorry to be frank. But it is you two that will be cold," she responded without missing a beat. She seemed worried.

We sat there a few minutes more. The two folks in the back, which I had guessed were from the Hochman side, came up, knelt at the casket, and said their goodbyes. They kissed Laura and me, too, since I was sitting in the front row.

"I'm sorry about what I said," she whispered. "It was ever thus. Decided by Fortune, don't you think?" She paused. "And what will yours be? I saw a palm reader's salon tonight, just down the street. I don't believe in them, and yet..." she said, with just an inkling of a smile. "She said I was unlucky in love. Not very original, if true."

I just watched her lips. She had chosen a dark red lipstick for the wake. And, nevertheless, with her dead brother within spitting distance, she had aroused me. When I met her eyes again, she was staring at me.

"When will you come?"

"We're leaving with you."

A smile crossed her lips.

"We don't expect to be in Italy long. Technically, it is for a consultation, forty-eight to seventy-two hours. We have no powers of law, obviously, and we are only to observe and assist with information."

"Of course. You are not the CIA."

I did a double take, not knowing if she was joking or not. After I realized she was serious, I said, "I'd like to ask a big favor of you, cop to cop, since we are not, as you say, CIA."

She looked at me directly. "Don't worry. I'll arrange for two pistols. You'll have them as soon as we land. Of course, if you must fire a shot, then I know nothing about it. Understood?"

I nodded quickly.

I rose to leave and moved to the casket one last time. I leaned over and—I don't know why—kissed the corpse on both cheeks. I ran my forefinger lightly down his soft silk black tie, straightening the knot. He held the real key to all this, and he was dead. As I left, Laura again pulled me in for the double kiss. She stood and held on to my hand tightly. I kissed her on both cheeks. She allowed me to linger a moment in her lilacs. I felt her chest against me.

*   *   *

When I hit the street, I saw the sign for Jackie's Palm Reading on 78th off First. What the fuck, I had time. It was a darkened little storefront, five steps down. The only light was from Jackie's neon sign in the front window. Nobody was around. Then there was a voice, high pitched from the back room, behind a curtain.

"Sister Jackie is in. Von moment," a woman said.

I sat in the moth-eaten couch up front. The ground floor sitting room was kept gray by the large window shades behind the sign. The couch was actually a car front seat, reddish-black, weathered, and patched with duct tape.

"Jackie iz ready to receive you now. Please to come."

I walked behind the curtain to see Jackie sitting in a large wooden chair. She was fifty-ish and going bald. She wore what basically looked like a large brown bag. The dress was laced with blue and gold and green horizontal stripes, accenting her bulging circumference.

"Please to sit down, Mizter Polisman."

That unnerved me slightly. "How did you know that?" I said stupidly.

"I am Jackie, the one who knows. Vye you coming now?" she asked. She had small brown eyes, the whites more yellow than white. She looked Russian, with those Tartar eyes. "Voo-man problem?"

"A forty-eight-hour reading. Can you do that?"

"I doan think so. My powers come ven they come, sometimes beeg, sometimes not so beeg. Understand?" She pointed to a sign to my left. "No refund."

128

"I understand."

"Giving me now your hands," she said, putting out a huge paw of hers. It was plump and peasant brown. She massaged mine for a few seconds. Feeling the lines, squeezing the fingers. Finally, she picked the right hand and laid it out in front of me on the table between us.

"You are right-handed, yes?"

I nodded.

Then she placed her hand fully on top of mine for a moment and closed her eyes.

Maybe a bad idea. What the fuck was I doing?

She hummed and traced the lines in my hands a few times.

"You vorried."

"I think maybe I have made a mistake." I got up with her hand still holding mine.

"No, no," she cried. "You pay. You sid down. Not mistake. But you are goink to make mistake. Soon."

I sat down.

She looked straight at me. Peach fuzz hung from her jowly cheeks and even a brown tuft on her chin.

"Hyu going a-vay," she said. She must have sensed my hand tense at that and she smiled. "See. Jackie know."

"Where?" I challenged.

"I doan know dat," she said perfunctorily, as if I should know a seer can't give such precision.

"You go someplace…far." She dropped my hand and said. "I think maybe you not go."

"What?"

"Iz better you not to go."

"Why?"

"I doan know why. Better you not to go."

"I have to go."

"Yes, I know dat," she said, as if I were a fucking idiot. "But better not go. You vill lose someting of value to you over dere."

"That's it?"

"Please, I'm a reader of hands. There are no vords there written. Only feelings. I'm not telling you eggzactness."

"Come on. That's not enough."

Then she started muttering in another language. She stood up and her vastness became more evident. I wondered how that throne could even hold her. She seemed not just fat, but a scale-buster.

"Mizter Polisman. This not baloney bool-shit. You vant hear things you like, go to Mother Rita on Second Avenue. She tell you vhatever you vant to hear. Happy stories. Here, I tell da truth, even if you doan like," she said, sticking out her hand with finality. Her palm was tinged a light green from all the twenties that had crossed it.

When I got home, I called Harry.

"You good?" he asked.

"Yeah. Got news. Going to Italy. Met a woman I like."

"Work or pleasure?"

"Both," I said.

"Can't get any better than that," he replied. I could hear him exhale the cigar smoke out. But he was waiting for me. He wanted me to say how it could get better.

"It gets better."

"Yeah?" Harry said, playing the game.

"Two, nine, five, one," I said.

"Good, kid. I like those numbers. They sound lucky to me. I'll try them tomorrow in the lottery."

He hung up and I packed.

Giovedi Sera

It had been a bright spring day, the kind for which the Milanese yearn after their typically rainy and overcast winters. The thick satin curtains in the fourth-floor library were nearly closed, with just a halo of early evening sunshine flirting around the edges. Three C class armored Mercedes limos were again parked in the courtyard. The palazzo was quiet, even more so than the normally hushed workday, when employees on the floors below went about their business, as Italian Labor Day happened to fall on Thursday. Employees would take Friday, too, in order to make "il ponte," or the bridge to Saturday, for a long weekend. Italians loved bridges.

"It's strange how sometimes the lamb comes to the lion, isn't it, Senatore?" the Baron said, sitting on the long sofa.

The Senator was preoccupied and then winked at him. "Yes."

"It shows that God does indeed work in mysterious ways, Senatore."

The Senator walked over and sat down, not far from his colleague. "Well, I don't know if there is a God," he said, "so for now, you will have to do."

The little Baron giggled at that. "Mr. Bruno is waiting outside. He must understand there are to be no mistakes this time around. Adesso, giochiamo in casa, e niente autogol." ("We have the home field advantage now. No own goals.")

"Si, certo," The Senator added. He walked over to the library's front door, opened it, and waved lightly at the guard, fingers barely moving, the flick of a hand as bare, tired, and patrician acknowledgment. The guard bowed and went off, returning in a moment with Mr. Bruno. The Senator could have bent the first knuckle of his index finger just a millimeter and the guard would have noticed and understood its meaning.

"You may go," the Baron said in English to the guard, who again bowed and left.

"I had always thought the Stasi were so diligent, so efficient, men who followed orders in the old Prussian way," the Baron began, not talking to Bruno but The Senator, as if Bruno weren't there. The Senator, who'd stood up, then walked around the couch and sat down again, this time in a chair to the right of the Baron.

Bruno faced them and stood at attention, like an I-Bar. He said nothing, knowing that the Baron had not addressed him directly. He simply stared straight ahead, at the cold air above the head of the Baron.

The Baron continued, again glancing toward The Senator, "The ex-Stasi are not as good as we thought. Too little exercise, I suppose. Unfortunate. Once your master is gone, the whole thing goes to shit, doesn't it, Senator?" His voice began to rise at the end of the sentence, with an exaggerated emphasis on "shit," suggesting to Bruno that had the Baron been a young man, he would have had his hand tightly around Bruno's throat.

The Senator said nothing, eyeing Bruno.

"The major has underwhelmed us with his abilities so far," Baron said, finally addressing the younger man. Those blue eyes of his searched Bruno's face for a sign, anything that would tell him the man was no longer qualified for the job. A shiver, a quivering finger. "You killed a consulate employee in her home and firebombed a policeman's house. Yet none of this led to what we wanted."

The major remained at icy attention. There was a longish pause, then Major Bruno knew it was time to respond. "The black policeman always has a woman with him. The girl was unfortunate, but we didn't realize who she was until we were in the apartment and it was too late. We've been to the Consulate. She might have recognized us."

"Now those two policemen know what you look like, eh?" the Baron asked.

"Only the African has seen me."

"Are you sure?"

"Yes." Then, as if to placate his master with soothing news, the major added with perhaps a little too much enthusiasm, "I'm reasonably certain the Americans have the key. They are coming here and—"

"I know that!" the Baron shot at him. "Alitalia 601. It lands tomorrow morning at eight forty-five at Fiumicino."

"Yes."

"That's all you have to say?"

The major continued to look to the air above the Baron. "There will be no bodies. I promise you that."

"Be careful. Those who break their promises to me usually regret it a very long time."

"Usually, it's an eternity of sorrow," The Senator chimed in, unable to resist. He laughed and the Baron snorted loudly. "God at least has purgatory. The Baron, unfortunately, isn't so forgiving," The Senator added.

"Go. Do," The Baron said to the major, who did a military about face and walked toward the door.

"One more thing," The Baron yelled. The major stopped. "I'm sure you are not going to be foolish here. I don't want blood in the Roman streets, and, more importantly, since I can't trust you to be smart enough to consider this, you must anticipate their moves. So far, they have eluded you. Consider that they might not be carrying the key with them. It could well be in Italy still, and they might know where. Or they might not. Let them find for us what that little radar man has hidden all these years."

"Suicide wasn't it?" said The Senator in an amused tone.

"Yes," the Baron laughed. "The church teaches us that those who play God and take their own life go straight to hell. At least the maresciallo saved his family. A real Italian." He turned back to Bruno. "Verstehen Sie? Leave us."

The Baron and The Senator remained in the library for a few moments in quiet.

"I don't trust Bruno to do the job properly," the Baron said. "I've taken care to make certain our own people are involved, too."

The Senator nodded and said, "I wonder, my dear Baron, if we aren't wasting our time over this key."

"You know what that little bastard had," the Baron replied. "We should have suspected long ago that Muro knew about it."

"Yes, of course. But this is ancient history. Italy was a different place then. I wonder if it would cause such a fuss now."

"The people need a mystery," the Baron said. "It keeps them occupied, keeps them from stealing our wealth. What would the Americans do if they knew who really killed Kennedy? They'd probably rise up out of boredom."

"You're exaggerating, old friend. More likely, they'd yawn. As for Italy, I grant you that our countrymen all love a conspiracy, and solving it would be so deflating. But most of the people involved are dead...or dying. Neither of us has much time left."

"Speak for yourself, Senator," the Baron groused. "I have a legacy to protect. As do you."

"Will we enjoy it where we are going?"

"That's all merda. We're all dust in the end."

"My point, Baron. We must consider that the key may not be as fearsome to us as we believe. In the new Internet Age, information has a shelf life."

"All things must be considered in war," said the Baron, quoting his favorite philosopher.

"It reminds me of the story of Don Quixote and the lion. Do you know it?" Before the Baron could reply, he went on, "Let me retell it. I enjoy it so much. It comes to such a wonderful end."

The Baron grunted assent.

"The valorous and foolhardy knight came across a muleteer with a cart, wending its way across Spain from Oran. He carries two lions to be delivered to the king. One, a great old animal, sits in its cage, minding its own business, when Don Quixote gets the notion that he must battle the King of the Jungle and prove his courage. Of course, the mule driver and the gentleman with him are in a panic at the thought, and Sancho Panza is beside himself. They want to flee this ill-advised adventure and the knight's sidekick is certain that he will be devoured alive. There's terror in the air and they are unable to stop the great knight. Don Quixote rides up to the cage and the lion makes not a move. The iron door is flung open. At this point there are screams and wails from all corners." The Senator laughs, savoring the story.

"Tis doom. Don Quixote awaits the great beast. The lion opens his eyes a bit, sticks out his great pink tongue, and pokes his head—with a regal but aging mane—out of the cage. He gives the Knight of the Rueful Figure a big, wide yawn, long sharp teeth, shiny white in the sun, then turns around and lays his head down, going directly back to sleep."

The Baron gave a little horse neigh. "But, Senator, which one of us is Don Quixote and which the page?"

"Neither, my dear Baron. Don Quixote and Sancho Panza arrive tomorrow on Alitalia 601."

They laughed hard. The Senator went over to the curtains and pulled them open. The Gnome shielded his pale blue eyes from the fading sunlight that invaded the room.

CHAPTER 11

FRIDAY

After passing through customs at Leonardo da Vinci airport, Laura was about to go collect her brother's body when the Carabinieri officer assigned to us walked up. She seemed to know him and they exchanged a few words privately. "Good, thank you," was all I could make out Laura saying to the sergeant, who wore the order's traditional light blue shirt with dark blue pants with the jaunty red stripe down the side. He had a sidearm in a shiny black holster.

"This is Sergente Fiorino, Marco," Laura said, bringing him close by the elbow. "Your official escort."

That meant our official minder.

The sergeant smiled. He had deep blue eyes, blond hair, and very little beard to speak of. A few spider hairs. Standing maybe six feet, one inch, he couldn't have been more than twenty-five, and a little on the pallid side. From the north, probably.

"Good morning," he said in that British-accented English so many Italians were afflicted with. "I am very happy to be receiving you. We, I mean the maggiore, is very much wanting to talk to you about this case."

Turner tugged at my side at that. Like we had a lot. I was sure he was rolling his eyes behind me.

"I'm Detective Paul Rossi, NYPD, and this is my partner, Detective Hamilton—"

"P. Turner. Yes. I am very excited to meet you," Fiorino said. "The newspapers here have been full of your…" he looked at me for a second, "…I mean your daring exploits on the case. Wonderful how you have escaped the death squads they sent after you. I read that you might have a key lead to this case," he said. "That is how you call it, yes? A lead?"

I tried to hide a wince.

"We are going to try to help in any way we can. Lead is perhaps too ambitious."

Turner pushed lightly past me and shook hands with Marco, and then I did.

"Thanks, Marco. I think the papers have been exaggerating. You know how they are," Turner said, giving him a half smile, which was good enough to give poor pasty Marco a suntan, seemingly unexposed as he was to such high wattage power.

Laura interrupted, the smile on her face gone. "I must retrieve Gaetano. I'll see you at the inspectorate headquarters in a few hours. Marco will see to you. He'll take you to the hotel first, before the meeting at three p.m. with the SISMI major."

At that Marco clicked his heels and said, "Just wait out front here." And he was off.

When he was out of hearing distance, I turned to Turner. "Your fucking key remark to Gretzman continues to give me nightmares."

"How did I know it was going to clear the Atlantic?"

"And that is why I got rid of it."

"What?"

"I don't have it on me. And we shouldn't carry it around. If something should happen to us, there is a letter going to Laura about where it is."

"And if she's blown away along with us in a hunting party...or dirty?"

"There's another letter going to Peek-a-boo."

"Uh-huh," Turner said as we walked through the terminal. "I noticed you didn't tell your partner where it is."

"I'm telling you now. Muro has it."

"What? You gave it to her? What is wrong with you?" he shouted just a little too loudly. We exited the concourse and moved on toward the curb. Turner quieted down. "You mean Guy?"

"For a smart cop you're embarrassingly stumped," I said, flashing him a lot of teeth.

That's when he dropped his Gucci Maxi overnighter. He grabbed me by the chin, just as an old Roman lady might, and squeezed. "Very good, Paolo. *Molto bene*. Of course, it might not be so easy to retrieve but at least they won't nail us with it."

Marco pulled up in a big blue and red Land Rover Cruiser. It looked as if it were just out of the showroom. These guys liked to drive in style. He placed the bags in the back and we slid into the rear seats.

"Marco, we might be followed," I said as he threw it in drive.

"No problem." He pointed to the automatic nestled in its holder next to him, under the dash. It looked like an M16.

As we escaped the airport ring road, the commercial and cargo buildings disappeared and the land turned to farms. The light green fields whizzed by. Land tilled for thousands of years. At 10 a.m., the sun was still relatively low in the sky. Pointy green cypress trees were everywhere along the road, along with pine trees sculpted so the tops reminded me of large broccoli spears. All around were tractors and the ubiquitous three-wheeled blue Piaggio Ape, a motorized tricycle really, a modern donkey, glorified with various kinds of platforms above the two back wheels, sometimes a flatbed, sometimes an enclosed compartment. The pickups of Italy chugged along every road, from superhighways to ancient cobblestone streets. On our right were the train tracks that led to Rome.

About fifteen minutes into our ride, Marco said, "One other thing." Over the front seat and into my lap came a box covered in satiny paper and topped with a red and blue bow.

"Compliments of Laura," he said.

"Thanks very much," I said. Turner and I slipped the 9-mm Beretta 92s into the waistband of our belts. The one extra mag for each of us went into the breast pocket.

"Also," Marco said. "Please mind there are metal detectors at the inspectorate. Remember to leave the gifts in the truck. Okay?"

"No problem, Marco," Turner answered. "I knew I was going to like this country. Marco, I like your country very much."

He turned his head our way for a moment and gave us a quick smile, which turned quickly into a frown.

"What's wrong, Marco?" I asked.

"We are being followed already."

Turner and I turned around so synchronously that we looked mechanized. "Let's not make it so obvious, huh," I said. He turned forward. Marco kept his eye on the road. "Marco, you mean the little green car a few lengths behind us?"

"Yes, Fiat Bravo. The, how you call it, the *targa*…well it looks like a rental plate. That's what you say, correct? Plate?"

"No offense, but the guys messing with us tend to drive fast German cars," I said.

"That is okay, but this car has followed us since right out of the terminal."

"Marco, do you have binoculars in the truck?"

"Yes, of course." He pulled a small 10x32 out of the glove box and threw it back to me.

I bent forward and down, out of the Bravo's sightline, and then came up slowly with the glasses, hoping to peer over the top of the backseat and catch a glimpse.

"I see a guy with a black mustache and thick black-rimmed glasses. Nobody else in the car, but that's a mistake we made before."

"Friend of Jens?" Turner said.

I adjusted the glasses as best I could but the truck's bouncing ride wasn't helping. "This guy looks too small to be anything but a putz," I said.

"Please, what is putz?" Marco said from the front.

"Marco," Turner said, "are you absolutely sure this green Bravo has tailed us right out of the terminal?"

"Yes. Certain," he replied. "*Cento percento.*"

That's when I finally got the field glasses to work cleanly. "Pull over," I said loudly.

"What?" my car mates said together. The car swerved a bit, as Marco was surprised by my hollering.

"Pull over. Right now. Right now, Marco, please." I shook my head.

Turner pulled out his niner and Marco slammed on the brakes instead of slowing down as I had asked. Turner and I, without belts, jerked forward and the binoculars went out the side window. Marco went for the automatic.

"Wait. Wait. Stop," I said. "Put it away. Sorry. This motherfucker is not who you think."

Turner looked confused, that small furrow of brow and chin out.

Marco looked at me as if he thought I were crazed. "*Cosa succede? Perche gridi?*" ("What's up? Why are you yelling?"), Marco said.

The green Bravo had slowed down not far behind us and looked as if it were going to do a slow pass. When I was certain of the driver, I jumped out as he was pulling by. The driver hit the brakes.

"Get out. Get out of the car right now," I shouted. I had a mind to pull out my niner and shove the silver muzzle right up one of Gretzman's nostrils, but that would have brought even more attention to us arguing on the side of the road. "Do you know we were ready to blast you off the highway? My new Italian friend here has an M16. Get out of the car you…you fucking hack! Goddamn it. You are compromising us even now." I looked around for other cars that might have been following us, then walked around the front of the Bravo. Before I could pull him right through the side window, he jumped out and got the door between us.

"Easy, Rambo. I'm just doing my job," Gretzman said, tugging at the crappy caterpillar on his lip and grabbing the fake glasses as they slipped off. "Thought I'd try a new look," he said, smiling.

Turner emerged from the backseat. For once he wasn't laughing at or about Gretzman. Marco looked confused. His hand was on his holster.

"Hey, hack is not a nice thing to say. I don't think you realize how…" Always with the joke. Maybe Gretzman thought it would calm us down.

"Shut up," I said. "What are you doing here?" I put my pistol back in my waistband.

"Short straw, I guess," he said, faking a puzzled look at my gun. "Funny, Detective Rossi, I guess I don't know my international crime fighting treaties as well as I thought, 'cause I was sure you wouldn't be allowed to carry here in Italy. My error." When he saw we weren't laughing, he closed the front car door. "This is my story and I'm following it, like a good hack. You need my help. You're too busy fantasizing about La Wonder Woman."

I ignored what he said. "Since when does the *Post* do international stories?"

"Since they involve the NYPD. That's when. Anyway, what's the problem? You're the ones who stopped the show."

Turner looked to Marco and said, "Come, let's get back in the car and back to business."

"My partner's right," I said to Gretzman. I walked over to the Bravo and pulled out the keys from the steering column."

"Hey…don't. Come on. It's fucking hot out here. I don't know the language," he begged.

"Sorry, but I cannot allow you to compromise us. You are also a big fucking pain in the ass."

"Hey, my stories got you here."

"Now, I'm helping you out," I said. "You don't seem to understand how dangerous this is. You aren't tailing Paris Hilton and her Chihuahua. There are guys trying to send us to Hell and they won't let you get in the way."

"Thanks, Officer. Your bravery shall be forever remembered by all the people…"

I stifled an incredible urge to pistol whip this ass. That's something that might have happened in the old days, before I dropped the sauce.

So I took a deep breath, which I was supposed to do in situations where I'd love a drink. "I don't give a shit what you think of me. I'm doing you a favor," I said. And I moved back to the truck and got in.

"Let's go, Marco," Turner said.

I stuck my head out the window as we pulled away. "I'm going to leave these keys at the base of the next emergency phone station along the road. I don't know if it's ten feet or ten kilometers from here. Shit, I don't even know if they have 'em here, but that is where you'll find 'em," I shouted. I looked in the rearview and could see Marco had a few sweat beads on his forehead. "You do have emergency roadside phones here, right, Marco?"

"Yes, of course," he replied. "They come equipped with espresso machines, too," he added.

For a moment, he got me. After that, I started liking him, too. I eased back into the seat and watched in the rearview as Gretzman cursed us. He threw that stupid disguise onto the side of the road.

"Nice, Paolo," Turner said, staring straight ahead.

Forty minutes later, we shot up Viale Aventino and Via di San Gregorio, then around the cobblestone streets circling the Colosseo.

Huge crowds surrounded the ancient crumbling arena. Street performers wearing Roman costumes were mixed in with the tourists, like roosters among hens. Men with short red tunics and thick bronze thighs talked dirty to fat American females. "Let me show you my sword, baby." Ten minutes after passing the huge and beautifully grotesque Altar of the Nation, south of the Piazza Venezia, ridiculed by the Italians as The Wedding Cake, we found our hotel, La Chiara, not far from Piazza Navona, in the oldest part of town.

Turner wasted no time. "We have a few hours, Paolo. Let's take advantage."

"I'm bushed. Gretzman spoiled my morning, or what was left of it after that flight. Got no sleep. I just want to crash."

"Not me, partner. I'm heading out to the Pantheon."

"No, thanks. I'm here. We have a meeting at three."

"Got it," he said, already halfway out the door.

I unpacked and wondered what my dead grandfather would think. He left this place with a one-way boat ticket and a beat-up straw suitcase. I returned eighty years later, the same country, but different. He came from a tiny farming village near the Basilicata coast, when a man's wealth was measured in sons, donkeys, and land. These days, Morruggio was crawling with topless Brits and Germans sunning themselves on the rocky beaches, looking for the still untouched Italy.

Ten streets long and five wide, my *nonno* always prefaced each of his Old Country tales, holding up two hands and ten fingers first, then one hand. There was the cemetery at the edge of town as you entered from the main highway and a newer one constructed at the end of town as you left to return to the highway.

"Perfect," he used to say. Death coming in and death leaving, as if you needed any other signs of our *sfortuna*, he would laugh. He hated the place. Dirt poor. No jobs. Nothing. If it weren't for the rocks, there'd be nothing for the kids to play with. The bay was close by and he'd watched as more than one bored boy had died swimming in the stronger-than-it-looked surf, dashed against the stony outcroppings now dotted with those sunbathing tourists. "Rocks are much stronger than bone," he would say.

I opened the windowed doors that led to a small terrace overlooking the tiny square of Santa Chiara. Though it had been a bright sunny morning when we landed, the clouds had come on fast and it began to rain in heavy sheets, an early summer shower. Turner would get drenched, but naturally it wouldn't bother him. I had to unpack right away. He had to see the Pantheon right away.

It stopped raining just as it had started and then fifteen minutes later it began again. I closed the terrace doors and lay on my bed for some shut eye. Better to be well rested for a meeting where I basically didn't know what to expect. Maybe they would genuinely let us help them, or, as was common with cops of different jurisdictions, they'd resent it. It was bad enough the few times a case took me to New Jersey or upstate. Here we were three thousand miles away in another country hunting criminals they should have caught on their own. Our Roman reception just might be chilly.

An hour later, I heard a light knock. Rod in hand, I walked to the door and, standing to the side, said, "Who is it?"

"It's me, Laura."

I opened the door. She was wearing a black trench coat, despite the heat. She had a look on her face that I'd not seen before, sultry. Her shades were hanging on to her face just at the tip of her sharp nose. Those wonderful green eyes of hers, strangely paler now, peeked out over the tops of the sunglasses. She said nothing. She took a tiny step toward me and the coat opened a bit. She was wearing some kind of frilly bikini outfit. La Perla? The soft curve of her chest, the whites of her breasts, sent a shock directly to my loins.

I shuffled in retreat, in confusion. She jumped in the door and onto me like a bat on a bug, spreading her wings around me. And I fell backward slowly, as in a movie run at half speed.

144

Then more knocking on the door.

I woke up in an empty room. I went to the door, my clothes still on. I hadn't wet myself. A pipe dream, but enjoyable. Laura was slowly driving me crazy. Green eyes you could spot twenty feet away through a throng of women, men, and martinis. The first time you saw them, they dared you to talk to her.

It was Laura at the door. But she wasn't wearing a trench coat this time. No bikini undies. Just her carabinieri uniform, though the tight fit flattered her. Her military cap was sexy on her. Her normally straight black hair was curly wet from the rain and drooped into small ringlets onto her shoulders.

"Are you okay?" she asked, standing in the hallway. I had kept her out there a few seconds too long, staring at her in confusion.

"No. Yes. I'm okay. You've been here before," I said absently, my back to her as I walked away from the door.

I didn't hear her follow me in. I turned. "I'm sorry. I was in a deep sleep just now. I never can sleep on planes, so I was catching up. Economy class is a terrible way to travel." When I looked at her now, she had on a wicked kind of smile. She knew.

"Perhaps I should go." She stood still in the hall.

"No. Please come in. I was having a strange dream. That's why I'm so discombobulated."

She moved over the threshold. "What is this 'discombobulated'?"

"A ten-dollar word for 'confused.'"

As she passed me, I could detect the scent of lilacs again. I always thought a woman should wear just enough perfume to do that to a man. That you should only just get the tiniest whiff. It should make the tip of your tongue come out slightly for another sense, like a snake taking a pulse of the local prey.

"And what was this dream about?" she asked, barely restraining a smile. She turned and sat down on the couch. "Something to do with this case? I hope not."

I sat on the edge of the bed, facing her. "Just a dream. A nice dream but one of those where…" As it returned to my mind, I feared I would embarrass myself somehow, like some tongue-tied teen. "Never mind. Not important. Can I get you something from the mini bar? Water, beer, whatever."

"White wine."

I brought her a glass and poured some sparkling water for myself.

"No nice Italian wine for you," she said with a little bit of pride.

"Don't drink much," I said.

She arched her eyebrows for a moment and probably made the correct assumption. "Where's Hamilton?"

"He's out for a walk. Went to the Pantheon for a look-see."

"'Look-see,' she said, "another American phrase." Laura repeated "look-see," wrapping her wonderful lips around the word as if that might help her understand it.

I tried not to stare at them.

"Hamilton is interesting, is he not?" she said.

"Yeah. Never had a partner like him."

"You mean black?"

"No, I mean someone who in some ways isn't a cop at all, yet in others is one hundred percent cop, a cop's cop. I don't know how to explain it, but you're a policewoman…"

"I'm a cop," she corrected me.

"There's By-the-Book Turner. Do not fuck with him when the bullets fly. Do it right when you're on a pinch with him or don't come along to the fight. He actually knows how to take his weapon apart, clean it, and put it together again. I've forgotten all that. And sometimes we'll be in that car an hour waiting for some dogshit to come out of his doghouse and he'll be telling me about Sun Tzu's *The Art of War* and how we could apply it to policing. He's not gonna be a cop forever, unlike me."

"I like him," she said sweetly. Her nose wrinkled and her nostrils flared almost imperceptibly. I once had a girlfriend whose nostrils flared only when she came, and this came back to me just then.

"I know you like him. And so does he."

She put her glass down on the end table, and she shook her head. "Oh, no, please. I do not like him like that." Then she checked herself. "I suppose I could, but I find him more fascinating than attractive. An unusual specimen of a species that produces mostly mediocrity, no?"

"You mean cops?"

"I mean people."

"Yeah. I agree."

The rain had stopped again and I walked to the terrace doors to open them.

"You, on the other hand, have *grinta*," she said pointedly. "You do not like to give up when you want something, eh?"

I looked over to Laura and her eyes were watery. I didn't think it was my grinta. "How are you holding up?"

"Okay, I guess. I am worried about my parents. They have not taken it well. He was the firstborn."

"I'm sorry," I said.

"He will be buried tomorrow. In Ustica. That's why we came to Rome instead of Milan."

"What?" I asked. I tried not to sound shocked.

"Yes, in Ustica. Believe it or not, that is what his will said. He kept it at a safe box at MilanoBanca in Milan. It shouldn't be a surprise. It's a very quiet island. I'll be going alone. My parents are too old to go. There are no flights, only ferry service from Sicily, and I'll be gone for twenty-four hours. I hope you can manage without me."

"Well, we've got Marco…"

"And your Italian is not so bad, though you use a lot of dialect from the South, correct? Tell me, where is your family from? And was it your grandfather who came over to America?"

"Yes, Basilicata."

"Do you feel American or Italian?"

"I was born in the U.S. When I was a kid in school, I felt Italian. All of us were tribes then. Micks, Spics, Polacks, Guineas. Back then we were what our parents were. But I'm an American. Baseball, not soccer, is the beautiful game. I drink cappuccino at night."

She laughed. "A terrible habit of your people." She rose and walked to the terrace doors. "It's funny how that works. How people change. Gaetano had been in America many years and I noticed how he'd picked up American habits. His walk was different. He lost interest in *calcio* and in conspiracy theories, except for Ustica. He was a changed man, though I can't say for sure it was America. After Ustica, there were times when he seemed happy, but it was not genuine joy. Other times I would see him, and he was so depressed that I thought he would kill himself," she said, looking out on to the terrace.

I walked up behind her quietly. She was holding the doorknobs, one in each hand, the doors open and her between them.

"What did he tell you about Ustica?" I asked.

She turned, startled at my question. Or perhaps it was the tone.

"Nothing. He never told me anything," she said, as if she were worried that I had suspected her of knowing. She began to cry, and I thought she would either drop down or into my arms. I couldn't tell. I put my arms around her and held her lightly by the shoulders. She was looking down and wiping her tears. She looked at me and for a moment I thought she wanted me to kiss her. Maybe I was dreaming again or channeling my own desires. I would have loved to kiss those lips. The vulnerable look in her eye told me to do it, but it was the wrong vulnerable. It wasn't me that had weakened her knees. She started to lean into me.

That's when the door opened and in walked a happy, soul-of-a-beatnik detective, just back from a leisurely stroll around the Pantheon. I turned my head, still with both hands attached to Laura's shoulders. Despite our nine-hour plane ride and next to no sleep, he looked freshly pressed. A light green polo shirt over khaki pants over brown Prada loafers. And then the face. His eyes were positively jumping for joy in what he must have thought was the discovery of Laura and myself *in flagrante*. From his vantage point at the door fifteen feet away, it must have looked like we had just kissed when he barged in.

For a long moment he just stood there with that wide, the-devil-knows-all crack in his face…teeth out. He stopped two paces from the door.

"I'm sorry if I'm disturbing the party," he said, glancing briefly over at the open bottle of wine on top of the mini bar.

He inspected one glass, mine, smelled it, and touched the San Pellegrino bottle.

My hands dropped from Laura's shoulders. "How was the Pantheon?" I asked.

"Well," he said, moving to the minibar, next to the couch. He crouched and opened the door. "There wasn't an open bar there, unfortunately, among other things," he said, looking at Laura while pulling out a little Johnny Walker Black bottle, "and the Carabinieri stationed there weren't as attractive as the tenente, but I managed to find it interesting.

Made a stop at San Luigi dei Francesi, a church with two fine Caravaggios. The real deal, not like that fake in Salerno's office. One day, when he's working for me, I'll let him know about that. And I managed to squeeze in San Andrea Delle Valle, but there was no beautiful Tosca *there*…nor Cavaradossi or Scarpia." He plopped himself down on the couch, looking at Laura. There was now the thinnest bead of sweat on the forehead of a man who rarely sweated.

I detected just a trace of jealousy. Oh, he was happy thinking I was getting over, but I could tell he was oh-so slightly miffed that it wasn't him.

"Sending the devil to hell, are we?" Turner said to her. His voice was The Mellow. The one I often heard him thrust into the phone at our desks back at the One-Nine, the one for the fair sex only. "I understand the room next door is vacant. Perhaps I should take it."

Laura had recovered herself by then and she laughed out loud. A surprising sort of yell, as if she'd really been tickled. She walked over to the couch to pick up her hat, which was sitting next to Turner. "You are very interesting, Detective Turner. That's a famous line from an old Italian story by Boccaccio."

"As I said, I dabble in poetry on the side," my partner said, sipping his drink.

"Yes, but from what happened to poor Sylvia it was a good thing I didn't accept your invitation."

Turner winced. I smiled.

"The Boccaccio story is one of a monk and a young virgin in the desert," Laura said. "We all have to read Boccaccio in school here, or at least make believe we have read it. It is…how you say in English…" she closed her eyes a second, as if looking inside her brain for the word, "…a naughty story. A virgin goes to the monk's hut in the desert and…" Laura was trying to put on her hat, fix her hair under it, and give the explanation of the story at the same time, and not managing it well. "Ah, well, you can guess the rest."

"Why don't you let me tell our philistine here the rest of the story, Lieutenant Muro," Turner said. "I saw that Marco is downstairs."

"I will wait with Marco in the lobby, so you'll be able to get ready. A presto," she said, slipping out the door.

"You know Boccaccio?" I said.

"Not really. Never grabbed me like it did my father. That 'Send the devil to hell' was a line in a friend's poem, a spectacularly pretentious friend. After he read it aloud at St. Mark's, I had to look it up. I have to admit, though, 'sending the devil to hell' is a wonderful euphemism."

I sat next to Turner. "A monk and a virgin?"

"Well, she wasn't for long, Paolo."

Chapter 12

Friday Afternoon

At about 3 p.m., we emerged into the heady sunshine of an early Roman afternoon in May, already late for our first appointment. The rain clouds had stomped in but tiptoed out. Besides the street buskers and taxi drivers, there were few locals to be seen at first. Mainly tourists and pickpockets, gypsy kids looking for an easy mark. Then the store gates went up, raising the noise level, as the Romans came back from long lunches. The thing about Rome was the ochre. Lots of European cities have block after block of beautiful seventeenth-century palazzos. The quaint local bakers and butchers don't set Rome apart from Paris. Roman monuments are unique, but the Caesars left their marks across the Continent. Some of the best Roman architecture was in Turkey.

It was the ochre palette that held me. There was no end of buildings in different shades of it. Some with a rust tinge, others brown or tangerine. Still others had a yellow fade or a mauve hue, as if somehow the weather and aging combined and conspired to make each palazzo different. We passed a sprinkle of Fascist-era granite buildings, each standing out in a shadowy prominence, like an ugly heiress at a debutante ball. The Inspectorate was originally a black-shirt building, with a huge, stylized eagle at the top. Pieces of the frieze had been hacked out on either side of the bird. The now infamous *fasces* were removed after the war.

Palm trees gave Rome its dreamy character, an easy stage on which fables were played out. They stood as quiet reminders that this city was the westernmost outpost of the Byzantine East. Romans know their city is sister to Athens and Istanbul, Alexandria and Jerusalem, and only a distant cousin to Paris and London.

We met with SISMI at the Inspectorate, a carabinieri station, because foreigners aren't allowed into SISMI buildings. The Servizio Informazioni e Sicurezza Militare wanted just us, so Laura would meet up with us later. Marco made it as far as the decrepit, windowless conference room, with white walls, peeling in spots, and bare except for one photo. It was a photo of seventy-two-year-old PierFranco Berodi, the prime minister, wearing a slick grin. He was nicknamed Il Ciuffone, or the thick-haired one, for having a luscious plume of black locks adorning his skull—which served him well at elections—at an age when all of his political opponents together were lucky to have enough hair to keep one single comb busy. But his enemies and Italians in general preferred to call him Il Ciuchione, or the big jackass. In the corner was a limp Italian tricolor on a flag stand.

Bright white lights, which seemed more for interrogation than a foreign delegation, lit the room. The three of us sat, waiting for the major on cold metal chairs. The black table was bare save for two ashtrays filled to the brim with butts. Marco took out his cigarettes but the pack was empty. Turner offered him a Rothmans. Marco stared at it, then smiled and lit one.

Major Ettore burst into the room from another door down the other end. The door swung open, squeaking loudly on its hinges. With him came one other man, clipboard in hand. Outside that doorway I saw momentarily, before the door slammed shut, a couple of men standing, peering into our room. They looked away when our eyes met.

Ettore shut the door. "Welcome, gentleman," he said in Italian. "My name is Maggiore Giovanni Ettore." The other man introduced himself quickly as the translator. We stood and shook hands all around.

Ettore nodded to Marco and asked him in Italian to leave. "I'll wait for you with Laura," Marco said as he left, squashing his Rothmans into an ashtray, spilling out ash.

Ettore looked to be about forty-five, dark chestnut hair with sprays of gray around his sideburns and temples. Brown eyes and bronze skin that made you think he was a Lazio farmer under the sun most of the day, not a military inspector or a lawyer. He wore a mustache that had sprouted some lines of silver and a beard neatly trimmed to his chin, salt and pepper, or *brizzolati*, as the Italians called it. He was wearing a jacket and tie, not a uniform, which surprised me. I could tell from Turner's expression that he also was wary, expecting a uniform. And then I saw the thick gold ring with a big, blood red rock in it, just like Consul General di Gagliano's.

"Are you with SISMI?" Turner asked through the translator.

"Yes. I work without a uniform generally. I'm an investigator. A major, officially, but a lawyer, not a spy, not like James Bond, anyway." He laughed.

We said nothing.

Ettore seemed to sense our unease. He turned and placed his suede jacket with big brown elbow patches on the chair nearby. He sat directly across from us and threw down a manila folder he'd been carrying under his arm.

"Detectives Turner and Rossi, yes?" We nodded after the translation. I tried not to nod too early or give any sign that I understood what he said before the translator did his thing. He put down his pencil on the folder and held each end between his fingers, looking down at the table, as if he were thinking of something to say. "Gentlemen, the Italian government is interested in the information you might have on the Ustica case. The whole reason you are here is to tell us what you know. In this folder is a description of what has happened to you over the last week—as far as we know, of course. There are plenty of lacunae, spaces that you perhaps could fill in?"

"We'll try," I said after the translator finished.

"Good. And as a show of good faith," he said, "I will tell you first, as much as I can legally, of what we know. How's that?"

SISMI knew where Muro was on the night of the plane crash. "We believe he and the other pilot, Captain Cofari, were in the air."

"But," I interjected.

"Yes," Ettore said with a wave of his hand. "At the public trial, Muro said he was on the ground. That was long ago." Ettore stopped and closed his eyes a moment. He twirled the pencil in his hand. "Cofari, as you might know, killed himself just a few months after the plane went down. There were rumors back then that Cofari, who was the focus of the probe, had seen the explosion but could not tell the source. Many speculated publicly that Muro or Cofari were the culprits. Muro was living beyond his means, and the money was coming from a bank in Lugano, Switzerland, but we could not trace it further than that, at least on a legal basis. The marriage to Hochman wealth had complicated things," the major said.

"We don't believe that Muro downed the plane," Ettore said. Then he dropped two thin files on the table, one for each of us in English. "Read these summaries while I attend to something quickly. You will not be able to take the reports from this room," he said. He left through the door he came in.

May 1, 2002
Confidential
Summary for NYPD. Detectives Paul Rossi and Hamilton P. Turner Only
Prepared by Maggiore Ettore, G. SISMI
Pilots: Col. Muro, Gaetano. Capt. Cofari, Angelo.

The June 27, 1980 Ciampino ground log says Muro and the other pilot flew out that night, but the exact time of the flights remains a question. They returned to Ciampino, Cofari first, and each of their F-104s was missing ordnance, a Sparrow missile. Both pilots had said they'd taken off that way, missing the full weapon complement, because they were scrambled so quickly. The weapons log backs them up. It happens, so there's no way of knowing for certain. Tampering with logs cannot be ruled out.

In 1980, many powerful people, inside the government and out, didn't want it solved. The current government doesn't care one way or another. With elections coming soon, our PM Berodi would like to have an answer, to the extent that he could claim credit by blaming the other side, or anybody else, for that matter. But if he doesn't like the answer, well then perhaps your trip will have been a waste of time.

After numerous investigations, SISMI, NATO, Parliament, information from opened Soviet archives on Libya, commanders and generals hauled up before magistrates, the only solid evidence we have on Itavia Flight 870 is that there was an explosion on that plane. It took seven years to find the black box, and recovery of fuselage pieces went on for years more. It established only that there was definitely some kind of explosion. Whether the blast was internal or external, accidental or intentional, cannot be determined and may never be. There are, of course, many theories. But eighty-one people died, and only God knows why.

When Ettore returned, I asked him what he thought happened.

"I believe they saw something criminal," Ettore said. "I can't prove it. This case is twenty-two years old and I've been involved almost since the very beginning." He replied even before the translator finished my question. Then he took the files from us.

"With conspiracy theories you can go anywhere—the prospective is infinite. With the deadly but likely dull facts, only boredom." He paused. "We enjoy the scandal itself far more than finding out. Not knowing who shot Kennedy is far more exciting than knowing, wouldn't you say? Beh, what I think doesn't matter. It's what you might know that matters now."

Turner and I looked at each other. I was unsure about how to proceed. Ettore didn't inspire trust. There was the red rock on his finger. It didn't look like a harmless civic group ring. I wasn't sure he still cared about this case, after so many fruitless years of work.

"In terms of quantity, we certainly don't have what SISMI has," I said. "But we might know something." Ettore looked at me for some hint. "We have reason to believe some undiscovered evidence, possibly strong evidence, still exists somewhere in Italy," I ventured. "That's what we are looking for." What could we give him, short of the key itself, that he didn't know already? The key was a no-no. We couldn't trust the guy with it. We didn't know whom he was working for. I folded my arms.

"Undiscovered evidence?" Ettore said, musing on it a bit and not looking at either one of us. "What kind?"

"I can't tell you right now."

"I see," Ettore replied patiently. "Do you know where this evidence is?"

"No," Turner answered, and then elaborated, "Not yet. But we expect to find out soon."

"How do you know there is evidence if you don't what it is or where it is? You are foreigners. How do you know it is important?"

Turner brought his hands together in front of his mouth, his index fingers pointed in a church spire, and tapped his lips lightly. "We have some idea. Why, I cannot tell you."

I turned away, fearful of what was coming next. I was pretty sure Ettore was going to throw us out.

"So, let me make certain that I understand," Ettore said calmly. "You think there is important undiscovered evidence, yes?"

We nodded.

"But you don't know what it is? And you don't know where it is?"

"Yes," we answered in unison. Then we looked at each other.

"And...you don't wish to tell me, the official representative of the Italian government in this case?" Ettore got up from his chair and I thought he was going to grab his jacket and walk out, but instead he just moved to the far end of the room, his back to us. He turned. "But you are sure it is important evidence."

The major bent over the table and put his hands on either end. "Detective Rossi. Detective Turner. I hope you are not going to tell me that you have *La Chiave d'Oro*," he said.

Turner and I didn't look at each other. I might have flushed a little crimson at the mention of The Golden Key.

"Yes. It's famous. Like the Holy Grail. No one knows where it is, but we all are certain that it *is*. The key that solves one of the most horrific crimes in modern Italian history. Surely, there must be a key. That's what the Italian public believes. Wants to believe, anyway. Gives us some hope. We need hope, like everyone else."

The translator was having a tough time keeping up with Ettore, who was now upset. His face was crimson, neck muscles tight.

"The papers have gone on about it for years. It's been found several times already, you must know. Several journalists here have located La Chiave and made a nice career out of it. I know one who's bought herself a nice house in Amalfi from her book sales on it. And the Key has led nowhere. If the Key exists—and I don't think it does—I'm certain its discovery would lead only to more papers being sold, not the truth."

We sat motionless. He looked at us for some clue. He wanted it to be something other than a key, I'm sure. He'd almost had me convinced the key was worthless. That's when I started thinking that maybe that's what *he* wanted us to think. Who the fuck knew? We were in an Italian fun house. I didn't know if this guy was dirty or clean.

"No, Major. It's not a key," I said, finally breaking the silence. I had to say it. First, we couldn't tell him. And second, it was obvious he'd have sent us home if we had.

"Good. The reporters downstairs waiting for me—they will be very disappointed," he said with a nasty but satisfied smile. It was clear he was relishing that prospect. "Everyone knows you are here and why. The Americans always have the answers. We Italians have been conditioned to expect that. I will enjoy seeing their faces when I tell them you don't have La Chiave. There will be frowns and hooting noises. Disbelief. Accusations of a cover-up, right to my face," he said, bringing a finger up to his nose. "I could write the stories myself right now. But let's forget about the key and focus on what you have. Let's try that."

"Can't do that," I said quickly. I thought he would blow, but he didn't.

He laughed walking back to our side of the table. "I see. You expect to solve this crime on your own. In a foreign country, where you are being watched twenty-four seven—and not just by us—where you don't speak the language and where, I'm guessing, you trust no one?"

Silence.

"I realize you don't trust me. I'd probably do the same thing in your position, but you'll get nowhere without cooperation. And I really do hope it's not a key."

More silence.

"You know, I could have you sent back immediately...but I won't do that. I'm going to show you a little trust. Perhaps you will return the favor. You'll have forty-eight hours. No more. After that your invitation is revoked and I'll have you put on the first plane back to America. And I'm not going to give you a detail of men, either. I can't waste the people's money on you without some reasonable basis."

"Major Ettore, all I can say is we have some information from Muro and it seems genuine. Because of the way we found it. People have been murdered for it. He hid it in America and we discovered it during the investigation of his murder. Let's just say our method of discovery was not sanctioned by the law," I said looking directly at him. Ettore showed nothing. "The fact that Hochman's apartment was pulled apart inch by inch suggests somebody very powerful knows or believes there is evidence somewhere in Italy that could lead to—"

Before I could finish, Ettore interrupted, "You're on your own. You can have Marco but that's all. He'll keep you out of trouble, at least. I was rather hoping that you Americans had something. I'm Italian after all. Like Pontius Pilate, I wash my hands of it," he said, dramatizing his statement with his hands. Ettore picked up his jacket and the files he'd let us read, bowed slightly to us, and then, as if it had just come to him, he pulled out a business card and threw it on the table so that it slid like a playing card right to me.

"One other thing. No weapons, eh!" he said. He turned and left through the door he came in. Outside, the same two guys were still standing, and they began conferring with him right away in lowered voices. The translator, who followed Ettore, shut the door.

Turner looked at me but I kept looking straight ahead. "Man, I thought elbow patches went out years ago. Did you see the ring?" he asked. "Makes me nervous. Di Gagliano's lodge brother."

"Yeah," I said.

A moment later, Marco entered and asked us if everything was alright. I grunted a yes. We got up and shuffled out. The carabinieri station house could have been plopped right down where the One-Nine was, with almost nobody knowing the difference. The same plain gray walls with municipal green trim. Holding pens with trannies and heroin addicts, and crappy offices for management. Only difference: Santissimo mini-espresso machines scattered like water coolers all around. Marco stopped for an espresso and pulled a couple for us, too.

We walked ahead, out of Marco's earshot. "Now what?" I said.

"You're the one who said we have strong evidence," he said, taking a sip.

"Follow the key and the letter," I said, looking around us for eavesdroppers. "We have the real key, paid for in blood. They know there's a key. The fucker who killed Sylvia told you so."

Turner nodded. "*They* who?"

"One mystery at a time, Ham. We have a key and Dottori's address, No. 11, Piazza Navona. Let's go there. Maybe the wife still lives there."

"It won't be a total loss. There's a Bernini sculpture there. The Four Rivers of the Earth. There's even a black man in the sculpture, Paolo."

Marco returned, Laura in tow, waiting for us.

"Time to go," I said.

Laura was looking better and better to me as the days wore on. She'd let out her hair, previously bunched up wet under her hat, and it tightly followed the line of her jaw, coming to a point at her chin and framing her face. The word "fetching" kept coming to mind, like a finger pushed into my back, daring me to do something about it. Her cap sat on top of her head, a badge on the front of it, with a shiny, silvery flame, the carabinieri symbol.

"And where are we going?" Laura said. Marco followed the three of us.

"Piazza Navona."

"To see the Bernini?" she asked.

"No. We're looking for a widow," I said. "Preferably one who wants to clear her husband's name of suspicion."

Turner pulled out his Rothmans and passed one to Laura. She finally deigned to smoke a Canadian cigarette. We ducked out the back to avoid a press scrum, and out to a street full of honking buses and Vespa mopeds and even SUVs, far more of those giants than I would have imagined popular in a place where the streets were made for chariots and where gasoline was so dear.

On the way over, Turner asked, "What are the chances she still lives there?"

"Not that bad actually," I said. "Who gives up an apartment on Piazza Navona? Not for all the gold in the Vatican."

Laura, sitting in the back with Turner, looked mystified. I didn't want to tell her with Marco around. I wasn't even sure I wanted to tell her at all, but at this point it looked like she had assigned herself to the case, too. Her brother was involved, but if I asked her why she was with us, that would make it seem like I didn't trust her. I should have asked Ettore about her. She shrugged her shoulders, as if going along with the game.

No. 11 was at the far end of the piazza, where nearby a street actor swathed in a tight silvery wrap, with a silver painted face and Statue of Liberty crown, stood motionless on a pedestal a few feet in front of the door. Someone threw him a coin and he moved an inch and tooted a horn for about five seconds.

On the building intercom, there it was: Dottori, Apartment 5. Turner and I made no sign to Marco about whom we would see. I asked Marco to stand watch at the front door facing the piazza. Better to keep him on a need to know basis. He seemed to be the only cop without an ax to grind, and we needed him to guard the entrance. We might have been followed.

Someone came out just as we entered the lobby and opened the main door for us as she exited. We walked up three flights to number 5.

On the first landing, Laura pulled us over. "Who's Dottori and why are we seeing him?"

"Her," I said. Turner rolled his eyes.

"She. Whatever. You have no authority to do investigations," she said.

At that, Turner and I began walking up the stairs again. She cursed, and a little too loudly, but gave in. I turned and put my finger to my lips.

"At least tell me what's going on," she whispered. "You could get myself and Marco in some difficulties here. Who knows what this woman will do when she finds out who you really are?"

That's when Turner grabbed me by the elbow. "She's right. Paolo, you're good but you can't pull off being an Italian cop. No way. Dottori will see through that faster than you can say, 'Forza Italia.' We need Laura."

Turner was right. I motioned her over and we huddled on the landing. "Mrs. Dottori is the wife of Alfredo Dottori, the head radar man at the Marsala airbase in Sicily. Your brother apparently knew him and they corresponded. We found a letter at Hochman's apartment from Dottori to Guy dated 1982 that hints at some Ustica evidence both knew about and kept hidden." I didn't tell her about the key. "Dottori committed suicide right after he mailed the letter."

"Do you have the letter?" Laura asked.

I tapped my vest pocket.

"May I read it?"

"I know what it says," I said, perhaps a bit coldly.

We walked to her door and Laura knocked. There was no response at first but then we heard a pair of slippers sliding slowly to the door. A woman opened the door a crack. What hair I could see was totally white. One eye was visible through the slim opening, and she peered at Laura, then me, then Turner, where her gaze remained a moment. She quickly closed the door before Laura could say anything.

Behind the door, the sound of the slippers sliding along a floor moved away and Laura began to plead in Italian, "Please, signora. We would like to speak to you about your husband." The slippers stopped a moment and then they again moved away. Laura looked at me.

"Try again," I whispered.

"Signora, please," Laura said with more supplication. "We have a letter from him that we'd like to show you."

From the apartment came a sound like an interior door opened then closed again quickly. I looked at Turner.

The slippers returned. The woman opened the door. Out of the apartment came a faint, stale smell of old papers and moldy books mixed with a little cigarette smoke. I saw two cats running for safety.

"I needed to put on something presentable," she said in Italian. "I don't often get visitors anymore. And so many at once," she added, looking Turner and me over again. "I've been burglarized so many times. Damned drug addicts. An old woman alone must be careful. And so, to what do I owe my good fortune?" She had put on a thin blue robe. The cuffs of her white pajamas peeked from the sleeves here and there. By the creases that amply lined her face she looked to be about seventy. Well-fed but not fat, she walked with a barely perceptible limp. The hall was lined with bookshelves, lots of oversized books.

"Signora, we'd like to ask you some questions about your husband."

"He hasn't been around much lately," she said. She kept her hand on her door.

I thought she was being funny, but I wasn't certain. Crazy Old Lady was possible, too.

"It's about Ustica," Laura said.

Laura motioned to my vest pocket. I pulled out the letter and showed her the envelope. She read the return address and relented. She took it and looked it over quickly. "I need my eyeglasses, but it looks like his handwriting," she said in Italian, turning and walking back along the hallway, leaving the door open.

Though she made no sign to follow inside, we did. "I know it's about Ustica. I read the papers. No one's been around for a long time asking questions. Lots of people did when Alfredo was alive, sometimes uninvited, but after he left us, they stopped coming. We were living in Sicily then—awful people those Sicilians—except for my husband, practically Africans they are," she said matter-of-factly. Then she wheeled and, not knowing Turner didn't understand a word, said to him, "Please. I meant no offense. It's what we Romans say."

Turner looked at me for an explanation.

I shook my head with a half-smile. "I'll tell you later," I said. He knew we needed her.

"After Ustica, we moved back to Rome, where I'm from," she said.

"This apartment has been in my family for four generations, though we've come down a bit."

She brought us into her living room, which had windows on the piazza. Laura introduced us as two American investigators of Muro's murder. She knew Gaetano and had read about the crime in New York. Mrs. Dottori told us to sit while she went into the kitchen, returning with her eyeglasses and a plate of biscotti.

"I'm going to make some coffee so you just sit and wait here. Only a moment," she said, turning slowly, her hand on her right hip, which seemed to give her some trouble, and walked back to the kitchen. The apartment faced east, so at 5 p.m. there wasn't so much direct sunlight and the rooms had a shadowy look.

Turner and I sat on the couch, while Laura took one of the two seats at the table. My partner pulled out a small notebook.

"You going to take notes in Italian?"

"I wouldn't mind having a place on Piazza Navona," he said, ignoring my question and walking over to the window. "She's got a great view of the Bernini fountain and the river Nile in particular. Ah, the Veiled One," Turner said to no one in particular.

Mrs. Dottori returned in a few minutes, carrying a silver coffeepot and a tray of four white demitasse cups, each trimmed with a thin filigree of gold. She placed them on the low table and waved Turner and me over. She poured the coffee and placed two small cubes of sugar on the saucer next to the cup, on the opposite side of the small spoon, then handed it over. Turner started scribbling in his notebook. Mrs. Dottori's eyebrows were raised in confusion.

"Is my coffee so interesting?" she asked, and Laura translated.

"No, ma'am," he replied in English, shaking his head. He was hesitant but then said with a grin, "I'm also a poet and, well, something just hit me, and I had to get it down." Laura translated again. I looked the other way in embarrassment. I wanted to grab that book of his and throw it into the piazza.

"Ah, poetry," she said. "How beautiful. A policeman poet. I think the world would be a better place with more of these, don't you?" she said. Laura laughed and explained it to Turner. I nodded and gave a taut smile to Laura to get the ball rolling.

"Can you tell us anything about the letter?" I said, and Laura translated.

She picked it up from the coffee table and read it to herself. "Not beyond what it says. It's certainly from Alfredo, though." She put it down.

The air went out of all three of us, but she had more to say.

"Gaetano and Alfredo were friends. They met for the first time after Ustica. Both were questioned endlessly after the accident. For a Milanese and a Sicilian, they got along well. Talked a lot on the phone, at first anyway. Then Alfredo started getting a little crazy in the head and refused to use the phone with him. 'They are listening,' he used to say. They met in person occasionally here in Rome, downstairs at the fountain, sometimes somewhere else. Alfredo wouldn't tell me much. He said he wanted to protect me."

"What did Alfredo tell you about Ustica and the colonnello?" Laura asked.

"Nothing. I wish he had told me something, maybe then I would understand why he killed himself," she said. She blinked back tears.

"Tell us about Alfredo," Laura said gently. "Tell us about the man who loved you, who gave you his all, for whom you were the world. Tell me, another woman." This was Laura's intent. And it worked.

"Alfredo was an engineer by training and a Maresciallo in the Aeronautica," she said, pride stiffening up her voice. "He commanded the radar station in Marsala, in Sicily. This you must know," she said, looking at all of us. "Anyway, there's not much to tell. He was a wonderful man, and all the talk after Ustica about his hiding the radar tapes is slander."

"The missing eight minutes," I said.

"Yes. He would not do that. I'm sure the higher ups did it, the bastards at NATO, or the Communists, or the fat cat capitalists, or maybe the government forced him. Who knows what purpose the accident served? My husband was a good man," she said, and this time she broke. She put her head in her hands. Laura was getting teary-eyed. We sat uncomfortably for a few moments on the couch.

Laura touched Mrs. Dottori's forearm. "Tell us about your husband. Not Ustica. Something else. What did he like to do? Did he like the cinema? Ice cream, that sort of thing."

Mrs. Dottori brightened a bit. She wiped her face again and smiled. "He was a wonderful man. Very good to me. I think he only cheated on me a few times, not like your typical Italian man."

Turner continued to scribble God knows what.

"Alfredo wasn't only an *ingengnere*. He loved literature, too," she said, this time pointedly at Turner, who put down his pen. "You see all the books here. He was what you call an amateur. His specialty was medieval Italian writers, Dante, Boccaccio, and such. Many of these books here are either special editions of their works or books about those writers. Alfredo himself wrote one on *The Decameron*. That was his specialty." She paused and put down the handkerchief, having regained her composure now. "It was called *Use of the Fool in The Decameron*. It didn't sell many copies, but he won a little award. Yes, Boccaccio was his favorite, as I'm sure you figured out."

"*Perche?*" Laura and I replied in unison.

Mrs. Dottori laughed at that outburst. "Well, look at his letter. Haven't you read it?"

I practically jumped from the couch to the table in one leap, scaring the shit out of Mrs. Dottori.

I grabbed the letter, rereading it quickly. "*Cosa c'e'?* Mrs. Dottori. What is it?" I said, mixing my English and Italian.

"I didn't know you could speak Italian," she said to me. "How nice. Agente Laura said..."

It was clear from my face that I didn't give a damn about that.

"Right here," she said, taking back the letter: "It says, 'the fourth story of the fourth day.'" She looked at us as if it would be entirely obvious to a fourteen-year-old Italian high school kid. "*The Decameron.* The fourth story of the fourth day. That's one of the book's one hundred stories, and it happened to be Alfredo's favorite. He'd read it aloud from time to time. Sometimes a wife must put up with things. I still remember it now, twenty years after his passing. It's the story of doomed love long ago, during the Middle Ages, between a beautiful Saracen princess from Tunis and Gerbino, a Christian prince of Sicily. It's such a wonderful story. Very sad ending, though, as these mixed marriages must. Perhaps I can read it to you. I'll grab one of Alfredo's books," she said, getting up.

"No, Signora Dottori. There's no need," Laura said, holding up her hand and looking at us, but Mrs. Dottori was already limping her way down the hall.

"I remember that story, one of the saddest tales in the book. I told you that I had to study Boccaccio," Laura said to me. She wore a wan smile. "Paolo," she said, "had you given me the letter earlier, I could have saved us a lot of time. The fourth story of the fourth day. The beautiful princess is murdered on the high seas between Sicily and Sardinia."

"What are you getting at?" I said.

"After the princess is murdered, Gerbino buries her on a small island in the Mediterranean."

"Ustica!" said Mrs. Dottori as she returned in triumph, her timing perfect. "*Ecco,*" she said pointing to a spot on the page.

Laura took the book from her and read it, translating directly into English: "Then, letting them take up the fair lady's body from the sea, long and with many tears, he kept it and steering for Sicily, buried it honorably in Ustica, after which he returned home, the woefullest man alive."

"I wish that Gaetano could return home," Laura whispered. She began to cry. Mrs. Dottori, standing, put her arm around Laura's shoulder. She teared up as well.

Laura handed the still open book back to Mrs. Dottori. As she did, what appeared to be a bookmark fell out. But it wasn't a bookmark.

"Well, look at this," Mrs. Dottori said, picking up the paper from the floor.

Turner got up and went to the window again, scribbling. I came up behind him and tugged his jacket, a black and gray hounds tooth linen affair.

Mrs. Dottori stood up. "Just like Alfredo to leave a poem behind that he didn't want me to see. Of course, he put it in here because he knew I'd never read the book after having heard the story so many times.

Laura looked at me.

"May I read it?" she said quietly to Mrs. Dottori.

"Of course," she said, handing the paper to her. "Alfredo would love nothing more than a beautiful young lady reading his poems."

Laura began and translated into English as she read.

What Little Was Known, by Alfredo Dottori 1982

On a mild summer night in June, 1980, across an untroubled Tyrrhenian Sea

the sun set in a cloudless sky, its fading power still barring the oncoming night

The full moon hung there, a pale, papery white, like a child's playschool cutout.

A Libyan MiG 23 flew into Italian air space, chased by two Italian F-104 Starfighters

Little chance had they of catching the more advanced MiG

Above them, two pilots—one in a U.S.-NATO F-14, another in a French Mirage from the carrier Clemenceau

watched the hunt, both waiting, hoping, for a kill order on the

MiG.

At 20:45 the intercept order was given. Caught in the middle,

Like a lamb unawares, was an Italian DC9 commercial airliner quietly making its way to Sicily.

By 21:15, bodies and luggage bobbed lightly in the water below.

In a five-mile swath—halfway between Naples and Palermo, the ancient

Capitals of Norman Sicily—lay 81 lives snuffed out.

A few had died from the blast. Others were sucked out of the plane as it depressurized.

The rest expired on impact with the water, after ten minutes of a ride likely so hellish that, Italians later said,

Surely the victims deserved a place in heaven, all sins forgiven

Large chunks of the fuselage swayed for a minute with the seas. Some bodies floated in the Tyrrhenian, arms out,

Christ-like, just as if they were in the air, before slowly dropping down

When dawn broke the helicopters came for survivors, before the rescue boats.

A few suitcases and seat cushions, a small piece of a wing

The Itavia DC9 crew never radioed for help.

The plane disappeared from the radar screens right before the eyes of the air traffic controllers on the mainland and in Marsala, Sicily

A white blip, then no blip.

And a few days later, a Libyan MiG 23 was discovered crashed on a remote Sicilian mountainside,

Ah, but the Italian government and NATO said it had nothing to do with the downed DC9

Nothing. The MiG pilot's partly decomposed body and his jet were rushed back to Libya without an investigation

Even had the government been inclined to investigate.

To this day, after so many years and numerous investigations, no

169

one knows how or why

That airliner vanished from the radar screen, like a magician's coin, on a beautiful summer night—except those that do.

"Strange little poem isn't it?" Mrs. Dottori said, as she began to tear again. "The strange thing is," she went on, "that the plane was not raised from the sea floor for over a decade."

That got Laura tearing again. "By which time," she added between sniffles, "whatever evidence was left was useless."

"I guess we're going to Ustica," I said to Ham. "The fourth story of the fourth day is a Decameron reference, and the story ends in…"

"Ustica. It's a shame we don't know what the fuck we are looking for. I understand it's not easy to get to," he said quietly to the window, not turning to look at me.

"We're looking for a princess, Detective Turner. A Saracen Princess. How hard can that be?"

"Maybe you should tell Laura about the key, Paolo. Come entirely clean?" Ham whispered.

"Don't know just yet," I said. "She's going to be surprised enough when I tell her we are going to Ustica with her."

When Laura pulled herself together, we made our goodbyes quickly. It was sad leaving Mrs. Dottori. I didn't think she would get another visitor for a while. She kissed all three of us on both cheeks, as if we were old friends. "*Buona fortuna, regazzi.*"

I was surprised to find Marco right at Mrs. Dottori's door when I opened it and I must have looked it.

"I was just coming to get you," he said. "There is a man watching the building. When I went toward him, he left abruptly. I did not see his face clearly. There's a back entrance on Via dell'Anima. We'll use that to leave."

My estimation of Marco went up another notch. "No black Mercedes?" I said to him, walking alongside of him and down the steps. Laura and Turner were behind us.

"No, just a man making believe he was reading the *International Herald Tribune* on a bench out front. He's been sneaking glances at the front door. Let's not take chances," Marco said, shepherding us down the narrow stairs and out the back entrance.

Sabato Sera

The Baron sat in his office next to the library. Folders littered his desk, the stacks so high that the Gnome could be seen only through the spaces between the piles. Each folder was thick, clasped with an old-fashioned brown rubber cord: merger scenarios, investigations of clients and competitors, reports on enemies and anyone trying to buy up shares of the companies he controlled.

His secretary knocked. The Baron didn't like intercoms. The buzzing noise annoyed him. "Il Senatore is on the phone," she said, and he picked up the extension.

"They're here," Montone said.

"Yes," the Baron replied wearily. The Senator had always been less sure of himself than he let on. The curse of the arriviste, the Baron thought. The Senator cared about popular opinion. "Our men are watching them very closely. They went to see the radar man's wife today. What do you think of that, my friend?"

"I think you have what you wanted," The Senator said.

"Almost. I'll let the line out some more. Bruno didn't give them enough credit. We won't make that mistake. The key is useless if we don't know where the tapes are. Perhaps the Rueful Knight and Sancho Panza can lead us to the tapes, eh, Senator?"

There was silence on the line as each man, not entirely confident of the other's motives, thought about the tapes.

"After twenty-two years I'm tired of having my balls in a twist over these tapes," the Baron said in a rare unveiling of his unease. "We are

close. To be rid of them once and for all would make the few years I have left pleasurable again. Berodi, that shit of a prime minister, keeps nagging me about them. And I don't entirely trust him. I'm sure if he got them first, he'd crucify us."

"He's a liar," The Senator said. "Worse, a socialist. He'd pimp his granny to the Turks for a vote. I don't trust him."

"Don't you have anything on him? This should have been done years ago."

"All we have are his mistresses," Montone said.

"Gesu Cristo, this isn't America. There's got to be something good. Il Ciuchione isn't a fucking altar boy. If we don't get something soon, he's going to become difficult to handle."

"I know that, Baron. I have people here and in Switzerland working on his bank accounts. We'll have something. We are being creative."

"Good," replied the Baron, settling into a better mood. "Soon Mr. Berodi will be put in his harness, and the Ustica tapes will become the myth everyone believes them to be."

Chapter 13

Saturday Night

I sat on the bed that evening when a call came in. I was hoping to hear from Libby, but that was foolish since I didn't tell them where I was going and what I was doing. I figured they needed a break from me.

We had to catch a plane to Palermo and a ferry in the morning to Ustica. We hadn't told Laura yet. Like Marco, she was still on a need to know basis. I was thinking with my dick lately, but so far had managed to keep her in the dark and it in my pants. I couldn't tell if she was dirty, only that she was fine. I was angry with myself for this.

"You going to get that or what?" Turner asked, stepping out of the bathroom in his robe after a shower.

I picked up the receiver.

"Ciao, baby," Gretzman said. "Know any good restaurants in Ustica?"

"You're misinformed. The cops don't trust us. They don't think we bring anything to the table."

"They don't know about the key. I went to Mrs. Dottori after you did. Very nice lady. Her homemade biscotti are so good. Did you try them?"

I didn't reply.

"I thought that would get your attention. Told me the whole story of your visit. She seems lonely. By the way, she likes Turner more than you, even though you're a paisan. She likes artist types. Smart women always do. Anyway, I know you are going to Ustica, but I'm not sure why. It'll come to me. That's what they pay me for. I figure that key has to open a lock somewhere. Don't bother looking for me on the plane. I'm about to board a jet to sunny Palermo."

That's when I hung up. As I did, I could hear that giggly, smug Yale boy laugh.

"Who was that?" Turner said, adjusting the knot in his tie.

"Gretzman."

"White boy doesn't know when to stop, does he?"

"He doesn't know how far in it he's sunk. He thinks his little press card will protect him from a big nasty." I thought about calling Ettore to have Gretzman picked up but decided against it. I didn't think Ettore would even take my call.

We grabbed our bags and went down to the lobby. Turner bought cigarettes and I waited for him inside the front door. Marco was in the Land Rover, sitting quietly as usual. He didn't notice me. He was busy polishing his gun. It gleamed black in the hotel lights. Then he loaded it, put in a magazine, then took it out, put in another mag and took it out, as if he were practicing. I don't know what he was expecting, but he was sure making me more nervous. Turner came back and saw me staring at Marco. He gave me a quizzical look.

"I'm watching our bodyguard. He seems thorough," I said, continuing to stare at our driver.

Turner looked at me, crooked his lips left, and arched an eyebrow. "Come on, Paolo. Gretzman's got you all in a tizzy."

I laughed as we got into the car.

"What is so funny?" Marco said, putting down his piece.

That damn British accent kept throwing me. "Nothing, Marco," I said.

He shrugged his shoulders amiably.

"You didn't tell Laura that we are going to Ustica, right?"

"No, but I had to tell my superiors, of course. Maggiore Ettore. He was not pleased, I must tell you. They are fighting over it right now, so I suggest we finish our dinner quickly and get to the plane before they change their idea."

I smiled at Marco's novel use of the word idea.

We ate at Samuele's that night, a place not far from our hotel. When she arrived, Laura looked lissome, a blood red Nehru blouse over black jeans, and holding a big black motorcycle helmet under her arm. Her neck seemed longer and more graceful in civvies. She was breaking me down. I wished we weren't cops. I wished at least that we were not on the same case, that we were living in the same country, the same house even. Just looking at her bare arm was affecting me in a way that, if not suppressed soon, could take me to a land of honey and trouble.

Turner whispered to me, "It's getting obvious that you have it bad."

I wondered if she had noticed.

At dinner no mention of the key was made. Marco ate with us, so that wasn't possible. Throughout the meal, my partner kept looking at me expectantly. There seemed to be no way to do it with Marco around. There wasn't enough time, and it was a tightly packed restaurant, with our neighbors and spies, most probably, on top of us.

After dessert, Laura said she wanted to have a cigarette outside. I joined her. It was early evening yet. A throng moved down the street, like a blob that shifted together left or right as it encountered a Nigerian hawking fake Gucci bags or a Senegalese with *autentico* African wood sculptures. *Motorini* flew by loudly. We weren't far from the Pantheon.

I pointed to a quieter, narrow side street around the corner and we walked over. It was dark. She handed me a pack of Club Slims, with two cigarettes out, and a lighter, which was embossed with the initials

G.M. It was windy, and the flame went out, so I gently cupped my hands on top of hers. They were thin and light, her nails unpainted. I moved my focus from the end of my cigarette to her eyes. She met me for a second and then looked away. In the evening and under Roman street lamplight, they looked more *glauco* than absinthe green.

"I have to tell you something," I said. God, that sounded stupid. I felt like a thirteen-year-old. Thinking and meta-thinking. What should I say? What was she thinking? She didn't respond. I could tell nothing from her face. For all I knew, she was thinking about her brother, or about her last lay, or dessert.

"We're going to Ustica with you."

She turned sideways to me and looked away. She had her right arm up, the hand holding the cigarette, and the other folded around her body, left hand on the right hip, toward me, as if she were hugging herself. Cigarette smoke wafted lazily upward and disappeared.

"And why are you doing this?" she said, not looking at me. "Or should I ask, since you like to tell me things at the last minute, whose game are you playing? What side are you on?"

"I could ask the same thing of you," I said.

She looked at me hard now, the first flash of anger I'd seen from her since New York. "I'm not working for the police on this or the government. I'm not working for Gladio or any other shadowy and possibly non-existent groups. Understand? I'm working for myself, for my brother…for my family. He was mixed up in this, yes, but he didn't do anything wrong."

"How do you know that?"

"I know that," she said, her voice raising and wavering simultaneously. "I know my brother. I grew up with him. He was *un uomo per bene*. A good man. He didn't shoot any airliner down. That is what I'm trying to prove." Her tone suggested she wasn't entirely convinced of that.

I weighed everything in my head. It was now or never. We had to tell her. I had to have access to Muro's casket and that wasn't going to be easy without her. He'd be in the ground tomorrow. There was no tomorrow.

"What is it that you have to tell me?" she asked. She moved over to a bench and sat. I sat next to her, our knees touching.

"The letter to your brother from Dottori included a small key."

Her eyes went big and she snorted.

"I have it. It's hidden."

Her face had moved from quiet sadness to disbelief, almost pity. "Oh, *Dio*. Not you, too. La Chiave? You haven't fallen for that? Don't you know the stories about the key?"

I began to doubt her again. "The key came in the letter Dottori sent to Muro twenty years ago. It was unopened. But I'm sure your brother knew what was in it. You didn't see Dorothy's ransacked apartment or her dead body. The goons in New York were after it. It must be the real thing. They are after it now."

Laura shook her head. "They could be wrong, too."

"The Holy Grail exists and we have it. I have no idea where it leads. God, we don't even know where to look on Ustica, but that's the place for sure. The note and Dottori's background...hell, your brother's burial request proves it."

She sat there without a word for a good two minutes, staring at me. "Is that why the American reporter is following us?"

She pouted and it seemed on purpose. Despite thinking—or knowing—this, the reptilian part of my brain was at that moment in control and it was starting to get real bad for me. The reptile knew she knew and didn't care.

"He found out accidentally. I *don't* trust him, but I am certain of his intentions and Turner's but nobody else," I said pointedly.

She straightened out her knees to move closer. I felt a tingle from her soft shoulder brushing me, her thigh against mine. She put one finger under my chin and nudged it toward her face. "My intentions are pure," she said quietly and without drama.

I heard someone coughing hard just a few feet away.

"We thought maybe you went back to the hotel," Turner said. Then he sat next to me.

I put my head down and smirked, and Laura looked the other way. I had the feeling she was holding back a laugh.

"Your timing is always impeccable, Detective Hamilton P. Turner," she said, not looking at him.

"Marco's in the car. He appears to be in a rush. Let's go," he said.

"I know about La Chiave," she said, finally turning to Turner. "Just one more thing. Where is this key?"

"That remains classified," I said, walking away.

Rounding the corner of the next street, we reached the Land Rover, where Marco was speaking into his cell phone. As I got to the truck, I heard him say, "A little patience, *bella*. Ciao, *bella*."

Turner jumped into the car and I was about to follow when Laura pulled on my jacket.

"I have my motorcycle. Why not ride with me?"

Marco wasn't happy about it. "I'm responsible for you two," he said, afraid something would happen to me. He turned to Laura. "Tenente, I'm supposed to be taking care of them. You know that. You're not even supposed to be involved. This is irregular," he said to her in Italian.

"*Cazzo*, the whole fucking thing is irregular," she replied.

He relented and nodded to me. I handed him my ordinance since he was going to have to check it before the flight. I was hoping for a nice solid Harley, something that said get out of the way. But it turned out to be a lithe racing bike, a black and red Ducati with raised fenders and small seats. Riding a motorcycle in any big city was a death wish. In Rome, you might as well prepay for your plot.

She sat on the bike like a pro, like it was formed to fit her legs, and then she raced the engine. The roar set off complaints from the apartment window above us. She unhitched a second helmet from the bike and adjusted the straps for me. "I don't use this one much," she said matter-of-factly.

I got on, and it seemed to me that it was really just one seat. Shit, I was right on her ass. I could practically feel the rivets of her jeans. This position was making me comfortable in my mind but uncomfortable in my groin. I was hoping my hardness would not be too obvious, but it was probably too late for that.

"Put your hands around my waist and hold tight," she said.

I must have seemed a bit hesitant.

"Come on," she said. "I have to get to the airport in time to make sure Gaetano is on the plane."

I just grabbed around her waist, tightly interlocking my hands and resting them just above her belt buckle. I was trying to stay higher than that and lower than her breasts. But we were bent forward, and when the bike hit a road bump I could feel them nudge against my forearms, where my hairs tingled with each brush. I wondered if this whole thing was intentional. Maybe she liked me for more than helping her find her brother's killer.

I lay my head sideways against the nape of her neck. Her black hair flowed out of the helmet, fine wisps of it whipping my face lightly. I could smell the lilac again. I squeezed her tight and she responded. I closed my eyes there for a moment, a warm Roman evening, and then looked up at green palm tree branches whizzing by as we screamed down Via del Corso, the huge white Wedding Cake in the distance ahead of us. It was as if I were ascending toward a strange gray white heaven. "I really like this," I said, trying to be heard above the road din and wind.

"That Mercedes is following us," she said loudly but calmly.

"What?" I'd heard but the wind made it hard to be sure.

"Don't look back," she said. We'd left the Land Rover way behind and now a black Mercedes was tailing us. I turned my head around anyway. I could almost make out the guy on the passenger side. He

179

looked like the third man back in Harlem. Couldn't be certain. He had a cell phone to his ear. We were going fifty, it seemed, and each bump made me instinctively face forward and grab her more tightly. They made no attempt to get closer. No metal came out, so I wondered if maybe Laura was a bit paranoid. Rome was crawling with Mercedes.

"Are you sure?" I shouted.

"Yes." We did a last second ninety-degree turn into a narrow street, one of those found all over Rome, into which only motorcycles and compact cars could fit. As we shot down the road, I looked back and saw the Mercedes slam hard on its brakes back where we'd turned from Via del Corso. A few Romans gave us the finger as we sped by. Forty-five minutes later we arrived at Ciampino airport. Turner and Marco walked up to us at the gate.

Marco asked for Laura, but I told him she was at the Alitalia cargo desk to check on Muro's casket. Usually level-headed, he seemed angry for once.

Turner took me by the arm, a little too obviously. "I have to talk to you," he whispered, and pulled me away.

"If you're trying to hide something from Marco, you're doing a shitty job of it."

"I don't like him anymore," Turner said. "He spent nearly the whole ride to the airport on his cell phone. Once or twice he used your name, Laura's name, my name…seemed to be arguing with the other side. I don't like it."

"He was angry about us splitting up. Protocol. He's covering his ass. He probably knew how fast Laura likes to ride and was worried I'd fall off and die," I said.

"I don't understand Italian but I don't think he was talking to his superiors. At least not the ones we know about. This is going to sound crazy, man," he said, "but at one point I heard German coming out the other end of that phone of his."

"Maybe he understands German. Lots of Italians speak two

languages. For all you know his mother is German and he was bitching to her about us. Come on."

Turner seemed satisfied, but barely. The rest of the evening he didn't look happy. Laura sat at a window seat, next to me on the aisle. She didn't say much.

About twenty minutes before we landed, she said, "This is it. You can barely make out the lights of Ustica below." She pointed through the double paned glass. "This is where that plane went down, in the commercial corridor just fifteen minutes outside Palermo. This was about where Gaetano was flying...and watching. Those dreams of his were so terrible. I don't know how he lived with them for so many years. Those poor people. For what?"

I took her hand. She lay her head against my shoulder. I felt a tear on my skin and thought for a moment it seemed just as when Angela used to cry when I came home with bruises or worse.

    *   *   *

The taxi ride to the hotel was quieter than our other excursions with Marco. Turner and I had our eyes out for a black Mercedes.

"Something wrong?" Marco asked. He'd noticed us looking around.

"Nothing," I said. I got the feeling Marco was dissatisfied with the answer.

Twenty minutes later we said our good nights at the hotel and five minutes after that Turner was already asleep in his bed in the room we shared.

Laura kept invading my thoughts. I tried imagining her in a potato sack, or taking money from Gladio, anything to put her out of my mind. It didn't work. I sat up on the side of the bed.

Though early May, it was already warm in Palermo. I could hear the Vespas, hundreds of metallic night crickets, whirring outside on the street past our window. I walked over and opened the enormous floor-to-ceiling window shutters, green and slatted. They opened onto a *terrazzino* just big enough for two to stand. They creaked loudly as

I pushed them out, and I feared Turner would awaken. But the street noise covered me. We were downtown, on Via Francesco Crispi, just off the ferry port. The *Stazione Marittima*, with *Grandi Traghetti* and *Siremar* ferries, some huge, some small, and parked three deep for the night, was visible from the balcony. The ocean was black in the distance and I saw lights from a ship on the horizon. Out there somewhere was Ustica.

I heard a cough and looked to my right. Laura's room was next door. Her arms hung over her terrace's balustrade. The rest of her was just inside. A thin line of gray cigarette smoke skipped away silently and up into the night sky. She hadn't noticed me. I wondered what she was thinking about. Her brother probably. This was it. He was going into the ground.

I remembered when my dad died. For days after his heart attack, I didn't believe he was gone. Like a kid, every time I saw his body, there was this crazy voice in my head, a hope really, that he wasn't dead. That he was sleeping. That he was going to get up from that hospital bed, from the casket in church and at the wake, and everything would be okay again.

I wondered if Laura thought much about me. It felt so good to hold her on the motorcycle. And that smell. I looked over to the right again. More smoke, but this time her head was out far enough for me to see her profile. I watched it, waiting for her to turn my way, but she never did. That gave me a feeling that she knew I was there.

It was midnight and the street noise began to die down. I could hear Turner breathing. Laura closed her shutters. It was now or never. I crept across my room to the door and opened it silently. The bright lights hit me from the hallway and blinded me for a moment.

Standing in front of her door, I took a deep breath. No sounds came from her room. Last chance. Husband your self-respect or roll the dice? I knocked very lightly. Too lightly. If you're going to play craps, then throw the dice hard. It felt like ten minutes had passed but it had been just one. My fingertips were sweaty. Someone in a blue suit came around the corner and passed by me in the hallway. He took a quick look at me and moved on.

Just as I raised my arm to knock again, I heard a rustling. "Just a moment," I heard Laura whisper. She opened the door wide enough for her head to peep out, her eyes blinking repeatedly from the bright hallway light. She rubbed them and some of her black hair plopped over her face.

"Are you alright?" she asked. She didn't seem angry or put out.

"Yeah. I'm fine," I lied. It was as if my feet were on fire. Funny how I could be steady with the lead pinging around me, or when chasing an angry pimp or drug dealer down a dark alley, but none of those skills could help me now. "I was worried about you," I said. "I saw you hanging out on your terrazzino."

I saw her whole face. She had on a robe that opened slightly. I looked down and could see the white of her panty peeping out.

"Worried about me?" she replied, smiling sweetly and opening the door some more. "Oh," she said, sleepiness fading, getting my gaze up from the crotch line. "What do you mean? Has something happened?" A small note of worry came into her voice at the end.

"No. I was...I was at my window just now and I saw you there, smoking. It's late. I thought perhaps you were upset about Gaetano."

She looked at me and I could tell she was weighing the situation. It was the point in a relationship my partner calls The Transit of Venus. The female inspecting. Was this a good thing? What would be the repercussions?

"*Avanti*," she said, and opened the door just enough for a slowly widening NYPD detective to slide through. I walked past her and shut the door.

I didn't know which way to go. Sit on the couch? Did she want to talk first? Or just talk? Go straight toward the bed? I moved in just a few steps, non-committal. We could have gone either way, to the couch or to the bed. Let her decide.

She came up behind me and put her arms around me and hugged herself to me, burying her face in my back. I couldn't tell if she was happy or sad. Thinking about me or Gaetano. She made no noises.

Finally, a low "*Mi piaci molto,*" came out, the words tiptoeing up my back, across my shoulders and finally resting on my ear. "*Mi piaci molto,*" she said again.

She relaxed her embrace and I turned to face her, still inside her arms. "Do you know what that means?" she asked.

"Yes," I said. "I'm rusty when it comes to the verb *piacere*. Haven't had a chance to use it much lately."

"Me too," she said, reaching up with her hands to bring my face to hers.

Her lips were softer than I had imagined. I tasted salt briefly, a residue of a tear in the corner of her smile. She kissed me with a ferocity I had never felt, as if she meant to jump right inside my head. I picked her up and she wrapped her legs around me, like a human bivalve. She lay her head against my chest and I felt her bosom against me and her breathing. We didn't go to the couch.

Chapter 14

In the hall, a passing bellhop eyed me as I sneaked out of Laura's room that morning and returned to mine. A moment later I was under the covers. It was wonderful. She was passionate, lovely to behold. My personal love messiah. But this was terrible. I was compromised, getting involved not only with another cop but one that wasn't entirely a third party to the case. I could see Gretzman laughing already, all for a night of pussy. I liked her more and more each minute. Those eyes. The way she held me, the way she seemed hurt if I didn't trust her. I'd have bet she was a great shot, too. It was like having the perfect cop partner. I looked over at Turner, who was breathing deeply.

I'd left our terrace doors open. It was raining so I rose quietly and closed the doors. As I did, I saw the familiar cigarette smoke rings wafting out of Laura's room again, her arms again hanging languidly over the balustrade, almost as if she'd been there all night. The bay was darkened by clouds that were rolling in fast and tight. Lightning flashed on the horizon.

Merchants were opening their stores and the rumble of steel gates being rolled up worked its way through the air. Just below our terrace a light blue Ape was parked in front of the local *pescheria*, with two

185

fat, deeply black-haired men in dirty aprons discussing the day's catch, at least from what I could make out from two floors up. The Ape held a dozen large blue buckets of water and fish in the back. To the right in the harbor was the Ustica ferry. I wondered if Gaetano's body was already loaded on it. I remembered that I had to get that key back. We needed access to the casket.

When I got out of the shower, Turner was scribbling in his little composition notebook. "She was here. Did you see her?" he said, looking up distractedly.

"What?" I snapped, sounding a bit guilty.

He gave me a quizzical face, eyebrows up. It was not the question that I had thought it was. In fact, it wasn't even a question.

"I was saying," he said, rolling his eyes and sitting in the semi-damp chair near the window, "that my muse was here."

"Uh-huh."

"Who'd you *think* I waz talking 'bout?" he said.

I didn't answer. I picked out a shirt, pants, socks, and a tie.

He laughed and got up from the chair. "You lookin' guilty to me, Paolo," he said, walking by me. Then he stopped and made like a dog sniffing the air. From a pile of my clothes on the floor he picked up the T-shirt I'd been wearing last night. "Smells like lilac to me, Paolo," he said, walking into the bathroom. Even with the door shut his shower singing came through. "Ho-jo-to-ho! Heia-ha-ha! "

*   *   *

Ferrymen were loading cars onto the boat when the four of us arrived at the landing. Marco dropped us and took the Land Rover on board at the stern. We stood on the dock, a light mist coming down now.

I turned to Laura. "I think I should tell you where the key is," I said.

"I'm not sure I want to know," she said.

"I understand, but you have to know now. I hope you won't be angry with me."

Laura looked at me for an answer. If I hadn't known better, it looked like a satisfied smirk. "Why would I be angry with you?"

"It's in Gaetano's casket. That was the safest place. No one would look there. And if something had happened to Turner and me, well, there was an envelope back home that would have been sent to you and Mayor Salerno with directions to the key."

"In the casket?" she said, furrowing her black eyebrows a bit. She put her hands to her face. I thought she was going to cry on me, but she laughed. "Mio dio. Siamo in un film di Hollywood."

"I slipped it into the knot of his tie," I explained, a little embarrassed. "At the wake, when I bent over and kissed him. The key fit perfectly."

We shuffled up the gangway. There were probably only ten other people coming aboard. It was raining harder now. Some of the boatmen had umbrellas.

"It's not going to be so easy to get the key," she said.

"Why?" I asked.

"First, the casket is in the hold, God knows where. And that's not the worst of it."

"What?" I said.

"The casket is sealed. You must know this. Health code."

Shit, we were going to have to pry it open, not an attractive prospect. I could just see the horrified look on Laura's face as we huffed and puffed and broke open the casket and Guy's body flopped out. With what tools? "Marco would have to be distracted," I said.

Just then he walked up. "I heard my name."

"Yeah, we were wondering what was keeping you," I said.

"Not so easy to park a truck on this little boat. They usually only take cars. I had to put the official carabinieri face on. *Molto grave,*" said the cop with few whiskers.

Must have been his uniform. Italians loved uniforms.

The two-hour boat ride gave enough time to locate the casket. There was no way Marco would allow us out of his sight for long.

187

Turner volunteered to stay with him. He was convinced that Marco, like Ettore, was not to be trusted. My partner wanted to find out what he could by talking to him alone.

"Laura and I are going for a stroll around the boat," I said.

Surprise registered on Marco's face. He was figuring out what was happening between Laura and me.

Down the far end of the ferry was the cargo door with a sign: Admittance to crew only. We opened it quickly and jumped in. There was a platform with a narrow ship's ladder that led down to the hold below decks. Someone was there. He couldn't see us yet and started climbing the ladder.

Laura grabbed me and started kissing me and moaning, not loudly but just enough that the man heard us as he pulled himself up to the platform. He was big, with a few days' stubble on his face.

"Come on, folks, can't you wait till we get to the island?" he grumbled in Italian. We didn't respond and Laura really went at it. She started to unzip her sweater. "Oh, Holy Mother of God," he said. "Look, you're not supposed to be here..." We continued to ignore him. Finally, he gave in. "Well, don't be all day about it. I don't want to see you still here when I make my rounds again," he said, opening the door and stepping out on to the deck.

As the door slammed shut, I laughed. But Laura didn't stop right away. We went at it some more. "Um. Laura...he's gone now."

"Yes," I know that. "I have eyes in the back of my head."

I gingerly stood her up and whispered, "Later," into her ear.

We moved down the ladder into the hold. The lighting was bad, and the few big pieces of freight were strapped down. We stumbled through the hold about half the length of the ship before we found the casket...caskets, both strapped to the side of the hull, one above the other. It was dark. They looked the same.

"How can there be two fucking caskets?" I said, a little too loudly. She shushed me. It was possible there were other men in the hold. We stood still a moment to see if my outburst had attracted any attention. We heard rats scurrying about.

"Other people die too," she said.

"Can you recognize which one?"

"I think so," she said with a nod. The ship was starting to sway lightly, and as she passed me she fell onto me. I kissed her before she moved to the caskets. I was hoping it would be the one on top, because the bottom casket—the way it was situated—was not going to be simple to get at. I went off in search of something to crack open the casket. Next to a fire extinguisher and attached to the wall was a gaffing hook, a long, thick piece of metal with a metal claw on one end and tapered on the other. I lugged it over.

When I returned, she was still eyeing both, then she ran her hand lightly along the side of the top casket. She kissed her hand and then laid that kiss gently on the top casket. That was my sign.

"You're certain?" I asked.

She nodded and stepped back. "It had metal corners. Hochman insisted. The bottom one doesn't."

I brought the tapered end to the lip of the top casket. It was a little too thick to slip in easily so I had to push. I didn't want to overdo it for fear of smashing up the casket and upsetting Laura.

I turned around to her. "You don't have to watch. Why don't you wait for me at the ladder and keep guard?"

"That's okay."

I levered the tapered end into the casket, but without much success. I could have rammed it, but that would wreck the casket and maybe attract attention. We needed a strong push rather than a punch. I looked at Laura.

She grabbed the blunt end of the pole.

"On three," I said.

This time I could feel the metal easing its way in. After about ten seconds, we heard a cracking noise, and then a whoosh of air entering the casket. The gaffer went in some more and the casket lid opened a few inches. I looked behind me to Laura. I thought she'd be more upset than she was. She was tough.

"Go to the ladder," I practically ordered her. This time she gave in. I didn't want to open the lid too much for fear of destroying whatever held it closed. Against all horror movie wisdom, I snaked my arm into the casket, the gaffer propping the lid open. I could barely move my hand inside. Nothing—for too long a time. Jesus, they fucking stole the body. I shoved my arm in as far as I could and finally hit something. It was an ear, and I knew it was Gaetano because I felt the military epaulets on his shoulder. I tried to stay away from the face. Had to stay away from the face.

I felt my way across his chest to his tie. I was up to my bicep. It was not going to be possible to get much further in. Slipped my middle and forefingers under the tie knot. In a moment the key was in my hand and my arm was out of the casket. After I pulled out the gaffer, the lid was not going down, so I leaned on it hard and it slowly closed. I tried the lid again, to test it, and it held.

Just then Laura came running back. "He's coming again." She jumped, doing a flying leap so that her legs wrapped around me, and she landed hugging me, her thighs squeezing my pelvis. She almost sent us sprawling to the ground. I bumped my head on a pipe hanging from the low ceiling. I instinctively rubbed my head with one hand and held her with the other.

"I'm sorry," she whispered.

"That's the limit, *regazzi*," the same cargo man growled in Italian. "This isn't a cheap hotel. I understand love. I'm not hardhearted, but there's a time and a place for everything. *Fuori! Fuori!*" he said.

"Okay, okay," I said.

"I'm sorry," Laura said as we walked by him. "We're newlyweds honeymooning on Ustica."

"What's this gaffer doing here on the floor?" he asked as we walked away.

We didn't respond.

He gave a little grunt. "You're lucky I don't report you to the captain," he said as we made our way to the ladder.

In the interior passenger lounge in the top deck, we found Turner and Marco discussing Wagner. Turner glanced at me for a sign and I nodded. He looked relieved.

"Marco is an opera fan, Paolo."

"Not surprising," I said.

"What is surprising, though, is that he prefers Wagner to Verdi," Turner said.

"So?" I shrugged. "You love Wagner."

"Yes, but I'm an American. Verdi is…a god here. For Italians. His music is in their blood. It's the first thing they hear while suckling at their mother's breast and often the last thing they hear before they die."

"I find Verdi a little sentimental, perhaps," Marco explained.

"Oh," Turner said, looking away and bringing his hands together, "please don't give us the organ grinder bullshit."

"No, no," Marco protested. "I would never say that about our greatest composer. It's just that his topics are too often just love alone. Important, yes, but Wagner takes on the great myths of his nation, not just carnal passions." Suddenly Marco became animated and pointed across to the other side of the boat. "Hey, look. That man." In his excitement he fell into Italian before quickly switching back: "*E' tornato*. I mean he's returned."

We all turned to see a slight fellow in black pants and raincoat running outside on the deck and then down the steps. He had on a hat pulled down to his ears.

"What, Marco?"

"I think that's the fellow from Piazza Navona. The man watching the front door of the building you went to. Signora Dottori's apartment."

Right away, I looked to Turner. He'd heard precisely what Marco

191

had said, too.

"Are you sure?" I said to our bodyguard.

"I only saw his face for a moment. Very white, like he was sickly. But he has the same red Ducati baseball hat," Marco replied.

We jumped up and ran after the man with the hat. I was about to go for my pistol when I realized where we were. Bounding out of the passenger lounge and to the deck, we scared the few passengers that there were. "*Cosa c'e? Cosa?*" came the shouts. Once outside, the rain made it a little difficult to see.

"I'll take the stern," Turner said, running down the port side of the boat. Marco followed him.

No one was on the foredeck outside. I ran to the bow. There was a ladder that led to the helm, but I doubted he took that route. Then I saw the toe of a shoe sticking out from behind a stanchion. He was between that and the gunwale. I nodded to Laura and she had her hand on her black holster. I crept up to the stanchion, grabbed the leg, and pulled.

"Easy, tiger," the man said.

"You dopey fuck," I said.

"Easy. Easy," Gretzman said. He was drenched.

"I told you to stay out of this. Go home. You're going to get us and maybe yourself killed. What part of that sentence don't you understand?"

"Just following the story."

I grabbed him hard by the lapels and shoved him up, perp-like, against the stanchion, so that he was on his toes. It was time to be persuasive. His hat flew off and into the Tyrrhenian below us. "You think this is a joke?"

I thought it would shake him up. He was still flippant. "Shit. I liked that hat," he said, looking over the side. "Hello, signorina policewoman," he said to Laura, who had walked up behind me. "Come on, let go, Rossi. I haven't done anything and you're not the law here.

Though I see," he looked down at my belt inside my jacket, "that you're still carrying. Your writ runs to Ustica, does it? Shit, I should call the carabinieri myself. You got no right."

"Go ahead. *She's* a carabinieri," I said, motioning with my head to Laura behind me. "What have you been writing about us, scribe? I haven't seen your rag in days."

"Ever hear of the Internet?" he said. "I haven't written anything. I'm keeping to the deal. And I have news for you."

I loosened my grip just a little, so that his feet were flat on the deck.

"I wouldn't trust that other cop with you, Marco. Not only is he not as pretty as your new girlfriend," he said, smiling at Laura, "he's on the phone a lot whenever you're not with him. I've been watching. For an Italian cop, he sure talks a lot of German."

Laura's eyes narrowed at that, and before I could ask her about it, Turner and Marco ran up.

Gretzman shouted, "Let me go." To Marco, he shouted, "Officer, please tell this man to let me go."

I looked over at Marco. "Do you want me to arrest this man?" he asked me.

"Arrest *me*?" Gretzman blurted out, incredulous.

"No. He's a journalist," I said, sarcastically accenting the "journ" part long and hard. "He's written about the Muro murders. Put us in the paper several times. How would you like that, Marco? He could put you on the map in New York."

"The map?" Marco questioned, not understanding. "They taught us at the academy not to talk to reporters. Always, 'No comment.' They are not to be trusted."

"Exactly," I answered, looking at Gretzman. I let him go. To the right, off the port side, I saw Ustica a few miles away. The rain had let up. The land was black, a lava rock jutting up from the sea. There were houses hugging the sides, and a main road winding its way up the mountain from the dock. The boat gave a blast on its horn, and

Gretzman saw his chance and stepped out from the semicircle of cops around him.

Marco looked at me, and I said, "Forget it."

"Go home," I called after Gretzman as he walked back to the passenger lounge. "We're just burying Muro. There's nothing happening here."

"Screw you," he answered without even looking back, and then disappeared into the lounge.

"What are we going to do with him?" Turner asked.

"Marco, can you restrain him on the boat? Accidentally handcuff him to a railing or something?"

"I could arrest him," he said with doglike desire to please, "and take him to the local police on Ustica, but that would take time. I can't keep him on the boat."

"We haven't got a lot of time. Forget it. Next time, if we have to, we'll cuff him."

Turner nodded in agreement.

We came upon the port. "Ustica used to be a pirate haven for hundreds of years," my partner said. "And a penal colony till not too long ago. Isn't that right?" he said to Laura, who shrugged.

"I must go below deck to get the truck," Marco announced, and went off.

"We'll meet on the dock," I said.

After Marco was gone, Turner, watching the dockhands throw thick ropes to the ferry crewmen, said to no one in particular, "Did you happen to hear what Marco said when he first saw Gretzman?" The boat engines roared in reverse and we lurched toward the bow.

"Yeah, I heard it," I said, watching the ropes being tied.

Laura looked at us. "Please don't keep me in the dark again."

"I'm sorry, Laura. We aren't going to do that anymore. Marco said he saw Gretzman outside Dottori's house."

"Yes. So?"

"We never told him whom we were going to see, and we didn't buzz the intercom. How'd he know we were there to see Dottori?"

Laura thought about this a moment. "What are you saying?"

"Either he's just Ettore's boy keeping an eye on us and he'll grab the key as soon as he sees it. Or...maybe worse," I said.

"But Dottori's name *is* on the intercom. That's where he saw it."

"We intentionally *never* told Marco which apartment or the name," I said, looking at Turner, who nodded with me.

"He came right up to her door, remember?" Laura said, thinking she had me.

"Exactly. No name on her door. How did he know Dottori and which door?" I replied. "Did you tell him?" It slipped out before I could stop myself.

She frowned and stepped back. "Well, he must have figured it out, that's all. Dottori's name has been mentioned in the papers."

"Marco was in diapers when the papers were hot on this story," I said.

"He knows you're here for Ustica," Laura answered. She seemed unconvinced by her own argument. "I know Marco, he's a young carabinieri. Very smart, international background, and looking to impress people."

"Impress whom?" Turner said.

*   *   *

As the ferry engines went silent, a small black hearse pulled up to the dock and waited in the cargo loading area. It was Sunday morning so church bells were pealing. We filed off the ship and found Marco sitting in his shiny Land Rover. He was reading a day-old pink-papered *Il Gazzettino dello Sport*. He smiled when we approached.

"You're the boss, now," Marco said to Laura.

"I'll check with the hearse driver to make sure he's clear on what to do. We must pick up the priest. They will be in a hurry to return for the other casket later. There are no refrigeration facilities on the dock," she said.

Turner and I sat uneasily in the backseat.

The rain had stopped. This being a Sunday morning in Italy, the city was shut quiet but for the church and the one *pasticceria* cafe. There seemed to be no young people at all here. Silver hair dominated. No baby carriages, no kids. Ustica was tiny, a satellite of a remote larger island. It was beautiful, too, and the black lava rocks probably would shine bright on a sunnier day, but there wasn't much in the way of beaches. Day old papers were probably the best you could find. At a café nearby, several men were gathered around a table, playing cards under the awning, an old brown wooden cane or two lying against the wall. All of them wore suit jackets or sweater vests, though no ties. They were all clean-shaven, with their hair combed neatly. At least those who had some.

It was a scene right from Morruggio, in Basilicata. Angela had come along the first time I'd visited my grandparents' village, twenty-five years ago, before we'd gotten married. On the bus ride into town, I was recognized by someone who had never seen me before but claimed to be my second cousin. Unlike the geezers in Ustica, the men in Morruggio played dominoes. I walked up, rather timidly, unsure of my Italian. They seemed a single organism. All domino action stopped and ten eyes looked up at us with small-town wariness. In the best standard Italian I could muster I told them I was looking for my *nonno's* brother. I got cold looks, but when I repeated myself in dialect, the stares disappeared. When I told them the name of the man I was looking for, Rocco Rossi, that's when the excitement broke.

"*Venite! Venite!*" one commanded. He waved us to follow him. The man, GianLuca Dentibianchi—I remembered his name still, Whiteteeth—took us to a garage. He brought out a motorcycle with a sidecar, an antique, the kind from World War II movies. He motioned to Angela to get into the sidecar, and when she hesitated momentarily, he seemed to know why. He pulled out a white handkerchief and made a big deal out of dusting off the seat, bowing and pointing. Angela jumped in, putting her rucksack in her lap. I hopped on behind GianLuca and off we roared through town, and right through its single flashing yellow light, with nary a thought for any cars crossing our path. In a minute we were at Rocco Rossi's house and GianLuca hopped off the bike and took Angela's pack so she could get out.

"*Benvenuti a Morruggio*," he said, bowed, and then zoomed off.

Someone waved a hand in front of my face. "Angela, cut it out," I said.

"Angela who?" Laura said. She was standing outside the Land Rover on the dock in Ustica, and waving her right hand directly before me. It was delicate but sinewy, the hand she used to shoot. I'd been staring so long at the old men in Ustica that I'd lost track.

"Angela? No. I mean…" I said.

"Come on, let's go," Laura said, jumping in the front seat. "We'll follow the hearse. We pick up the priest at the *Duomo* and then straight to the cemetery." The hearse turned onto the main drag and we followed, up the incline. It was quiet in the car until we reached San Michele, Ustica's Duomo.

"Parents still not coming?" I asked Laura.

"They could not bring themselves," she replied. "My mother was too upset. I'm still worried about her."

"I see," I said, not satisfied. I didn't entirely believe her. No Italian mother I knew would refuse to go to the funeral of her first-born son, not even if he was a pedophile mass murderer of twelve-year-old honor students.

The priest, who hadn't missed many meals, showed up vested in regulation black hassock and white-laced surplice. He hadn't bothered to shave for old Gaetano, with a thick five o'clock shadow, lush even, matching the hair on his head. His cheeks were dimpled. With that stubble he reminded me of Fred Flintstone. At a probable forty, he might have been the youngest man on the island. He was sweating slightly and put a purple and black leather box—with the tools of the trade—on his lap.

"*Buon giorno, figli miei*," he said, giving a small smile. Hellos all around followed. He didn't seem particularly interested in Gaetano. Perhaps he knew who the box held.

The road went up for a while before we reached a flat plateau and then we moved along the side of the old volcano, along a dirt road. We passed the cemetery front gates, which needed repair. They seemed permanently open and hanging onto their brick posts by a single bolt. The place looked a mess. More than one headstone had fallen over; vines clung to many of them.

The cars rolled to a sharp stop. We exited wordlessly. Just off the road was a freshly dug grave, Gaetano's final resting place. Dirt was piled high on one side and we gathered around the other. Turner and I helped the driver and his assistant put the casket on a gurney. They brought it to the lip of the hole in the ground. Just seven people here for Guy, six of them for work reasons. The hole was deep and black at the bottom, caught in the shade of the dirt mound next to it.

I looked around the cemetery, which, like the town, hugged the side of the mountain. The rain clouds hadn't left and kept the sea a dark green. Nothing plowed it on the horizon. On the switchback fifteen feet below us, an Ape was parked with a blond wooden casket in the flat bed. There were two levels to the burial grounds, with another freshly dug and open grave on the level right below us. There was a yellow mini-backhoe and wooden breastworks surrounding it. Plenty of monumental sepulchers—for a small island like Ustica—dotted the cemetery. Donato, La Calsa, Onofrio were the names inscribed, some ornately with trellises or roses, on the arch above the metal door guarding the tombs.

The padre took his implements out of the purple and black box at his feet.

He was at the ready, at the head of the hole, his thurible on a small chain at his left side and a small, fat, weathered prayer book in his right hand. Four of us, Turner, myself, the driver, and his assistant held the casket over the hole by way of two ropes under it. I feared that if we didn't do this exactly right, the unsealed casket would let poor Gaetano topple right out. The padre gave a short prayer, then some kind of poem in Italian.

I wasn't sure of his Italian. It was a different dialect, yet the poem sounded like...well I couldn't believe it. I shook my head. It couldn't be. Yet it was. I thought he had thrown in the words from *I'm Going Home*, the finale of *The Rocky Horror Picture Show*. Since it was in Italian, it wasn't easy to tell right off, but after a few seconds I was certain.

The priest said, "Cards for Sorrow. Cards for Pain. 'Cause I've seen blue skies through the tears in my eyes. And I realize I'm going home. I'm going home." It seemed like the hearse driver was mouthing the words, too, as if he also knew them by heart.

I looked at the priest and he winked at me. It was fast but it happened. Turner didn't understand and the others looked bored and uninterested in what the *prete* was mouthing. Laura probably wasn't even listening.

He signaled us to let the casket down slowly and we did, as he waved the thurible over it. Laura walked away and rested her hand against a tombstone nearby. More prayers came out of the priest's mouth. Then an Amen and he slapped the book shut. Done. Gaetano was officially in the choir eternal. Or maybe somewhere else.

"Gather the ropes, boys," the priest said to the driver and assistant. "Let's go. I have a couple more today."

Turner walked over to me. He said in a low voice, "I saw a Gerbino monument on the way in. Giant thing. Looks like a mausoleum. Could it really be the prince in the Boccaccio story?"

"Don't know, but we're looking for a princess." As soon as it came out of my mouth, I knew that I had just said about the weirdest thing an NYPD detective could ever say on official business.

Laura turned and was making her way to us, wiping the tears and some mascara from her eyes.

"Where's Gerbino?" I asked Turner before she got close.

He pointed it out, about one hundred yards away, down the hill and one level below us, along the switchback toward the front gate. It was situated similarly near the edge of the second level, overlooking the first level of the cemetery.

"And the princess?" I said with a straight face.

"No sign of her," he said, "unless you are referring to the one that's walking over to us now."

"Let's take a look at Gerbino." I said.

He nodded.

"What about Gerbino?" Laura said, touching me on the shoulder. "What are we looking for?"

"We'll know when we find it," Turner said, moving down the road. "And maybe not."

"Funny priest," I said to Laura, who was between my partner and me. Marco walked behind.

"He should have shaved. On this small rock, you don't have much choice," she said. "He complained to me that Marco was supposed to drive him back."

"How did you get the hearse driver to cooperate?" I said.

"Realistic tears at a well-chosen time work wonders on men," she said without a smile. Her head tilted at a slight angle and the dark sunglasses she wore brought out her Lolita potential.

We arrived at Gerbino's final resting place. Plain but large, it was made of granite. Guarding the entrance was a metal door that looked like it hadn't been opened in many decades. Thick vines had grown in and out of the crevices between the door and the granite, arms holding the door fast. That made me think this was not a likely place for what we were looking for. The lock on the door was massive and ancient, more 1200s than 1900s.

Even if Muro's key worked, we were going to need a chainsaw to cut those vines. High weeds lined the tomb's perimeter. Behind it some ten feet or so, and partly obstructed by the overgrown vegetation, was another grave marked by a tombstone.

"No sign of a princess," Turner said, pushing the weeds out of the way and running his hand softly along the granite, whose surface was roughened by time. "Very nice—once."

"Maybe she's buried with Gerbino," Laura offered. She looked closely at the epitaph, but it was worn down and unreadable. "The words are probably Latin," she said. "Marco, do you read Latin?"

He shook his head. He was uncomfortable, sensing we had designs on the grave. "Why are we here, regazzi?" Marco said. "The burial is over. Let's go."

I walked over to Marco and motioned him to sit with me on the step in front of Gerbino's door. He complied reluctantly.

"What's this about?" he said.

"Marco, my friend," I said, putting my arm around his shoulder. "What I'm about to tell you is going to be very hard to believe but believe it you must."

He took off his hat and wiped his brow. It was nearing noon and getting humid. The clouds were breaking. A patch of sweat stained dark blue at his armpit was visible.

"Are you familiar with the Ustica disaster?"

"Of course. All Italians are. It's unsolved."

"Bingo," I said.

"Over twenty years. So?" he asked, looking now at Turner.

"You might find this difficult to believe," I said, "I mean why would two New York cops be involved in such a case. We hardly know anything about it, about the history, the crooked politicians and industrialists, the Mafia, the Red Brigades, the bad cops that might be involved. We really know nothing. And yet," I said, shaking my finger in the air, as if to underline the whole thing, "we might."

201

Marco looked at Laura for some explanation, but she gave nothing. "You are telling me that you know who shot down the plane?" Marco said. He screwed up his face, with the corner of his left eyebrow pointing downward in skepticism.

"No, we don't know."

His face relaxed.

"Marco, we are going to need your help. I can tell you a little more, but you will have to humor a crazy idea of mine. We might have to do something that is a little unusual…perhaps illegal. Nothing serious. It's something teenagers do around the world when they are bored and live near a cemetery."

"I don't know. Major Ettore would probably not like this. This could cause difficulties for me." Marco looked away, then back. "You promise it is not a serious crime?"

"I promise. The evidence we have came from someone involved in the Ustica disaster. We got our hands on it in New York. I'll tell you when it's time. No one knows about it. Not your superiors, not the Italian government, not even the U.S. government."

"Ah, *La Chiave*," he said. "The newspapers were right. There is a key." He looked like a kid on Christmas morning.

I moved to Gerbino's door.

"Wait," Marco said aloud. "I'd rather not see this. Anyway, you will need something to cut those vines around the door. I'll go see what we have in the truck." He walked off toward the car, one level above us.

At first, I was happily surprised not to have Ettore's man spying on us. But then Turner shook his head and put up his hands. "What now? Where the fuck is he going? I don't like this, Paolo. Anyway, our key's a bitty thing. It's not going to work a medieval lock."

"We have to try," I said, as did Laura at the very same time. We all looked at each other. "Let's do this quick. Keep an eye on Marco," I said, turning to the business at hand. The lock was blackened by weather and tough to figure out. There was no hole in the front for the key, nor the back, nor the side. I flipped it upside down and there on the bottom was what looked like a keyhole. I wiped as much grime and age as I could from it. I looked at Laura, her eyes big.

I put the key to the hole. It didn't fit at first, but I massaged and jimmied it until the key slid in. Once in, the key seemed too small. I pushed so hard that I almost lost the key inside the lock.

"You're right, partner," I said.

Before Turner could open his mouth, Laura said, a little too insistently, almost like an order, "Keep trying. It's an old lock." She grimaced. It wasn't a look on her that I liked.

"More like not the right lock," Turner said. He was shaking his head, and I knew his head shake was about Laura.

Five minutes of wheedling, cajoling, and cursing that lock did nothing. I turned to them. "No dice."

"What about some oil?" Laura said.

"Forget it," I said. "I can tell by the way it feels that this is not the lock for this key. Anyway, we are looking for a princess, not a prince." I sat down on the mausoleum's front step and Laura sat next to me.

"Try it again," she said loudly, even more insistent. There was an edge to it I wasn't liking.

"Where the fuck is Marco? How long does it take to check the fucking truck?" Turner shouted. "We are looking for a princess, not a prince," he said, walking off. "I don't trust that white boy, Paolo. He's taking too long."

I put the key in my pocket. Turner went to the back of Gerbino's tomb. Laura sat unhappily on the step next to me and folded her arms. A tight little smile did nothing to hide her impatience.

"What about us?" I said. "Regardless of what happens, I'm going back to the States, whether it's tomorrow, two days or two weeks, I'm going back. Then what?"

"I don't know," she said, looking away. "You live there. I live here. Not much that can be done. I would like you to stay. Maybe you want me to go to America. Neither is going to happen. Let's enjoy it while we can."

Just then, Turner screamed.

I jumped, thinking he was hurt. The yell came from around the back of Gerbino's tomb.

"Arabic!" he yelled a second time.

We ran around back.

"Arabic! Arabic! Arabic!" Turner said.

We found him clawing at the tomb behind, another mausoleum, though smaller than Gerbino's. The weeds had so covered it that it looked like a tombstone. It was a good way submerged, too, as if the ground had been slowly sucking it down over the centuries.

Turner said nothing more, just kept pushing away the weeds until we, too, could clearly see what he had. Faded, very faded, but it was Arabic script.

"How could this be? A Muslim in a Christian cemetery?" I said.

"The princess was from North Africa, Tunis, right? Arab," Turner said, not as a question but as a fact. "She was Arab. That's Gerbino. This has got to be her grave." He pulled the thick weeds that blocked the front door of the crypt. It was made of the same stone as Gerbino's and looked to be just about as old.

"Look at the lintel," he said. In the excitement over finding the Arabic script covering the door itself, we'd missed the arch above it. The writing in stone was weathered, and clearly it was the Latin alphabet. Turner wiped the grime from it.

"La Sa" were the first four letters. The rest couldn't be deciphered, and then the last two letters: "na." "La Saracena," I said quietly.

Laura jumped at Turner and kissed him square on the lips.

CHAPTER 15

SUNDAY: NOON

We stood before the princess' cenotaph and I rubbed the back of my neck, damp with sweat and mist. Maybe there was something in there that would solve the crime...or just a ragged shroud wrapped around a few bones and a pile of dust. After our visit to Mrs. Dottori, I'd read the fourth story of the fourth day. Doomed love between a Christian prince and a Muslim princess, each having never so much as glimpsed each other until their first—and last—meeting. She heard stories of his valor and fell in love with him sight unseen, and he the same after hearing she was "one of the fairest creatures ever fashioned by nature." Just as Gerbino had her in sight—her name is never revealed—La Saracena was brutally murdered before his very eyes by allies of her father, who wanted to marry her off to the King of Granada.

"I feel a little weird doing this," I said.

"What about those eighty-one people who died without burial, their spirits skulking about, only to haunt my brother for years. Haunted to death," Laura said.

I pulled the key out. Unlike Gerbino's, the lock on this mausoleum was modern and heart shaped. Thick copper and broad. The key slipped in, as if sucked in. I popped the lock. *Click.*

Turner started to giggle. I felt Laura's breath on me. "The door's only big enough for one at a time," I said. After removing the padlock from the hooks holding the door closed, I slipped it into my jacket breast pocket.

I pushed the metal door, which creaked on its hinges. It opened slowly and gray light filled a small part of the entryway. Cold, dank air rushed out at me.

"What are you waiting for?" Laura said. Again, a little too hard.

She jabbed her flashlight into the tomb, threading her arm between me and the doorway. It felt like she might push me out of the way to get in.

I stepped in and down about a foot. The floor was grainy, granite pebbles all over. There were two stained glass windows, about twelve inches square on each lateral wall, and in the back was a stone altar. The tomb itself measured about twelve feet by twelve feet. With the princess and the three of us in there, not much room was left. The walls were covered in Arabic. On that altar was a sarcophagus. Laura flashed the light on it. It, too, was covered in Arabic script.

We were strangely quiet at first. I pointed to the stone casket.

"I suppose we are going to have to open this one, too," Laura said with not a little sarcasm.

"I don't think it's possible without tools," I said. "That's a stone lid. It probably weighs hundreds of pounds. I doubt Maresciallo Dottori messed with it."

Turner examined the room. He felt along the walls, looking for a sign, anything. We were in the right place, it seemed, but we didn't know what we were looking for. He pointed to an ornate candleholder hanging from the ceiling on metal chains. It, too, had Arabic script in silver filigree metalwork surrounding the glass, which enclosed a wax candle.

Once you lit the candle, the words could be read, I imagined. It hung just a bit too high for us to reach quickly and there was nothing to stand on. "We could use Mo Malik right about now," I said to no one in particular. Mohammad Malik was the One-Nine's new terrorism liaison.

"Ah, shit," Turner said, pulling his hand away from the wall quickly, as if bitten.

"What?" I said.

"We are not the only living things in this place. There are no poisonous spiders in Italy, right?"

No one answered.

I moved closer to the stone coffin. My eyes adjusted. "Yes!"

"What?" my partners said.

I pointed. "La Saracena" was written across the side of the lid in Latin letters about an inch high.

I grabbed Laura and brought her face right up to the words. She shone the light on them and smiled. Turner gave a whoop, then got serious.

He gave the mausoleum a full turn. "There are no more clues, Paolino," he said. "We have the key. We're in the right place. Where's the sign that says, 'Here are the radar tapes'?"

"If that's what it is," Laura interjected.

"Of course that's what it is," I replied, getting loud and testy with her for the first time since we kissed. "For Chrissake, the guy was the head of radar at the air traffic station for the area. It's the fucking radar tapes. And it better be the tapes and not another fucking Boccaccio clue."

Turner chimed in, "This is getting me nervous. This whole thing is bad. Marco is out there. What is taking him so long? He was just supposed to get a cutting tool. Maybe he's on the phone to Ettore. Paolo, one of us should be on watch. This could be a Gladio trap."

"He doesn't know we're in here," I said.

Right then and there, if I'd been told the world was going to end in ten minutes or that the CIA had killed Kennedy, I would have believed all that and more compared to what happened next. Gretzman came flying into the crypt, as if tossed in, then slipped and rolled the rest of the way to the altar, screaming, "We got problems," and threw himself flat on the floor.

"Speaking of fucking mistakes," I said. I pulled out my pistol for the first time on this trip and brought it to his temple, safety on. Gretzman hugged the ground.

"Don't waste a bullet on me. You're gonna need every one you got."

I grabbed him by the belt and attempted to force him up, but he'd have none of it. "Let me go, fascist jerk. Yeah, I know about your little Mussolini bust…we are in a bad way. I didn't run in here 'cause I enjoy your company," he said. "I'll admit the chick cop is very nice, but there are two very black Mercedes coming up the road at Mach 1 and they are definitely in a rush to see some dead people," Gretzman said, throwing himself down again.

Outside, tires squealed loudly on the cemetery's asphalt road. Doors opened and men started yelling in German-accented English, "Get out, get out fast."

I looked at Turner.

"We should send you out, motherfucker, with a white flag," I yelled at Gretzman. He lay motionless. "They probably followed you."

Gretzman gave me a "Yeah right" snort. "They fucking know your every move, Mr. Marlowe."

Before his last word died in the dark, the loud pings of bullets pierced the air. They came in the front, came in through the small windows, and ricocheted all around. We all lay as flat as possible on the tomb floor, which was below ground level. I felt small pieces of the walls, dislodged by bullets, flake off and hit me in the face and on the forearms. One dented slug fell harmlessly right in front of my face, so close that I could still smell the hot, acrid gunpowder on it.

"Not good, Paolo," Turner said to me above the din. He looked at Laura, "Don't you have radio connection to Marco?"

She shook her head.

"Fucking Marco, where is he?" Turner yelled. "He's probably in with them, the bastard."

"He could radio for help from the truck," I said, little hope in my voice.

"Help?" Turner said. "The three of us are the biggest collection of cops this rock has ever seen."

"We just have to stay put. Marco *will* radio for help." I didn't sound very convinced because, like Turner, I had some suspicions about him. Maybe he didn't want to take them on alone. Two cars with four guns, maybe even eight. Tough odds. For the Teutons too—the doorway was wide enough just for one—we could pick them off as they came in. They were mercenaries, not prepared to die. There was a good chance all of us would die just for a key that leads to nothing, on a piece of shit island in the middle of nowhere.

The onslaught stopped.

Gretzman moaned. "Motherfucker…I'm bleeding."

I inched over to him. "Throw me the light." I motioned to Laura. I put the flashlight on his wound, shading it with my hand in the hope it could not be seen by the Germans. It didn't look like he'd taken a full-on hit. Maybe a ricochet in the shoulder. I ripped up part of his shirt and held it to the wound. "Hold that until we get out."

"If we get out." He winced. Gretzman rolled on to his back and moaned some more.

"Shut up," Turner said.

I made the mistake of leaving the flashlight next to Gretzman. He grabbed and started idly shining it around the crypt. "Nice tomb," he moaned.

"Cut that out, asshole," I whispered. And then I noticed the candle when the light was on it. "Something's there," I said, looking intently at the lamp.

Gretzman tried to get up. "You are certifiable, Gretzman. I don't give a shit about you. If they pick you off, it's one less worry, but I don't want them to start shooting again. Get the fuck down," I said in a loud whisper. Gretzman winced and doubled over from the pain.

"One of you has to give me a boost up. Just a quick boost," I said. Laura and Turner didn't respond.

"I'll be down in one second. *What the fuck did we come here for?*"

"Paolo, the bullets could start flying any second."

I looked around for a stick. Anything that I could use. Nothing. "Do you want the tapes or not?" I hissed.

Turner put out clasped hands. In a second I was rummaging around the candleholder with my hands. "There's something. Almost got it…"

The Germans opened up again. Metal pinging. Those goddamn small pieces of brick and grit ricocheted off the walls and into my face. Turner dove for cover and I was left hanging from the candle. It broke from the ceiling and everything came raining down, me, candle pieces, and pointed shards. Laura and I rolled as tightly as possible against the other wall.

Then suddenly all was quiet again and the three of us looked at each other.

I flashed Turner a big grin. A black thing had landed at the base of my feet. I reached over and grabbed a black cloth bag with a drawstring. Inside was a wheel-shaped case, maybe the width of a hand across. Turner and Laura's eyes were on me as I pulled back the little leather strap with a snap clasp. When I opened the case, there they were, two little reels. I put the flashlight on them. They were the kind I remembered from those big bulky computers I saw on TV in the 1970s, at NASA in Houston when the Apollo rockets went up.

"Two tapes," I said quietly. "Numbered 1 and 2"

Turner put out the full smile, ear to ear, devil tails at either end.

"I'm not dead," Gretzman said. "If I could get up, I'd give you a big kiss."

One of the Germans shouted, "Come out. First throw your veapons, und den come out vit your handz up. Von at a time, pleaze. Ve have no time for games. Your lives are at stake here," he said.

"Well, it's nice that they are polite," Turner said, shoving himself into the front right corner and risking sitting up. He crawled to the doorway without exposing himself. "I make four. Two behind the Mercedes closest to us. One behind a tree and the other bent down behind a tombstone right close. I don't have full range of vision."

I slid over to the other side of the door to get a look the other way. "I don't see anyone else."

"Just four?" Laura asked.

"I hope," I said.

"You have sixty zeconds." He sounded like Arnold Schwarzenegger, like his pal Horst or Jens, or whatever the fuck his name was.

"One's going to the trunk," Turner said. "I don't think it's for flowers, Paolo. I think he's getting some heavy ordinance."

"One behind the tombstone, one behind the tree, two at the car, giusto?" Laura said.

"Yeah," Turner said, watching incredulously as she pulled herself to a crouched, ready position to the left side of the entryway, a Beretta in each hand. She took a deep breath.

"What the…" Before I could say, "fuck are you doing," she was out the door, like a cowboy in a Sergio Leone spaghetti western. The attack remounted and all of us ate the floor again. I took a ricochet in the thigh. It stung badly. I wasn't sure I would be able to run if it came to that.

Then it stopped quickly.

I squeezed as close to the door as I dared, to take a look.

Outside, there was what seemed to be confused yelling in German. "*Alt, alt, ist das Fraulein.*" ("Stop, stop, it's the girl.") I must have had a strange look on my face, because Turner said, "Hey, what's the matter? She hit?"

"No," I said, confused. "She ran to a gravesite that was under construction on the other side of Gerbino's mausoleum. And then she jumped over the parapet and breastworks and ran to a tree. The Germans didn't take a single shot at her. Now they are between her and us."

"Tosca has some *coglioni*. What's the matter?" Turner asked.

"I'm not sure, but it looked like they didn't *want* to shoot her. They weren't even looking her way. Only our way."

The shooting show outside recommenced. We instinctively ducked, but this time nothing was coming in. Instead the battle was blazing between Laura and the Germans. She'd created a diversion. A lot of screaming in German, and, strangely, a trace of surprise in their voices. "*Was ist das? Was ist das?*" Then another one said in German accented Italian, "*Ragazza che cazzo stai facendo?*" ("What the fuck are you doing, girl?")

"Well, they're shooting at her now," I shouted over the lead. "That's good enough for me. Let's summon the blood, partner. This is our chance."

Turner was practically up my ass as we ran out the door. My right leg felt like a hot blade was stuck in it, directly into my quadriceps. I ran. I hobbled. I ran.

"Hey, you bastards, don't leave me in here," Gretzman moaned. Turner rolled to the ground behind Gerbino's tomb. We were still within earshot of Gretzman. "You guys have to protect me. I'm an American citizen…" Then a low, sad, resigned, "Fuck."

One of the two Germans by the big tombstone nearest us was already down and out. There wasn't much left of his face. The other two Germans by the car were bent down on the far side. I spied their feet in the space under their car. One was shooting away from us, presumably at Laura, and the other was popping up and down, taking shots at us.

"I make three, repeat three perps, one down," I yelled.

"Confirmed. I don't see the fourth. No Laura."

I heard a couple of pops coming from the tree where we'd last seen her. "She's at nine o'clock, in that mound of dirt and wood. See it?"

Turner nodded.

"We have to split up. I can't run fast. Take the tapes." I threw the cloth bag to my partner. That brought out the guys at the car again and bullets whizzed by.

As fast as I could, I limped down the left side of Gerbino's tomb and crossed to a tree. Turner took off the other way and that was the last I saw of him. Both of us drew fire. From my position I glanced at the parapet where Laura had hidden. She didn't look my way. She was taking shots at the Germans.

I saw a shimmer of silver and an orange muzzle behind the large tombstone directly opposite her, from the partner of the first German that had gone down. Laura ducked and disappeared from view.

Bits and pieces of my tree were falling off, as if someone were chopping chunks out of the bark. God, they used big bullets. I heard shots on the other side of Gerbino's, but I couldn't tell who was giving and who was getting. I thought about Gretzman in the tomb, dying there. A great *Post* story he wouldn't be able to write, the poor schmuck.

The two Germans by the Mercedes nearest to me ran to the car behind it. They wanted a better sight of Laura. There was more shouting in German. The remaining guy behind the tombstone got up and tried to get back to his pals. He grabbed at his bloodied stomach. He shouldn't have gotten up. Laura jumped up from the parapet and let out a volley. The guy went down quickly in a heap.

There were two Germans now by the car, red with fear and cursing each other. It looked like the one wanted to leave but the other was shaking his head. A couple of shots came from the direction of the front of the car. Turner. They ducked down and I lost sight of them. I wanted to join in, but the pain from my thigh was making my aim unsteady. I took a couple of shots and managed to hit the side of the back car, then a tire. I hit as many tires as I could. It was now three to two, our favor, and Laura was turning out to be an Italian Annie

Oakley. I looked back at the parapet and she was gone.

A German got to the trunk of the first car and pulled out two Uzis. The machine guns barked, and my little tree was disintegrating around me. Going back to Saracena's tomb wasn't an option. The only cover was on the lower level. I had one chance to run and jump to it.

I thought about Libby. Angela wouldn't have to say a word. The minute Libby saw her mother, she'd know. Angela wouldn't cry. It was too late for that. But Libby would, and then Angela would cry at Libby's pain…maybe even a little bit for me, too. At this point, I was really feeling stupid, like maybe Dunne was right. All for a fucking murdered foreigner, and one who was probably dirty.

"God fucking dammit," I whispered as I took off. The slugs whistled from behind me, the dirt around me exploded in clumps. Then I was flat on my back. Felt like a hit to the chest. It hurt a lot. I forgot all about my thigh. I was paralyzed. The bullets stopped coming. The Germans thought I was dead. Maybe I was. I could feel my fingers, but I couldn't move them. I was looking at the cloudy sky. The hit turned me around as I fell, and I opened one eye. The Germans were moving slowly, almost at ease. I couldn't recognize their shouts. It was garbled, like a cassette tape played at low speed.

Was this the way it went? Sucked out of the world, inch by inch, with everything slowing to a tedious grind? Would my last seconds keep playing over and over, never ending? I just lay there watching, as if peering through an old-fashioned arcade Kinetoscope, the pictures flapping and clacking, one by one, in succession before me to form a silent action film. Out of the quiet came the *put-put-put* of that Ape flatbed coming up the road toward the Mercedes. I saw mud caked to its sides, but I couldn't see the driver. Sitting in the back was that blond casket we'd passed earlier. For me already.

My chest hurt. It felt like I'd taken a Mike Tyson left hook. The Germans had turned to watch the Ape, guns trained. With their attention elsewhere, I reached up with my left hand, and that I could move my arm amazed me. I hesitantly touched my chest. There seemed to be metal, sharpened and warm to the touch, coming out of my upper ribcage. Weird. I pricked my finger and pulled my hand away. I didn't feel any blood, either.

I asked myself how I got a full frontal shot to the chest when the Germans were on my right. I wasn't running that way. I ran toward the parapet and Laura. I was so tired that my arm fell away.

The renewed rapid report of their weapons made me instinctively shut my eyes, though I could hear that the bullets went away from me and toward the Ape. When I opened my eyes, it was over for the driver. The windshield, what was left of it, was splattered with blood from the groundskeeper. Poor fucker. Picked apart doing his job on a shithole speck of an island where nothing happened, and from a bunch of fucking foreigners, for no reason at all that he could know. Kind of like those folks on the Ustica plane. A quiet nothing and then bam, you're blown out of this world and into the next, the *al di la*.

Tears came to my eyes. No sign of Turner. I lay there eyeing the Germans, who were crouched down behind the first car. The Ape had smashed into the back of the second car. That casket lay there in the flatbed.

"Come to me," it said. The casket lid moved slightly. Maybe I *was* dead. Who else but the dead could see the dead? That's what my *nonno* always told me. The lid rose an inch and then dropped down again. After finishing off the Ape, its driver compartment emitting black smoke, the Germans had turned back in Turner's direction. I shut my eyes tight again, hoping they couldn't see my face.

Jesus, where the fuck *was* Marco? Really. The Germans shouted some more. I opened one eye a crack. The casket lid opened quickly and all the way up. I saw an arm in a light blue shirt come out. I blinked. My mouth opened as if to scream but nothing came out.

I couldn't have crawled into that casket because it was already occupied. Gaetano Muro's avenger jumped out of that casket like a

Marvel superhero. I thought Laura could fly the way she seemed to float over the top and front of the Ape, landing in front of it and behind the Germans. It was as if she were gliding on a wire, landing on one foot, with the other bent at the knee. All she needed were colorful red tights and the moment would have been complete.

The Germans never had a chance. Their faces registered a hopeless surprise, eyes wide, mouths halfway open, that she was shooting at them at all. Two shots and down they went. If I weren't dead or nearly dead, I'd have probably gotten hard. I wished I'd get hard, at least then I'd be sure I was alive. She went over to check them. It was quiet again, just as it was when we were sitting on Gerbino's front step. Low moans still came from La Saracena's crypt. Gretzman had managed to pick himself up and was standing, just barely, at the door's threshold. He was grabbing his shoulder, and the shirt was covered in blood now. We were either both dead or both alive, according to my *nonno*.

Chapter 16

Sunday Afternoon

I remember being weirdly happy, lying there. I hurt a lot, but I was happy. I reached up again, encouraged that my left arm responded to command, and tentatively felt my chest. La Saracena's lock was still in my shirt pocket. The sharp metal parts that I felt—like razor petals of a nasty flower—were, I realized, the splintered lock. A bullet had hit the lock head on. And not me. I thought about it again, because it was so nice. The bullet, intent on me, instead had hit the lock and stopped. It was the impact of the lock's pressure on my chest, not a slug, that hurt. Radar man Dottori's lock had saved me.

Then I saw her face. Those limpid green eyes looked down at me. Funny how things happened. I'd been dead three minutes before, and then I was staring up at this girl with the most beautiful gaze. It was the best high I had had in a very long time.

"You're alive?" she said, but almost as if she were surprised. She didn't wait for an answer and moved off right away, looking around, as if she feared another attack. She didn't sound so happy. Normally, if your new boyfriend isn't dead after maybe you thought he was, you might take that well. I really expected a smile from the girl. "Do you have the tapes?" was all she said, almost spat out, turning her back to me to search the surroundings.

"Are there more bad guys?" I groaned.

"No, I'm looking for Hamilton." She didn't sound so calm, either. And she didn't help me up. Laura then found my Beretta on the ground and slipped it in her belt.

Well, I supposed I didn't need it anymore, but that bothered me. "He's around...I hope," I said, trying and failing to get up. My vision had cleared. I looked down at my chest. "Nice of you to ask how I am," I said while dislodging the lock from my skin. I pulled some flesh with it. That fuckin hurt some more. My sternum throbbed when I breathed. I had a bruised banana-black outline of the lock on my chest, and inside the black bruise was all red, with blood just below the surface of my skin. "He went to the right and I haven't heard his gun in a while."

"That's because he's out of bullets," she said curtly, searching the cemetery for signs of Turner.

"You're good at math, too," I said.

She turned and said, "Get up." Again, a little harsher than necessary. I was beat up and maybe I couldn't hear right. I understood that maybe she was angry that she had to kill all the Germans. Fair enough. But this seemed excessive. My thigh was still giving me trouble.

"What's wrong?" I said.

"Get up," she said a second time. There was no mistaking it. She was not a happy cop. It was a scary kind of green in her eyes now. She walked over to the Germans again, to make certain they were all the way dead. She spoke to them as she stood over them. The angle wasn't good but I could have sworn she was mouthing, maybe crying, the words "Muori. Muori. Muori." ("Die. Die. Die.") Just like that. Three times. She cracked a wicked smile, mouth half open.

She came back to me, putting her face directly into mine. I thought she was going to plant a nice one on me, but instead she yelled, "I need the tapes, understand?" I was halfway standing up. She had grabbed my lapel, and her gun was still out, though pointed away.

"I understand. We're going to clear Gaetano." Maybe she finally broke under the pressure. "Hamilton has the tapes. We'll prove it to the world," I said. I was finally standing. Sort of. My thigh really hurt. I could now feel the drying rivulets of blood that had coursed down my leg. Around the wound, it was still wet.

She gave a sarcastic chuckle, not like any laugh I'd heard from her before, and then she paced toward the two crypts. Gretzman had collapsed again in front of La Saracena.

"Where's that fucking Marco?" I said to Laura. "Gretzman is going to need help right away, if it isn't already too late."

"Don't worry about the journalist," she said, standing over him. The way she said it chilled me.

For a moment, as she walked slowly around his prone body, pistol straight down at her side, I thought she was going to finish him off.

I fingered the lock that had saved my life. The Germans were using big slugs, .45s. I bent over, sending shooting pains all through my ribs and chest. I almost blacked out but held myself steady against a tree. The bullet was lodged in the metal. I couldn't see much of it, just the butt end sticking out. I brought it close to my face. I couldn't figure how they got me full on. I didn't remember facing them when I ran directly toward Laura's position.

Laura was again next to me. I hadn't noticed her come back. She startled me.

"You're a very lucky man," she said to me, her mouth up to my ear, her tone disbelieving. She took the lock from me and examined it, her face partly perplexed and partly amused. "Very lucky," she said, again whispering in my ear. I didn't get quite as excited as I normally might when a woman like that whispers in my ear—even in a cemetery. No. There was something different in the air, and it wasn't love. And she still had her gun out, in her hand. The battle was over. And when the fighting stopped, the warriors sheathed their guns. She knew the rules. My nerves were jittery.

Laura faced me, her back to Gerbino's, when Turner peeked around the crypt. I saw the muzzle of his gun, along the corner of the mausoleum wall. I wasn't sure what was going on with my girlfriend, so I tried to signal him with my eyes.

She whirled and assumed the kill position. Turner drew back.

"Hey, it's Turner," I said, but she ignored me. I raised my arm but the pain swelled.

"Out! Hands up," she yelled.

"Hey, girl. It's just me," Turner replied, confused.

"Don't come out, partner," I yelled. This was getting far too freaky. Laura turned the gun on me for a moment, her face almost ugly. I thought I was going down.

She jumped behind me, like a ninja, all in one bound. The tree was behind her and I was between her and Turner. She had put her arm around my neck, and I felt Mr. Beretta's cold nose flush against my right temple.

"Detective Turner, please come out," she said calmly.

He did another quick peek and knew the score.

I knew how to get out of these situations. A back kick to the groin, or, in the case of a woman, a hard left elbow to the ribs, and a quick grab of the muzzle with your right hand, all in one motion. I would never be able to do it. The pain was too much. The coldness of the gun muzzle on my skin was too difficult to overcome. It wasn't haphazardly pointed at my temple, halfway pointed into the air, the way a punk or a junkie might do it. She'd buried it into that little indentation in the skull, just next to the eye, and horizontal, so that the slightest provocation would cause that little fellow to explode right through both hemispheres.

"Let me guess," I said in a tired voice. "You're not Guy's sister. And last night…a fluke fuck."

She gave a short laugh. I felt her breath on my neck again.

"First you fuck me, then you kill me," I said.

Turner heard me. "Better than the other way around," he said

220

from behind Gerbino's crypt. "Maybe the girl's not happy with your performance."

Muro, or Laura, or whoever she was, was all business. "I will count to five. If I don't have the tapes in my hands, Detective Turner, you will be needing a new partner."

"Don't," I shouted. "Run. This bitch is going to kill us anyway. She plugged all the Germans, but not for us. Shit, she already took a shot at me." I waved the lock in my free hand. "Just run. Marco's got to be around. You can make it to the truck before she can."

I thought she would hit me with the gun, but she didn't. Instead, her grasp around my neck got tighter, python like. I dropped the lock.

"You know, *signorina* Muro, or whoever you are, Marco's still around."

"He has orders to stay at his truck," she barked. Then laughed. "I can take care of him."

"How about a deal? The tapes for Paolo?" Turner said.

"No deals, Detective Turner. I gave you that gun. I know how many bullets you have left. Zero. Save your partner and yourself." She began counting, "One, two…."

"How do I know you'll keep your end of the bargain?" Turner said.

"You don't," Laura said, stopping the clock for a moment. "You will just have to trust me."

"Give me a moment," he said.

"You have three left," she said. "Two, one…."

"Okay!" he shouted.

"A wise decision. I always knew you were smart. Too smart to be a policeman, perhaps," she said.

"Not smart enough it appears," Turner replied.

"Enough talk. Come out slowly. First throw the gun out. Then you walk out slowly, hands in the air, with the tapes in your hand and visible."

"Don't," I screamed again. "Fuck her."

"Too late for that now, my love," she murmured in my ear.

"She's got us, Paolo. I could never make it to the truck." Then a black handled Beretta flew through the air and thumped about five feet away from us. "I'm coming out. No fireworks."

I sagged in Laura's grip. "My leg hurts," I said, hoping to distract her. She kneed me in the back and I fell forward to the ground, moaning.

"Hey, Paolo?"

"Run. I'm a dead man," I said through the pain.

"Have no fear, Rossi is fine. Come out, Detective Turner. Slowly. Hands in the air, one step at a time, just as I asked, and we'll all be done in a moment." She had her pistol trained on me.

Turner saw me lying there. His hands were up and the canister holding the tapes was in his right hand.

"That's fine, Detective. Stop before you get to Detective Rossi and then throw me the tapes. Understood?"

He nodded and walked slowly toward me, stopping a few feet from me. "You all right?"

This was it. She wasn't going to skip leaving two witnesses. No. It was not going to be that way at all. I thought about Libby and I was going to cry. Somewhere in California, was she thinking of me? Was she worried about me? When my father died, I wasn't around, so I often thought about that exact time he passed on. What was I doing? Was I thinking of him? What was he thinking as his last breath rose out of him?

"I told you to…" I began, but my partner waved me off with a look.

"Tosca, you're not," he said to Laura.

Laura tilted her head, toying with him. "*Come?*"

"You definitely killed Scarpia, a few Scarpias," he said, looking over to the dead Germans around us. "Man, you even jumped over the parapet for old Paolo there," he said, pointing down to the grave on the level below us.

I winced. "Ham…" I sounded a little like Libby when I've

embarrassed her.

He looked at me and smiled, as if to say, "Be patient." He turned back to Laura. "You're a fine falcon, too…"

"And who is he," she shot back, pointing her gun at me, "Cavaradossi? And you, Angelotti?" Funny thing was she was playing along, as if Turner were really getting to her. She was a woman, and he was Turner, and he was getting to her. Who the fuck was she working for?

She waved the gun nonchalantly around in her right hand. "In the opera, Cavaradossi dies. By a bullet if I remember correctly."

"Tosca dies too," Turner said.

"I can assure you that I won't be killing myself for either of you." She stood there, reflective, the gun muzzle lightly touching those juicy lips of hers. "I don't care if you believe me or not. Gaetano was my brother and I'm going to clear our family's name. I don't trust you, or Ettore, or Gladio to help me. Gladio thinks I am working for them. In Italy, however, you must help yourself," she said. Then quietly, "Guarda," she smiled, "e' quasi ora."

I tried to stand up. "You're full of *merda*. I don't believe you," I said to her. "You're as dirty as Gladio."

"Don't move," Laura said, now aiming at me. "Stay down."

"Fuck you. You're going to shoot us anyway. I might as well die like a man. Go ahead. Do it," I said. "If you can. Or will you shoot me in the back?" I couldn't move too well but I began to hobble off. I figured she'd shoot and that would at least knock some sense into Turner's head. Maybe he would run off with the tapes.

"Stop," she said to me.

I kept moving, not looking back. I heard the click of the Beretta lever going back as she racked the slide. There was a shot. I cringed. No hit. I was afraid to look back. She'd probably taken out Turner. I turned and her hand was pointed in the air. A warning volley. So, this little honey was less steely than I thought. A real bad guy would have put us down by now. She now pointed the pistol at Turner's head.

"The tapes," she said.

Turner had undoubtedly made the same calculation about her. He faked a toss to her and threw the canister far past her. It landed about thirty feet away.

She watched it arc and then fall.

I couldn't see his face but I just knew he had on the full smile. I could feel the heat.

"Well, now," Turner said. "We seem to be at an impasse."

"Shut up," Laura said. "I'm going to walk to the tapes, and both of you are coming with me, slowly and always five feet behind."

"Negative, Lieutenant. Paolo and I have every intention of walking away from you alive. What we are playing here is called 'chicken' in America. I don't believe you're a freelancer in this. See, you can't be certain of what's in that canister. Probably the tapes are there. But what if they are not because I hid them ten minutes ago? You can kill us first, but alas, you might find the canister empty. You won't find them before the police get here. Your boss man won't like that. What's an empty-handed girl to do when Gladio asks her for the tapes? Let's not think about that. Now your best option—"

"Shut up," Laura said.

And that was the last thing I heard clearly. A deafening engine roar and wind came from lower down the mountain, from the cemetery section below us. It grew louder quickly and was accompanied by whirring rotors. A blue carabinieri helicopter appeared suddenly from below, angled with the tail up and the front low, hugging the mountainside. It bristled with black-suited figures holding long gun barrels, pointed out. It moved in and hovered just above the treetops. With its large forward cannons jutting forward from either side, it seemed a prehistoric monster about to grab its prey. Turner, his hands over his ears, yelled something to me, but I couldn't hear him. He was bent over, pressured by the air turbulence from the copter blades, then pointed toward Gerbino's crypt with one hand. I almost toppled over from the backwash. Laura had turned away from us to face the copter. She ducked behind the tree.

"*Fermatevi. Mani in alto,*" boomed a loudspeaker from the helicopter. Ropes fell out of the ship and men rappelled down, machine guns strapped to their backs. "Hands up," the voice shouted in English now.

It was a sick maze of cops and robbers where no one wore white or black. Turner and I scrambled back toward Gerbino's tomb. I looked back and Laura was in the shooter position. The gun's black mouth faced me, out of which a bullet would come for my head. I think she smiled. I turned away and there, about twenty feet away, was Marco. Finally, Marco was here. Thank God for Marco.

He was behind a tombstone with his weapon, that wonderful machine gun he kept in the front seat. I felt like screaming, "Where the fuck were you, Marco? Goddamn you, Marco, and your British accent." I was standing directly between Marco and Laura. His muzzle was also pointed directly at my head. He, too, wore a wide smile. His cap was pushed jauntily to one side, as if he were shooting in a game. I ate dirt again, throwing myself down with the kind of force I didn't think I had left. I cut my face on a rock. Turner was already up to Gerbino's. I covered the back of my head with my hands, waiting for my skull to be blown open.

The ground rumbled with the thudding of SWAT team boots hitting dirt. No shots had been fired yet. For a moment there was just the whooshing of the blades slowing down, like a dog panting. No voices. Nothing else. And then I heard two different reports: one clearly from a pistol, one from an automatic, then yelling. Orders in Italian by several shouting voices. I was so tired I couldn't understand a fucking thing.

Somebody lightly touched my leg. I lay still, with my hands over the back of my head. My head was intact. No brains that I could feel.

Then I heard a voice that sounded like Marco, but I wasn't sure. The blades were loud. He was talking in Italian to someone standing above me. "No, he's with us." Then I heard Turner's voice.

"Paolo, it's okay," he said, bending down to me. "Can you get up?" He grabbed me by the hand and pulled gently.

I looked up and rolled on my side. Turner was standing there with Marco and a SWAT guy next to him. "A holy trinity, if ever I saw one," I said, wiping the dirt out of my mouth. Turner helped me up. Back behind us Laura lay on the ground, two SWAT men standing over her. The helicopter had moved off and set down where there was some open space. I watched as a couple of regular powder blue Polizia Urbana Alfa Romeos sped up the road to us, followed by ambulances.

Behind us, near La Saracena's grave, Gretzman lay prone and motionless. He wasn't moaning, and from where we were standing, I couldn't see if his rib cage was moving. A SWAT guy was taking his pulse.

I limped over to Laura, leaving Turner and Marco behind, but the men in black motioned me off. I turned to Marco, and he gave them the thumbs-up for me. They backed off a bit. I bent down. Her face was no longer pretty, with one intact eye open, just as she was shoved into the *al di la*. I couldn't shut it. There was a bloody mess of brains splattered on the tree behind her. I walked silently back to Gerbino's tomb.

"I don't think she would have killed us," Turner said. "That's why I took the risk. Otherwise I would have been long gone."

"She had it in her," I said.

"I didn't say she was incapable…only that she wouldn't," he said, putting his hand on my shoulder.

"We're like the American cavalry, eh?" Marco said, his voice sounding a little too chipper for the occasion. There was a medal, maybe a promotion, in this for the rookie. His picture was going to be on the front page of every paper in Italy. Us, too, and I could just see

Dunne's neck veins bulging.

"You okay?" Turner asked me again.

"Think so." I touched my thigh. The bleeding had slowed but it still hurt.

He turned to our minder: "You know, Marco, you cut it pretty close. It would have been better if you had made an appearance earlier."

Marco seemed genuinely hurt by the remark.

"But, Detective Turner, I couldn't. I had orders. There were four of them, five if you count Tenente Muro. I heard the gunfire, but I didn't know where you were. I did not see you. You could have been dead already. I thought Detective Rossi was dead. What chance did I have against five? They had several automatic weapons." But his face showed something else.

"You mean that you didn't know about *us*, either, right?" I said. "You didn't trust us."

"It was a confusing situation. We knew about Tenente Muro, but we had very little information on you two," Marco said. "Major Ettore ordered me to stay at the truck until the helicopter came, and that's what I did. Through my rifle scope"—he pretended to hold a rifle and look through the telescopic lens—"I saw the tenente had a gun to Detective Rossi's head. But I couldn't fire. They were too close together and I was too far away. I could not risk coming closer and being seen. There was no way to get a clean shot until much later, when the copter arrived and all of you ran," he said.

"Talking about me, eh?" Ettore said in English, walking up from behind us. In his right hand he held the small cylindrical canister, which I'd completely forgotten about. The object of desire for investigators, dozens of families of the murdered, scores of Italian journalists, millions of Italians, and whoever sent the Germans and my late girlfriend.

I looked at my partner.

"Hey, I didn't tell them where to find it," Turner said quickly to me.

We looked at Marco.

"Major, I don't remember you speaking English at our first meeting in Rome," I said. "This country is full of surprises."

Ettore ignored me. He was smiling. Marco wasn't the only cop who was going to get a notch for this. He looked down at his feet a moment and then at us. "I'm sorry. I couldn't tell you much, for obvious reasons. We suspected Dottori had hidden the radar evidence, but we had no clues. We knew Gaetano Muro was involved. After Dottori's suicide... if that's what it was...the trail went cold for many years. But I had always suspected it. The business I gave you about the keys was true. We didn't know that there actually was a key, just that the radar logs from that evening had disappeared," he said, looking at the canister. The latch was off. "And when Tenente Muro showed up to help you out, well, we knew you were on to something."

"Why didn't you warn us she was no carabinieri?" Turner said.

Ettore exhaled. "First, she *is* a carabiniere, and is...was Muro's sister. Second, we needed time to find out how she'd penetrated the investigation. Unfortunately, there are people even in the carabinieri and SISMI who answer to outsiders and not to the chain of command, just as there are in the NYPD. I knew her presence meant your investigation was being taken seriously by those outsiders who no doubt were interested in the radar evidence, just as much, if not more than ourselves. Third, we had Marco, here, protecting you. Did you know he graduated in the top five percent of his class?"

"Who are the outsiders? Gladio?" I asked.

"Please, Detective Rossi. Let's not overblow this. There are corrupt people in our country, just as there are in America. Some of them have influence, power, that they shouldn't have in a democracy."

"How do we know you're not one of them?" I said. Out of the corner of my eye, I could see Marco frown.

Ettore let out a "Beh." That stung, evidently. "Anyway, I will suppose you must trust me."

I heard that too much lately. His manner dropped several degrees colder and he turned to go. "One more thing. On behalf of the country, SISMI, and the carabinieri, I thank you for helping us find this tape. Our gratitude allows us to overlook the fact that you carried and fired weapons illegally in Italy, a crime equivalent to what you call in your country a felony." He moved off a step and turned back to us.

"The thing that makes me a little uneasy is this," he said, scratching his temple. Ettore pulled out a reel, *one* reel, with the radar tape spooled through it, and held it aloft, examining it as if he could read the tape straightaway. "Now, I'm just a lawyer. Not a real policeman, mind you. And yet…" He put his hand around the reel, so that it was enclosed in the grip of his fingers. Then he held it up to me. "There's a number two marked on this spool."

We stood there wordlessly.

"I'm guessing there might be a number one tape somewhere. What do you think, eh?" he said, now looking at the marked side, turning it over a few times, then slipping the tape back into the canister.

"Logical," I said.

"We'll discuss this later, after we take your statements." Ettore turned and walked away, talking to no one in particular but loud enough for us to hear. "Don't waste that gratitude. Should you be hiding a tape number one, it will go difficult for you. The Italian people are quite welcoming. Very friendly. But if you cross them…" His voice trailed off. Despite his misgivings, he had a spring to his step. He walked away whistling, joked with some of the SWAT team men, then went to the road to talk to the local police, the Polizia Urbana, who had already put up yellow cordon tape along the road and were extending it on a perimeter around us.

"*La Vendetta*," Turner whispered in a guttural voice under his breath. "There is a Baron Scarpia in this thing after all."

I had to laugh. "That Tosca business was pretty good," I said.

"Hey, I knew she'd know. That's mother's milk here," Turner said.

"Bought us a few seconds. That's what we needed."

Marco seemed confused. "Please. Major Ettore is very happy with you, and you seem displeased."

I looked at Turner now that Ettore was gone. He stared straight into my eyes for a few seconds, then looked away. "Later," was all he said.

Now I knew that somewhere in a small radius of Turner's movements was reel number one, hidden. I wanted to ask him where. But Marco was never out of earshot and now there were dozens of folks walking around. Christ, they all spoke English for all I knew. I didn't want Turner to even look at the hiding place, for fear he'd give off a signal to them.

Two large panel trucks arrived. Out came the evidence collectors, four men in white suits, the back labeled *Polizia Scientifica* in bold black letters, booties, headgear, surgical masks, armed with freezer bags. Two others with video cameras followed.

A stretcher carrying Gretzman came by, and he waved at the attendants to stop. They put him down. The reporter had his right arm taped down tight to his body. The blood flow had been stanched, but his shirt was covered in dried blood. His forehead had an inch wide but not deep gash running across it and his left hand was encased in a temporary soft cast. He had on a huge smile though, which was about the last thing I expected. Then again, he was probably going to get a book out of this.

"I'm glad to see you guys. Hell, I'd be glad to see *Il Duce* himself after what I've just gone through," Gretzman said, looking right at me.

"You all right?" Turner asked. It was surprisingly heartfelt, too. My partner really did like him.

"I thought you were dead," I said, trying to liven things up.

"Can't get me down when I have a good story. Man, I could probably live on this in Italy. A nice little life, too. House in Tuscany. *pied a terre* in Rome. Talk show rounds. A book. Maybe my own TV

230

show. Not a bad thing, considering the showgirls around here. And that cute little newspaper reporter, well I'm sure her attitude toward me will get much warmer," Gretzman mused from the ground.

I looked away. "Glad you're not dead," was all I could muster.

"Thanks. I do believe Detective Rossi is starting to care," he said, and he tried to feign wiping a tear from his eye with his bandaged hand, but it was too painful and he stopped in mid-swipe. The attendant told him in Italian that it was better for him not to move. "No 'Thank you' for helping, eh?" Gretzman said to me.

I said nothing.

"Hey," Gretzman continued. "Who was that *pezzi grossi* with you just now? Mile wide smile."

"Nobody," I said.

Marco interjected, "Inspector Maggiore Ettore," his voice rising in excitement. "Now I recognize you," he said directly to Gretzman. "You were the fellow outside the building in Piazza Navona and on the ferry, correct?"

Gretzman just smiled. "Funny thing about Ettore and the alleged tape number two I heard him talk about."

The alleged was for Marco's ears. I knew where he was going with this, and I turned to Marco. "Could you please excuse us for a minute?" Marco, for once, seemed defiant, like a teen making his first stand. He was probably thinking he was part of our posse, the boys who solved Ustica. He didn't even respond and just walked away miffed.

Gretzman winced as he shifted in the stretcher. The Italian attendants were grumbling and getting antsy, wanting to get him back to the hospital and themselves to lunch probably. "Seems like the major has the wrong idea."

"What's that, Gretzman?" I probably should have shut up or walked away.

"Well, if I saw correctly, he had just one tape reel."

I remained silent. Turner walked over to Marco.

"I know it was dark in that crypt, but that generally doesn't affect my hearing. I distinctly heard you say 'tapes.' I think that you specified two."

I looked around. There was no one within earshot except the EMS guys. "Think what you want, Gretzman. Write what you want. I'm not going to correct your mistakes. An error like that can get you killed in this country. Us, too."

"I do believe you really care," Gretzman replied, putting his bandaged but movable left hand to his heart. "Don't worry about me, Detective Rossi."

"I don't," I shot back, wanting to end the conversation.

Gretzman looked at me, cocked his head to one side, and smiled. "*Andiamo*," he said aloud to his attendants, with an imperial wave of his left arm. He was about ten feet away, passing Laura's body, now covered in black plastic, when he yelled, "Sorry about your girlfriend, Detective Rossi." Moments later they loaded him into the ambulance and took off. Over by the Germans and Laura, the white suit guys were still bent over taking samples, shoe prints, blood, hair, and pictures, lots of pictures. They pulled the Ape driver out of his vehicle. One of the local cops was crying.

"You should get that leg looked at," Turner said to me.

We left for the local Polizia Urbana station, a tiny thing of four rooms and two cars outside. It was right in the center of town, across the street from the town's lone hospital and cinema. Playing at the theater that night was a showing of *The Rocky Horror Picture Show*. On the old-fashioned hand-lettered marquee was, "Don't dream it. Just be it," in English. I knew where the local padre would be that evening.

I had my leg looked at, and Ettore's men came to interview us at the station, but not until the late afternoon. He had the evidence now and was going to make the most of it. What we said didn't matter much. We were lame ducks to him, not knowing he didn't have both tapes. Maybe one was all that was needed to explain things.

232

The clouds broke and the sun came out around 4 p.m. We weren't all that far from North Africa and it didn't take long for the temperature to shoot up. There was no air conditioning in the station. When I asked about it, a cop said it was broken and that it had been broken for as long as he was working there. "Don't worry, it would be fixed eventually," he said sarcastically.

After question time was over, Marco came in to tell us that Ettore had arranged for a helicopter ride for us direct to Rome. "If we hurry, we could be in Rome tonight," he said. I guessed he missed his German girlfriend.

"The maggiore will be on TV tonight," he went on. "*The Mauro Costa Show*. He's making a special taping, then he goes on *Faccia A Faccia*, a political talk show which often ends up in a huge row between the guests."

"And I thought he didn't like the press."

Turner smirked.

"Marco," I said, and the weariness must have been telegraphed from my face. I was beginning to feel like a party-pooping parent. "We're gonna take the ferry back."

"But…"

"Don't worry, we'll make it. Anyway, what if the tape's a washout?"

Marco's face took a quizzical turn. His eyebrows scrunched up, and he looked to my partner, as if for a translator. "What means this 'washout'?"

"The tapes might not show anything at all. Have you thought of that possibility?" I think I said it too harshly.

Marco's face turned from questioning to what was almost pity. "But it doesn't matter what the tape shows or doesn't show," he said kindly, as if he were talking to someone on the cusp of senility, or maybe a dog. "For us, it matters only that it's *the* tape," he said.

We had to get the other tape.

"There's something we have to do…tonight…here. We need your

help, Marco," I said. I expected hesitation, a short talk about how he could get into lots of trouble. "*I guai*," I repeated in Italian.

Instead, he asked me if he had to keep it a secret from Ettore.

I said, "Yes," wearily, anticipating a no from him.

"In that case," Marco said, "yes." He was trying to give us a sign that he was with us. I guessed the excitement had changed him. It was his entrance fee. He wanted to be part of our gang.

CHAPTER 17

SUNDAY NIGHT

Marco agreed to come back with us to the cemetery that night, even though we didn't tell him why. After my leg, chest, and face were bandaged, we had an early dinner in town and waited until the sun began to set, around eight o'clock. There would still be a police detail up there guarding the crime scene. But we needed enough light for Turner to find the tape. At 8:15 we piled into the Land Rover and headed up to the grounds. I sat in the front alongside Marco, and Turner lay across the backseat, armed only with a small penlight. As we pulled up the switchback road to Gerbino's, I looked back and saw the town lights come on, candle flickers against a Mediterranean turning a sweet purple around us. The sky finally cleared and the moon rose in the east, bright yellow, the cracks in its face just becoming visible.

There was a Polizia Urbana Alfa Romeo at a point in the road that was directly across from Gerbino's. One blue was standing alongside it, smoking a cigarette and looking down at the town. It appeared to be only a one-man detail. Apart from the SWAT team, which left, there weren't too many cops on the island to begin with. He was on a cell phone as we pulled up past him. The cop looked at us, puzzled, and walked toward our truck even before we'd come to a halt. He had an automatic slung across his chest. He threw away the butt.

"We need to go about twenty feet past Gerbino's," Turner whispered.

"Roger that," Marco said. "Are we breaking into another tomb?" he asked, with not a little excitement.

I looked back at my partner to see his reaction to Marco's sudden adoption of American jargon and policing methods, and quickly realized my mistake, but not before Turner whispered a hard, "What the fuck you looking at, Paolo? You are going to give me away." I quickly turned forward again. "No. No breaking and entering this time, Marco."

"Okay, in position," Marco said. "He's coming. We need to get out before he gets to us. Detective Turner, you need to open your door slightly just as we do so he doesn't hear the lock unlatch." We jumped out but tried not to look jumpy.

. The cop had reached the back of the Land Rover before Marco greeted him and brought his progress to a halt. We were on either side of the truck facing him and blocking his way past the truck. Before we could even make pleasantries, the cop, who was about six foot three and easily two hundred and twenty pounds, complained loudly, "You are not supposed to be here," in Italian.

"You know who we are," Marco replied.

"And you know you aren't allowed in this area. So get back in the truck and leave. Don't make trouble for me," the cop said. He aimed his flashlight into the truck through the back window and I thought it was all up, but he was distracted and didn't see Turner, who got as low as he could on the car floor.

"Look…" Marco searched the cop's badge for a name, "…Rossi. Oh, Rossi," Marco said, turning to me. "He has the same name as you."

I smiled stupidly.

"Maybe you are related," he said, turning back to the cop, "to our American policeman Rossi. He was hurt in the shootout today."

"Yeah, and maybe we're both related to the star of the '82 World

Cup, but I don't have time for this," the cop shot back, almost in a snarl, before Marco could finish. "It's just me up here and I have to watch the whole fucking cemetery, so get back in your truck and move on."

"Okay, easy. You don't have to bite," Marco said apologetically.

"It's my fault, paisano," I said, hoping my Italian would be understandable.

He looked over at me. I pulled out a pack of Camels and offered him one. He took it and seemed to relax slightly. I pulled out my lighter and gave it to him.

"There was a woman killed here today," I said, scratching my head. "And..." I faked a stammer, "And...and, well..." I turned away, as if hiding a good cry.

"He just wants to go to the spot again," Marco jumped in, "where his girl died, that's all. Say a prayer or something."

Officer Rossi took another drag on his cigarette, spit out the smoke upward into the rapidly descending night air, and then looked over our truck again.

"Okay," he said with a half frown. "Sorry about your girl but make it fast. The *sergente*, a Milanese bastard, sometimes gets it into his head to check up on me, and if he finds you two here, my nuts are roasted, understand?"

We nodded and I pointed in the direction of the tree where Tenente Muro had breathed her last. We walked slowly over to give Turner as much time as we could, past the Polizia Urbana car, past where the bodies, the black Mercedes, and the shot-up Ape had all been earlier that day. All that was gone now. A couple of little white marker flags were sticking up out of the ground, left by the forensics team. Empty shells. Red flags in six spots. Dead bodies. One was right about where Laura's head had rested that day.

We had our backs to the truck now. I figured Turner was already out the door and on the way to the tape. I kneeled and kissed the ground, then whispered in English, "Oh, Laura. Why did you have to get mixed up in this?" On my knees, I put my hands flat against the ground.

That provoked Officer Rossi, "Sbrigatevi!" ("Move it!") Then he added, "Come on," in English, tapping me on the foot. I ignored that and he tapped me again. I got up slowly, hung my head low, and kept my hands at my side. I turned and faced him, so that now I could see the truck behind him.

"Do you have a woman?" I said to him in as sad a tone as I could muster. I rubbed my eyes, as if to wipe away a tear or two.

"I'm married," he answered gruffly. His back was to the truck and Turner's position.

"Do you love her?" I said.

"She's my wife," the cop replied.

It had gotten dark enough that I could occasionally make out Turner's bouncing light fifty or so feet away as he pointed it one way and then another. I tried to ignore it so Officer Rossi wouldn't notice a wandering eye. Marco was nervous and our friend sensed it. We were going to have to wrap this up quick. That's when I hit the right note.

"Do you have a girlfriend?" I asked Officer Rossi. I think it disarmed him. Had Marco asked him that, no doubt he would have told him to mind his own fucking business, but with me, he was civil.

"I know a woman in Palermo, if that's what you mean. I see her once in a while."

"And if she were killed?" I said.

"I'd be unhappy," he replied, adding, "but not for long. I'd find another skirt, and, friend, that's what I advise you to do. As quickly as possible."

The officer smiled a silly grin, as if he thought he'd just said the wisest thing in the world. "Yes. I'm sorry to be a hard ass, but this is a big case, though nobody is saying why. Do you guys know? I've heard it's about Ustica. Can that be? The plane crash twenty-two years ago?"

Now it was Marco's turn. "Well, we can't say anything about it,

Officer Rossi. You know, rules are rules," he said, emphasizing the last three words as a parry.

"Oh, come on. A return favor here," he said. "It could be big trouble for me, letting you back on the crime scene like I did," he said, almost like a begging child. "Give me something. Is it Ustica?"

At just that moment I saw Turner sneak back toward the Land Rover. In a moment he was inside the car.

"Well, thanks very much, Officer Rossi," I said. "We don't want to get you in hot water."

Marco and I continued walking back to the truck, but so did he.

"Come on," he repeated. "Ustica?"

I heard him right behind me and realized that if he came all the way to the side of the Land Rover, he'd spot Turner for sure. I stopped short, and, behind me, Officer Rossi almost walked into me.

Marco turned around to face me. The lines on his face had coalesced into worry. I motioned him to the truck with my eyes.

"Let me tell him, Marco," I said. Marco moved to the driver side and jumped in the car. Behind the Land Rover, I put my arm around Rossi's shoulder. "Tomorrow, Officer Rossi, you are going to read a lot of things in the newspaper. Not all of it will be true, but some of it will."

He looked me right in the eyes. It was Ustica, he was thinking. And like all Italy, he wanted to know and not know at the same time. He was afraid the answer would be too difficult to bear. He pushed the black muzzle of his automatic to one side. "Tell me," he whispered.

"Yes, it has to do with Ustica," I said quietly.

"Holy Mother of God," he exclaimed.

"Now listen. We haven't solved anything, just found some more clues."

Officer Rossi didn't look at me, just straight ahead. "After all these years," he murmured.

From the driver's seat Marco yelled, "Let's go. The last ferry leaves in a few minutes." There was no hint in his voice of anything. No indication of what Turner had found out there.

"I've got to go," I said to the cop, but he didn't pay me any mind. He was hypnotized into silence. I turned and got in the car. "We're clear," I said. I looked back out the window and out of the corner of my eye I saw Turner slumped down across the backseat foot wells. Something was wrong.

When we were out of the cop's sight, I turned. He looked sick. I didn't see anything in his hands.

He sat up on the backseat and looked out the window, at something that seemed far, far away. "It wasn't there, Paolo."

Marco jammed on the brakes and we jerked forward. Even he was surprised. He turned around. "What do you mean?" We had just passed the old iron gates of the cemetery entrance.

"Are you sure you went to the exact same place?" I asked Turner, ignoring Marco's question.

Turner just stared out the window. I thought he was going to cry.

"I left it at a grave by the name of Verdi, exactly fifteen tombstones from Gerbino." He was speaking just above a whisper, and a weird laugh came out. "It was made to order. The bullets were flying and there I was by a tombstone with the same name as the great one himself. Easy to remember. There was a bouquet of fresh flowers there, sitting on the grave in a little green container. I dumped the water out, put it at the bottom and put the flowers back on top. Perfect."

I was so crazed with confusion that I began to doubt my partner. I started to doubt myself. Who was there that was still alive? Did I miss someone? Did Ettore or Gladio have extra men around that we didn't see? There was just the three of us, plus Marco, who was way up at the truck until the end.

"Gretzman," I shouted. "That fucker."

"What are you talking about, partner?" Turner said. "He was practically dead."

"Maybe, and maybe he wasn't as hurt as he let on. He was the only person still alive—that we know of—in a position close enough to see what you were doing. He did it. He somehow, during all the shit going down, picked himself up and got the tape." There, I'd let out our secret.

"There *is* another tape?" Marco let out loudly. He looked straight ahead at the road, as if he didn't want to show his face.

"You sure you aren't letting your love for the reporter get in the way here, partner?" Turner asked. "I mean the guy was fucked up real bad."

"Not fucked up enough," I said. "We're through underestimating that guy. He followed us all the way from New York. He saw his opportunity with us occupied and took it. Didn't you see how happy he was even though he was so bandaged and banged up?" I put my hand to my forehead. "We've been played, Ham. Big time. He was taunting us. Remember he'd heard Ettore talk about one tape."

"If he stole the tape, why would he mention that?" Marco said.

"Because he's very smart and very arrogant," I answered. "He's got to have it."

Turner edged over to my way of thinking. "The scribe wasn't that far away. He certainly could have seen me," he said, "and I wasn't looking at him." He took his head in his hands, running his hands through his hair, as if he were trying to bring back the picture. "Yeah, I remember he'd tried to stand at one point. Then I saw him flat out. I don't recall whether his eyes were open."

"He saw you," I yelled, hoping my emphasis would bring it home to him.

"Yeah, yeah, yeah," Turner said, each successive "yeah" getting stronger, as if he were convincing himself.

"But he was so injured," Marco said. "He had to be carried off."

"There was nothing so terribly wrong with him that he couldn't do it," I said. Then I remembered Marco. "And what about you? Did you see him moving around?"

"Me? No," Marco said. "I was up by the truck. I could see no one."

His response had a scintilla of worry in it, as if we might suspect him. It surprised me. "When did you get back to the area? You know, when you shot Laura."

"I was ordered to stay at the truck until the helicopter arrived. And that's what I did. From my position, since I was higher up, I watched the helicopter churning across the sky, and as soon as they got close I ran down to your position, hoping she hadn't killed you. I saw the reporter on the ground and that's when I saw you and Turner running, and when I shot Laura. I didn't see Mr. Gretzman get up at all." Then, almost as an afterthought, he said, "But I didn't have my eyes on him at all times."

"He did get up," I said, my voice getting louder again. "He's got the other tape."

Marco put the truck in gear and we shot down to town. The hospital, more like a clinic, was run by some Franciscan nuns. We rushed in, flying by the front desk, and, instinctively, when I saw a woman walking down the corridor in a flowing black and white robe, I slowed down, as if I were back in St. Luke's grammar school.

"We're looking for a Mr. Gretzman," I told her in Italian. "He was hurt earlier today."

She looked confused. She'd probably never heard the name Gretzman in her life.

"The American from the cemetery," I added.

"He's in 105."

As we hurried down the hall, I could hear her calling after us, "*Signori, signori,* gli'orario di visita sono finite (Visiting hours are over)."

The way we burst into the room just about sent Gretzman out the window after what he'd been through. Took him a second to notice it was us and not folks who wanted to slash his throat.

"Where's the tape?" I yelled at him. I was right in his face. He must have been sleeping because his eyes were blinking furiously from the

242

light. I grabbed him by the one good shoulder and he let out a pained scream.

"Ow! Hey, get your fucking hands off me, black shirt," Gretzman shouted.

Turner put his hand on my back. "Paolo."

I composed myself, letting my hand slip from Gretzman, but I stayed right on top of him. "Where's the fucking tape?" I said as calmly as if I'd be asking him to pass the salt, all the words with serenity except when I said "fucking," which I shouted so loudly that the nun, who had followed us in, heard it. Her face turned red. I guess she understood some English.

"Geez," Gretzman said, lying back down in his bed, trying to put some distance between us. "You don't even knock. Unnecessary roughness penalty. You got the sister upset at your language. And I don't have to tell you—much as I'm touched by your visit—that visiting hours *are* over."

I didn't even look back, though I know the nun was behind me. "Gretzman, I'm going to ask you one more time. Where's the tape?"

"You know, I'm not sure I like you with that attitude." He motioned to the nun that he wanted us out, holding up his hand and waving it, then pointing to the door.

The nun came into the room. "I'm sorry, gentlemen, but it's too late for visitors now. The patient needs rest. You can come back tomorrow," she said in Italian.

That's when an unruffled Marco, with his dark blue uniform, the red stripes down the pants, and white shoulder sash, came through for us again. Marco looked every inch the authority he represented.

"Sister," he said in Italian. "We're here on police business. An investigation…you know…of the unfortunate events in the cemetery this morning."

She looked down and crossed herself. "Oh, how horrible. It's not enough the plane crash has forever linked this island to that plane

243

tragedy, now all these murders. It's such a quiet town, normally."

"We just need a moment with Mr. Gretzman. We won't be long and I promise we won't disturb the other patients."

She nodded and silently moved to the door. Before she exited, she said, "Is it true that this American man has something to do with that plane?" she said.

"That's what we're here to find out, Sister," Marco said, gently closing the door on her.

As soon as I heard the click, Turner and I went into action. Marco stood guard at the door. We opened every drawer and closet there was. There was a small night table by the wall. I emptied it and moved it away from the wall. Turner went into the bathroom and uprooted anything that wasn't attached. I opened the window and checked on the windowsill.

"What the fuck are you guys doing?" Gretzman shouted.

"Keep it down," Marco said.

I went through his jacket and pants. Nothing.

"Let's move him." We grabbed Gretzman to move him off the bed.

"This is bullshit!" he screamed. There was a knock at the door. The sister had returned, asking to know what was wrong.

Marco pulled out his Beretta and aimed it at Gretzman's forehead. The reporter froze and let us pull him off the bed. His protests turned to muttering as we slipped him into the chair nearby.

"That fucking hurts," he said. A wet red spot appeared on the bandage around his left hand, at the palm.

"Sister," Marco said through the door. "Everything is okay. Not to worry." He waved his pistol at Gretzman again.

"Todos okay…I mean *tutto* okay, Sister," Gretzman said reluctantly in the direction of the door. He started moaning again. "You guys think I have the tape, huh?" He smiled wickedly.

We said nothing. I turned over the bed and looked under the box spring and between the mattresses. Nothing. I thought about ripping them open, but he couldn't have had the time or the ability. There was nothing else in the room to check.

"You fucking lost it, didn't you," Gretzman said, and he laughed and then stopped because the shaking hurt him. "You fuck up, lose the tape, and right away I'm to blame."

"We didn't lose it. You took it."

"I did not," Gretzman shot back. "But I wish I had because at least we'd know where it was. By rights I should have it. If I had been able to get up from that crypt floor, I would have taken it."

"You have it. You're the only one who could have taken it from the hiding place."

"Yeah, well, you searched this place and it's not here. Why don't you check the ambulance? That's the only other place I been today since the cemetery. Hey, check my asshole while you're at it." He tried to bend over but couldn't.

I looked at Turner and Marco. We were adrift. He had to have it. Maybe he did hide it in the ambulance, though how would he retrieve it? I asked Marco to find out if Gretzman had any visitors and he went out to speak with the front desk.

"Can you at least put me back on the bed?" Gretzman asked. "I can hardly walk, and you guys think that I up and grabbed the tape while fucking bullets were flying. You're sick. I'm lucky to be alive. Fuckin' *Post* owes me hazardous work pay."

"You can walk," I grunted. We lifted him back to the bed. "He snuck it out somehow. Maybe a visitor who didn't check in," I said.

"What's wrong with you?" Turner asked Gretzman.

"Yeah, right," he said pointedly to me. "I got a ricochet hole in my arm," he moved his right shoulder forward as proof, "and my left hand's practically got a stigmata bullet wound."

I was calmer now and took a closer look at Gretzman. Face was cut up. Couple of stitches above the right eyebrow. Right shoulder in a cast and left hand completely bandaged over, so there was probably little use of it. Even if he had lifted the tape, it was unlikely he could even hold on to it, let alone hide it somewhere on an island he didn't know.

Marco returned. "No visitors," he said.

I slumped into his chair. Turner went to the window. He pulled out a Rothmans. No smoking in hospitals here was enforced the same way it was elsewhere in this country. If you could get away with it, you did it.

"Hey, you can't smoke in here," Gretzman said.

The clinic was on a bluff that overlooked the ocean, and we could hear the waves splashing against this piece of lava. We were screwed. Totally and with some finality.

"Maybe it was that Third Man, again," Gretzman said to me. "Or a Fourth Man," he giggled.

I sat there staring straight ahead. I just barely made out what Gretzman had said. The people who could have had the tape were right here in this room.

"Hey, there were a dozen SWAT guys around us. Maybe your friend Ettore has it," Gretzman said, pointing as best he could to the TV above his bed. It was on when we came in, but the sound was down.

"Turn it up," I said wearily.

"Yeah, right," Gretzman said, looking at his useless hands and holding them out as best he could. Marco took the remote and raised the volume.

It was Ettore in a nice suit on *The Mauro Costa Show*. The host was a fat little man who moved from guest to guest, bent over and practically whispering into each ear, as if they had secrets to keep but might reveal to the audience. But this night it was Ettore alone. Why a SISMI fellow would be on TV was not something I could figure, unless it was a signal of how important Ustica was in the Italian psyche. Maybe he wasn't SISMI. The government had to say something. It's been such a huge fuckup from day one.

"This action on Ustica today is somehow connected to the plane crash?" Costa asked.

"Yes, we believe that's true and we should have confirmation very soon."

"Is that because you are looking at the famous hidden radar tapes? My sources say you have them. You recovered them this morning on Ustica...of all places."

Ettore looked away from his host and smiled, and then he ignored the question, like the government spook he was. "Actually, the most important key to the case was found earlier today," he said. "I should say it's a person who stepped forward, after more than two decades, someone who knew one of the passengers. She'd heard about the shoot-out on the news today."

"Tell us more," Mauro cooed.

"This person, who worked at a bank in Bologna at the time and was a close friend of one of the unfortunate passengers on the plane, has given us information that leads us to believe..." Ettore paused, "... that the aircraft was intentionally destroyed to get one man on the plane." Ettore was looking straight into the camera. I figured he wanted to send a message to the right person.

From the television you could hear the audience gasp loudly. The cameras cut quickly to angry faces on some men, women crying. In Gretzman's room, the nun, who'd returned, was aghast. After a "Madonna *mia*," her mouth was open in a perfect O. Marco was silent.

Gretzman sensed something was up. "Whad'ee say?"

I waved at him and shushed him.

"And what of the radar tapes?" Costa murmured quietly to his guest.

But Ettore held tough and would have none of it. "I have no tapes that reveal anything." Strange kind of denial. *No tapes that reveal anything.* Maybe the tape was going to disappear again. Or his tape, number two, didn't show anything useful.

"And what of these Americans on the case? CIA?" Costa asked.

Turner heard "*Americani*" and asked if they were talking about us.

"The Americans," Ettore replied, "are following the murder of Colonel Muro in New York last week. Two of the guns found with the dead East Germans this morning on Ustica were the weapons that killed Colonel Muro, as well as his American wife and an Italian national who worked at the consulate in New York. That I can confirm."

"Well," I said to nobody in particular. "Thanks for telling us."

"What?" Turner said.

Marco explained to him what Ettore had said.

"Is Gladio involved in this?" Costa asked.

"I don't know," Ettore replied. "We are trying to find out. And that's all I can say." Then Ettore left the stage and the speculation that Costa was well known for began.

"Gentlemen, really. It's getting late," the nun said. "I must ask you to come back and visit tomorrow."

We shuffled out. "Take it easy, Gretzman," Turner said. I left without looking back. Marco waved at the patient.

Turner was the last one out, and as he moved to the doorway, Gretzman said, "Hey, can I talk to you?" I stopped in the hallway. "Not you, Rossi, just Turner. Alone."

"We're a unit," Turner said to him. "You got something to say to me, you can say it to both of us."

The nun was getting impatient.

"Yeah, well, you're not thinking this through," Gretzman said.

"Go on, listen to what he has to say," I said to Turner. "Don't worry about me." But it was too late. The nun barred the door, and my partner wasn't about to go through her.

"Too bad for you," Gretzman said as the door closed behind us.

Lunedi

The Baron left his home to walk to his office at exactly 7 a.m. every working day and exactly along the same route, just as he'd done for the past fifty years. He'd go south along Via Brera, where his eighteenth-century palazzo was located, then along Via Verdi. At the corner where Verdi met Via Alessandro Manzoni, at Il Teatro Della Scala, he'd make a right and walk around the front and along Manzoni—it was shorter to go behind the opera house but he enjoyed going around the front—and then a quick right to Via Filodrammatici.

Occasionally, novice reporters waylaid him along the path as the sun rose, thinking they'd pry some scoop out of his old hide, the great White Whale. The very first thing an aspiring Italian journalist learned was that one quote from the Baron would make a career. The second thing they learned was the sphinxlike qualities of the Baron. In that half century, he never once so much as even acknowledged any reporter's existence with a raised eyebrow or pursed mouth, let alone uttered a syllable in response to a question from such rabble.

The Baron, slightly hunched forward from eighty-five years on this earth, gnarled hands entwined behind his back, his head pointed downward, walked as if he were intently interested in his shoe tops. He knew the way so well he didn't have to look. It was said there was an indentation in the pavement along the route he took, exactly the width of a wan, seventy-kilo, octogenarian. During the 1970s and early 1980s, when the shooting started in Italy, the bank's head of security often tried to talk the Baron out of his method of travel, but the Baron—by that time "honorary" chairman of MilanoBanca, but firmly in control—would have none of it. "I'm nobody," he would say. What he meant was that nobody had the coglioni to touch him.

At that hour on a Monday—most shops were closed Mondays until noon—*the only people on the cobblestone streets in the center of Milan were old folks going to early mass, or an occasional worker from a pasticceria-café. The rest of town was shuttered.*

The Senator had arrived early, buoyed by excitement. In addition to his usual British tailored blue suit, The Senator wore a bright red tie, a sign of his happiness that day. A tray with biscotti and two espressos were on the coffee table near the couch in the Baron's office. He was never late, so the coffee never got cold. The Gnome walked in and sounded a small note of annoyance. He had told his secretary a million times that he didn't want anyone in the office when he arrived, but she, like all Italian secretaries, could not face down someone as powerful as The Senator unless someone more powerful, like the Baron, was present. The Senator had a wide smile on his face.

"You know I don't like red," the Baron harrumphed, coming in and glancing at The Senator. He hung up his coat on the rack by the door.

"I've heard the good news. I saw Costa last night," The Senator said, ignoring the Baron's ill treatment.

"I didn't know you were such an early riser," he said sarcastically.

"Baron, I am aware that your man has the tape."

The Baron liked that he'd said "your man," a submissive admission, the thing one of the weaker members of the pride would say to the head. "I spoke with him yesterday," the older man said. "He'll be here tonight. Finally, this will be over. We should never have sent those goddamn Germans." There was a hint of blame in his tone.

At that, The Senator looked away, toward the balcony that opened on the cortile. "Have you spoken with Prime Minister Berodi?"

"I hope Il Ciuchione reads the papers this morning and immediately shits his pants. He has a mouth like his weak colon. It can't stop spitting out merda. He can wait," said the Baron, who sat down on the couch and sipped his coffee. The Baron's legs dangled above the floor, and he moved them back and forth nervously, as a child might.

The Senator nodded. "And the Americans?"

"What about them?" the Baron shot back. His mood wasn't particularly good at first. He would have to go to a later mass because of the surprise intrusion, and he hated to have his routine upset.

"Exactly. What about them?" The Senator repeated.

The Baron grumbled at this. "No need to remove them now. They've served their purpose and I am assured they haven't seen the tapes. Killing them would only feed the investigation. They'll be back in the land of barbarians tomorrow, none the wiser."

"What if they keep snooping around?"

"They won't," the Baron said with finality. He put the blue and white demitasse cup down, placing it so that his family's crest—something The Senator's family, only one hundred and fifty years from its blacksmith origins, didn't have—faced his old ally. The Baron traced his family's lineage to Calogero Spaccaforte, a knight who had fought valiantly for and was granted a coat of arms by King Ferdinand I of the Two Sicilies in the eighteenth century, and then even further back to the Normans. The crest showed a standing lion, St. Mark's symbol, holding a long, thin cross in one paw and a bloody rapier in the other. The weapon was far larger than the cross.

The Senator, who avoided looking at the emblem even as it attracted his eye, stretched out slightly, his long legs bumping up against the coffee table. "It's a strange world, you know. Us taking care of this problem for Berodi. We should have let him and his party roast back then when the plane went down, when Berodi was just the mayor of Naples. But by helping him then, we now own him, and him a socialist, too."

"Sometimes you must make investments in communists," the Baron added. "Look at our investments in China. These are the bets that pay the best returns."

The Senator sensed the Baron's mood had improved. "Baron, I am the first to respect your silences, your not having told me everything over the years, as I trust your instincts and methods implicitly. But now that we...you have the tapes, perhaps you could explain why a hammer was *used to get Mr. Bancarotta on the plane instead of a pinprick."*

The Baron was obviously enjoying the moment. He felt expansive. "Now that you are seventy-five, I can tell you. Never trust anyone younger than seventy-five, I have always said," he joked. "If Verdi were alive, he'd make an opera of it and I would be the villain," the Baron said with the excitement usually reserved for his machinations.

The Baron sat back on the couch. He held the cup with his left hand and fingered it lightly with his right. He was silent for a moment, looking forward and never once toward The Senator until he was ready. He took the last sip of coffee and put down the cup. "Paradoxically, it was the only way not to attract attention to us," he said.

The Senator raised his white eyebrows slightly.

"Killing Bancarotta in a plane, with eighty other people was my idea," the Baron said. "No one would believe an airliner full of people would be downed for one man. A huge conspiracy machine sprang forth, fully formed and beautiful, like Aphrodite's birth. That diverted attention from him, keeping everyone busy following wild theories about NATO and Libya. And nobody cares about poor Mr. Bancarotta but his mother—and us.

"A more conventional, let us say, terrestrial removal, even had we made it look like an accident, would have been examined by the police, perhaps nosy reporters, working just on his death only. Clues would have been found on the ground instead of lost in the ocean. In that case, Bancarotta's nasty discoveries about our rather piggy Christian Democrat friends would have been exposed," the Baron said.

"Very industrious, that man. Avocato Bancarotta had gotten a hold of blind wire transfers, bearer bonds, found bills from front companies, deposit receipts from the Guernsey Islands, the Caymans, the Swiss. It was a paper trail as long as this country is old. We could not have had the Christian Democrats implode when we had no one to take their place. Without them, the government of the time would have been forced to ask the Communists to join a coalition with it. Our barbarian

American friends would have given us trouble if it came to that. And the Communists were not, at that time, yet accepting our generosity. They could not be allowed into the game then.

"It all could have been different." The Baron turned wistful, one of the few emotions he allowed himself. "If only Bancarotta had listened to reason."

The room went silent.

"But the TV show last evening. Costa. They now suspect that Bancarotta was killed..." The Senator said.

"Yes, yes," the Baron said, waving absentmindedly. "But my man has the tape now. Anyway, there were advantages to our plan," the Baron went on, more to hear himself revel in a successful plan than to tell The Senator. "First, it was the kind of thing the Red Brigades did, so I was sure they would get blamed. Second, and more importantly, we searched his office and his home and even his girlfriend's home after he left for the airport that day. It was the only way we could be certain that Mr. Bancarotta would have all his documents together with him and that we could destroy them all. The sea swallowed them. He was on his way to meet Palermo's head magistrate. That part also you knew already."

"And the Libyan MiGs?" The Senator asked.

The Baron got up and moved to his desk. He grabbed a folder and walked over to the coat rack by the door and grabbed his raincoat. A tiny smile came to his face. He seemed far off in thought.

"Colonel Gaddafi, as you know, owes us many favors. I allow him access to his own money for one thing." The Baron giggled. "The rest I cannot tell even you. Let's just say our trigger-happy cowboy Allies were spoiling for a fight with the 'great dictator' of Libya then." The Baron said the words "great dictator" with a scorn he once reserved for Mussolini.

"The Americans were being embarrassed by the Iranian hostage fiasco, so they took a very unreasonable risk that night against the Libyan MiGs and turned the whole thing into a very unfortunate accident...but extremely fortunate for us. And even though our Colonel Muro was not *responsible for Ustica, we had to throw a veil on it as if Muro had gone ahead and done what we had asked him to do that evening anyway. Muro knew he did nothing, was suspected for years, and went crazy. Just imagine if he had carried out our orders and had killed all eighty-one people. He would have broken much earlier. This was far better for us. God works in mysterious ways. And now that Muro is dead, there are just the three of us who know it. As I said, fortune favors the bold."*

The Baron opened the door with his right hand, on which was a gold ring with a large ruby, the color of pigeon's blood. "I'm going to Mass. Care to join me?"

"No," The Senator said. "Our stains are too deep, wouldn't you say?"

"It's not possible for man to discern Providence's long-term plans. I take solace in that," the Gnome said, shrugging his shoulders. He closed the door behind him, his light step echoing in the hallway outside.

Chapter 18

Monday Afternoon

When the phone rang, I was exhausted. We'd missed the last return ferry to Palermo but Marco arranged for a Carabinieri copter to take us back to Palermo Sunday night and we caught a late plane to Rome. I'd slept late. Turner was gone, probably sightseeing or testing out his newfound fifteen minutes of Italian fame on the local ladies. The sun was shining brightly through the large white-curtained windows. I wondered if I should answer it. Pretty much nobody knew where to find us. Except Ettore. I got up, hoping to get some news, hoping the tapes he had showed something.

"Hi, Daddy," the voice squealed on the other end. The connection was bad and she was so excited that her voice sounded different. Or could it have matured already in the few days away from me?

"Libby?" I said, still half asleep. I rubbed my face with my free hand and looked at the clock—3 p.m.

"Yes, Daddy. It's me. I'm so happy to hear your voice. Are you okay? We heard you were hurt."

"Peanut?" I said again.

"Yes, *Dad*, it's me," Libby said, and there was some more of the tone that I knew well, the barely suppressed humoring of an adult's befuddlement.

"No. I'm fine. Geez, it must be…" I looked again at the clock trying to do the math quickly. "Geez, it must be five a.m. in Cali."

"No, Daddy, it's just nine a.m. We're back in New York. When we heard you and Uncle Hamilton cracked the case and that you got those guys, Mom figured it was safe to come back. She didn't like Cali. The mayor's office called us. We took the red eye last night. We just got in." Then I heard some rustling behind her on the phone. I heard her say firmly to someone there, "Just another minute, please."

"Who's there with you? Your mother?"

"Yeah, there are a few people here. Everybody's pretty excited. I'm very proud of you, Dad. I think Mom is too, but she won't say it. You're okay, right?"

"Yes. Yes. We haven't actually solved much," I said. I sat up in bed. There was commotion in the background. I heard a voice that was recognizable whispering, "Let me speak to him, little girl. Please." The man was begging.

"The *Post* has a big picture of you and Uncle Hamilton on the front page today. They say you solved the biggest murder case in Italian history, Daddy. They're calling you the Italian Connection." She paused. "What's that mean?"

"Forget it. Remember what I told you about headlines. Listen, honey, where are you guys right now?" I asked. After what we'd seen here of Gladio, I wouldn't put it beyond them to kidnap Libby.

"We're in the…" The phone was passed to someone else.

"Detective Rossi?" Peek-a-boo's voice boomed over the line. "It's the mayor here. Got your whole family here and Turner's, too. Let's not forget your partner. Is he there? Love to talk to him, too."

"Well, Mr. Mayor, it's three p.m. here and he's gone out to do… some sightseeing."

"Of course. The case is closed. And anyway, that's why I'm calling.

Congratulations to both of you. Very good work. You've made all New Yorkers proud, Italian Americans, African Americans, everyone," he said, even louder, as if to emphasize it, I guessed, to Turner's family in the room with him, "and especially us Italian Americans. Remember that. 'Using your head, not breaking heads,' right?"

"Yes, Mr. Mayor. But we didn't get all the bad guys involved."

"Don't be modest. The lab says the bullets match. Each one has a match—Colonel Muro, his wife, Ms. Hochman…may she rest in peace…and that unfortunate Sylvia girl," the mayor went on, "the one with your partner that night. The bullets all came from the guns found with those Germans that took shots at you. Jens Dorman was the name of one of them, if memory serves. They are the killers and they are dead. Justice served without the court costs." He laughed into the phone. He was pretty taken with himself. The press was going to be good for him. Real good. The election was this fall. Then he turned serious again. "I'm sorry, but I understand one of the Italian policewomen was killed, too. A shame."

I thought of Laura's face then. "Well, sir, technically that's true. We're still trying to figure out her involvement," I said, not all that certain how far I wanted to go with this. "But the people who paid the Germans, we don't know who they are. They're still at large."

"Yes. But Ustica has nothing to do with us." There was a pause that was much more uncomfortable than it was long. "I don't want you investigating an Italian plane crash. The people killed on U.S. soil, on New York streets, that's what you were sent over for. Leave the rest to the Italian authorities. You're on New York City government business. Your stay doesn't allow for freelance investigations."

"Yes, Mr. Mayor," I said, sitting down on the edge of the bed. There was not much getting around it. The tape Turner had hidden was gone; Laura was dead; Ettore wasn't returning my calls; and the trail was cold. Gladio hadn't tried to kill us in the last twenty-four hours. At the very least, it meant they knew we didn't have the tape.

Just then, Turner sailed in through the door. From the look on his face I figured he'd gotten at least one phone number.

"Mr. Mayor, Detective Turner has just returned."

My partner smiled, devil tails all the way out. "The Mayor?" he mouthed to me and did this thing where he twirled the make-believe whisker ends of a make-believe mustache. It signified a good thing.

I'd cupped the receiver. "Peek-a-boo wants to congratulate you... us."

Turner put the phone to his ear, and I clasped my hands together above my head and shook them, mocking a winning boxer.

"Hello, Mr. Mayor," Turner said.

I walked away into the bathroom, where I could make out an occasional, "Sure, Mr. Mayor," and, "Be glad to help, Mr. Mayor," and, "Let's talk about that when I return." Then he talked to his mom and pops for a second, sounding like a boy, and hung up.

Turner shouted from the main room, "That's one happy pol. He thanked me on his behalf of all New Yorkers and especially...."

"African American New Yorkers," I chimed in.

"You should have come with me today, Paolo. Fucking lazy. That's another reason why you don't get laid. Do you know several ladies recognized me just from the ten seconds we were on the news? I'm sitting at a café right outside the Piazza del Popolo, you know, near the twin churches that aren't actually twins, and the women are raining onto my table like baby gypsies, boy, *baby gypsies*. And me with no *um*brella," he said with an "oh shucks" accent on the first syllable. "I got some new big black sunglasses. I'm telling you, we are going to need them."

I came out of the bathroom and kept a straight face. I threw my bag on the bed and began to pack. "Yeah, for all three hours we got left. Marco said the plane leaves Fiumicino at six. He's coming at four to get us."

"I sense that my partner is mad." He took off his jacket and threw himself down on the couch.

"Fuck yeah, I'm pissed. Everyone thinks this case is closed and it's not. Where the hell is Ettore? Fucking SISMI. He's as dirty as the rest of 'em probably. Probably not even SISMI. We were close, partner, real close," I said, holding my half-clenched hand up, "and we let it slip out."

It was quiet while I continued to pack. "You mean *I* let it slip out of our hands," Turner said, picking at a tooth with a toothpick and looking toward the window.

"That's not what I said," I said, throwing my clothes into the bag.

"But that's what you *mean*, partner," Turner said. "I've never seen you pack without folding your clothes. Highly unusual."

"Wrong," I said, but really he was partly right. "Somehow *we* fucked up. The bad guys…the real bad guys got away."

"I know that," Turner said absently. "What do you want to do now, Paolo? Our tour of duty is up. No more keys. No more clues. The tape is gone. Our welcome worn. All we got are economy class tickets back to New York City."

"Let's go over it one more time."

"Paolo, we've been over this three times already. I still have to pack"

"Come on, humor me, just once more. Until Marco's here. Come on."

I sat at the table and took out a piece of paper, and roughly sketched everyone's position in the cemetery: the Land Rover, the cars, the two crypts, the road, the Ape, the tombstone where Turner hid the tape, and the level below us, everything about as good as I could muster.

Turner pulled himself over reluctantly. We went over the movements and elapsed time as best we could remember. The result was the same: Gretzman was the only one who could have had the tapes. Neither the SWAT guys nor Ettore could have seen Turner or confiscated it. Turner had hidden the tape a full minute before the copter had appeared, he said, and just *before* the run-in with Laura and minutes before the cavalry and Marco arrived. It would have been an extraordinary stroke of luck for them to find the hidden tape. Gretzman was at La Saracena's crypt and Marco was at the top of the hill by the Land Rover, too far away to have seen Turner.

"Unless Ettore's men somehow stumbled onto it, the scribe is the only one who could have seen me," Turner said reluctantly.

"He has to have the fucking tape. He has to have it," I said, banging the desk a little too hard.

"You saw his hands. He was bad. He doesn't have it."

"Hamilton," I said, turning to him. "Somehow, someway he got the tape. Maybe adrenaline did it for him. We can't underestimate him. For all we know, he bribed the ambulance drivers or had somebody at the clinic there waiting for him. Do you think he came all this way alone?" I said, perhaps a little too loudly.

Turner rolled his eyes and got up. He was having none of it. "We been over this already. You saw there was nobody in the car with him at the airport."

"That's nothing. Reinforcements of some type."

Turner looked away. "Partner, you have to get a hold of yourself. You know we have been dealing with forces much larger than ourselves. The kind of people that have tentacles throughout SISMI and the carabinieri. Hell, this fucking room is probably bugged right now. They've pretty much known every move we've made and had somebody there to watch us. Shit, maybe you work for them."

"Cut that fuckin' out," I shot out.

"Sorry. But you have to let go of this. It's over. The dead people are accounted for. The murderers are dead, too."

"Not all of them," I said. "What about those eighty-one people on the plane?"

"Paolo, that's not our problem. We came to solve three NYC murders. And we done done it. The rest would have been gravy," he said, opening his luggage case and throwing it on the bed. He started to pack and I moved over to the couch. It was quiet, a fucked up, uncomfortable quiet. He was angry now, too.

"Peek-a-boo wants me to work on his Senate election campaign this fall," Turner said, trying to lighten the mood. "Now that I...we are supercops, he wants me to give a few speeches to the people—my people, that is, da pooooor black folks," Turner said, filling up his shoulder travel bag.

"Sounds like a good idea," I said without paying much attention. And then I realized that I didn't know my partner's affiliation. Like most white folks, I'd just assumed that he was a Democrat. "You are going to work for a Republican?" I asked.

"I *am* a Republican," he retorted, not missing a beat in his packing.

And it just hung there, as if a funny looking owl had flown into the room and just sat on a perch. I watched him a moment.

"Never heard of a black Republican?" he said a bit defensively.

"Kind of rare."

"Now, maybe. But not 100 years ago. Well, I'm an unusual guy. When I show up at local Republican Party meetings, the fuss made for me is a mega-fuss, man. Like I say, hambone, there's still a lot you don't know about me. Now you know one of my dirty little secrets," he said, closing his bags up.

Thirty minutes later, the phone rang. Marco was downstairs with the car. The ride to Fiumicino airport was a quiet one. Marco seemed sad to see us go. He didn't say much. We were running late and he was focused on getting us there in time. I was unhappy to leave Italy. I watched *il Colosseo* recede in the side mirror as the defeated troops left the Eternal City. Turner sat in the back alone with his arms folded. He seemed deep in thought and didn't look at me once. I worried that maybe I offended him by assuming he was a Democrat. Silly, but he was touchy about certain things.

"Seems funny without Laura in the car," he blurted suddenly.

Dead air.

"I mean, I know she was bad and all, but we were a good team, the four of us. Like the International Mod Squad," Turner said. "I always liked Linc. Got a cousin named Lincoln."

It was quiet for another mile.

"Hey, Marco. When did you know Laura was bad?" he asked.

I turned around to see what was up. It was a funny time to be asking such a question. Turner was intent on something.

Marco didn't answer.

"Hey, Marco," I said, "did you know Laura was bad?"

"Why are you asking me these questions?" Marco finally replied. His tone was on the edge of defensive.

"I'm a cop. I'm just curious," Turner said.

"Ettore kept me in the dark almost to the very end. Just like you. He told me over the truck radio at the cemetery just before the helicopters arrived." He'd never said Ettore's name without the maggiore.

That seemed to satisfy Turner for a minute. But then he said, "Last night you said you saw Laura holding Paolo hostage, that you couldn't get a clear shot, and that's how you knew she was bad."

"Yes. No. I *knew* but that was a guess during the heat of battle. What I saw was her gun to Detective Rossi's head. That was clear through the scope, but I'm no marksman. And anyway, I am reminding you that I didn't know what to think about you, either. I was…how you say…in the dark on everybody. Everything unofficial. When Major—I mean now Colonel Ettore told me you were with us, then it was *ufficiale*."

Turner didn't reply or say another word for the rest of our trip.

Marco's tone was definitely not kosher and getting more and more defensive. I couldn't figure it. There was a creepy feeling in the air and I was glad when we parked. All of us jumped out quickly, as if there were a bad smell in the truck.

Before Marco came around from the other side, Turner whispered to me, "He's dirty. I had the story on this guy from the get-go."

I shook my head.

"Yes," Turner repeated emphatically with his eyes.

Marco insisted on seeing us get our boarding tickets and walking us right up to the security check point. Seemed unnecessary. His excuse was that with him we could get right through to the front of the long line, which is exactly what we did. It was almost as if he couldn't wait to get rid of us.

Turner kept whispering to me whenever Marco was out of earshot, "We've got to lose him."

I was damn sure we wouldn't be able to lose Marco, who seemed to be making certain we got to our plane. By the time we reached the security checkpoint for passengers, he seemed so intent that for a moment I got the feeling he would try to come aboard and personally secure our seatbelts himself. But we made our goodbyes there before the carry-on luggage screeners. Marco even kissed me on both cheeks, Italian style. When he pulled away from hugging me, his jacket opened slightly and I saw something that I didn't expect. Inside his vest pocket, an airline ticket peeped out.

"I'm very glad to have met you," Marco said. "I hope that I can come to New York and observe you working firsthand."

"Marco," I said, "Thanks for all your help, and especially your excellent marksmanship." Turner was almost sulking.

He laughed as we parted. Marco waited there, wanting to make certain we were through security.

"Just as soon as we get through the checkpoint and he leaves, we've got to come right back out. We've got to follow him," Turner whispered.

"Aw, come on. This is ridiculous," I said, throwing my bag on the conveyor for the X-ray machine. I took off my shoes.

"Look," Turner said, "I'm gonna tell you fast. You have to believe me because we've got to follow Marco to wherever he's going."

"You are talking crazy," I whispered. At the table past the checkpoint, Turner looked back. Marco waved to us and left.

Turner spoke as if his life depended on it. "Paolo, there's some cognitive dissonance here, otherwise known as jive talk. Marco said when he walked up to us right after the SWAT copter arrived that he saw Laura holding you hostage. Remember? He said that's when he *knew* she was bad."

I nodded. "Yeah, he just repeated that on the way here."

"But he keeps saying that he was ordered to stay at the truck, and that's what he did, until the copters came and we saw him pop the Tenente with the automatic. But, Paolo, if he *clearly* saw Laura holding you hostage…" my partner said.

"Through his fucking scope," I interrupted. "Jesus. Then he saw you hide the tape through that scope. That was three, maybe five minutes earlier than when the copter arrived."

"Now you're talking my talk," Turner said.

"Then he ran down and picked up the canister with tape number one on the way to the kill shot for Laura. Fuck," I said, and a little too loudly. One of the security guards came over and asked if anything was wrong. "Marco slipped up yesterday by acknowledging that he saw Laura holding me, and he couldn't change his story today because he knew we'd call him on it."

Turner's face said checkmate.

"He was there," I said, shaking my head. "He saw you, and *he* took the fucking tape. I cannot believe this. Partner, he probably had it right there in the car with us and was laughing at the American cops. Oh fuck!"

"What?" Turner said.

"He had an airline ticket in his vest pocket. I saw it."

We moved down the concourse toward the departing gates as fast as we could without running and attracting attention. We exited through the baggage area, one level down from the departure area.

"Take the tags off your bag. Put them down on the carrousel and leave them," I said. "Put these shades on. Leave the jackets, too. Marco would recognize our threads."

We returned to the departures concourse, with giant groups of

Americans, Germans, Spaniards, Chinese, and Japanese blocking our way in just about every direction. But Marco's progress was probably similarly slowed.

"Where's the money at in this country?" I said.

"Milan."

"That's where he's going," I said. "I'm guessing he will deliver the tape personally." We ran to the nearest departures monitor. "Alitalia planes leave for Milan every thirty minutes from gate ten. The next one leaves in twenty-five minutes. We've got to buy tickets for Milan."

"Not much of a plan," Turner said, shaking his head with doubt.

"This is all we got, partner."

He nodded and we bought the tickets.

There was no reason to know with certainty that Marco was bagging us. Top five percent in his class. Ettore was the guy who had one of the tapes and he told us nothing. I grabbed three newspapers so we could reconnoiter with some cover. We couldn't let Marco see us. We sat down, heads buried in the papers at the bank of seats nearest but not at the gate ten lounge, just in case he was already in there. We broke up the gate area into sections, each of us sweeping them visually for Marco.

"Two o'clock, coming out of the men's room," he said. There was Marco, out of uniform and in civvies now. He carried a small overnight bag. Marco looked around, practically right at us and through us. He wasn't expecting to see us, so he didn't. He went to the café on the other side of the gate and went in.

"We have to split up. Less risk that we'll be recognized that way," Turner said.

"Okay. We meet on the other side."

"One more thing," Turner said as he rose and walked away. "I'll be back in a sec."

Activity at the gate quickened. Boarding began.

A minute later, a big, ugly, floppy hat landed in my lap. "I'll see you in the city of fashion," he said, walking toward the gate. He already had his hat on, pulled down on his head, with wraparound sunglasses.

Hamilton Petrarch Turner wearing a floppy hat. Well, that was like George Clooney in overalls, something that could happen, but not something you wanted to see. Mine said AC Milan, red and black. "I don't even like soccer," I mumbled, and put on the hat. I searched my pockets for change for an *aranciata* and found Ettore's business card. A colonel now, and probably that was just the beginning. General couldn't be far off, regardless of what came out of this.

Somebody in this mess had to be clean. If Marco's dirty, then maybe Ettore is clean, despite all my misgivings about him. He was pretty high in SISMI. They could have wanted this swept away just as much as Gladio...that fucking red ring. There wasn't much time. I called him. I had no real logical reason. It was an Italian fun house, a merry-go-round of truth. We had no authority, no guns now. Even if we caught up with Marco, what would we do? Go *mano a mano* with him on the plane? And the people meeting him probably wouldn't be very happy to see us.

"Colonel Ettore," the voice answered.

"Colonel suits you," I said in English.

"Well, Detective. Where are you? I thought you'd be on a plane back home already."

"Me, too."

On his side of the phone, I heard a woman's complaining voice in Italian: "Why do they have to call you on your first day off in months?" Ettore shushed her.

"What seems to be the matter, then? The protocol has run out. You are staying beyond the agreement? A vacation?"

"Colonel Ettore, I don't have much time, and—"

"You don't trust me, do you, Detective Rossi?"

"Frankly, every time I've trusted someone in this country, it's turned out to be wrong."

"The odds are in your favor now, I suppose," Ettore laughed. He seemed genuine.

"We had the second tape," I blurted.

"Lo *imaginavo*," ("I figured") he said quietly with a bit of despair. "Had?"

"It's been stolen from us."

There was a pause on the line. "And now you want me to help you, eh?"

At the gate, passengers were starting to gather in a line of sorts. Italians really didn't understand the concept. An Italian line more resembled a rugby scrimmage. A huge semi-circle of people immediately formed in front of the gate.

"I don't have much time," I said again.

"What if I told you a little story?" Ettore said. "Something that might convince you."

"They're getting on the plane."

"Who? You're at the airport still?"

"Yes. I've got to go."

"Listen quickly," Ettore said, and some nervousness crept into his voice. "The plane was downed for one man, and one man only."

"Yeah, I know that. Goddamn it. I saw the Costa show last night," I said, and I was getting a little too loud. Some folks walking by gave me a strange look.

"Let me finish. What you don't know is that the man, the target, was a *procuratore*, an investigating magistrate in Bologna by the name of Bancarotta. He was looking into bank dealings by a Luigi Colavito, who was Prime Minister at the time of the plane crash, a politically weak Christian Democrat. This was during the Cold War. Bancarotta's girlfriend at the time, who worked at the bank, came forward yesterday after the news of the shoot-up at the cemetery. She says now that he had discovered documents that showed Colavito had accepted money from Gladio. It was funneled through La Cosa Nostra in Sicily, money

267

and votes. Offshore bank accounts. She thinks the procuratore made copies and hid them well. Too well, so far. We are working on that. It would take too long to explain. Bancarotta was on that plane to see the head magistrate in Sicily and present the evidence for an indictment." Ettore paused. "Mr. Colavito is still alive and politically very well today. Do you happen to know who he is today?"

That's when my heart sank. "*Il Presidente della Repubblica*," I answered.

"Very good. You know your international politics. He is also the biggest supporter of the current Prime Minister, an *arlecchino* (clown) by the name of Berodi. They are marionettes of the Gnome, the Baron Enzo Spaccaforte, the chairman of MilanoBanca."

People were boarding. "Why are you telling me this?" I said.

"I'd like to get that tape. I don't know what's on it. Maybe something. Maybe nothing, like the one I have. That's the Lord's truth, but I'd like to know. The Italian people deserve to know. The families of Mr. Bancarotta and the eighty other people who died need to know. Colavito and Spaccaforte must face justice."

I had to spill it. There was no way we'd get that tape back on our own. "Colonel Ettore, I've got to go. We're on Alitalia 2440 to Milan, following Marco. We think he took the tape from us."

Ettore didn't respond right away. I just heard a deep breath. "*Gesu Cristo*. We'll be there when you land," he said. "Do nothing until you get a signal from me. I don't have to tell you that Sergente Fiorino is likely dealing with people who would make Attila the Hun blush."

I hung up the phone, put on my new floppy hat and sunglasses, and walked slowly to the lounge, hoping not to walk into Fiorino. I saw Marco get up and move to the gate. Turner and I followed.

A stewardess with drinks moved ahead of us into the first-class compartment, where Marco was seated at the window. As she bent over to hand him champagne, we slipped past him into economy class. Flight 2440 was supposed to take off at seven p.m., and the jet pulled away from the gate on time. But we went nowhere for forty-five minutes, trapped in the plane at the gate. The pilot said a minor mechanical issue was being repaired. On the other side, at Linate Airport, we sat in the airplane after it landed another thirty minutes on the tarmac. Within minutes of touchdown, everyone on the plane was gabbing into a cell phone. Both delays were Ettore's doing, I figured. It was after nine o'clock when we filed out of the plane.

Chapter 19

Monday Night

I went over our every move during the flight. Maybe Ettore was the baddie, another puppet of the Baron. I had made the trade, but I was having second thoughts. Wasn't it possible that Ettore was the one who worked for Gladio? What about Marco? I played devil's advocate in my mind. Maybe he was taking the tape—and we weren't certain he had it—to the only clean person in Italy, not to the Baron. Just maybe I gave the game away to Ettore when I called him. Why didn't Marco tell us? To protect us? He's a smart kid. He didn't want us killed. It's dangerous. Maybe they both were bad. The whole country could be working for Gladio, for all I knew.

A woman in the aisle pushed passed me, her shiny beige Gucci bag bumping up against my head, bringing me out of my trance. I peeked into the aisle and saw Turner ease out of his seat. There were already too many people standing to see Marco in the first-class cabin.

I wasn't sure how Turner would take me letting Ettore in on the deal. When I exited the plane, I noticed we weren't at a gate, but somewhere on the tarmac, with a huge green and white bus waiting for us outside. From the plane door, at the top of the gangway steps, I saw Turner enter the bus. The jet's engines hummed quietly and slowly to a cool down.

I followed and edged up close to Turner, his face deep in the paper. I looked at my newspaper, whispering, "I called Ettore." I heard a rustling and turned toward him, peeping around the edge of my *Corriere*. After the transport doors closed with a loud pneumatic "foooooosh," the bus lurched forward and I leaned into the man behind me, who cursed under his breath. I grabbed one of the handles hanging from the ceiling.

"He's going to be there," I said, just mouthing the words.

"Where?" My partner's eyes narrowed slightly, just enough to deliver his doubt.

I shrugged my shoulders. "There. Wherever Marco goes," I whispered.

A minute later, the bus came to an abrupt halt and the doors opened, disgorging people from all sides in a scrum, as passengers scrambled to get to the concourse doors and the taxis outside.

Up ahead, Marco walked briskly through the doors and into the airport concourse. We followed. I wondered why there wasn't a car right on the tarmac for him. If he were really dealing with Gladio, that's what I'd expect. Maybe we'd done something stupid.

We stayed as close to Marco as was possible. Then he did a funny thing. He dropped a candy wrapper by a garbage bin and bent over as if to pick it up. He reached around the trash can and pulled out a small white bag and put it into his pocket in one motion. The candy wrapper he left behind.

"D'ju see that?" I said.

"I didn't see what he grabbed but I'm sure it's metal," Turner said. Marco straightened up quickly and walked briskly through the front doors of the concourse to the taxi area. We had to run to keep up. As we came out, Marco jumped into a taxi. Luckily, the Italian cultural and anarchic refusal to stand in an orderly line has its advantages and we ran for the nearest free car, cutting in front of a half dozen people who were simultaneously angered by and impressed at our boldness. The driver looked like a stoner, with long brown hair in a ponytail, big black sunglasses, a red beret, and tie-dye shirt. I thought he was going to try to sell us some pot.

"Follow that cab ahead on the left, the one about to exit the concourse," I ordered in Italian. The driver put on a wide smile, as if he'd be waiting all his life for such a film noir order from a man whose accent in Italian was obviously American. He threw it lustily in gear.

"*Certamente, babo,*" he said, and just a little too enthusiastically, it occurred to me. He'd called me Pops. We shot out of the airport roundabout and were on a wide but dimly lit road that led to Milan, with a park on the right side and factories on the left. The airport was just outside the city, and in a few minutes we were on Viale Corsica.

On the seat next to me, my partner leaned forward, trying to keep an eye on Marco's cab. "He's two cars ahead of us. I got the tag. MI 724 957."

Meanwhile, the driver, who was turning to look back at us more times than was necessary, continued to have a huge smile on his face. Stoner though he might have been, he was doing too good a job. Soon enough, we were right on Marco's tail.

"That's too close," I said.

He looked back at me. "No problem," he replied in English, and my body edged forward as our speed dropped noticeably.

"I know you two," he said in Italian.

Turner wanted to know what the driver said and I told him.

"I know you," he said again, keeping one eye forward on Marco and one on us. He took a hard left onto Via Sforza, his wheels screeching. We lurched rightward in the backseat.

"You are those American police, yes?" he said in Italian. "Ustica, right? I saw your pictures on the TV news. CIA?" He grabbed a newspaper lying on the front seat opened to a page with our mugs and waved it at us. "CIA, yes?"

"CIA? No. We're policeman from New York," I said to the driver.

"Right, right, *destra*," Turner yelled suddenly.

"No problem," the driver said again in English, and we veered right onto Corso di Porta Romana. "Who's the guy we are following?" the driver asked, switching back to Italian.

"Nobody," I replied.

He looked back at me and winked. He was getting me nervous, looking backward all the time instead of forward. He was one of those cabbies who didn't realize he could talk to someone in the backseat without looking directly at them. He liked that I said "nobody." It confirmed, no doubt, his wildest theory about the chase. No one chases a nobody, so it was definitely a somebody ahead of us. "I hope you ketch no-*body*," he said in heavily accented English, flashing his scraggly teeth.

Marco's cab made a right on Via Mazzini and started to slow as it got to the Piazza del Duomo on the right.

"We have to stop behind him. Don't pass him," I said to the driver. Marco's cab stopped at the piazza, not far from a subway entrance.

"Pull over," Turner yelled. We came to a halt about fifty feet behind Marco. Turner and I scrunched down behind the front seats.

"Okay, okay," the driver yelled back. "I don't want break this to you, but we were followed, too."

I quickly looked behind me but there was no car to be seen.

He saw me. "They're gone already. Two black cars. I hope they are with you," he said, smiling.

"Mercedes?" I said in a panic.

"No," the driver replied, "Alfas, I think. Why?" he said, this time looking at me like he was a little sorry for me. He turned on the inside light, but Turner yelled "No!" and he shut it off. "Your nobody is out the door," the cabbie said.

Marco was walking off. I gave our driver thirty euros. In the large, open Duomo piazza, he wasn't going to get away.

"Thanks," the driver said, making the V-peace sign with his right hand. "Good luck, CIA. *Forza Italia!*" he said, a little too loudly.

Lit up dirty gray by the streetlights, the huge, white, triangle-topped Duomo glistened with statues, gargoyles, and pointy spires on nearly every inch of its outside walls. There were folks milling around the square on a quiet Monday evening in the spring, but mostly there were teenage boys on skateboards, testing their skills on the marble steps. A couple of peddlers were having a smoke near the subway entrance, their faux Vuitton bags and Prada shoes still laid out neatly on blankets. Others used contraptions that could be folded up quickly with their goods the minute a blue was spotted.

Turner and I exited the car. Marco was far enough away that he wouldn't have recognized us. He sauntered toward the Duomo. He seemed to be in no rush.

"Hallo, hallo, Prada. *Scarpe.* Nice Prada shoe," said a *clandestini*—what the Italians called illegal immigrants—in heavily-accented English as we passed them. God, even the immigrants knew we weren't Italian.

"Hey, Mother A-free-ca," the other, maybe from Ghana, maybe Senegal, said to Turner, hoping to get some solidarity attention, but my partner was having none of it.

"This boy going to church?" Turner said skeptically of Marco—who was walking toward the Duomo.

We let him get a little further away. And then we split up again. I walked to the right, Turner left. Marco continued across the plaza, as if he were going right to the front of the Duomo. About halfway across he made a sharp left and walked toward the large arcade that lined the plaza. Beyond that was the Galleria di Vittorio Emanuelle II, Italy's original mall. He stopped just under the arcade's thick arches before going into the Galleria. I froze at first, then kept moving in case he looked over. I continued slowly to the right, tacking left, not letting our boy get too far away. Turner was down the far end of the arcade and he stood behind one of the columns, out of Marco's sight. Marco lit a cigarette and stood there a few minutes, smoking.

Did he sell out his country or was he about to bust this thing wide open? He looked at his wristwatch a couple of times. Then he looked over at me, right at me, and I looked away, continuing to walk to the right. When I turned back, he was gone and Turner was running toward the entrance to the Galleria. So I ran, too. When I nearly reached the entrance, I stopped. I feared Marco might be just inside. Turner stood at the entrance. I motioned, "What gives?" with my hands, and he cricked his head slightly to the left, pointing to where Marco had entered. He pointed to his eye with a finger, meaning he had spotted Marco, then walked in slowly, and I moved in a minute later.

I had to remove my sunglasses. While the Italians had perfected the art of seeing at night through darkened glasses, I could not. It meant I'd have to stay way back of Marco and keep my newspaper handy. I tugged at my floppy hat so it came all the way down as far as possible on my head. I was certain I looked like an asshole by local standards. Some of the skateboard boys had pointed at me, screaming, "*Deficiente.*" It had always been one of my very favorite words in Italian. It meant idiot, mentally deficient, backward, a fool, an asshole, but said properly, with the right tone, it was so much more, that you were simply beyond hope of intelligence.

The light was bright inside the Galleria though most of the shops were closed. Turner wandered past the window of a bookshop down the other end, which gave out on the other entrance, Piazza La Scala. His back was to me. I entered the Galleria slowly but couldn't see Marco. There was a Burgy still open, an Italian McDonald's, with tables and chairs outside. I made my way to a table and sat. I couldn't make Marco. I pulled up my paper and occasionally peeked at Turner. I assumed he had a bead on him since he stood calmly down the end. For the most part, the Galleria was unpopulated. A few couples chatting. In the center, some men were making a racket taking down something that appeared to be a temporary tourism kiosk.

Turner barely lifted his chin to indicate that Marco was in Il Salotto, a café a bit further down from us. I saw tables outside the café, but he wasn't sitting there. I sat tight, not knowing if this would be minutes or hours. I was hungry. A couple sat next to me with burgers and Cokes, and the smell was getting to me, reminding me of home. A country where everyone wasn't trying to kill me. The man whispered into the woman's ear and she giggled and fake slapped him. That seemed to really rev him up and he gave her a tight kiss. I looked away. They left.

Turner moved slowly along, pretending to window-shop. He moved past a point directly across from the café and was now at the exit from the side of the Galleria that gave onto Piazza La Scala. Across the way was La Scala itself. The Altar of Opera. I had a feeling he wanted to take a look at it while he could.

That couple next to me left an unopened bag of chips on their table. I grabbed it. I was really hungry. They didn't feed you on short flights anymore. The couple went past the workmen in the center and stopped. They danced around a spot on the floor, looking down at something. She put her hand to her mouth, laughing. Then she dug her heel into a spot on the floor and spun around on one heel. Then he did the same thing. It was the Bull's Balls. The Galleria had signs of the zodiac in mosaics on the floor. Tourists and Milanese spun around on their right heel on the balls of Taurus for good luck.

Someone came by my table and accidentally dropped his cell phone onto it.

"*Scusi*," I said.

The man, who had a military style buzz haircut under his hat, kept moving.

"Hey, you dropped your..."

But he didn't stop. He went out of the table area and down the hall without a word. I raised the phone to my face, confused, as if expecting some little man with a gun to jump out of it. Then it rang. The tone was a pop tune, a Madonna song from the '80s, *Like a Virgin*. I looked at the readout. It was Ettore's cell phone. He was somewhere around here, as were his men, one of whom I realized had delivered the phone to me. I let it ring a few times, and then answered.

"Colonel," I said.

"Really, Detective Rossi, we mustn't be feeding you too well here if you have to eat someone else's Burgy leftovers."

I smiled, and looked around slowly, hoping to pick him up, but that wasn't possible. He could have been in any of the stores or in the offices above, which had dozens of windows onto the Galleria. My eye caught the barrel-shaped vault above at the center of the cross.

Ettore went on: "I want you and your partner to cease surveillance. We're all around you and I don't want to risk Marco's recognizing you, or you getting killed. We'll take it from here."

"Thanks, but no thanks," I said. I certainly wasn't having any of that after everything we'd gone through to get this far.

"Still not sure what side I'm on, eh, Detective Rossi?" Ettore said. There was faint weariness in his voice. He was a man very close to a long-sought prey. I could fuck it up.

"It's my tape," I said. I looked up at Turner, who was milling in the same spot at the end of the Galleria, past *il Salotto*. It seemed like he could see me but I wasn't one hundred percent sure. "I can't even reach my partner, anyway," I added.

"Your fucking tape?" he screamed into the phone. I pulled the phone away from my ear. There was a longish pause. I saw two men milling around directly opposite Turner. They looked like Ettore's men.

"Cease surveillance," he said. "There's a risk you'll ruin it for us, and that you'll get killed in the process. That is not in our agreed protocol. Thanks for getting us here, but this might get extremely unpleasant soon." Ettore's patience was wearing thin. I heard it in his voice. "We don't want to pick him up until he meets his handler. We want him, the tape, and the other side. Is that clear! You must stand out of the way," he shouted. "Stand down."

I didn't bother replying and he hung up without another word.

It still smelled. If we didn't follow Marco, we wouldn't see the tape. If Ettore really wasn't clean and they got him without us, the tape would disappear. If we didn't get the tape, chances were it might never get seen. I didn't know my left from my right at this point. Ettore was okay, not okay.

I felt the vertigo coming on and put my hands to my face, covering my eyes in case things started to spin. They did. I felt nauseated. Godawful. I grabbed the sides of the table hard. Saliva came up first and the rest wouldn't be long. I rested my head on the table. God knows what Turner was thinking. He knew he couldn't come over to me.

I don't know how long I did this. Maybe three minutes. Maybe thirty. When I pulled my hands away from my mug, there was a well-dressed waiter standing before me. Burgy didn't have wait staff. He said "*Salve*," to me, and put down his tray, which had an espresso coffee on it and a small plate of biscotti. On the handkerchief in his pocket the words "Il Salotto" were smartly stitched in yellow thread.

The waiter pointed at a note under the coffee saucer, bowed, and left. I pulled a white folded piece of paper out and opened it.

It's been nice working with you and Detective Turner. I have learned a great deal. However, I must bid you adieu. Please don't follow me anymore. It will likely mean your life.

All Best,

Marco Fiorino, Sergente.

I looked up and there was our man, giving me a little wave before turning right and moving off to the Piazza La Scala entrance, where Turner stood. For what seemed like a slow motion few seconds, I sat there looking at the fucker. I was laughing at myself. He thought it'd been a nice little game, and now he'd won, and wouldn't we just leave him alone. I forgot my fondness for him, what little was left. He wanted to humiliate us. The motherfucker. In a single motion I jumped out of my seat, crumpled the note in my hand, sent the table flying and the few people still around scattering. The cell phone fell to the floor, breaking into pieces. I hurdled the balustrade that roped off the tabled area from the Galleria and made for Marco. No time for the Bull's Balls.

Marco met my partner and socked him hard at the La Scala exit with a surprisingly fast and solid punch. Turner landed on his ass, as if hit by a bolt. Marco was out into the piazza. I came up to Turner and pulled him up. There was some yelling by men inside the shops. They came out and I could see the glint of silver-black in their hands, but they didn't go after Marco straight away.

Turner looked woozy. "You alright?" I asked.

"Yeah," he said, rubbing his goateed chin. "Who knew the kid had a monster left hook?"

Marco ran past the Da Vinci statue in the piazza and crossed Via Manzoni in front of La Scala.

Was Ettore letting Marco go, or giving him more line? His men inside the Galleria, or at least the people I thought were his men, were waving at us to come back inside the Galleria. They weren't visible to Marco, who looked back at us standing near Leonardo, and he smiled as he crossed the street in a slight crouch. He had a Beretta in his right hand, close to his pant leg, as if to hide it as much as he could.

"It's now or never, partner," I said. We took off after Marco. A dirty orange streetcar of ancient vintage rolled by and stopped right in front of La Scala. We lost Marco behind it. A couple of men jumped off the tram and tried to stop us but we ran right around them.

"Stop! *Alt! Fermatevi!*" men were screaming at us from several points in the street. There were no uniforms, only men in plain clothes. I couldn't tell who was who. Bad guys, good guys. Shit. Then there was the wail of the Italian carabinieri sirens, and several blue and red striped Alfas roared up onto the pavement of Piazza La Scala, just missing Leonardo's big, boxy pedestal.

At that moment, a human dam burst and throngs of people began streaming from all three front doors of La Scala. The opera had ended five minutes before. Marco disappeared into the crowd of tuxedoes and evening gowns. They enveloped him quickly, as if he were a single-cell bacterium surrounded and digested by a larger amoeba.

Turner put his hand to his face for a moment, laughed, and then looked over at me.

"Beautiful," I said, trying to spot Marco in the crowd. Above us I could hear a whirring helicopter. Its spotlight was crisscrossing the front of La Scala. Some of the opera goers probably thought it was just some kind of celebrity-searching TV news klieg light.

"I overheard someone coming out of the bookstore earlier say it's the Wags tonight. Lohengrin," Turner said, shaking his head, as if to say, "If only I'd known." "We missed it. You don't see that one done too often anymore."

Meanwhile, the carabinieri, or SISMI, or whatever, went wading in full force. Scuffles were breaking out all over the street in front of the theater. You've never seen hubris till you've seen a bunch of poshes being treated like common criminals. Women shoved to the side, to the ground, screaming, "*Vergogna!*" ("Shame!") Their men, most of them pushing sixty and seventy, wheezing at the cops, trying to maintain some semblance of manhood in front of what must have looked to them as a melee, plain and simple.

"I guess Colonel Ettore hadn't figured on this. Perhaps he's not an opera buff," Turner said, almost cackling.

I eyed the crowd. "Come on, we can't lose him. He's somewhere in there."

Another streetcar arrived from the other direction, from city center, clanking its tocsin loudly. The tuxes fell dangerously in front of it on the tracks. Women tried to pull them up. It was an unreal riot. Finally, way over on the right, outside the crowd, leaning over a police car and speaking into a small headphone mic, I spotted Ettore. Then he pushed the microphone from his face and yelled at his men, pointing to the left side of La Scala, where ran Via Filodramattici, a name which means the street of theater lovers. Some of his men tried to run that way but the crowd blocked their path. Others took the long route around the crowd, and a few ran down Via Verdi, probably to come up around the back. Turner and I were still outside the ever-growing crowd and we edged along to the left.

"Ettore pointed left," I said.

"There," Turner said, also pointing to the left. Marco was trying to extricate himself from the mass of people surrounding the front of La Scala.

"Walk. Don't run," I yelled. The crowd buzz was loud.

We moved along and around the now stranded streetcar. Out the front window of the tram, the driver was standing, fuming at the folks blocking his way on the tracks. "Out of the way, fucking capitalists!" he screamed. "First you get the Ferraris by stealing our wealth, now you want the workers' transportation. Out of the way," he yelled, clanking the bell. For a moment I really thought he might start to run over the suits or break into the *Internationale*.

Marco freed himself from the scrum and looked back for Ettore's men. Somehow he must have grabbed someone's tuxedo jacket and top hat and put it on, hoping for some kind of cover. We saw him walk coolly down Via Filodrammatici, a dead-end street. We followed.

He was about twenty feet from us. He didn't turn around. Our footsteps were drowned out by the crowd. He still held that pistol in his right hand and a small box in his left.

Should we run up and get our heads blown off? Reason with him? Surely, he'd recognize that he's trapped. The street got narrower as we went along. It was very dark, as the whole right side of the street was taken up by the solid walls of La Scala, so there was no window light thrown on the street. Down at the end of the street sat a large gray palazzo in a small square to the left of La Scala, fronted by massive wooden doors with medieval brass hinges. It had small, delicate arabesque window arches going all the way up to the fourth and top floor, where one light was shining. It had no address number.

Turner and I crept along, he on the left, while I was on the right, slinking along La Scala's brick face. Marco had one hand up to his ear. A cell phone. He slowed down. Then, incredibly, he stopped and looked at the doors on the street, as if he weren't sure of the building he wanted. He was looking for an address. He didn't know where he was going. Finally, he faced again toward the large palazzo, put the phone away, and started walking to it.

I pointed to the palazzo. We started to run when Marco was ten feet from the front door. He was going to close the deal.

And then the deal blew apart.

CHAPTER 20

MONDAY NIGHT

It lasted probably all of ten seconds. There was no warning from Ettore's people, no screams to "Stop, put your hands up!" Nothing. Seemed like every cannon within twenty miles of Milan had been rounded up, loaded at the far end of the street, and let go at once. Turner and I were horizontal in a second. I was once again eating Italy's fine dirt. The ordnance was going precisely down the middle of the street, where Marco was located. I looked over at Turner, who had his hands over his head. That seemed like a good idea and I did the same. I peeked behind me and saw wispy blue smoke from guns emitting lead and orange tracers. There were screams coming from in front of the opera house, the patrons frightened by the firepower.

As best I could, lying prone, I looked down the street again. I figured Marco was already dead. He'd made it somehow to a large column in front of the palazzo and was hiding behind it, but he was bleeding every which way. His top hat had fallen to the street and rolled down the steps. Ettore's men at the La Scala end could not see him behind the column. There was no more crowd noise.

Suddenly, the shooting stopped, and Ettore yelled, "*Alt, Sergente Fiorino!*" The chopper was right above the rooftops. Men were rappelling down from it. They were down Marco's end of the street. Funny, but right at that moment I looked up at the palazzo and noticed

283

that light on the fourth floor was out. I don't know why I noticed that in the middle of this lead fest, but I did.

"Stop, Marco," Ettore yelled again.

Marco made no reply. He was done. He was unlikely to take any shots in his condition, bent on one knee behind the column, about three feet from the front door. He was talking to someone, or to himself, I wasn't sure. One of the men who'd rappelled down, his sight trained on him, told him to come away from the door. Marco coughed up blood. He had one arm against the column and looked like he was going to make a jump for it to the palazzo door. That's when I noticed one of the big oak doors was already opened a crack. He was talking to someone at the door, but I couldn't see who it was.

"*Alt*, Marco," Ettore said. "This is the last time."

Marco lunged toward the front doors but didn't make it. He fell to the ground just in front. The undertaker wasn't going to have to drain him. He lay there face up and Ettore's men rushed up to him. Two came over to Turner and me, one on each of us. I lay there and saw dozens of feet rushing by me.

"Stop him. Get the box from his hand, now!" Ettore screamed as he ran by me on the way to where Marco lay. "Get the tape!"

Marco lay in front of that large weathered door. The klieg lights' shine bounced off the golden strap hinges, three on each side of the two doors where they met the front wall. From behind the door, right at the base, a hand came out, as if the person to whom the hand was attached was kneeling just behind the door. It was a right hand, of a size that suggested it belonged to a child, but it was gnarled, its skin mottled with age.

It came out like a little animal itself, with a consciousness all its own, moving with intention. It had a ring with a thick gold band and a bright ruby, just like di Gagliano's and Ettore's. The rock glinted blood red in the spotlights. The hand's fingertips gripped the box held in Marco's young and now lifeless palm. It pulled. Marco didn't yield at first. I thought maybe Marco was still alive, but another tug by the hand brought the box out of Marco's grasp. The sergeant's hand fell back to the ground, and the box along with that wizened mitt disappeared behind the door, which then closed quietly.

At most it took a few seconds. Ettore leaped toward Marco's prone body with his own hand outstretched. He was practically flying through the air like a fullback toward the goal line, but he was too late, and he landed on top of Marco. It seemed like none of his men knew what he was doing or why. He'd obviously wanted to keep everyone he could out of the loop to protect the security of the operation. His men were nearer to Marco. Had just one of them known what Ettore wanted, the colonel would likely have finally gotten hold of the tape. So close to his grasp, and then it was gone. Or was this the way he had wanted it to end?

Now that the lead storm ended, the world came back and a rumble from the crowd in front of La Scala was heard. Women crying. Men yelling. Cops and the SWAT team screamed commands to each other. Secure the area. Two more klieg lights were brought up, and one shone brightly on Marco. Ettore sat dejectedly near him on the two steps that went up the palazzo, Marco's top hat in his hand. Now that I could look at it for more than a moment, it seemed an old, stately building, a scene from the end of an opera, the blood so red from the lights that it seemed fake. But what did I know about the opera?

I lay there wondering why the fuck they didn't bust down that door. I couldn't have been the only one who saw what happened. If that box held the tape, and surely it did, it was inside that building. Get the policemen's second-best friend, otherwise known as the battering ram.

Turner tried to get up but the SWAT guy told him to stay down. I got the same reception.

"Hey, Ettore," I yelled, pointing at his men. He waved them off with a disgusted flick of his hand, and Turner and I rose. I felt bad for the colonel. This was not going to go down well with his bosses. Forget about General Ettore.

I walked slowly over to Ettore. Turner shook dirt off his jacket and followed.

This is a moment where nothing you say can be adequate, so I said nothing.

Ettore sat motionless for the most part, acknowledging us with the slightest movement of his eyebrows. He was wearing a thick, black anti-projectile vest over SWAT black khakis, all covered with Marco's blood. He stared straight at the ground, facing forward, with Marco to his left. He looked as if he'd lost his best friend, and in a way, he had.

Ettore knew what I was thinking. "We can't go in the building," he said without looking up at me. "Not just because we didn't have a *mandato di perquisizione*, a...what do you call it?" He rotated one finger in the air.

"Search warrant," I said.

"Yes. We didn't know where Marco was going. Should have guessed it but didn't. That's my fault. But even had we known, it would have been no use."

"What are you talking about?" I said, perhaps a little too harshly, a little too much like a cop who thought he knew better. But I didn't.

Ettore didn't get mad. Didn't make a face. Didn't tell me to fuck off, which was what I deserved. He just pointed behind him, to the door into which the gnarled hand had retreated. "Look at this place," he said.

I searched the tall doors for an answer. They'd taken a few hits and the owner wasn't going to like that. The column, too, had been etched by lead. There was no street number on the building. I got the feeling the owners cultivated anonymity. He continued pointing, knowing that I hadn't figured it out.

"Look, Paolo, look," Ettore said.

It was the first time he'd addressed either of us by our given names. "Look," he said, one more time, quietly.

To the right of the doorway, a bit higher than eye level, was a gold

286

plaque fixed to the wall. It was probably three inches high by six inches long, not much bigger than a nameplate you'd see on a desk. Etched on it in blue lettering was the word "MilanoBanca." Nothing else.

"Headquarters," Ettore said dejectedly. He began to raise himself up.

"Of Gladio?" I said.

"Some say," Ettore said. He began to walk away slowly, down toward La Scala and the crowds. The carabinieri had been able to cordon the street off, but beyond the sawhorses the crowd stood, staring down toward us. They knew what building it was. They were strangely quiet now, as if all of them were wondering, "Well, Ettore, did you get the tape? Did you solve the crime of the century?"

Then I said the stupid thing. It was necessary that in such a situation someone say something stupid. So I did.

"Ettore, why don't we get the *perquisizione* (warrant) now?"

The colonel didn't stop, didn't even turn around. He just took his hand and pointed over his shoulder again. I would have bet every dollar I had that he was laughing as he walked away from us, a soft, knowing, sad laugh, one that said, "Go read your history books, boys. Discover the way things really work around here."

I turned to look at the palazzo a last time. At the fourth floor, that same light was back on again. The window was open now, and now that I was closer, it was not a window but a terrace door that was open. And I thought I heard laughter wafting out of that room. Not loud and boisterous, but that confident laughter the servants would hear coming from upstairs in the mansion.

An ambulance silently made its way down Via Filodrammatici, dodging knots of SWAT boys and armored policemen. It backed up to Marco and two men jumped out. These ambulance guys never discussed the deceased; it was just another body to them. These two, as they put the corpse on a stretcher, covered him, and hauled him into the ambulance, had a long discussion on the benefits to Inter, one of the local teams, of a new Spanish striker named Diego Milagro. One of them looked at me and asked if Inter had won that night, but just as the words were out of his mouth, he realized I wasn't Italian and turned away without so much as, "Never mind." They never once looked at poor Marco or asked about him.

"Kind of sad about Marco," Turner said as they loaded his body.

"I thought you didn't like him," I said.

"Yeah, I know. I didn't trust him, but I still kind of liked him all the same, you know. You ever get that feeling about somebody?"

"Yes," I said, nodding. "I think of my ex like that...among other women."

My partner sat on the step where Ettore had been. I sat next to him, trying to avoid Marco's blood.

"We could have attended Lohengrin tonight, you know. I think it was the last opera of the season," he said. He rubbed his arms against the night air, which was getting cooler.

"Do the bad guys win in Lohenbrau?"

"Lohengrin," Turner corrected. "Well, yes and no. Let's say the good guy loses the girl on account of a mistake she makes, and then she dies at the end."

"Nice," I said. "They always die at the end, don't they?"

"Life is a lot like the opera," my partner said to no one in particular. "That's why people like it. Yeah, the music is great, but just when you think the stuff that happens in Tosca is improbable, it happens in real life," he said. He was quiet for a moment. "You think Ettore will ever get those guys?"

"No. The Pope'll convert to Buddhism before anybody gets the ruling class of puppeteers. Even more true in this country. The funny thing is they thought they did in '92 with the Mani Pulite investigations. Fat chance."

"You sound like a socialist, Paolo. You surprise me." Turner gave me a three-quarter smile.

288

"Not at all. Just a realist."

An old church bell began to toll softly somewhere nearby. Eleven bells quietly marking the hour, mocking our fuckup.

And from that night in Milan on, church bells reminded me of Ustica and the wretchedness of death undeserved.

*   *   *

We walked back through La Galleria like two disappointed hunting dogs, trying not to make eye contact. I turned my right heel on the Bull's Balls, but immediately felt the vertigo coming on again, so I stopped. Turner was so down he didn't even give it a try.

We found Ettore standing at the bar in La Salotto, sipping a coffee. It seemed to me that he'd aged some just in the few days that I'd known him. More gray hair in the temples, maybe. I looked at Turner, unsure whether we should join him, but Ettore waved us over with a smile. After what he'd just been through, I was amazed he could still manage to move those facial muscles.

"How do you like Italy now?" he said, offering us a cigarette.

Neither of us answered.

"You are wondering about the MilanoBanca business, eh, l'assenza del mandato di perquisizione? ("The lack of a warrant.")

Again we said nothing.

"Italy's a funny place," he continued, almost as if he were talking to no one in particular, or to a great big audience in front of him. "We hate the powerful, but we respect them. And most especially, we are jealous of them. We don't really think, 'Oh, if only we were all equal.' We leave that hypocrisy to the French. We are not really egalitarians. No, the Italian says, 'If only I were more powerful than the other guy, my neighbor. Then I'd show him,'" he said, taking another sip.

"You know, the Baron is the most despised yet most envied man in all of Italy. He's much more respected than the Prime Minister, Berodi, that monkey-faced idiot, or his illegitimate political father, Presidente Colavito. Those two are just politicos. They could be thrown out

289

tomorrow. Even bad angels owe their power to someone greater." Ettore looked not heavenward but in the direction of Via Filodrammatici, in a mock saintly manner, hands together in prayer.

Ettore called for drinks. When I took a Diet Coke, Ettore nodded.

"To the little bastard himself," the Italian said. "*Lo Gnomo*. All Italians know this: *Il Papa potrebbe condannarti, ma ci vuole la sigla dello Gnomo.* My English is not so good, but it roughly translates as: The Pope may condemn you, but it means nothing until the Gnome signs off." Then, almost as if he weren't talking to us, "If we envy a man like that, can we be honorable?"

That word always got my attention. "You're being a little hard on the paisans."

"Who's the Gnome?" Turner asked, losing track of the characters in this drama.

"That's our little nickname for the Baron, Enzo Spaccaforte, honorary chairman of MilanoBanca," Ettore said, stopping for a moment. "Short and from a backward island, like Napoleon, and just as powerful in this country. Whose hand do you think it was coming out of the door tonight?"

"You saw that?" I asked.

"Yes and no," Ettore answered. "I know you saw it, so I will acknowledge it to you, but if the reporters ask, I will answer, 'No, there was no hand.' And if you tell the press you saw a hand take the box from Marco's dying grasp, I will simply deny it."

The looks on our faces made Ettore grin. "Had I gotten my hands on that tape…" He looked at us, pursed his lips, and nodded slightly, as if to remind us that we had once held it in our hands. "Ah, well, anyway…with no tape, what's the point of telling reporters that there was one, but, sorry, I lost it to the Baron? It adds to his power and detracts from ours. Perhaps we'll find another way, but until then, there is no tape. I don't know why you didn't trust me."

"Maybe it was the unusual red ring on your hand," I said. "It's just like the one di Gagliano had in New York, and the one on the hand that came out of the door tonight."

Ettore groaned. He brought his hand up to his face. "This too I didn't anticipate from you."

"What's that mean?" I said.

"That you would notice something like that. My father worked for the Baron, long and hard. I met *lo Gnomo* more than a few times when I was a child. He scared me terribly, with those blue eyes of his. The Baron killed my father—no proof, of course—when he no longer had any use for him. There were many things my father knew. He got too close to the Gnome, it seems. That's when 'accidents' seem to happen to his people. Car crash in my father's case. I wear my father's ring as a reminder of what I need to do, what I owe my father's memory. Crazy as it sounds, I will not take it off until I get the Baron."

"I'm sorry," I said.

"Not your fault," Ettore said, rubbing his face.

"You can't just let him get away with that," I said. And the moment the words came out of my mouth I was sorry I'd said it.

Ettore didn't take offense. "He's gotten away with much more in the past. Maneuvering his loyal followers into the Prime Minister's chair, merging feuding or bankrupt companies, screwing workers and investors alike, buying huge tracts of property just before the government needs them. I've often imagined what would happen if I had the evidence that proved the Baron was the head puppeteer in this *spectacolo* called Italy. The funny thing is that this is something we instinctively know, and we've not objected much so far, so why would we begin to do so? And what's more, the tape is likely to prove nothing."

"Let's say," he went on, "for argument sake, it shows a missile hit that plane back in 1980. What then? Would it show who sent it? Probably not. Even if it did that, let's say it came from an Italian F-104, say Cofari or Muro, or even an American NATO plane. It will be called an unfortunate accident. After twenty-two years, then what? Or maybe it was a bomb. For all we know, perhaps the La Brigata Rossa or the Libyans did do it. Well, the papers would have a wonderful time. Most of the people responsible are dead, and the others will get themselves good lawyers. And the Baron is —*l'Intoccabile*, an Untouchable, a caste in Italy that is the zenith not the bottom. It's not even a caste. That would imply there are others."

"To get a *mandato* against MilanoBanca, even assuming it was possible, would likely cost me my job, if not my life. I might have tried it if I were one hundred percent convinced it would be successful. But there's more chance that an American soccer team will win the Serie A cup," he said with a resigned laugh. "I won't risk all for such a low payoff."

To me it sounded like a justification for failure, something with which I was not unfamiliar. We all did it. You couldn't get the bad guy so you say he was not gettable anyway. It's allowed, but not forever. "Then why bother in the first place?" I said.

"Because of my father and because it's my job. It's not just the eighty-one dead, sorry as I am for them and their families. I would like to deliver justice to them. But there are eighty-one *clandestini* drowning every month off the Italian coasts trying to get here from North Africa or Albania. Nobody gives a shit for them. Just these eighty-one who were in a plane crash long ago. A lovely mystery that can go on and on, intriguing American cops, beguiling Italians, the way they love to be seduced. And it would satisfy me to have the tape, to perhaps understand the deed."

"And yes, I would deeply enjoy denting the Baron's ship, however insignificant that damage might be—for we'd never get him to serve a day in jail. Here, it's nearly impossible to put any eighty-five-year-old behind bars, even a former Nazi, let alone the Baron. More than anything in the world, I want him to die unhappy from la *brutta figura*, to pay for those eighty-one people...and countless others. That, for him, would be far worse than any jail sentence. Do you understand *la brutta figura?*" he asked, finishing off his cigarette and stubbing it out. The barista came over and told us he was closing up.

"Italians like to *fare la bella figura*," he said, "to cut a good figure, to look important and to be looked up to, respected, feared. It's more important than money. To look bad doing something is about the worst thing that can happen to an Italian. You lose respect. People talk loudly behind your back. If I had the radar tape, then maybe I could make the Baron *fa una cattivissima figura*, make him look very, very bad. Nothing would satisfy me more than that. At his age, he might die of that alone," he laughed.

"What now?"

"We'll keep an eye on Marco's parents, his girlfriend. See if they fall into some money. The Baron is scrupulous about paying his debts. And then there's Bancarotta's girlfriend. She may remember more with some encouragement. Perhaps the lawyer did make copies of the evidence he was taking to the Sicilian magistrate. Perhaps he told her. I met her briefly yesterday in Rome, just before you called me. Guilt is a wonderful thing.

"She knew all this time, more than twenty years, why the plane was shot down. She apparently told no one. It's been eating her alive and now she feels better. Hah." Ettore brought his hands to his stomach and rubbed it, as if it ached. "She may know more than she's let on. Perhaps she *has* more than she's let on. We've already put her into hiding. Of course, the Baron has tentacles in SISMI, and you were right to worry about that—though not about me," he said with a soft laugh. "We shall see."

Ettore, who was leaning on the bar, stood up and motioned us to the door. The bar's lights went out. The Galleria itself was nearly deserted now. As we walked to the door, I turned to Ettore, "I'm sorry about the tape."

"We didn't know whom to trust," Turner said. "So I hid it. But I didn't know the SISMI cavalry was coming. Otherwise, I would have kept the tapes together."

When we exited the Galleria, Ettore said, "I have a surprise for you. A little while ago, I spoke with your superior, a Tenente Dunne, I think he said his name is. Yes?"

We nodded. Turner made a guttural sound, something that might come out of an animated character, the villain in a kiddy cartoon.

"They are anxious for you to return. In fact, they were wondering why you weren't on the plane that you were supposed to be on," Ettore said. He tilted his head a bit, as if he didn't understand. "They are under the impression that you have solved a great crime."

"Well," I said, "they're happy we got Muro's killers. You know...the Germans."

"Ahh, yes, I see," Ettore said. "Well, that is something, isn't it? That was your job, your crime to solve. Find those bad guys."

Nobody said anything after that for a while. Ettore's last words just hung there like a subtitle to a pathetic scene. We walked with him to his car, though Turner and I really didn't know what to do. It was 11:30 p.m., our bags were in Rome, we had no hotel and we were supposed to be in New York already.

"Anyway," Ettore said absently, picking up the thread of our conversation from ten minutes before. "They want you home right away, it appears. I believe your official delegated authority has run out, so we are breaking all kinds of protocol now. Come, we'll drop you off at the airport. There's a SISMI Gulfstream waiting for you. You'll be home in no time."

I felt like protesting. I wanted to go back through Rome one more time. I had badly wanted to see the cypress trees near *il Colosseo*.

Eight- and one-half hours later, we landed at Kennedy aboard a sleek fifteen-seater, courtesy of the Italian secret service. No one was at the airport to greet us. No mayor. No band. No nothing.

Martedi Matina

The Senator for Life practically floated into the Baron's office at 10 a.m. Tuesday, his appointed hour. He was, as usual, meticulously dressed, his Saville Row suit an understated navy blue that matched his eyes, which twinkled with excitement.

He was worth at least one billion euros, lorded over hundreds of thousands of employees, but nothing had made him quite as excited as this. "Congratulations," he said, rushing into the room. He sat next to the Baron on the couch and grabbed the espresso cup all in one motion. He was so happy that he wasn't bothered by the Spaccaforte coat of arms on the delicate demitasse ceramic.

The Baron just grunted, but a contented grunt. He was smiling but wished to keep The Senator in his place. The Senator was almost common in his manner, coming in so excited. The fact that he sat down next to him on the couch instead of across from him already bothered him.

"Once we got our own men involved, it was a fait accompli," the Baron said, an unsubtle reminder that the Germans were The Senator's idea.

"I'm surprised there wasn't a front-page picture in Il Corriere of your hand coming out the door," The Senator laughed.

"I might have fancied that," the Gnome replied. "But I do like the photos they had." He held up a copy of Il Corriere in one hand and La Repubblica in the other. On the front page of both was a nearly identical picture of Ettore sitting dejectedly on the front steps of MilanoBanca's palazzo, a bloodied and torn black top hat at his feet. The loss of the tape was as good as etched in his face, notwithstanding his later denial. "He's less intelligent than his upstart father," the Baron said of Ettore. "I see the same airs." The little Baron hadn't expected a shootout right in his front yard. He wondered if Marco, or even The Senator, had sold him out.

"A shame you had to eliminate Tenente Muro. Such a pretty girl."

"Beh," went the Baron, looking blankly in front of him, as if he were *off somewhere else.* "I didn't trust her. My one mistake was recruiting someone who had an emotional attachment, and then she ran the risk of another. She was not in complete control of the situation. I had the feeling she would turn on us. The fool. In any event, our backup performed very well. It was a good thing our left hand didn't know what the right was doing, eh. The little minx might've gotten Marco to his knees as well." *The female never had the attraction that power did for him. His will obeyed was a feeling better than any woman could ever give him.*

The Senator quietly bristled. Colonel Muro was the Gnome's man. The whole thing was a fiasco occasioned by Colonel Muro, he thought.

Then the Baron remembered he'd summoned The Senator and turned to his ally. "Enough of the celebrations. I called you here for a reason. These two policemen from New York reminded me of something I'd read not long ago. I wanted to discuss it with you."

The Senator stopped smiling. He leaned slightly forward, in the Baron's direction.

"The mayor there, what's his name?"

"In New York?" *The Senator said, surprised.* "Salerno. I know him. I've run into him at various functions there. I'm hosting a benefit in New York in a few days. He will be making remarks. The Italian American Cultural League."

"Excellent. And don't they say this Salerno might be president of the U.S. someday?"

"Well, yes, he's papabile, if that's what you mean. Anyway, you will like this about him: his people are from Sicily originally."

"What I remember is that he has a Caravaggio in his office. There was some sort of scandal, no? About how a barbarian politician could get a hold of such a work. He's a lover of Italian opera and art?"

"Yes, he is. It's a fake, of course," *The Senator said.* "I know the Manhattan dealer who sold it to him. You can practically count the number of known, bona fide Caravaggios on your hands and feet."

"I know that," *the Baron replied testily.* "That's not my point. I don't *care a fig if it's real or not," he practically shouted.*

The Senator sat back from the Baron, not quite alarmed, but almost. He raised his gray eyebrows, as if to say, "Well, what is your point?" something The Senator could never say to the Baron.

"Make use of all those museum boards you serve on," the Baron said. He rarely gave direct orders to The Senator, but this was very important to him. "Why don't you arrange for some Caravaggios to visit New York? Let the mayor take the credit."

"Baron, I know the man. I know his reputation. He can't be bought."

"He can't be bought easily, perhaps," the Baron shot back quickly. "But every man has his price. Salerno's might be high, but undoubtedly he has one."

The Senator shrugged his shoulders, not wishing to contradict the Baron. "Three thousand miles of water is just the beginning of the differences between Italy and the U.S.," The Senator said.

"Don't overestimate the barbarians. They love money more than we do, and that's saying a lot." The Baron trained his Sicilian eyes on The Senator. "I think it would be extremely useful to have the future president of the U.S. as a personal friend, eh?"

When the Baron looked away, The Senator relaxed. The audacity of the idea to bribe a future American president was what separated him from the Baron, and he knew it.

"After you arrange for the Caravaggios, why don't you send il sindaco, Mr. Salerno, a Michelangelo."

The Senator's jaw dropped.

"Just an ink drawing. It's an opening bid. Let's see where Mr. Salerno's price range lies," the Baron said. "I happen to own a Michelangelo. It's a rough sketch of an old hand, gnarled and reaching for an apple. It will do nicely."

The Baron laughed so hard at his own joke that he felt a hard twinge in his eighty-five-year-old heart.

Chapter 21

Tuesday

After a long flight of no sleep and little shuteye at my apartment all day, I reported to the One-Nine at 4 p.m. Dunne had decided to greet me by playing the Italian national anthem over the precinct loudspeaker system. He'd put a bunch of little red, white, and green flags all over our desks. I felt everyone's eyes on me, as I walked to my desk.

Dunne was on top of me before I could even sit down. He threw a fat manila file on my desk. "You and Turner are on this. Today. See Murcer about the particulars before he leaves later for his little bungalow upstate." It was his way of saying our asses belonged to him again.

Turner entered a moment later to the sound of the Italian national anthem once again piped in over the loudspeaker system. He, however, hummed right along with it, never once concerned that Dunne was trying to mock us. "Why the long face, Paolo?" he said to me as he sat down.

I pointed to the manila folder on my desk. "Our next job," I said, shrugging my shoulders. "How much to you want to bet it's a teenage drug dealer at the Westin Academy?"

"Ft. Thurston Howell III not good enough for you anymore, eh? How you gonna keep the cop on the beat after he's seen Rome?"

I nodded.

"You like dee Mercedes following you?" he said in a singsong Jamaican accent.

"Yeah, kinda," I answered.

"And you liked Laura not a little? Even though she was going to kill you, and more importantly, me, too?"

"Well, I admit that was a downside, but until then it was going well. I liked her a lot. We still aren't sure who she was working for. Who knows, it might have gone down differently if Marco hadn't shot her."

"And now, all we've got is..."

"Fucking Dunne," I replied before he could finish his sentence. Turner sat at his desk and leafed through the folders.

I called Harry.

"Hello," he said. The same voice as before, gruff but more bark than bite.

"It's me."

"I know. Ciao, baby. You're back. Missed you. How was the trip?" he said. His little white poodle, which he named St. Bernard, yipped in the background.

"We got a few bad guys. Not all of them. I made it out alive."

"Yeah. I read that in the *Post*. Nice. But I asked you how the trip was."

"Two years, ten months, and...six days."

"Attaboy. Now you're talking accomplishments," he said, saying the last word as only a former stevedore could, as if I were closing in on Joe DiMaggio's fifty-six-game hitting streak, something real.

*   *   *

The next couple of weeks went like that. I did miss that Muro case. The mystery. Needing to get a read on each and every person, cop and civilian, that I was up against. It got so bad that I even looked forward to calls from Gretzman, who had returned not long after us, his wounds healed. It had affected the scribe as well. I could tell. He stopped trying to antagonize me, something I knew he took great pleasure in.

Dunne, on the other hand, seemed the happiest I'd ever seen him. It was as if he had the power to suck up the bad karma coming out of us and transform it into good karma for himself.

I couldn't sleep much. We hadn't solved Ustica. Deep down that bothered me, and Turner, and Gretzman, too. We caught some tuna but the great white got away, even if everyone thought we'd solved the Muro murder. At one point, a few days after our homecoming, the mayor threw a little press reception for us. It was a short ceremony, outdoors on the steps of City Hall in the bright sunshine. We got medaled. Libby was there, proud of her dad. Peek-a-boo seemed to be in a rush, but even so he noticed my mood and, when the program ended, he asked me about it.

"Hard to say, sir," I answered him. "Appreciate the fanfare. But we feel like we didn't really get to the bottom of it."

"You mean Ustica?" the mayor said.

I nodded.

"That was not your charge, Detective Rossi. Love it as I do, Italy is not our country. They've been looking into it for years. They know who did it. He's not been brought to justice for a reason. If you didn't know that before, you know it now."

"I can't help feeling we could have busted it. We were outsiders. That was helpful, in a way. No axes to grind. No preconceived notions. We trusted no one, which in the end hurt us, but it served for a time, and anyway, I wouldn't make that mistake again."

Peek-a-boo seemed intrigued by this. He looked at me as if maybe I were just crazy enough to be useful. He waved at David Holden, his chief of staff, and told him to come over.

He pulled me by the arm up the steps and away from the reporters. "I think very highly of you and your partner," he said, but in a way that was more like he was still thinking about something else.

"Thanks," I said.

He put his hand to his chin absently when Holden arrived.

"Mayor. I don't like to rush you," said the Second Brain, "but you've got a noon with Councilman Stephens, a one o'clock luncheon with the head of the teachers' union all the way uptown at the Four Seasons, and a three o'clock with the Brooklyn Republican Club."

"Yes, Holden. Let's go. But I want you to set up something with these two detectives in the next few days. I've got something in mind, but it has to ferment, okay?" he said, looking at me.

"You know where to find us," I said. The mayor turned and was gone. Holden just gave me a kind of bored look, one more note in his agenda. They walked away in a hurry and I saw Holden tell something to an aide, pointing at me.

The next few weeks, I found myself often sitting at my desk, staring at nothing in particular. We had to make a run to Scores—a stripper was found brutally separated from her assets, a nice girl from Nebraska, the neighbors said. They're all nice girls—but I just couldn't get it up for the case. Maybe I was done.

In late June, Turner and I were stepping out to lunch when Dunne summoned us into his office. His puss was more sour than usual. I couldn't think of any transgressions we'd be punished for, but then I wasn't with Turner one hundred percent of the time.

He closed the door. Bad sign. He didn't tell us to sit down. Worse sign. We sat.

"I got a piece of information this morning that I'm not particularly happy about," Dunne said. He put his hands together and then leaned forward at his desk, toward us. He pulled out a memo and laid it on the desk facing us. From the look of him, despite what he said, I didn't think he was totally unhappy with that piece of paper. "It's from 1 Police Plaza," he said, pushing it to me.

The Commissioner's departmental seal was at the top. It was brief, a couple of paragraphs long.

Patrick Dunne,

Squad Leader,

Detective Boro Manhattan, 19th precinct.

Dear Pat:

The mayor's office has directed me to temporarily detach Detectives First Grade Paul Rossi and Hamilton P. Turner from your command. Have them see David Holden in the mayor's office on July 8 at 9 a.m. They'll be attached ad hoc to Central Command. The mayor's office has not made clear how long this assignment will last, so if you want replacements, please put in a request ASAP.

All best,

Tom Standhope,

Deputy Police Commissioner.

P.S. Hope Cindy and the boys are well.

I handed the note quietly to Turner. Standhope—now I finally knew who Dunne's godfather was.

"I don't know what the fuck this is about, but I'd be lying if I told you I was heartbroken," he said. "I don't give a shit if you never come back and I hope you don't. You solved a few cases. Fine. But I never liked your attitudes," he said, looking at Turner now. "The only thing that pisses me off is that your leaving is not by my hand. That's all. Dismissed," he said.

We got up quietly and left without looking back at Dunne. Turner was ahead of me, so I couldn't see his face. I figured he'd have the biggest smile I'd ever seen, but when I caught up to him, there was no sign of it.

"Aren't you happy?" I said, grabbing his arm and stopping him.

"Ecstatic," he said quietly, and started walking again toward our desks. The rest of the crew knew we were in Dunne's office for something. They looked at us expectantly.

"You have a funny way of showing ecstasy," I said.

He stopped again and looked at me. "Partner, you really are

302

a white hambone sometimes. You know that you can be so happy sometimes that showing it would be a mistake. A bad move. *Bruta figura.* I hate that motherfucker more than anyone in the world, and worse, I don't respect him. To show him or anyone in this building that I was happy to leave would be an admission of emotional weakness that I cannot allow. I don't want him or anyone else thinking even for a millisecond that he might have gotten to me, that he mattered, even the least itty-bitty bit, that's all."

I showed ecstatic, a grin wide enough for the both of us. We returned to our desks. Turner pulled a flat cardboard moving box out from under his desk. It had been there all along. He folded it into position and started piling things into it.

*   *   *

At the appointed hour, we showed up in Holden's office, a cubicle off to the side of the Mayor's office. It wasn't very big but it had a door. There was a picture of the president on one wall and the mayor on another. There were a couple of old New York etchings on the wall behind his desk, just like the ones in the boss's office. "Sit down," Holden said in a voice somewhere between unfriendly and arrogant. "I'll get the mayor." He left without even looking up at us.

Peek-a-boo came in a minute later, shook our hands, and sat on Holden's desk.

"How long do I have till the conference call?" he said to Holden.

He looked at his watch. "Fifteen, twenty max, sir," he replied.

The mayor held his hands to his face for a moment, then looked up at us. "Okay. I don't have a lot of time, boys. I'm going to make you a proposition."

We nodded.

"A few weeks ago, I was at a benefit dinner given by the Italian American Cultural League, and who should I run into but the great Giovanni Montone. The Italian industrialist, the biggest probably. One of the richest men in the world. They call him *Il Senatore*, The Senator.

"He's as dirty as they come, of course, but he wants to do something for New York after 9/11. He calls it his second home. Makes me want to cry," the mayor said in mock fashion, holding his hand to his heart. "Now he wants to bring a whole slew of Caravaggios to New York, a monster show."

Turner perked up at that.

"But that's not why I brought you here. The Senator gave me a gift that I must show you. Holden, please. It's on the mantle behind my desk, in brown paper wrapping."

When Holden returned, the mayor gingerly took the package from him, then gently pulled the paper off a small framed charcoal pencil drawing, about twelve inches by twelve inches. "Look at this. Isn't it wonderful? It's a Michelangelo drawing of an old man's hand reaching for an apple. Really exquisite. Look at the delicate lines in his forefinger. The musculature. Now, Signor Montone *gave* it to me." The mayor smiled mischievously. "I mean the city, on behalf of some Italian industrial group, Colfin." He carefully put the drawing on the desk so it faced us. Turner bent over, studied it.

"Here's the thing. I had Sy Hochman over to dinner a couple of nights ago. Poor guy. He's really broken up over Dorothy. Anyway, I showed him this drawing. And guess what he tells me?"

"He told you it was his," I said.

'That's right," the mayor said, a little surprised. "Says it was in his family for years, but his parents had to leave it behind when they fled Amsterdam sixty-three years ago two minutes ahead of the Nazis. He's used investigators for years to try to get back some of the art looted from his family and others but couldn't find this one.

"What's all this mean, you ask, right? Right," the mayor said, looking at us for confirmation. "Two things. First, you heard about the old art dealer murdered on East 97th ten days ago? Tarantino was the name, I think. Right?" Salerno said. He glanced at Holden "Only Old Masters and Italian Renaissance stuff. Old school European, won a fencing gold medal in the 1952 Olympics, right, Holden? The *Post* headline was the Master Fencer. I liked that."

Holden ignored him.

"That was two Fridays ago," I said. I'd heard about it from a buddy in the Two-Three.

"Turns out this art dealer isn't entirely clean," the mayor said. "This art dealer had a lot of rich important friends here and in Europe. Many of the dealers are Italians, as you might expect, given that country's trove of stuff. Hochman knew Tarantino, but says he never bought from Tarantino's gallery." The mayor gave a laughing, disbelieving "humph."

"Anyway, here's the second thing. You two are going to head up a special art felony squad. I have a feeling, and I'm pretty good at sensing this kind of stuff, that stolen art is going to be big for the next coupla years. You'll be attached to Central Command, but the whole city will be your beat.

"If Hochman is right, this city is teeming with stolen art. All I want you two to do," he said, first looking directly at Turner, then at me, "is find a couple of rich guys, preferably Americans and New Yorkers, who have knowingly bought some stolen art, and deliver them. If you happen to make some collars by November, so much the better. But that's not an order." He smiled a politician's smile. "And if it turns out to be art looted by the Nazis, well then, set up my senatorial inauguration party."

It was quiet for about five seconds.

Before we could reply, the mayor said, "Great. You will love this detail. Who knows, maybe you'll need to go to Europe again," he said, winking and quickly moving out the door. "Sorry, I have a call with the governor, fucking Wop bastard…" We didn't hear the rest because he was already out the door into his office. And then, quick as a rat, he popped his head back in. "Detective Turner. I almost forgot. You still interested in my campaign?"

My partner nodded.

"I've got to be at a church service Sunday morning in Bed Stuy." He looked to his aide. "David?"

Holden gave a barely perceptible eyebrow acknowledgement.

The mayor went back to Turner: "Want to join me there?"

"Of course," Turner said without missing a beat.

"Ask Holden about the details. I don't know the address. Gotta go." Peek-a-boo disappeared without looking back. Holden followed him out.

We sat for about ten minutes, like two kids in detention waiting to be dismissed. Nobody came back.

"We know the way out," I said to no one in particular, and got up. Seemed to be a lot of recent college grads running around with files and laptops. One of the requirements to work on Peek-a-boo's staff apparently was to be a hottie of about twenty-two with expensively cut, dusky hair, long pretty legs, and the desire to show them. Maybe politics wasn't the only reason Turner was interested, or Holden for that matter.

"What do you think about our new job?" Turner said.

"Not sure I actually accepted," I replied as we walked out of City Hall. "I don't know," I said and that was the truth. "I don't know if I like the idea of getting shot at over a Michelangelo."

"As opposed to a pimp?" Turner said. "What's the alternative, Paolo? Going back to One-Nine, to Dunne, to being surrounded by shitheads waiting to retire."

We meandered over to City Hall Park. For once it wasn't full of protesters of one kind or another, and on such a lovely day, it almost seemed a shame there weren't any trannies around. I got a hot dog and sat down.

"What do I know about *art*?" I said, picking up the conversation. "Remember that B-list artist guy with a big studio on First and 63rd, the old lumber warehouse? He worked big metal sculptures there, and one, a huge pyramid he was creating, fell on him when the winch broke."

"Yeah." Turner smiled a little guilty smile. "Killed by ten tons of *art*," he blurted out in a voice dripping with undisguised sarcasm, in homage to my short fifteen minutes of fame, when I'd said the same thing on a WENS news radio report of the death, so many years ago. I still have a tape of it. We both laughed hard at Turner's version. "But you have me as a partner," he went on. "I know enough about *art* for us both."

I turned to Turner, who preferred falafel to hot dogs. "There's only one reason I'm tempted." He kept eating his pita sandwich. "If *Il Senatore* is involved, then I'd bet the Baron is, too. I'd like another crack at them."

"'Set your sights high, my boy,' my mother always said," Turner said.

"I'm in," I said tersely, looking straight ahead. I wasn't sure it was a great idea, but Turner was right. It was a good idea and that was enough. Going back to Ft. Thurston was not appealing. I finished my dog, threw the napkin in a bin nearby, and rose to go. Turner stared at me. Probably the best smile I'd ever seen him put on.

He grabbed me by the chin, squeezing my cheeks like an old Roman lady would. For a second, I thought he might kiss me. "Paolo, I think we're going to like this gig."

I didn't reply. I didn't know. As a cop, most of the time, you didn't know. Most of the time, you guessed, and hoped you guessed right. We strolled out of City Hall Park, turned left and north toward the Brooklyn Bridge, just up the street, and walked up to 1 Police Plaza.

ACKNOWLEDGMENTS

Novel writing is a solitary affair but I have been fortunate to have many people in my corner over the years. In great part it is thanks to them that The Man in Milan was born. I'd like to single out the following people for their unstinting and unconditional support: Lisa Dierbeck, Giovanni Racanelli, Giuseppina Racanelli, Priya Doraswamy, Jason Pinter, Jonathan Santlofer, Megan Abbot, Edwin Finn, James Anderson, Rocky Totino and Elana Goren, Janet Dierbeck, Lee Child, Laura Lippman, Kopin Tan, Maria Teresa Cometto, Glauco Maggi, the Crime Fiction Academy, the Racanelli-Piazza-Mossa-Adamo clan, Richard Zahradnik, Jack Hersch, and Lloyd Khaner. Undoubtedly, I missed someone, so I ask forgiveness. Any errors, translations or otherwise, in the book are mine alone.

While the Ustica airliner crash is unfortunately a real and still unsolved tragedy some forty years later, this book is a work of fiction. All the characters, situations and places in this novel are purely imagined by me. There is no NYPD investigation of the Ustica incident, no Baron, etc. The only fact represented in this novel are that 81 innocent people died and no one knows how or why. The story, all names, characters, and incidents portrayed in this novel are fictitious. No identification with actual persons (living or deceased), places, buildings, and products is intended or should be inferred.

ABOUT THE AUTHOR

Vito Racanelli's short stories have appeared in numerous publications, including the Akashic Books' *Mondays Are Murder* series; the *Boiler*; the *Literarian*; *Newtown Literary*; *KGB Bar Lit Magazine*; Brilliantflashfiction.com; *Dark Corners*; a *great weather for Media* short story collection, and *River and South Review*. His works have also been performed at Liar's League NYC and broadcast by BBC4, as part of its Sunday afternoon story series.

His *A Trip to the Trees Place* was nominated for a Pushcart Prize. He was a 2013 and 2018 Fish Publishing Flash Fiction Story Prize finalist, placed a "notable" story in the Gemini 2016 Short Story contest, and was participant in the 2013 Pen World Festival. Vito's non-fiction has appeared in *The Wall Street Journal*, *The Newark Star Ledger*, *San Francisco Chronicle*, and the *Far Eastern Economic Review*, among other newspapers. He is a *Barron's* Staff Writer, and is regularly interviewed by U.S. and European TV and radio programs such as WABC, BBC, and CNBC. He was the Associated Press-Dow Jones News Bureau Chief, in Italy 2/94-10/9, and led the bureau's wide range of coverage of Italian financial markets and news.

He lives in New York City.